A NEW YORK STATE OF FRIGHT

HORROR STORIES FROM THE EMPIRE STATE

A New York State of Fright

Horror Stories from the Empire State

Edited by James Chambers, April Grey, and Robert Masterson

Hippocampus Press

New York

Contents

Introduction

New York bears many names.

The Empire State. The Knickerbocker State.

Its capital, Albany, is the Cradle of the Union, and Buffalo is The Nickel City or The City of No Illusions. Canandaigua means The Chosen Spot, Jamestown is The Pearl City, and if you visit Rochester, you're in The Flour City, The Flower City, or good old Ra-Cha-Cha. Saratoga Springs is The Spa City; Schenectady, Electric City; Syracuse, Salt City; and Utica is The City that God Forgot.

Then, of course, there's New York City and its five boroughs.

Brooklyn, The Fourth Largest City in the World or Crooklyn. The Bronx, Da Broncks, The Birthplace of Hip-Hop, and home to the House That Ruth Built. Staten Island, The Forgotten Borough, The Borough of Parks, and Queens, The World's Borough, located squarely on Strong Island (as is Brooklyn, though few like to admit it for fear of suburban taint from Nassau and Suffolk counties).

And The City.

Even people in the other four boroughs call Manhattan simply The City.

Bagdad on the Subway. The Big Apple. Capital of the World. The City of Dreams. The City That Never Sleeps. The City So Nice, They Named It Twice. The Crossroads of the World. Empire City. Fear City. Fun City. Gotham. The Melting Pot. Metropolis. If You Can Make It There, You Can Make It Anywhere. And my personal favorite . . .

. . . The Big Onion.

It's an old-school nickname few people use these days. To my mind, it captures the soul of New York City and State better than all the others. Onions have layers. They're tough. They can grow pretty much anywhere, and they do so in many varieties. Cut them wrong, they'll bring tears to your eyes. Cook them right, they're sweet and savory. Skin them, the exposed layer only dries and hardens. Onions embody the grime and delight, the depth and deceptive transparency, the paradoxical toughness and sweetness, the powerful flavors of New York and its residents. It's an ugly, honest, perfect nickname for the state this book represents. It hints at why horror fiction—often ugly, always honest—finds a perfect setting in New York.

The stories collected in *A New York State of Fright* come from authors all over the state. Each one offers a unique perspective on New York and showcases a unique voice. Many of the authors are lifetime New Yorkers, some transplants from other parts of the world. New Yorkers don't quibble about that. We are a city and state of immigrants. If you live here, you're a New Yorker, no matter where you came from. Not that New Yorkers aren't interested; we're just too busy to care. You get yourself here, and we'll take you as you came. Life here moves too fast to do otherwise.

Hence the saying, "A New York minute," because in any given 60 seconds more happens in New York than in some entire countries. In fact, New York's population exceeds that of most countries. If you drop the state onto a list of countries by population, New York falls somewhere around number 60 out of more than 200, a touch short of Sri Lanka and a touch ahead of Romania. The City alone, with about 8.5 million people, exceeds the population of many nations around the world—and that's counting only full-time residents, not the additional two to three million visitors and commuters who pour in daily.

In New York it's a survival tactic to skip the niceties. Need directions on Seventh Avenue? Ask someone straight up. They'll tell you where to go, maybe even flash a quick smile. Don't bother with "Excuse me," or "Can I ask you a question," or "Sorry to bother you, but . . ." New Yorkers have no time for that and will hurry on past. Get to the point. Tear the scab off fast and sharp. New Yorkers live the way horror writers write: in the thick of humanity and without blinders to its many sins and wonders.

It's an ugly world out there sometimes. New Yorkers waste no time denying it. Tackle the horror head on, drag it kicking and screaming into the light, confront it, and get on with relishing all that is good and beautiful in life before the next dark, frightening thing comes along. If you were in New York on 9/11, you understand how the City comes together when it's hurting. If you were in New York during the Northeast Blackout of 2003, if you saw the crowds gathered in the streets listening to the news on car radios, if you walked with thousands across the 59th Street Bridge, as I did, to make your way home, you understand there's camaraderie to being a New Yorker, pride in sticking together.

This is a city and a state that has witnessed all manner of darkness and evil from serial killers and corrupt government machines, from natural disasters to gas explosions, from common street crime to terrorist attacks, from winters so harsh it seemed they'd never end to summers so hot the fumes from trash baking on the streets wiggle in the air—and yet few people who live here would rather live anywhere else.

A New York State of Fright is a love note to that spirit. A disturbing, gory, sometimes twisted love note, true, but then we are horror writers and can only give this place our best, truest homage.

The spark of this anthology ignited within the New York chapter of the Horror Writers Association (HWA; www.horror.org). This is not an official HWA anthology, but it's safe to say this book would not exist without the enthusiasm and support of New York's HWA members, many of whom contributed stories. Our local HWA members have participated in literary events, book fairs, author readings, and horror conventions to help promote the horror genre and the work of New York authors. The chapter has become a small force on New York's vast literary scene. It felt right when conceiving this book to direct our efforts toward strengthening New York's writing community—thus it was decided to direct all proceeds from this anthology to Girls Write Now (www.girlswritenow.com).

Girls Write Now mentors underserved young women to help them find their voices through the power of writing and community. For twenty years Girls Write Now has matched teen girls with women professional writers and media makers as personal mentors. Their mentees—more than 90 percent girls of color and 90 percent high-need—publish in outlets such as the *New York Times*,

Newsweek, and *BuzzFeed*; perform at Lincoln Center and the United Nations; and earn hundreds of scholastic art and writing awards. The White House has distinguished Girls Write Now three times as one of the nation's top youth programs, and twice the Nonprofit Excellence Awards have named it one of New York's top ten nonprofits.

What better way for a bunch of horror writers to support New York's literary community than by lending a hand to its up-and-coming generation of unique voices? To encourage a group that helps girls confront whatever darkness may be in their lives through writing?

While most things happen quickly in New York, this anthology wasn't one of them. All our contributors wanted to make sure we produced the best book possible and to capture as much of New York as we could in a single volume. The editors worked closely with many of the authors to polish, refine, and hone their stories for publication. Many of the tales underwent rounds of critique and feedback in our local writing groups before being submitted. At the same time, we reached out to other authors in the state to invite contributions, and many came through with wonderful, horrific tales included here. Some who couldn't due to time constraints, prior writing commitments, and other reasons offered their generous encouragement and support—and who knows? Maybe they'll be on board for a second volume of New York horror.

In that sense, this book should be read as an introduction, not a comprehensive survey to the horror fiction of New York. It includes work by several Bram Stoker Award–winning authors and nominees, a Horror Grandmaster and Lifetime Achievement Award recipient, the recipients of many other awards and honors—right alongside new voices building their writing careers. It's a great starting point for readers. For anyone who enjoys these stories there remain many other powerful voices in New York dark fiction to unearth and read.

Horror fiction runs deep in New York's DNA.

One of the first great works of American horror, "The Legend of Sleepy Hollow," was written and set here. Edgar Allan Poe spent years living in the Bronx and working in The City. H. P. Lovecraft lived in Brooklyn for several years and set several of his stories in The City, including the classic "Cool Air." Richard Matheson was raised in Brooklyn, where he read *Dracula*, the inspiration for *I Am Legend*. Horror great Peter Straub lives here, and for many years so did Whitley Strieber, whose classics *Communion* and *The Wolfen* take place in New York. Ira Levin, author of *Rosemary's Baby*, was a native New Yorker, as is Jeffrey Konvitz, author of *The Sentinel*. John Skipp and Craig Spector set their vampire novel *The Light at the End* in New York City, and Jack Ketchum placed *Ladies Night* and many short stories here. This is only a small sampling of classics where horror and New York intersect. There are many, many more and many contemporary New York horror writers to seek out. There's enough horror fiction coming out of New York to suggest we change our state tag line from "I Love New York!" to "I Love to Be Scared!"

On behalf of our editorial team and all our contributors, I hope all those reading this book do indeed enjoy a good scare. There are plenty to be found within these pages. The stories here will take readers into some of the niche universes that comprise New York: the fashion world of Midtown Manhattan; ethnic rivalries among crosstown mystics; the loneliness of a New York street existence; an abandoned upstate construction site with a dark past; the fearsome quirks of the northern wilderness; the extremes of a city punished by nature; the layers of unpleasant history buried beneath modern parks and buildings; lost moments from a famous boardwalk; a vision of the city where the walking dead are another fact of life; dark and razor-sharp satire of the gap between rich and poor; forgotten relics of the old city warehoused in Brooklyn; and many other grim, sinister, and poignant visions. The stories here represent myriad facets of New York, glimpses into its dark undercurrents—and yet they offer only a taste.

I thank you, dear reader. Our editorial team thanks you, our contributors and publisher thank you for your interest in New York horror fiction, for picking up and reading this book, for supporting Girls Write Now, the local literary community, and its efforts to tame the shadows of life. We also acknowledge the generous commitment of our contributors and our cover artist and the support of the award-winning New York specialty press Hippocampus Press and publisher Derrick Hussey for their enthusiasm, professionalism, and patience making this project a reality.

We thank you for choosing to peel back a few layers of the Big Onion with us, braving what tears and tastes they may bring. We hope you enjoy what you find within these pages and feel inspired to seek out more.

—JAMES CHAMBERS

April 2018, Northport, NY

Heels

Gina cut through the throng like a shark, the fashionable spikes grac-
ing her feet unhindered by the uneven pavement. The lunch crowd
unzipped before her as she plowed forward, elbowing anyone who
dared stand in her way. Only the destination mattered. In a couple of
weeks, the Macy's Thanksgiving Day parade would march through
here. The tourists were already peppering the sidewalks, their odious
smartphones in hand. Occasionally, one would materialize in her
path and attempt to snap a selfie. Gina barreled through them like
bowling pins, enjoying their satisfying _oomphs_ as she made contact.
She passed a hot dog cart. The aroma of Sabrett's best made her
swoon with hunger, but food would have to wait. She still had fifteen pounds to go, and missing a meal could only help. Ignoring the
temptation, she turned onto West 29th Street.

The tiny thrift shop sat in the middle of the block, hidden between two clothing importers, easily missed if you weren't looking
for it. Only a hint of pale blue lettering remained on the sign above
the entrance, daring its reader to decipher it. The dirty shop window
blocked most of the natural light. The boxes on the other side of the
glass removed any possibility of seeing inside.

Gina had no idea how the woman kept her doors open; addicts
like her, she supposed. She opened the door, and the small brass bell
above it tinkled. The familiar combination of stale air and fabric made
her smile. She didn't know why—anyone who worked in the garment
district knew that smell. She imagined she could identify every type of
material just by scent. She inhaled deeply and worked her way past
the piles of clothes stacked haphazardly by one wall, careful not to
topple the towers of discolored, sagging shoe boxes on the other.

"So? Are they in?" Gina asked.

The silver-haired woman behind the counter grinned with her gap-toothed smile. A gold tooth gleamed in the dim fluorescent light. Sharp, penetrating, almost violet eyes looked out from a face deeply lined by the passage of time. In the fifteen years that she'd been coming here, Gina had never asked the woman anything personal other than her name, Malka.

"They came in this morning, as I promised they would." Malka reached under the counter and brought out a shoebox. She placed it on the pockmarked wooden surface. Unlike the ones on display, this box was new. Gina's heart leaped at the sight of the famous signature, *Louboutin.* Malka stalled for a minute before lifting the lid, then revealed its contents.

Gina gasped. These were even more stunning in person than when she'd first glimpsed them in the designer's line sheets six months before. The famous red soles contrasted the black, yellow, and blue patent leather above it magnificently. *What was it with shoes?* A new pair gave her such a high. But not just any shoe would do; only unique, beautifully crafted, spectacular heels. She picked up the right one and examined it. The inspection was an important part of her ritual, determining the shoe's pedigree. She had no intention of buying fakes. In New York, counterfeit goods were commonplace, and even though Malka never let her down, she would do her due diligence. *A $1,000 shoe for $400. How did the woman do it? Where did she get them? Who was she kidding? She didn't care.*

"So? You happy?" Malka asked.

"Over the moon."

"Good! You like them." Malka bent down and got her sales book.

On the shelf behind the old woman, a torn shopping bag caught Gina's eye. A beautifully crafted, phosphorescent, multi-colored heel jutted out from one of the tears; the swirls of color reminded her of a puddle of antifreeze.

"Could I see the shoes in that bag?" Gina pointed.

"What bag?"

"Behind you. On the shelf."

The woman turned. She saw what Gina pointed to and shook her head. "No, no," she said, agitated. "That's nothing. Not for sale.

You wouldn't like them."

"I just want to take a peek." The woman shook her head.

"They're garbage. *Nothing but trash.*" She took her pen and began writing out the receipt. "You have to get back to work. Let me give you a receipt."

Her stubborn refusal made Gina more determined.

"C'mon, that's not fair. Just for a second."

Malka shook her head again.

"Look, I understand. I just want to *see* them. I *need* to see them. What's the harm?"

"Not for sale. Forget them."

Malka began writing again.

BOOM!

An ear-shattering crash erupted from the front of the store, startling them both. Malka immediately grabbed what looked like a small bat from beneath the counter and came around, shouting in an unknown language. She flung open the front door and ran out.

Gina took advantage of the distraction, extended her body across the counter, and reached for the paper bag. She dumped out its contents. The most amazing cross-strap pumps tumbled out, with what had to be at least a five-inch vamp heel. She gently laid a hand on their surface. A deep sigh of pleasure escaped her lips when she made contact. An unexpected shudder spread throughout her body, leaving her flushed and embarrassed. The shoes were hot to the touch, pulsing beneath her fingers. She could not identify the material. It looked like patent leather but felt more intimate and familiar— velvety. She detected a layer of soft, silky fur on their surface, very understated. How could they be shiny, almost translucent and have fur on them? Most of the shoe appeared black but, when observed, additional colors revealed themselves: deep reds, midnight blues, even strokes of magenta. The various hues undulated, mesmerizing and soothing, like an underwater eel. As she watched the colors mixed to reveal new combinations. An illusion surely, but hypnotic nonetheless. She could not have said why, but she felt certain many hands, and layers, had built this shoe.

She examined the stilettos carefully. Malka had lied to her. These were new. Never worn. Not a mark or scuff anywhere.

The more she held the pumps, the more she coveted them.
Impulsively, she took off her own shoes and slipped them on.
A perfect fit.

She glanced down. She felt powerful, tall. Her four-foot-eleven-inch frame was now that of an Amazon, at least in her mind. And wasn't that what was important, after all? How a shoe made you *feel*?

She laid her worn heels on the counter and looked at the Louboutins, laughing at herself for ever thinking they were special. They were pauper's shoes in comparison to what she had on.

She slipped out of the store, briefly turning to see if she could see the store owner. A small crowd stood in front. Malka crouched in the center, looking down at three dead white doves. The spots of blood on the glass matched the blood on the birds' feathers. A chill traveled down Gina's spine. She turned back and hurried off.

*   *   *

Gina walked into her office. Before she could take her jacket off, Paula appeared by her desk. "Did you get the comps to the printer?"

"Jeez! I just got back from lunch. Give me a minute!"

"Did you go to your Salvation Army place and buy yourself something special?" Paula said, her voice dripping saccharin. Gina glared at her. Paula, nonplussed, looked around.

"Where are they? Wasn't today the day?"

Gina remained quiet. She felt possessive over her new purchase. How many times did Paula comment on her "silly" trips? *Why not buy the shoes she wanted, when she wanted? All this effort. Too much work. Blah, blah, blah.* Paula cared not a whit about budgets, salaries, or living within her means. She came from a wealthy family. Plus, her rich admirers made sure she would never feel the sting of a pinched wallet.

"Well! What do we have here?" Paula's eyes widened. She ogled Gina's feet.

"¡Aiii! ¡Carajo! What ju go there? Take them off. I want to see!" With a sigh, Gina took off her shoes and handed them to Paula.

She discovered, delightedly, that Paula was stumped. Even with her encyclopedic knowledge of fashion and styles, she could not identify the designer. She turned the shoes this way and that. Peeked inside, inspected the bottoms, ran her hand on the seams of the shoes. She stared back. Paula's eyes glittered with something Gina had never seen in her boss.

Jealousy.

"¿Ju got this at jor woman?" Paula's Colombian accent thickened unconsciously when she got excited. Gina hovered protectively, shielding the shoes, although she was not sure as to why.

"¡Ah! ¡Fuck-me choos!" Paula gave a bawdy cackle. After a minute, she tilted her head. "So, who's the designer?"

"I don't know. Can't figure it out. Doesn't have any of the known marks. But when I saw them, I had to have them."

"I can believe it. The catalog can wait a few minutes. Go ahead, put them back on. Lemme see!"

Gina slipped her feet back into the shoes. She felt as sexy as Paula.

Yes, sexy and—

—*alluring.*

Glamorous, even.

She'd been the chubby girl in school, the smart girl in high school, but never the hot girl. Now, the short, zaftig girl with frizzy blond hair disappeared and morphed into *this*. Nothing changed and everything changed. *¡Jeezuus!* The endorphins raged through her body, like an overheated locomotion. Could a pair of shoes make you feel that way? This pair could.

They stared at each other in silence for a couple of seconds. Then Paula broke the spell. "C'mon, back to work. Chop-chop." Gina sat back into her chair and resumed working on the catalog, grinning like a fool.

* * *

She looked at the clock. 10:00 P.M. That's it. She called it a night. Everyone else had left. She yawned and rubbed her sore shoulders, picked up her purse, then bent down, ready to switch her shoes. Then she remembered. Right. *These* were her shoes now.

She crossed Seventh Avenue—Fashion Avenue, although much of the production and fashion had long ago moved offshore—then turned on 34th Street. She headed toward the subway, to the Q train to Brooklyn.

As she reached the corner, she stopped. Why? She wore what could arguably be called *the* most fantastic footwear she'd ever scored. Barely thirty and not bad-looking. Why rush to an empty apartment in Midwood? What was she, *eighty?* Wednesday. Hump Day. The middle of the week. Time to break things up.

What club did Paula rave about last week, after Fashion Week? *Encontre.* That's it. She looked up the address on her iPhone, then called for an Uber. What the hell—these puppies would be broken in, in style.

The black car let her off in front of the club. The purple neon letters blazed the club's name, promising an unforgettable night. This was *the* hottest club in the meat-packing district—hell, in all New York, as far as she knew. An enormous line waited by the entrance. She walked toward the back of the line, then stopped. What if she skipped the line altogether? Time to put her new-found confidence to the test.

She approached the enormous doorman feeling electric; charged; *alive.* He saw her, turned, and unhooked the velvet rope, then stood aside to let her pass. She breezed by, acknowledging the gesture with a smile. Gina never experienced anything like it. She buzzed like a low-humming generator. She entered the darkness and allowed her eyes to adjust. The pounding beat slammed into her body like a living thing. She felt her pulse speed up to match the music's rhythm. She walked over, checked her Burberry, and made her way to the main floor.

*   *   *

Was it really 4:00 A.M.? The time had flown. She felt giddy and more than a little drunk. The moment she entered the club men, and some women, treated her like a celebrity. A carousel of beautiful flesh presented itself. They bought her drinks; danced, flattered her, and made her laugh. Sometime in the night, she had locked lips with a stunning, tanned blond girl. Deeper into the evening, she screwed some sexy, shirtless, abs-laden actor in the bathroom. In the *bathroom!* She, of the Catholic school upbringing!

She crossed to the other side of the street before ordering another Uber. A group spilled out of the club's door, laughing. They noticed Gina.

"Hey!" one of the girls called out. Gina looked in their direction. "Want to join us? We're going for breakfast around the corner!"

She hadn't had a bite since breakfast the previous day, "Sure!"

She stepped off the curb to cross the street. Halfway through, one of her heels caught between two cobblestones. She looked down and wiggled her foot, trying to dislodge it. As she did, the crowd on the sidewalk began shouting, then screaming.

She looked up, confused. What were they saying? And why were they yelling?

She didn't have time to register the warning. The SUV hit her full force, tossing her fifteen feet into the air, directly onto an oncoming delivery truck. As she tumbled off the grille, her head hit the cobblestones, and everything went black.

*   *   *

She opened her eyes. She didn't know how much time had passed. She couldn't see. A muffled, keening wail sounded somewhere in the distance, filtered through heavy cotton . . . *Where am I?* She could not get her bearings. *Am I sitting? Lying down?* Her heart pounded; she could hear it clearly. *What happened?* Then her vision cleared. The thick, dark corona receded from her eyes and she could see again. She was propped against a mailbox, on the sidewalk, but she could not make sense of what *else* she saw. Her legs were splayed out in front of her but—

Yes . . . her legs . . . yes . . . but . . . but—

—the *back* of her calves now faced her.

*   *   *

A crowd surrounded her. She tried to stand, but the paramedic pressed down on her shoulder gently, shaking his head.

"You need to remain calm, ma'am." He examined her carefully, taking her pressure, intent on keeping her still. "Do you know where you are? What is your name, ma'am?"

What was up with the *ma'am* thing? She was no ma'am, *way* too young for that, thank you very much. Gina took a deep breath. The realization that her pelvis had flipped 180 degrees threatened to spill into her consciousness and blot out everything else. She concentrated on her breathing, controlling it, slowing it down. *That's it. Deep breaths.* She didn't feel any pain. *Why* didn't she feel any pain? Was she in shock or, worse, paralyzed? She looked around. Other than the marionetting of her legs, nothing seemed broken. What about blood? Shouldn't there be *blood*? *Why wasn't she bleeding?* She didn't see any cuts—or bruises, for that matter. All those faces looking down at her. Earlier that night she'd been their queen: untouchable; unbreakable; confident. Now she lay on a dirty sidewalk like a discarded, broken doll. Then a real moment of panic. Where were her *shoes*? With relief, she saw them at the end of her feet, albeit facing the wrong way. She tried to move again and found she now could. The paramedic pinned her down in alarm. *"Ma'am!"* But this time she'd have none of it. She knew it looked bad, but her body said: GO. So she did.

She shook off his hand and, using the mailbox as support, she planted a palm on its surface and the other on the sidewalk. She got up—awkwardly at first, like a toddler, then more confidently. Then she rotated her torso, making it now face the same direction as her legs.

The crowd gasped. Gina took a deep, satisfying breath. *¡Toldja!*

She dusted herself off. Her dress was torn in places, but nowhere immodest.

The two paramedics stood frozen, then broke their paralysis and rushed up, insisting they take her to the hospital. She refused . . . Unconvinced, the female pushed the issue. Gina would have none of it. She gathered her bag and left.

*　　*　　*

She sat on the edge of her bed, relieved to be home. Had any of it happened? *All of it?* The entire event felt imaginary. She glanced at her bedside clock: 6:00 A.M. In a couple of hours she would have to go to work. *No way.* Paula would kill her, but she'd call in sick. She'd make up some excuse, which her boss would not believe, and then get back into bed. *Yeah, that would work.* She hadn't taken a day off in over eight months. She didn't feel guilty.

She looked at her feet and could not believe the shoes hadn't flown off somewhere during the accident—that there'd *been* an accident in the first place was incredible. That forlorn shoe, abandoned in the middle of the road, always the first image appearing on the news. The tragedy resonated in your psyche long after the newscast was over, reminding you a person been catapulted out of their shoes. But hers . . . well . . .

. . . there they were.

Still on.

Still beautiful.

She reached down and began removing the right pump.

As soon as the back of the shoe slipped off, a blindingly sharp, white-hot stab of pain shot up her leg and into her pelvis, impaling itself into her brain, sucking her breath away. She covered her mouth and stifled a scream. Her leg deformed and bent; the skin of her shin stretched, thinned then split. The ruptured vessels tore open, releasing a river of blood. Her shin cracked, then splintered, with a nauseating *crunch*. White shards of bone protruded, like broken beach fencing. The pain blinded her and she staggered forward, collapsing on the floor. She was losing blood rapidly. It seeped into her thick pile carpet. She began to drift out of consciousness. She gathered her strength and leaned forward slowly. Then, with concentrated effort, she pushed the shoe back on. Within seconds, her leg reverted. The injuries closed, then disappeared. The pain evaporated. In horror, she watched as the blood in the carpet now moved toward the shoes.

When her mind cleared, she examined the shoes more carefully. The events of the night had nearly destroyed her, and yet the shoes were unblemished: not a mark on them. She turned her foot so she could observe the soles: pristine, like new.

And then she knew.

The realization hit and shook her to her very core. The shoes had kept her alive, *were* keeping her alive. The shoes now *owned* her.

All of it happened.

All of it.

True.

Her life would never be the same, all because she had stolen these damned shoes.

Exhausted, she laid back on the bed, fully clothed, and thought of it no more as sleep closed in.

* * *

Gina tried returning the shoes, the very next day. When she arrived at the shop, a gruff-looking man greeted her. He sat behind the counter, glowering.

"Where's Malka?" she asked.

"What?"

"Malka. The woman who owns this store."

The man shook his head. "I've been here for twenty years. You need keys?"

"Huh?"

Gina looked around. None of Malka's stock remained.

The old woman and her stuff were gone, as if they'd never existed. Gina's hope vanished as Malka had.

She took one last look at the store sign, expecting to see the faded print, but instead, the sign now displayed: *Armin's Locksmith.*

She left, defeated.

* * *

She navigated through the passing weeks, terrified of losing a shoe.

She learned to shower in them. She slept in them. There was no respite for her. Since that very first night, she dared not take them off—she did everything in them. She was damned, and she knew it.

As the days passed, deep fatigue set in. Her calves hurt constantly. She developed shin splints. She began to limp as blisters grew and burst repeatedly. The process repeated itself weekly. She bought a cane. Her legs trembled with the effort of walking, or standing, on what were essentially six-inch stilts. Her feet would occasionally bleed, but the shoes absorbed the blood before she was aware of it. She discovered this disturbing phenomenon while getting ready for work one morning. A spot of blood appeared on her white bathroom carpet. When she glanced at her feet, she saw a thick, bubbling line of blood on the top edge of her left shoe. As she watched, it spread above the leather, then reversed course and disappeared. The shoes always looked brighter and shinier after a feeding. That's what she'd started calling it: *feeding*. Now she knew why the shoes didn't heal her blisters and cuts. They needed nourishment. They were leeches and they were self-maintaining.

"What's happened to you? Why you wear those shoes all the time?" Paula asked. "I know you have hundreds of pairs. What's going on? This is not like you." Paula did not look worried, simply curious. Worry would have required that she care.

"I just like these the best," Gina said quietly.

Paula shrugged and went back to her office.

As time passed, Gina's toenails grew inside the heels. Since she could not cut them, she let them grow unfettered until they filled the empty crevices, eventually curling into themselves. They grew into her skin, sliced into her toes, bloodying them further. The shoes happily fed on that too.

Six months after the night at the club, she ran into an acquaintance.

"Gina!" The woman, a designer from one of the other houses, stopped and gave Gina a couple of air kisses. "Well, you lost a lot of weight! You look fantastic!" Gina could see the lie on the woman's face. In truth, the last time she had dared peer into a mirror, she barely recognized the pale, gaunt creature, with deep, dark hollows staring back. She felt especially frail, her weight loss being the only *positive* thing to come out of this mess. She easily fit into a size zero now, the envy of Seventh Avenue.

"Claire, great to see you." Gina smiled, trying to look excited. Then the designer caught sight of Gina's shoes.

"Mon Dieu! Ceux-ci sont superbes!"

Gina grimaced at the compliment, then turned and hobbled off.

A month later, Gina found herself working late again. The layout for the new styles had to be handed to the printer first thing in the morning . . . She was alone. Everyone was gone. She stood up to get another roll of material and felt weak. She sat back down. She looked across the room. The samples seemed so far away, and she was so tired. She just had to get the last piece of material for the comp. *One more swatch and I'll be finished. Then I can go home.* She stood up and began moving forward. She didn't notice the roll of fabric that had fallen across her path until it was too late. Her heel caught on a corner of the roll, tangling itself in the material. She fell backward, landing hard and hitting her head on the marble floor. She lay there, stunned, for a moment. She steadied her breath; then she felt it: a light breeze across the right heel of her foot, from the fan across the way. In a flash, she realized one of her shoes had come loose. Before she could adjust it, it dropped off completely.

She froze.

For a moment nothing happened.

Then a tremor passed through her body, impaling her with fright.

She began convulsing, twisting. The flesh on her leg split open, revealing a mass of bone, muscle, tissue, tendons, arteries, and veins that shattered and burst. With an awful *crack*, her femur exploded out of her thigh, tearing through her skirt, drenching it in the dark, hot blood. The warm, coppery scent overwhelmed her senses.

The other pump slipped off.

Her entire body now shuddered with violent spasms. Her ribcage ruptured, then collapsed onto itself. Her left arm twisted at an impossible angle, then snapped, unable to bend any further. Her lower jaw shattered, then hung, dislocated, against her neck. Her pelvis lifted, then turned enough to break her spine. Blood, tissue, and viscera bathed the room in gore. And yet, she resisted her fate, refusing to die. Her chest heaved violently and shook with the effort, but as her life drained out, her eyes glazed over and she gave up the fight.

*   *   *

The large bloodied mass once known as Gina began to make its way to where the shoes lay. Slurping, the shoes began their feast.

*   *   *

Paula dropped her Marc Jacobs on the desk, annoyed. As usual, the girl was late. She would have to have a talk with her. She stepped into the ante-office to get the swatch card comps. There, in the middle of the spotless room, sat Gina's stilettos, alluring as ever. If anything, they seemed more spectacular than before. She admired them—no, lusted after them. She unconsciously moved toward where they stood. She sat in Gina's chair and reached for them.

What the hell . . . what was the harm? They would be amazing on her. Besides, the girl would never know.

East Side Devil

John C. Foster

The devil walked down 7th Street with a matador's strut and a beauty mark on his cheek, looking for the building marked 269. When he found the spot he rang the bell, and an old couple opened the door. Their day went downhill after that.

He pulled a thin leather glove over the knuckles of his right hand, the other glove held in his white teeth until he adjusted the first to his satisfaction. He repeated the process with his left as the bearded man tied to the chair squirmed, rattling the chair legs on the peeling linoleum of the kitchen floor. The prisoner was trying to speak around the gag, but the devil was busy.

They called this particular devil Spanish because he could pull a confession out of anyone. An Inquisition reference, right? Tall and narrow-hipped, he favored tight gray slacks with flared cuffs and a loose, cream-colored shirt. When he looked in the mirror he thought *toreador* and spun as he imagined a bullfighter might.

A poncho with a vaguely Mexican design went over his shoulder; it furthered the image and kept his shirt clean.

It was all about communicating. Everything was. That's what the Oracle told him that first day in Queens, in a kitchen not unlike the one in which he stood today.

"Hear you're telling fortunes, Moishe," Spanish said to the bearded man. "Reading tea leaves without permission. Without giving over anything to Astoria."

The old Hassid's eyes bulged with his effort to speak, his beard bristling as if with electricity.

Spanish turned to the small stack of old books in the sink and pushed two fragile scrolls in alongside them. Kabbalah. Worthless

Old-World babble.

"It's all crap," Spanish said, lighting a match. "You know this is all crap for the rubes, right?" He dropped the match, and the sink filled with fire as the ancient words burned.

Moishe screamed behind his gag.

"So you said your bit. Now you ready to hear what the Oracle's got to say?"

Sweat poured down Moishe's face, shining in the light of the fire.

Spanish stepped in with a stiff jab that broke the old Hassid's nose. Blood speckled the poncho as Spanish twisted at the hips and knocked the bound man onto the floor, chair and all. Spanish heard pounding from the apartment below as he righted Moishe with a grunt of effort.

"You ready to listen?"

Moishe nodded, bloody and weeping.

"You got something to say?"

Moishe nodded furiously and Spanish slipped fingers beneath the gag, dragging it down over the old man's bottom lip.

"Please, please." The words emerged through bubbles of blood.

Spanish grinned. "You look like the Sunday funnies. You know, they got the words coming out in bubbles?"

Moishe didn't understand him or didn't hear, just said, "You don't want to do this—"

"Whoa whoa whoa," Spanish said, backing up and holding his hands out in a warding gesture. "Shhhhh." He leaned forward and jerked the gag back into Moishe's mouth.

"There's one Oracle, Moishe. That's the message, right? There's only one Oracle and you ain't it."

Spanish turned to where the wife was tied up on another kitchen chair he'd liberated from their table. She was slumped and motionless with a pillowcase over her head, but the flickering fire made her shadow jump from wall to wall.

Spanish sniffed and set to work.

*   *   *

He peeled off the bloody gloves and wrapped them in the soiled poncho as he hurried down from the third-floor walkup. He pushed out the door of the old tenement and down the short flight of steps to the cracked sidewalk. They'd be found soon enough. New York City's Lower East Side was a tight-knit community and word would spread.

He sauntered up the shithole that was Avenue B and, when he saw a gutter he liked, kicked the gory gloves down the drain. The poncho found a new home in a dumpster a block later. He caught his reflection while passing a glass storefront and slowed his walk to a saunter.

Ten minutes later he was on an uptown Q train to 34th Street, where he'd left his Ford. A couple of older black guys moved down the train car in between the passengers and did a fair doo-wop act, earning some quarters. They gave Spanish one look, the way he held on to the pole overhead and let his body sway with the train, and passed him by without holding out the hat.

At Herald Square he hopped off the train and joined the human millipede trudging up the stairs through a miasma of urine and marijuana smoke. He waved a hand in front of his face as the crowd dispersed along the broad sidewalk. New York could be disgusting when it wanted to be.

The phone booth was covered in loops of graffiti but wasn't otherwise too befouled. He dropped a dime, dialing a number in Queens that rang a dozen times before he hung up. A bum asked him for change and he sniffed, staring at the bent man until he shuffled away.

"Disgusting," he said to himself.

His car was a beautiful yellow machine with elegant fins, shining bright against the drab city grime in a way that just screamed *class*. He smirked at the ticket under his wiper blade and dropped it in the street before climbing behind the wheel. Adjusted the rearview mirror and reached up to smooth his hair.

"Shit."

All that business in a stuffy tenement and he'd worked up a sweat. A half-circle of perspiration darkened the fabric beneath his armpit. A quick glance at the other arm confirmed that the infraction had occurred on both sides.

He keyed the ignition and spun the FM dial until he found Tito

Puente, rolled down the window and looked over his left shoulder until a delivery truck gave him an opening and he eased into the flow. He'd have to stop in Brooklyn for a change of clothes.

*   *   *

Drops of water struck the phone as he dragged his finger through seven semicircles on the rotary dial. He was naked after his shower, hair slicked back and enjoying the breeze that billowed the curtains of his fifth-story apartment.

After a shower, he preferred to air dry. Better for his skin.

He hung up, puzzled but not too much. Thought she must have had a run of clients. Wives who wanted to know whether their husbands were cheating. Young men who wanted to know if a girl would say yes. Madame Christina, the Oracle of Astoria, also known as Greek Town.

She found him when he was still Kowalski, showed him how to recreate himself. How everything about him could and should deliver a message. She gave him the name *Spanish* and spread the word about his abilities. Brought him deeper and deeper into the vision business and the loan sharking until he was the only one she needed.

She was all *he* needed, somewhere between mother and lover, teacher and friend. She lavished him with knowledge and gifts, and he killed for her.

After several years passed by, she revealed that she was not Greek but Cypriot, native of Cyprus, an island perpetually torn between Greece and Turkey. He found out with a little digging of his own that she was a Turk through and through. That did nothing for her business, so she became Greek.

Her fortune-telling was a front but also seasoning for the character she portrayed. It didn't take much to spread the word through the Greek criminal set that she knew more than she should about people. Saw when someone was going to move against her before they even considered it themselves.

Her reputation spread through the Greek Orthodox and Hassidic neighborhoods where superstition was as real as taxes and traffic jams.

Spanish opened up both closet doors and considered pants.

Chose black, tight at the hips, flaring at the bottom over sharp-toed boots.

He spun through a few dance steps and debated a red shirt, which would be great for the clubs later that night but a bit much for business. He settled on blue linen so he could avoid any more sweat stains. Slipped a five-shot .32 revolver into the belt at the small of his back and put on a black leather vest over that. A stiletto went into his right boot.

The radio was chattering about the war in Korea, and he shut it off. Spanish didn't give two shits about Korea save one thing: he didn't have to go. The Oracle saw to that.

He shifted his hips in place as music drifted in from the street while he tried calling Christina again. Got nowhere and decided just to head on over. If she was with a client he'd use the back stairs and wait in her apartment.

*   *   *

He left his car on the street. A bell began its mournful tolling as he passed the front steps of a Greek Orthodox Church. He glanced up to see if there was a wedding, but saw only closed doors bound in iron. The neighborhood was crawling with churches. Perfect for business.

He stopped in at a counter where they knew him and tapped a manicured nail against the glass, the damned bell still tolling outside. They wrapped a couple of spanakopita in wax paper, dropped them into a paper sack. Waved him away and the young man he knew as Kasper said things like, "Your money's no good here!" when he tried to pay.

They knew him.

It was a half-and-half street, storefront businesses and two or three stories of apartments above. Not a lot of cabs in the neighborhood, mostly families. He looked through the grimy glass of a *New York Times* box on the corner and took in the headlines. More Korea. He walked on.

The sign was still lit in the plate glass window, MADAME CHRISTINA'S—FORTUNES TOLD in garish purple neon.

He slipped around the corner through the alley, avoiding the wet channel that ran down the middle and cursing a rat that darted across his path.

The staircase in back shook as he took it two steps at a time until he stood on the small platform outside the door. He hated how many keys he had to carry because they ruined the line of his pocket, but Christina was a big believer in security. So he fished out the ring and went down the locks. Only the bottom lock on the knob itself was secured, which was odd, and he opened the scratched metal door.

He flipped the wall switch and nothing happened. "Shit." Felt his way through the pitch black and wished she wouldn't pull the curtains all the time. He found the kitchen table by touch and tossed the keys on it. Heard them slide and fall off the edge. "Dammit." He stepped carefully, scuffing his boots across the tiles as he made his way toward the sink and the light overhead.

He sniffed and his useless eyes grew wide at the stink of body odor.

"Who—"

A rush in the darkness was more heard than seen and then hands were on him, grabbing and punching. He lashed out, screaming, "Do you know who I am?" and reached for the gun at his back but felt it snatched away before his questing fingers could find it. A fist collided with his jaw and his knees went weak.

He went down beneath a dog pile.

"Turn on a light!" a hoarse voice shouted as a cloth sack was pulled over his head. He struggled when they pulled him up but was punched in the kidney for his efforts. He went limp as they half carried him, boot heels dragging on the tiles.

*   *   *

There was a car ride full of honking horns and muttered voices. Then stairs. A slammed door. A familiar smell.

They sat him in a chair and tied him to it.

He heard male voices. Something squeaking as it was wheeled into the room. Smelled smoke.

"Do you know who I am?" he snarled and they snatched off the hood in answer.

His balls shrank when he recognized Moishe's kitchen. Smelled the ashes from the sink. Saw blood on the floor, still sticky.

His eyes were drawn to the black metal of a charcoal grill on a tripod of metal legs. Billows of white smoke rose up from it and he could feel the warmth of smoldering coals. See the shimmer of heat in the air over its open mouth. He blinked away tears and tried to understand what he saw beyond the charcoal grill.

"Christina!" he shouted and she shook in place, bound to the same chair that had so recently held Moishe's wife. They had stripped the Oracle save for a cloth gag in her mouth, and her black hair was wild around her face.

"We know who you are," an old man's voice said, the words thickened by a life on the Aegean. Spanish saw a broad-shouldered, bearded man in elegant red robes with gold crosses. His eyes burned beneath thick black brows, and the hair on his head was the color of iron. He was a priest. Greek Orthodox. Spanish knew him.

"We know who you are," another old man said, also bearded, a yarmulke on his balding head. He was clad in a black suit with a thigh-length coat, a white length of cloth draped around his neck, the Star of David stitched into it at both ends.

Behind the rabbi and the Orthodox priest, Spanish saw several young men with hard eyes. Among them the same Kasper who had told him his money was no good.

"You're hurting our people," the Greek said.

"You're hurting our people," the rabbi said.

Beads of greasy sweat slid down his face, but Spanish pushed out a strangled laugh. "A priest and a rabbi walk into a bar," he said, flashing his bright, white teeth.

The rabbi placed a heavy copper bowl atop the coals and an earthy stink filled the room. Spanish tried to continue the joke but could produce only a dry, clicking sound. He felt his bladder let go.

"You're hurting our people," the rabbi said, his accent honeyed with desert sounds. "And we have decided to send a message."

"I understand, I understand, really I do—"

A fist struck his ear and Spanish stopped babbling.

"Not for you, little fish," the Greek said, admiring the coals. "This will be a message heard by all your kind."

"No-no-no—" A work-roughened hand covered his mouth until a dish towel was stuffed between his teeth, deep enough that he nearly choked.

The kitchen lights went off then and all he could see were two old men lit from below in cruel, flickering orange. It was a vision from an older time, terrifyingly pagan. The firelight drew harsh lines on their faces as they looked at Spanish. Their eyes caught the glow of the coals.

The two holy men each lifted held a hand over the copper bowl. "We will send such a message," they said in unison.

Spanish saw the crowd behind the holy men milling at a disturbance, shuffling to make space.

The bodies of his victims were carried into the kitchen and placed on the floor. They were naked, and Spanish saw that they had been bathed.

The rabbi dipped a hand into the bubbling metal pot atop the coals and scooped forth a dripping handful of clay. He knelt with an old man's care and rubbed the clay across Moishe's bare chest. Beside him, the Greek priest also knelt, spreading clay onto Moishe's wife.

Fear filled the kitchen, thick enough to smell. Not just his own; he caught the reek of it from the gathered crowd.

When the bodies were plastered in clay, the Greek priest rose and offered a hand to the rabbi, who nodded in thanks.

Words were spoken, ancient sounds that hurt the ear.

A foul presence filled the air, and Spanish felt his stomach rebel.

Moishe sat up, globs of clay dropping free. Slowly, awkwardly, he stood. An anonymous, raw thing of earth.

His wife sat up beside him, smooth and unformed. A being of mud.

Their featureless earthen faces turned to Spanish.

"You will bedevil us no more," the holy men said.

Spanish screamed through the gag as the two dripping figures shuffled toward him.

Loathsome in New York

Monica O'Rourke

Arthur Dove crossed Sixth Avenue, avoiding with equal care the frozen mounds of dog waste and mini–ice sculptures of spit and rain that refused to melt, even when temperatures crested above the freezing point.

He never considered himself a bigot. Not really, when he was surrounded by neighbors numbering in the millions. He liked and disliked equally, he would likely say if asked, and really, so he believed. Arthur viewed the homeless with equal disdain. Their race didn't matter—he despised them all. He wasn't to blame for their station in life, and he certainly wasn't the Cavalry. Yet with unmitigated gall came the jutting palms, soliciting alms, for the Great Unwashed lined the streets like trashcans.

Most never bothered to speak—not to Arthur, anyway. They rattled their cups in his face as he passed, and he never failed to wonder how they all managed to have coins to rattle if they were so damned poor.

Heading west toward Seventh Avenue, he passed the former welfare building, now shuttered due to lack of funding. At the bank, the grinning homeless man hovering at the entrance yanked open the door, as if this gesture was somehow equal to a day's work.

Tucking his neck into his collar, Arthur bristled past the disheveled doorman. Funny . . . when Arthur held a door for someone, he didn't expect to get paid for it.

After using the ATM, he headed toward his job.

The streets were overpopulated with homeless these days. Everywhere he looked, indigent: rooting through trash, huddled in doorways, camping out on subway gratings that blew stale, warm recycled air from the bowels of the city.

Their stench seemed to be worsening as well. What once had been a fading odor of unwashed bodies and spoiled garbage imbedded in filthy pores now mingled with the distinct smell of something putrid, like gangrenous flesh under a broiler.

Still they persisted in opening doors and waving plastic cups and upturned hands. Often he found himself holding his breath as he hurried on his way.

*   *   *

The old woman had constructed a cardboard shanty on the church steps. Her head was swathed in rags, and crumpled newspaper protruded from her patchwork shoes.

But it wasn't her plight that had made Arthur stop. Lying at her feet was a German shepherd mutt, filthy checkered bandana tied about his neck. Human suffering he could overlook, but seeing the poor, helpless animal—a victim of circumstance and not choice—was unsettling.

"What are you feeding him?" Arthur blurted, pulling the lapels of his camel hair coat closer together, yanking on his moleskin gloves.

"Anything he want," she cackled, plopping with a groan to the back steps of the church.

"It's bad enough you have to be here. Does the poor dog have to suffer too?" Arthur looked around, embarrassed to be having a discussion with one of *them*.

She stared at him defiantly and then threw back her shoulders. "Mistah, he all I got in the world. Why I wanna give that up?"

"He deserves a good home."

"He got a good home! 'Sides, don't I deserve that too?"

Arthur was taken aback. "I, well, I guess. Sure. I suppose."

"You 'spose? You think I ain't as worthy as a ol' dog?" Her accent, a peculiar combination of Georgia and Brooklyn, made long drawls of her words.

"That isn't what I meant. You could take him to the pound. They'd take care of him."

"They sure would. They'd gas him right quick, old mutt like this.

Ain't no one gonna take care of him like I can. Just gimme some money so's I can buy him a meaty bone."

Arthur pulled his hat over his ears and stomped away. How gullible did she think he was? She'd surely just buy booze or drugs with any money he gave her.

After work, he passed the church again on his way to catch the bus. She was there, reading a magazine, the dog stretched out at her feet.

He easily dismissed her, the old drunk, wasting space and air on the church steps, probably neglecting that poor old dog.

His doorman greeted him, handing him his mail and dry cleaning, and the elevator attendant delivered him to the fifth floor.

Inside his apartment, Arthur tossed his mail on the table and draped the dry cleaning on the foyer chair. The maid had forgotten to change the dead flowers again. Third time this month. He'd have to consider replacing her, which was a shame, so close to the holidays.

The apartment was too warm. He opened the living-room window, the frigid November air rushing in like an uninvited guest. His view of Central Park would be better if he lived on a higher floor, but he could still appreciate the scenery. To his right, small dots skated on Wollman Rink. On his left, tourists milled around and posed in front of Pulitzer Fountain.

He couldn't stop thinking about the dog, wondered if there was a way to rescue it, maybe even bring it home. But there was a strict no-pets policy on his lease, and even owning fish was frowned upon by the board of directors.

The next morning he passed them yet again. It had snowed the night before, and a light layer of powder coated the cardboard home.

He hoped the dog was okay. "Hello? You in there?"

The woman stuck her head out into the frozen air. "What you want?"

"Uh . . . just checking on the dog."

"Hmmph! The dog just fine!"

Without another word, Arthur hurried away.

He passed them twice a day for several weeks, every day feeling pangs of guilt for not giving her money for the dog, but every day managing to overcome his guilt.

One morning he stopped in a convenience store at Union Square, purchased a couple of blankets, and brought them to her.

"One for you, one for the dog," he said. At least this way she couldn't spend his hard-earned money on booze. "Merry Christmas."

She smiled, graciously accepting the blankets. "Know what I'm gonna do? I'm gonna sell his blanket and buy me some wine."

Arthur gasped, and she burst out laughing. "Ain't that what you think I'm gonna do?"

His cheeks flushed, and he laughed.

"It's okay, son. You kin think what you want. You went and did a real nice thing, bringing us these here blankets. That's all that matters, you see?"

He lifted his collar and ducked his head into his coat and hurried home. But this time he felt no guilt, only a comforting warmth.

He searched his cupboards for food to bring them. His counter was littered with cans of sauces, gourmet jellies, and tins of meats like squid and mussels, and he realized she probably had vastly different tastes. Besides, how would she open all those cans?

The market around the corner not only delivered, they took his order over the phone and shopped for him: one of the privileges of shopping in a Madison Avenue market where a quart of milk cost upward of five dollars.

The following morning he quietly placed the bags—filled with such items as cereal, crackers, vegetables, fruit, and dog food—beside her cardboard house, hoping not to disturb the dog—or her. On the bottom of one of the bags he left a twenty.

On his way home, she waved at him and bit into a cracker, throwing back her head and laughing. He laughed along with her but didn't stop on his way. He wanted her to have the moment. To stop now would have been intrusive.

Every day he arrived at her hovel a little earlier and stayed a bit longer. He learned her name was Lucy, and the dog's name was Val.

"Me and Val been t'getha fa'eva," she told him over a Styrofoam cup of coffee. "He one old dog." She stroked his dirty coat, and Val licked her palm.

Arthur smiled but didn't touch the dog. It was a little . . . gritty . . . for his taste.

"If you don't mind a personal question . . . how'd you end up out here?" Over the months, scenarios had played out in his head, visions of drunken brawls in corner bars, of jail scenes and custody cases ending badly.

She sighed, rubbing her palms on the knees of her tattered jeans. "Been out here years now. I was in the hospital. Complications from die-beetus. Run up a ton of them doctorin' bills. Couldn't keep up. So I lost my apartment, lost everything. I still owe a lot of money for that stay!"

"Oh." He bit his lip and chewed on the chapped skin. "No family?"

"Nope. Ain't got one."

"Nobody at all?"

"Just Val here."

"Diabetes, Lucy? Isn't that serious?" He remembered his grand-mother, who was about as heavy as Lucy. Gramma eventually went blind and even lost a leg because of diabetes.

"Sometimes. But I ain't worried. I got it for years now. Some-times, if I feel like I'm gonna pass out, I go to the ER. They give me a shot and I'm fine again."

"What about a shelter? Or welfare? Surely someone could help—"

Lucy laughed, waving her hand at him. "G'on, I ain't no charity case! Don't you worry none about me, Ahtha. I be fine."

He closed his eyes, lowering his head. "Is there any way I can help?"

"You been just wonderful to me, son. Like you was my own flesh and blood. You a real good man, and I don't need nothing else! I got everything I need in the worl' right here. Now you g'on and get to work, Ahtha."

That evening, instead of walking up 14th Street and passing the church, he went around to 13th Street. He couldn't face her again so soon.

He made it home that night and slammed his front door shut, standing in the dark foyer. The ticking of the grandfather clock in the study and lightly muffled traffic noises from five stories below were the only sounds in the apartment. He prepared a cup of tea. He wasn't hungry—hadn't had much of an appetite lately.

Roaming from room to room . . . to room . . . to room, he threw open doors, stared at opulence as if it were alien to him, as though he hadn't grown up enmeshed in it.

The answering machine in the kitchen blinked incessantly with scores of unheard and unanswered calls. He pressed the play button and realized the calls were days old—a week? Invitations to holiday parties, to squash games, to weekends in the Hamptons with colleagues and friends. Somewhere he'd lost touch with the world and was at a loss to remember when. He'd never been so profoundly depressed before. It had become so easy to ignore everything in his life. He considered himself lucky he was able to function at work.

Lucy. Val. For once he wasn't putting the dog before the human.

Another five days went by before Arthur allowed himself to walk up 14th Street again, on his way to work. That morning he didn't have food for her, or money. No blankets, no clothes. In his hand he held one tiny object. One gift.

The box was gone. All that remained where Lucy's life had been was Val, lying obediently on the step as if anticipating the return of his master.

"Val?" The dog's ears pricked up at the sound of his name. "Where's Lucy, Val?" Arthur patted the dog's head with a gloved palm. He slumped to the church steps and waited.

A short while later a priest came out of the rectory at the side of the church. Arthur rushed over to greet him. "I'm sorry to impose, Father, but do you know what happened to the woman who was living on these steps?"

"I'm sorry," the priest said, winding his scarf around his head, trying to block the gusting winds. "She passed away a few days ago. Did you know her?"

Arthur nodded, turning away from the priest, dropping to the church steps. His eyes felt damp and he blamed the powerful wind, because he knew he wouldn't cry, had forgotten how. Arthur would never cry over something like this. No tears wasted on a throwaway person.

Shoulders heaving, water somehow dripped from his face. But there were no tears, just water, nothing much at all.

In his palm sat his gift for Lucy, and he stared at the worthless piece of metal. A key. He had planned to welcome her into his home.

"Come on, Val," he said sadly. The least he could do was take care of her dog. Forget about the tenant board of directors. He'd move if he had to.

"Val? Come."

But Val refused to move.

Arthur held out his hand and tried to coax the dog from the corner of the steps. Val whimpered and lay there, studying Arthur.

"What's wrong, Val? Come on, let's go home."

Val lay his head on his front paws and lifted his eyes.

Kneeling before the dog, Arthur removed his glove and hesitantly stroked the dirty gray fur. He jerked his hand away, surprised at how cold the dog's skin felt. Of course it was winter, and he realized this, but the skin beneath the animal's flesh should have been warm, not as icy cold as the temperature of the outside air.

Arthur offered his hand to Val. The dog ran his tongue over Arthur's palm, and he jerked his hand away. No hot breath panted onto his skin. The lick from that tongue had felt like a caress from a slab of refrigerated beef.

"What's wrong?" he whispered, backing away from the docile creature. Despite its acquiescent nature, something about the animal frightened Arthur. Something was unnerving, and the fact that he couldn't quite figure it out was that much more upsetting.

He backed down the steps and onto the sidewalk, colliding with a collection of trash bags the homeless had already picked through for bottles and cans to return for their nickel deposit. Despite the frigid air, the trash reeked of rotting food and baggies of dog waste.

Arthur wandered up the block, feeling almost drunk, stumbling along like those same loathsome homeless. Unlike him they were bums, as he would have been quick to point out not very long ago.

Head reeling, he leaned into a lamppost, clinging desperately for support, pressing his flushed face against its cooling surface. Knees trembling, they betrayed him and he collapsed, clawing at the pole.

He lifted his head, which now sported a lump the size of an egg and was now in considerable pain. He couldn't remember whether he'd blacked out but suspected he probably had.

Someone helped him to his feet. He turned to offer thanks and came face to face with a homeless man, tattered clothing reeking of cheap booze and unwashed body odor. Somehow it didn't seem so bad.

The man clasped Arthur's hand between his and shook vigorously.

"Thank you," Arthur muttered, touching his bump with his free hand. "I appreciate the help. I-I—"

He yanked his hand away, suddenly realizing how cold the touch was. The chill of the homeless man's touch sent waves of nausea through Arthur's body.

"Are you okay?" Arthur whispered. "Do you need a doctor?"

The man chuckled, wiping his beard with his palm. "I don't think that would help me none. Thanks anyhow."

Arthur thrust his hands into his trouser pockets, rooting around until he found his money clip. "Here." He peeled off several bills. "Have dinner on me."

The man accepted the money and stood a little taller, pulled at his shirt in an attempt to stretch it over his ample belly.

Stretching out his hand toward Arthur, his sullied sleeve rode up the length of his arm.

Arthur gasped at the site of the bluish flesh, mottled with scars and road-mapped with bulging purplish veins.

It was almost as if the man had no circulation.

"Won't you reconsider?" Arthur asked, unable to take his eyes off the decomposing flesh. "A-about a doctor, I mean."

Dark ribbons of vein sluiced the vagabond's face and neck.

"My God . . ." Arthur muttered. "What are you?"

"What kind of question is that?" The man didn't appear offended, although he shook his head and wandered off, leaving a stunned Arthur behind to gape.

During the walk home, Arthur noticed the spirited people clogging the streets, herded along like so much cattle, headed toward God-knows-where in such an incredible hurry.

He felt a great sadness wash over him like the waves of a polluted ocean. No one made eye contact, no one knew he existed. In such an overcrowded city, he felt so alone.

His doorman greeted him because he was paid to . . . paid to know his name, to hand him his newspaper, mail, dry cleaning. There was a borderline obscenity in the unfamiliar familiarity.

Feeling despondent, he let himself into his apartment and heated a can of expensive gourmet soup. The taste was wretched, the worst meal he'd ever had.

The phone rang and the machine picked up the call, recording it in silence, since Arthur had turned down the volume ages ago. Except for work and Lucy, he couldn't recall having a conversation in weeks.

Sunlight filtering in through the kitchen window marked the passage of time, as late afternoon became evening. Strips of moonlight coated the pastel foyer walls.

Shortly after, Arthur got up off the floor and went to bed.

Except for the occasional trip to the bathroom and the occasional detour to the bar in the living room, he stayed in bed for three days, feeling sorry for himself, sorrier for everyone else. The answering machine collected his calls, and his uncharged cellphone sat untouched somewhere on his desk. He wondered if he still had a job to return to. But while that thought terrified him, it wasn't a compelling enough reason to climb out of bed.

Eventually, a compelling-enough reason came to him. *Val.* Somehow he would get the dog off the streets.

He pulled on some clothes and ran out the door, rushing downtown along Fifth Avenue, trying to hail a cab. Across the avenue he spotted one, and he darted into traffic to catch it.

Tires squealed as drivers slammed on brakes in an attempt not to run Arthur down in the street. He threw up his hands, palms out in a *stop* gesture, hoping this would halt the tons of metal rushing toward him.

The cab he was after had driven off, and finding another one in rush-hour traffic was less likely than finding the lost Ark. He didn't bother looking for another one and opted to walk downtown instead.

A short time later he was at the church steps.

Val was gone.

Arthur moaned, slamming his fist into his side in frustration. He was too late. Someone had already taken Val away.

He sat on the steps, elbows on his knees, face cupped in his palms, and he morosely watched everyone rush by.

"Excuse me, do you have—" Several times he attempted to ask someone the time, but no one gave him a glance. No one responded at all. He tried to remember if he'd ever been in that much of a hurry.

The streets seemed so much more crowded these days. The homeless seemed different as well. They were more . . . well, human, a trait he'd never noticed before. They had always just *been*. Part of the streets, filthy-gray extensions of a slab of concrete. Non-people. But now he could see their humanity and he could almost tell, just by looking at them, the sort of people they might have once been.

Shoulders slumped, he walked toward home. He'd failed. First Lucy, and now Val.

A familiar voice called his name. "Ahtha? That you?"

He turned. Lucy and Val stood several feet away.

As if trying to clear their apparitions from his failing eyesight, he blinked repeatedly. But try as he might, he couldn't make them disappear.

"What are you doing here?" he cried, throwing his hands up, rushing toward them.

He grabbed Lucy's broad shoulders, certain that she would disappear before he made contact, even more certain that he was losing his mind and imagining this whole thing. But she didn't disappear, and he pulled her close, hugging her.

"Oh Lucy, Lucy! How can this be? I thought you were dead!"

She held his arms and pushed him back so she could look into his eyes.

"What do you mean, Ahtha?"

"I mean, where have you been hiding? Val! Oh, you found Val." He knelt down and stroked the dog's head.

"You sure got me confused," Lucy said, laughing.

"I have?" He stood up again. "I just meant . . . where have you been? I was worried about you."

"Ain't that sweet! But you know where I been, ain't you? Been laid up in a slab in this here city's morgue. That's where they sends all indigents."

"What are you talking about?"

She studied him for a moment. "Ain't you noticed nothing? Ain't you seen some strange things?"

The noises in the city—endless blarings from a never-ending succession of cars, sirens racing through hopelessly congested streets, whistles and screams and jackhammers, oh my!—seemed to have become a ritornelle of acceptable background noise.

Of course he'd noticed. The ever-growing populace of homeless cluttering the streets like discarded newspaper, blowing in the wind as unneeded and unwanted as litter. He'd noticed that the homeless no longer meant Bowery Bums staggering up the streets drunk, paper bag hiding the Thunderbird in one fist. Homeless now included families, moms with young kids and babies, people who looked poor yet maintained an air of dignity despite their unfortunate station.

But the odd part—and he wondered if this was something new, or if he'd just never noticed it before—the odd part was that many didn't appear to be . . . well, alive.

Lucy stood by his side, a broad smile on her full, cocoa face, yet there was something different now. The Lucy he had last seen, weeks earlier on the steps of the church living in a cardboard box, was not the woman who stood by him now.

Her rich chocolate skin had taken on a grayish pallor, like a dusting of chalk or baby powder. Her lips were tinged blue, the whites of her eyes splotched with streaks of vermilion and saffron.

Yet there was still a smile in those wise old eyes.

"Ain't no more room for us, baby. We gots to take to the streets and make the best of it."

"I'm sorry," he said, feeling sad for her circumstances, wondering if she'd be able to survive indoors, in his apartment. Would she decay in the warmth?

"Don't be sorry, baby. Just make do. When d'you suppose it happened? Or do you already know?"

"What?"

She took his hands and clasped them between hers. "You don't know. Do you?"

He squeezed his eyes half shut and shook his head, shrugging.

"Think back, baby. When did it happen?"

"When did what ha—" But then he remembered running for the cab, darting into Fifth Avenue traffic. The minivan plowing into him, his body hurtling through the air, smashing into a lamppost. For the remaining seconds of his life he heard screams, and sirens in the distance. He'd savored hope of being saved. He'd felt no pain, he remembered. *So how bad can it be*, he'd wondered, *if it didn't even hurt?*

He looked down at his arms, at the gray-blue tinge of his skin.

"Let's go find a place to sleep," she said, taking his hand and leading him into Central Park, Val following closely behind.

The Chosen Place

Patrick Freivald

When they find my body maybe they'll think it's murder, a broken girl on broken beams, and they'll investigate. Maybe they'll learn the truth. It's too much to hope for justice, but I guess despite everything I'm still young enough, vain enough, to hope that hope anyway. Fourteen is too short a time, in my years or your weeks, and I'm so, so sorry.

The Haudenosaunee chose the wrong side in the Revolutionary War, and at George Washington's command General Sullivan did his best to exterminate them, destroying every village as they burned their way from Tioga to the Genesee River. No deaths were reported at Canandaigua in 1789, but the Continentals burned all the buildings, the fields and orchards, so that the proud confederacy of six nations "may not be merely overrun but destroyed."

George Washington said that. Ordered that.

What an asshole.

At the north end of Canandaigua Lake—Canandaigua is a bastardization of Ganundagwa or "The Chosen Place" in Onondowaga, and we stole both the place and the name—a building's huge skeleton stands on the exact spot of the original village. The North Shore Project boasts five oversized stories of steel girders and just enough platforms to remain dangerous, surrounded by chain link meant to keep out teenagers and troublemakers. Mired in politics and money, it broods over the North Shore breweries and restaurants, a decrepit monument to greed and stupidity that the locals try to pretend isn't there. I think it was supposed to be a luxury hotel for a shithole town with a dying economy.

It's easy to get inside. There's a spot on the shoreline where the chain link has come free of the sand. You can crawl under—well, you can't but I can, and I have, only scraping my back a little bit. After that you take one of the iron fire escapes up the side of the building and you can sit on the top floor and watch the waves. Only at night, though, and no smoking or someone will see you and you'll get a ticket. Cops love ignoring the drugs and abuse in favor of handing out tickets for stupid shit, but this, yeah, maybe ticketing for this was okay. You could die up here—one misstep, one gust of wind you weren't expecting, and bye, Felicia.

It's freezing on the sixth floor, with no walls to block the wind. Cold but peaceful in a loud sort of way, and though I only wore it for the pockets I'm glad I have my coat. The waves crash against the bones of two civilizations, one dead and one dying, and you can see lights from houses twinkling ten miles down the shoreline. People laugh and talk down at the brewery, their voices smeared by the wind but their spirits undaunted, and over at the Shell stadium some concert blared country music from some touring band, mediocre rock 'n' roll with a steel guitar's twang stretching like taffy over the sky. Peaceful, but it would also be beautiful without the greasy smells from Taco Bell and McDonald's and the Chinese place, the musty, fishy funk from the inlet, the rotten trash in the dumpsters behind the apartments. All that stink rises up like smoke around the North Shore skeleton, sixty feet up and a lifetime away, a memento mori of Sullivan's destruction jammed in my nose and burning my throat. It turned my stomach more than the tweaker on the first floor, and he probably hadn't showered in weeks.

I'm sorry. I don't know if my nausea makes you uncomfortable. Can you feel it in there? Do you even have a stomach yet to turn, or a gag reflex to gag? I should have paid more attention in Health Class, maybe I'd know. But history was always my thing. If I could live in the past I wouldn't have to live in the present.

Sullivan's orders were to destroy everything, kill all the men and take as many women and children captive as they could. Washington wanted to enslave the entire population, drag them in chains to the East Coast, broken and on bended knee, and then breed them into extinction. Early French settlers had named them the ihrokoa, the Iroquois, a pidgin word that meant "the killing people." The Omàmiwinini, Algonquin, hated the Haudenosaunee and had warred against them for generations, and were all too happy to paint their neighbors as murderous savages, to help the French to drive them west and south. In return the French gave them firearms and syphilis.

And it didn't work. The Haudenosaunee, allied with the Dutch and the English, proved too strong and drove the Omàmiwinini north.

The Iroquois had a fierce reputation and had raided white settlements for years, especially now with their Loyalist allies. But in the face of Sullivan's might the killing people ran, scrambling to flee with their families across the frontier and into what would later be Canada. What the Algonquin couldn't do in a century our fledgling country did in ten weeks, and almost without a fight. Some forces you can't stand up to, no matter how fierce your will, no matter how strong your resolve. To stand is to die, or worse. There's always worse. Sullivan broke them and burned them out, but took no captives. We can only imagine Washington's disappointment.

There goes the clock tower, 11:00 P.M., the last chime until morning, European order imposed even on the days themselves. Time for a drink.

My curfew was ten, and by now I know he's furious. He always wants me where he can see me, where boys can't be pawing at my little breasts and that space between my legs. Not so little now, and bigger every day. Sweaters aren't enough anymore, and we both know what he'll do when I start showing. Do you think he'd use a doctor or a knife? Do you think at all?

I see him now, pacing, screaming at Mom, screaming hateful words at me even though I'm not there. Calling me, lips frothing as hate spills from them across electric lines. Whore. Slut. Bitch. Cunt. All those things he wishes I would be so he could justify what he's done, what he's doing, and what he wants to do again. When the other is the enemy you can do anything to them and stand righteous, at least in your own mind.

I'd dropped my phone in the water—I don't need it anymore.

I kissed a boy once, in sixth grade. It was nice and sweet and made me feel good and I wanted to do it again the next day. But he told his friends and they teased him until he stopped talking to me. I didn't dare tell. It was common for the British to live with and inter-breed with the natives, but most of their children passed for white. What would you pass for, if tonight wasn't tonight?

He'll call the police. The other police, his buddies. He wouldn't want to find me himself; that's too easy. If his friends found me they could shame me on the ride home and then he could shame me in front of them, and then shame me again when we got inside. He was probably hard just thinking about it, rubbing himself when he thought my mother wasn't looking.

She knew. She just couldn't stop it.

Sullivan had frustrated Washington, taking months to provision his armies where Washington had wanted a lightning strike. He thought that the longer they delayed, the greater a chance the Haudenosaunee would find out and prepare a defense. He needn't have worried: they knew right away, they'd always known thanks to spies in his office. But in the face of impending destruction they went to the British for help, and the British didn't believe them, or pretended not to believe them.

I can't blame her for pretending not to believe me.

I mean, I can, but who cares? She's the one who has to live with it. With him.

The winter of 1779 was particularly harsh, and the displaced Haudenosaunee huddled around Fort Niagara in desperate camps. They had little food and less shelter, and if the British brought in food and supplies to help them it hadn't been nearly enough—they had a war to fight, and ten thousand men, women, and children too weak or too cowardly to fight an overwhelming enemy proved to be quite a burden. Disease and starvation scoured the camps, and thousands didn't survive to spring. Pioneers were still finding bodies three years later, huddled against wind and winter, or long picked clean by the carrion crows and turkey vultures.

Seagulls. They're what gave me the idea. The name doesn't fit—they should be called dumpster gulls. They don't live near the sea and eat garbage almost exclusively, scavenging French fries or pieces of ice cream cones from parking lots, fast food bags out of refuse bins. Flying rats, they'd descend on anything that even looked like food, sometimes even knocking stuff right out of your hand. And then they'd fight over it, calling out their high-pitched, hyperventilating shrieks. The crows and vultures can barely get a beak in edgewise.

There's more than one way to flee an unstoppable force. There was probably another way and I'm sorry I'm not strong enough to see it. I'm sorry I couldn't be what you'd need me to be.

I don't know how much Oxy it takes, but twenty should be more than enough.

I don't want Mom to find me in my bedroom, or some little kid riding his bike along the shore stumbling upon what's left of me. I don't want my father—your father—to find us first, to hide what evidence a DNA test might reveal.

The birds will let them know I'm here. Someone will see them, gathered around my Chosen Place, my Canandaigua, and they'll find me, and in the autopsy they'll find you.

The Hunting of the Kipsy:
A Cryptozoological Report

Hal Johnson

It's been 2500 years since the fish ate Jonah, and it will be another six or seven months before Leviathan swallows the world; in between these termini, sea monsters have been consistent nuisances to mankind, disrupting shipping lanes and vomiting on beaches.

Scarcely more affable are their low-sodium analogues, the lake monsters. The terrible Loch Ness Monster is the example best known to the layman, but cryptozoologists are frankly embarrassed by its popularity. If you are the sort of person whose favorite author is Shakespeare or favorite movie is *Citizen Kane*, then ho-hum, the Loch Ness Monster is for you. The more discerning of our cryptozoological community gravitate towards the study of the yobgorgle (*Megasus pinkwateri*) in Lake Ontario, or the ogopogo (*Hydrophidius naitaca*) in Lake Okanagan, to name just two.

I tell you this because I, the greatest of all cryptozoologists, have made my name studying those fearsome creatures that dwell between the devil of the lake and the deep blue sea of the deep blue sea, creatures that frolic and sport—or more accurately lurk and brood, for they are fearsome creatures, after all—in the tidal marshes and the brackish backwash of estuaries. I have watched the serpent Willatuk play hacky sack in Puget Sound, and I have ear-tagged Oliver Cromwhale as it swam up the Thames.

There is one brackish creature I have never laid eyes on, though, nor has any man or woman alive. This is the elusive kipsy (*Flumenoferox poughkeepsiensis*), a river monster of the lower Hudson. Whether there is one kipsy, like the lonely Nessie, or many, like the innumerable morags spilling like vermin out of Loch Morar, the literature does not know. Certainly *something serpentine* sank the S.S. *Normandie* in New York Harbor. *Something fearsome* pulled down the Holland and Lincoln Bridges that once spanned the Hudson, forcing the Port Authority to send commuters home through hastily-dug tunnels.

It was those tunnels that attracted a man some call the master of all monster-hunters, the king of cryptozoologists: I refer, of course, to Saxony's own Georg Philipp Friedrich, freiherr von Hardenberg (deceased). A bear of a man he was, rippling with terrifying muscles that twitched and throbbed of their own accord, whether he wished them to or not. Even his tongue and his eyeballs were ripped. A polymath, a poet, a man of culture, he was known as the terror of three continents:

- In Libya, he had bitten an amphisbaena in half, reducing it to the humiliating state of being two normal snakes.
- In India, he defeated a rakshasa at Indian leg-wrestling (fact: rakshasa cannot arm wrestle, because their hands are attached backwards, palm out).
- In his native Saxony, he had given a hickey to the Tannenberg Venus.

Like all good monster hunters he had a stage name; fearsome creatures everywhere quailed in terror when their spiky, poisonous ears heard it. Who cored the manticore? Who deuced on the medusa? Who cold-cocked the cockatrice? Of course it was *Novalis.*

Indeed, few men knew tunnels as well as he, thanks to his youthful experiences bagging Paracelsian gnomes in Saxon salt mines. Small wonder the sub-Hudsonic tunnels, engineering feats and much safer than those ill-advised bridges, attracted his attention. Also, he said, he wanted to see if the New World possessed creatures as fearsome as the Old. He was cocky, but we were all much cockier back then. Eagerly he swam across the Atlantic like Beowulf racing Breca, a cutlass in one hand to slice up krakens.

"Welcome to New York," the Welcome Wagon said, as Novalis dragged his hulking body up out of the harbor.

"Vich vay iss the bibliothek?" said Novalis. He may have said it with a slight accent, but of course for a man of culture such as the scion of the von Hardenbergs, mastering the English idiom was a cakewalk. *A strudel walk,* they say in Saxony. Soon he was dry and sitting in the research library. He had tried to net the stone lions by the stairs before he entered, but of course that was a big misunderstanding.

Novalis was nothing if not thorough, yet his research into the ethnology, diet, mating habits, and potential crepuscularity of the kipsy proved only how little information there was. Even the *Encyclopedia Americana,* for its "kipsy" entry, contained only one word.

Dangerous.

"Bah!" said Novalis (and, again, with a little bit of an accent); "no monster shall be the danger of me," which was technically to prove true. He untangled his net from poor Fortitude and purchased, with ancestral gold, a small dinghy and a couple of oars. By day he would row far up the Hudson, and at night he would let the current carry him down. As he rested beneath the starry sky, he would whittle the ends of the oars into spear points, for fishing and self-defense. And always he kept his eye open, for monkey-mermaids, for narwhals, for Coney Islanders, and especially for a kipsy.

There is more to fear in the wild stretches of the Hudson than just an estuary monster. Every day the sun rose over a tangle of quaint piers oozing deadly gentrification and then set over Palisades teeming with savage natives. In the distance, the East River glowed radioactively. Most deadly of all, some say, are the complicated tides that spiral around Long Island Sound, the bays, innumerable rivers and kills, and the New York Bight of the Atlantic as their water all tries to go, Three Stooges–style, through the same door at once. Novalis's little boat would spin in circles, and only his good right arm, ropy and writhing at the oars, drew him to safety. He had hair'sbreadth escapes and dramatic monologues. He dodged ferries and ducked under cannon fire (from Jersey City). He accidentally glimpsed Lady Liberty's ankles, quite scandalous in those days. But he saw no kipsy.

Undaunted, Novalis started rowing further afield, up the little kills on Staten Island or into the tangled streams that flow into the Hudson via the Croton Reservoir. Along these twisting banks he finally spotted kipsy spoor: droppings filled with the fanny packs and sunscreened noses of tourists.

When a fox or a fugitive wishes to elude a tracker, he runs into the all-obliterating water; imagine then how difficult it is to track a creature *that never leaves the water at all.* But Novalis had tracked great rocs on the wing, by the imprints their feathers left in clouded skies; and mere water was no hindrance to him. He stopped to unload most of his supplies, the tent and the food and the croquet set piled up on shore, and, his dinghy lightened, he crept silently upstream. The kipsy, when he encountered it, showed its teeth and swamped the boat, but Novalis had his pointed oars and his good right arm. It is not easy to get a serpentine creature with no limbs in a full nelson, but Novalis managed it. My pen scarcely dares to describe the contest. Literally, it leaks ink, like terror-sweat, when I try. But soon the great beast was unconscious, and Novalis sat astride its buoyant body, with one unshattered oar poling his way downstream. He whistled as he floated. He had already become the only human ever to capture a kipsy alive, the crowning moment of his storied career. He sailed his slumbering craft past a tent and a croquet set. He sailed under hanging fronds and through bright marigolds. He sailed past a tent and a croquet set.

"That is odd," thought Novalis, to himself. When he was just thinking, he had no accent, of course.

Hanging fronds again, marigolds again. Novalis began to get worried about the amount of time this was taking. It would hardly go well for him were the kipsy to regain consciousness before they reached the cages he'd had built at the Dyckman marina. Croquet. Fronds. Croquet.

Finally Novalis realized he'd somehow lucked into one of those fabled circular rivers that upstate New York is littered with. He decided to strike out overland, dragging the kipsy as he went; but when he tried to hoist the two-ton beast onto his shoulders with his good right arm, he found that arm surprisingly weak. By the time he realized that his left arm was the stronger, the kipsy had groggily opened its eyes. Quick as a flash it slithered through marshland and disappeared down a burrow. A crestfallen Georg Philipp Friedrich, freiherr von Hardenberg trudged back to civilization.

"That vasn't zo bad," he said to himself. He could always try again. But when he reached Manhattan and consulted the "bibliothek" he learned to his horror that the river he had rowed down, the anonymous hidden river he would never again find, must not have been circular after all, but instead looped in a figure eight, with a half-twist, like a Möbius strip.

Such an arrangement means little to the uninitiated; but Novalis was a polymath, and he understood the dread implications at a glance. Traveling along a Möbius strip, elementary topology tells us, flips a body's right and left, mirror-style. Depending how many times Novalis had gone around . . .

Nervously, just to be sure, Novalis drew from his pocket, with his twiggish right arm, some scrawled doggerel notes for a sonnet he'd been composing for Chancellor Bismarck. The sweat trembling in beads on his brow suddenly trickled down into his eyes, and he blinked it away. At first glance everything looked fine and normal: the name Otto, with a heart around it, remained at the top of the page. But then he saw—his hammering heart shook the right side of his body—that the rest of the paper was filled with Leonardo mirror writing. With his left arm Novalis struck the library carrel in grief, shivering it to splinters.

Worst of all was the shame, the way children would gawk as Novalis held a pen in his left hand or entered a room left-foot forwards. "What's wrong with that man, Daddy?" they would say, and Daddy would tell them it was not polite to stare. But almost as bad was the way food, prepared by right-handed chefs and (perhaps more importantly) packed with chemically dextrorotatory sugars, refused to nourish his backwards body. Novalis was a fine chemist— he could use words like *dextrorotatory* without looking them up first—and he knew he was doomed. What grim irony, he probably thought, that the foremost scientist of his day should be undone by science itself, by the trivial intersection of nutrition and chirality. Even water stuck in his throat, choking him, thanks to the dread Coriolis effect.

Of course he returned to the Croton Reservoir in search of the Möbius river, but he kept rowing the boat in the wrong direction and never got very far at all. Rapidly his mighty body withered. His eyeballs, which had once pulsed with musculature, now rattled about like raisins in their hollow sockets. A German who cannot eat sugar is not long for this world. He could not even swim home. By steamer they shipped him back to Saxony, and all New York gathered at the harbor to wave their handkerchiefs in salute for the brave man who had come so far to risk so much. "We'll never forget you," everyone lied, and then promptly returned to mugging one another.

Young von Hardenberg, Novalis no longer, tossed off some more poems and salty epigrams in his last days, and everyone said, with the flattery we owe the dying, that they were very good. Soon enough, at the age of twenty-eight, Georg Philipp Friedrich, freiherr von Hardenberg, in a giant bed with downy white covers in Weissenfels, shriveled away to nothing at all. His last words were of the kipsy—did the kipsy wither and die, too?

(Turns out she did not; von Hardenberg had wasted his life.)

With his passing I was finally able to take out of storage the brass plaque that said #1 MONSTER HUNTER. Briefly I polished it on my knee and hung it on my door at last.

And that is my secret: I leave the kipsy be. From that moment till the present day, and even for six or seven months into the future, I will remain the greatest of all cryptozoologists.

A Few Leaves from the Travelogue of Doctor Julius Jonsson, Cryptobotanist and Hylesoprotolist: Bay Ridge, or, The Belief in the Undead Still Exists in New York

Erik T. Johnson

. . . a mild April night when I found myself approaching the community of Bay Ridge from the West. My horse Lethe and I went along the Brooklyn-Queens-Expressway, or BQE. From high atop the asphalt road, the windows of run-down apartment buildings ran brightly by my feet, and high-rise apartment complexes loomed ahead, the most boring use of rectangular shapes imaginable, like diagrams in elementary geometry texts. Costco Price-Club, where the natives go to shop at wholesale prices, was quickly lost to view below as I rode on by two neon women framed by glowing X's atop a warehouse on Third Avenue. Soon the signs for car dealerships appeared on my right. Name brands fought for the very air, but I ignored their scuffle and continued to the 86th Street exit, where I hoped to find some rare plants growing by the curb. Unusual things often grow undetected near the ends of roads, because when people approach the end of a path they look to what is beyond it rather than at the path itself.

Alas, I had come to yet another community lacking in cryptobotanical specimens. The highway opened onto a land of concrete paths and brick buildings. Numbers rather than names marked the streets. This quantitative approach to direction hinted at a lack of depth, a bad sign because seeds cannot flourish without it. Not a tree lined those indexed streets! It was a hard year to be a botanist, and a worse time to be a traveling one. (Forgive me, my poor reader, for repeating this phrase for the hundredth time in this travelogue. As I mentioned in Chapter Two, I have spent most of my life hating the written word, and I fear my writing awkward as a result—this sentence being no exception!) All I found by the highway exit was some *Ranunculi* and *Regnellidia*, squashed beneath the shade of ubiquitous air-conditioning units protruding from the apartments above. Without any rare herbs to gather and peddle, I would once more have to rely on my hylesoprotolist studies to earn me a Comfort Inn's rest.

The streets were empty as though it were a holiday, or a plague season. It was late.

Suddenly I heard a mob shouting over toward Fifth Avenue. Cautiously I jumped back onto Lethe and we advanced, her hooves masked by the noise of discord. The crowd was located two blocks up and to the left, on Fifth Avenue between 86th and 87th Streets. We passed a Greek deli, a Chinese laundry, an Arabic video rental, and a pizzeria, so that before I came upon the natives I was aware of some of the faces I might see. It had rained earlier and the street was smooth and shiny as apple skin. Soon the wet shadows of people gesticulating wildly were thrown across our path by orange flickering streetlights. They were right around the corner.

I decided to circle the block and get a safer view of the crowd from the other side.

How to describe the houses of Bay Ridge in this travelogue! There are a few decent, two-family homes of brick, Tudor, or brownstone style, but these are the exception. Most of them look like children who have been playing dress-up in their mommy's bedroom and have gone too far in an attempt to be colorful. In one dwelling, Lethe and I saw pale yellow siding, an ochre stoop, and bright lemon-curtained windows. It looked as though the owners had based their look upon a swatch of yellows from the home-decorating center of a hardware store. One also saw plastic flowers planted among colored stones—a botanical outrage. I noticed Halloween decorations on doors, though it was the second month of spring. Lawn jockeys, Virgin Marys resting among bushes, BEWARE OF DOG signs, grand baroque Italian banisters for unimpressive stairways, and American flags completed the bewildering look of the neighborhood. From all this it was easy to see that the natives were colorblind, forgetful, and wanted to believe in something that could be pointed at with a finger. I was to discover that the last part of my supposition, at least, was indeed correct.

Presently the scene of confusion was before us. A crowd of all sorts was gathered before an Off-Track Betting service. The butts of cheap cigars covered the street as if they'd fallen with the rain. Some of the excitable group had flashlights, and these roved the night like spastic sunbeams.

A series of loud voices stood out from the general chaos.

"He crosses 93rd Street with wide strides!"

"He grabbed my ass!"

"He throws me over the turnstile, so that I get a ticket every time I go to take the R train!"

"He steals quarters from parking meters!"

"Kill the zombie!"

"He's not a zombie, he's a vampire!"

"Vampire, zombie, whatevah! Kill the freakin' thing!"

Sensing a hylesoprotolistic opportunity, I tethered Lethe to a STOP sign and joined the gathering.

"Where is the vampire in question?" I asked a colorblind widow wearing navy blue.

"That's just the thing! If I could only tell you!" she said, throwing her arms up in the air.

"Then why may I ask are we all gathered outside the OTB?"

She looked at me with annoyance.

"Uck! How do I know?"

"You *know* through the operations of the crowd, Madame. They are a many-legged brain that may disperse at any moment, like a dance company's dramatization of dementia praecox."

She ignored me and returned to waving her arms aerobically.

I spied a boy of about eight, who risked being trampled as he collected cigar butts and put them in a *Century 21* shopping bag.

"What are you doing there, young man?"

"I'm smoking," he said.

"Do you know why we are outside this OTB? Where is the vampire?"

"He used to live above the OTB. He played the ponies all day. Then he died a mean drunk."

"What was his name?"

The boy laughed.

"It was funny! It was Bark-a-loo!"

The name brought eucalyptus and lupins to my mind, and I frowned with longing so that he laughed even harder.

But there was something else about that surname.

My mind has been trained to recall the oddest of details. Certainly my scientific knowledge was full of them, but faithful readers of this travelogue will also recall the minutiae involved in the uses my father put to a combination of saltwater and the movements of red ants, and the way in which I located Flatbush Avenue by my careful noting of the position of certain candy wrappers in the wind.

Now I remembered: the smallest cemetery in Brooklyn is the Revolutionary Cemetery, at the corner of Narrows and Mackay Place. Only members of the Barkaloo family are buried there.

"To Narrows and Mackay!" I cried, and the crowd, at seeing a stranger so confident in their world, followed me with their flashlights, as though I had gathered them there to begin with for this purpose alone.

Fill a dark night with people and it grows strange and magical as a tank overpopulated with countless lobsters at a seafood restaurant. It is not hard to lose one's head over such easy wonders. But I knew I must remain calm and kept my mind on nothing but the goal as we journeyed south.

The Revolutionary Cemetery was small indeed—perhaps the size of two grand pianos resting side by side. Elms and maples threw redundant darkness over us as I tied Lethe to a parking meter and swung open the waist-high gates.

I heard voices at my back.

"Look—there he is!"

"That's the stranger!"

"No, that's Barkaloo. We better get out of here."

"It's nice out."

"Hey—Barkaloo lived over an OTB!"

"So?"

"So that's about horses, betting on horses!"

"Shut up!"

"No, wait! And this guy has a horse. Who else has a horse in Bay Ridge?"

"It's freakin' weird!"

"It *is* Barkaloo—he's going to invite us into his home and kill us!"

"But he lived over the OTB."

"Now he lives in the graveyard!"

I had to act fast.

"People, people, please!" I cried. "I've found something!"

It is a fact that a crowd shutting their mouths all at once is quieter than a single person doing the same, just as many prayers uttered at once are stronger than one. I took command of this powerful silence.

"A freshly opened grave!"

I did not lie. A grave had recently been violated. Mounds of dirt and coffin-splinters were strewn at my feet. It reminded me of the detritus of a shipwreck.

The curious, the brave, the frightened, and the dumb surrounded me to peer at the hole.

"There's nobody in it!"

"Barkaloo is on the loose!"

"This one here with the horse is Barkaloo, I'm telling you."

"Yeah, he's tricked us!"

And now I have reached the point of my narrative, dear reader, that I promised to reveal in Chapter Two of this travelogue, some four hundred-odd pages ago. That is, the reason why a man who swore his life through that he should have nothing to do with written history has produced the example in your hands.

Fear is a perpetual motion machine. Only a fool would not flee a mob powered by such a device. But in the sky there were clouds that roamed restless and black, and they fled from a glowing moon as if they were shadows. And when the clouds were gone I could see a small stalk emerging from the bottom of the open grave before me.

It was pure white with a lightly veined surface. I had never seen its like before.

How wrong I had been about the cryptobotantical possibilities of Bay Ridge!

Enchanted with this specimen, I was more than startled when they tossed me in the grave. The dirt fell upon me full of holes, so that it seemed they flung shovels of moonlight mixed with earth. I heard Lethe neigh in fright, a car screeching and then hitting something with a dull sound, falsetto screaming. And then I could hear no more and my eyes went blind as pebbles. . . .

* * *

I do not know the name of the man who dug me out of that pit. Before I saw him I felt his long fingernails on my face, gently wiping, soft as a woman's hair. He was exceedingly obese, bald as a blade of grass, and his eyes lacked pupils. He wore an olive raincoat filled with holes. I associated the color with the phrase "I'll live." And for a moment I thought he must be God.

The crowd was gone.

After he unearthed me, my rescuer stood mutely at the foot of the grave. Too dazed to thank him, I dug the white-stalked plant out from the soil beneath me and ran down toward the shore, nearly slipping in a pool of horse blood at the corner.

I stood under the Verrazano Bridge, which loomed in the fog like a giant harp. I finally decided on tending to the plant in the nearby Dyker Golf Course, where a man can easily hide among the thick vegetation. I played gardener there for a week, looking ragged as a vampire myself as I watched my find grow.

It bloomed in fantastic ways, rapidly developing large rectangular leaves that sprung from a flat, hard spine. They were colored a milky white and very smooth to touch. The leaves appeared successively, sometimes a hundred a day, until there were thousands of them.

In the past I would take a hitherto unseen plant and investigate its properties, grinding parts of it into a balm, a powder, and a potion, and then test these medicaments following Agrippa's Capricornian methods.

But I could think of nothing else to do with this marvelous thing than write the history of its discovery upon its very leaves. Ink flows so easily on the fragile surface.

It has not been an easy task to complete. The day after I began this travelogue, I was awoken by the sound of another mob. And now I will relate how hylesoprotolism saved my life yet again.

The wind . . .

A Nightmare on 34th Street

Steven Van Patten

"Are you going to tell me where these friends of yours are, or are you going down for all one hundred and forty-eight murders?"

Miles Ford looked more like the lead in a romantic comedy than a tough guy. But despite his affable appearance, Mr. Ford had been found holding a samurai sword in a famous department store filled with dead bodies. Answers were needed.

"I didn't kill anyone. At least, no one human."

Detective Greg Chapman took a deep breath. "Yeah, I heard the story you gave my guys. You need to sell that shit to the Sci-Fi Channel. But I figure you'll tell me what really happened eventually for the simple fact that you don't seem like the 'comfortable going to jail' type."

"Thank you. I think."

"In the meantime, you want some water?"

"Yes, please."

The room they were in looked like the ones on television cop shows. Of course, the cop shows never let on that an interrogation room smelled like a mix of paint thinner, sweat, and flatulence.

Miles took the small plastic cup from the detective's hands and gulped down the water in three quick swallows.

"We didn't murder anyone," he volunteered. "We were there to save people."

Chapman laughed as he rolled up the sleeves of his button-down dress shirt. "Well, if that's the case, I gotta tell ya, you really suck at saving people. So why were *really* you in Macy's?"

"My friends and I were assisting someone fight the creatures you saw."

"Did that someone tell you where those things came from?"

"It wasn't specifically mentioned, but I just assumed they came from hell." Miles made eye contact with Chapman for the first time.

The detective stared back at Miles in silent annoyance for ten seconds before saying, "I gotta warn you, if you stick with that bullshit supernatural story, you're going to end up doing shock therapy in Bellevue for the next three weeks."

"You don't have proof I did anything," Miles said. "And without proof you'll have to let me go eventually."

"Look, asshole, I've got one hundred and forty-eight dead bodies, some of which look like genetically enhanced government experiments, all in the world's biggest department store! So all I have to do is obey my captain and the frightened citizens of this city. If that means bending the rules so your stay is long and uncomfortable, then so be it!"

"Isn't there security footage?" Miles asked. "Why don't you go check that? I'll wait here, Mr. Patriot Act."

Anger filled Chapman's eyes. With a sweep of his hand, which had a large tattoo of an anchor on it, he pushed a yellow notepad and a pen in front of Miles.

"You know, that's a great idea. I'm going to visit the officers compiling the video. And when the footage shows what really happened, we'll all know for sure. Personally, I hope you didn't kill anyone. Mainly because I can't tell you how much I would love to take your ass to Bellevue myself. That way, I can sign you in personally. Hell, I might even stick around and watch them light your smart ass up. You'll probably be drooling like a stroke victim for the rest of your miserable, little life."

Chapman turned to leave the room. "I suggest you start writing down what really happened on that notepad. It'll make it easier to figure out what do with you when I get back." He slammed the door behind him before making his way to the adjoining room where Captain Willis stood watching Miles behind a two-way mirror. "What do you think?"

"He looks relieved that you're gone," Willis said. "He didn't seem frightened of you. I think this poor bastard believes he and his invisible friends are demon killers."

"Any word from the lab?"

"Nothing yet on the corpses, human or otherwise," Willis answered. "We are flipping his phone and hacking his emails. With any luck, we'll find the mental health professional who's looking for this prick."

"Great," Chapman turned to leave, then thought better of it. "Cap, what if this shit is true? I mean, you saw those bodies just like I did. What the entire fuck, boss?"

Willis turned and watched as Miles began writing in the notepad. "If this asshole is telling the truth, we are in for a long fucking week."

"Hopefully, he's just nuts."

"Hopefully."

*　　*　　*

It made sense I was the easiest one for them to find. My mother still lives on the old block, where I grew up playing kickball and chasing the neighborhood girls with Albert, Reggie, and Nick. Everyone, including me, had since moved away, but my mother is still hanging in there. She's one of the last African-Americans not to succumb to the increased cost of living brought on by the smothering cloud of gentrification that has permeated Brooklyn in recent years. Needless to say, I was surprised to run into Albert Abeke just as I was leaving my mother's condo. I was even more shocked that, after a friendly greeting, my childhood friend struck me over the head, kidnapped me, and tied me to a bed in his home in Long Island.

When I came to I knew where I was, because I had been to the house a dozen times. As adults, Albert and I had maintained our close friendship. He'd even raised his son, Jonah, to call me "uncle."

"Nick and Reggie are on their way," said Albert, standing over me. "I hacked into your phone to call them. I should bring you up to speed before they get here."

I noticed Albert's wife, Maxine, and his son, Jonah, watching the scenario from a few feet away. They both looked terrified and had clearly been crying. When I asked what was going on, Jonah was the first one to respond. "I'm so sorry about this, Uncle Miles."

"Why's the boy apologizing?" I asked, looking at Maxine. "He didn't kidnap me, did he?"

"No," Albert answered. "He is apologizing for reading an incantation from an old book of magic spells, which in turn has set terrible events in motion. These events have forced me to take over my great-grandson's body and kidnap you."

"Say what now?"

"You're not talking to Albert." Maxine finally found her voice. "His great-grandfather, Baratunde Abeke, from his Nigerian side of the family, has possessed him." She sobbed.

Ten-year-old Jonah said, "I was going through Dad's things and I found this book. When I read out loud a man appeared. He tried to kill us and Dad became possessed.

"You know what? Ya'll crazy people need to untie me!"

"Not until you agree to help me fight the Nameless One!"

"Albert, the only person I am fighting is you when I get off of this bed!" I had noticed that Albert's Nigerian accent, practically nonexistent by the time he turned thirteen years old, was more pronounced than ever.

"Didn't the woman just tell you I am not Albert?"

"He knows everything that Albert knows, and Albert is still in there somewhere," Maxine explained. "That's how he came up with the idea of recruiting you guys to help him. Albert feels he had the best friendship with you, Nick, and Reggie."

"Okay, so it looks like you've all lost your minds."

I was about to make a second flippant remark when the person I thought was Albert said, "Enough of this. I know how to convince him!"

And that was when Baratunde jumped out of Albert's body and leaped into mine. The first disturbing thing about this violation was the odor. My nostrils were filled with old-man-from-Nigeria smell and some unknown-to-me food seasoning that I imagine the old man was fond of when he was alive. Having never been possessed before, my first reaction was utter panic.

"Albert said you would be hard to convince," a very calm, deep voice sounded in my head.

"Out! Out! Out!" I cried.

Baratunde obeyed me, left my body, and jumped back into his great-grandson's. Then they had to untie me and turn me on my side, because I was choking on my own vomit. Once I'd pulled myself together, a tearful Jonah apologized again.

"Well, no need to cry," I told him. "How were you supposed to know your dad was descended from the African Harry Potter?"

Maxine helped to clean me up and gave me a bottle of mouthwash just as Reggie and Nick arrived. About ten minutes and two more possessions later, I was handing the bottle of mouthwash to Reggie and Nick.

If anyone looked ready to save the world it was certainly not Nick. Married life left him looking well fed and at least thirty pounds overweight for a man of five foot eight. Plus, he'd let his hair grow down to his shoulders. Nick is Filipino, but with the hair and the suit he'd worn to our impromptu séance, I couldn't tell if the look he was going for was Asian metal band or Japanese anime character.

Despite being a black man raised by a very liberal-minded mother during the Ronald Reagan era, Reggie had moved to upstate New York to become a police officer. He had also gone full-on Republican. His love affair with firearms ran so deep he was actually comfortable walking around gun shows while white guys wearing 'I Shoot Niggers' T-shirts browsed AK-47s next to him. It's probably why we haven't talked much in our adult years. I just didn't understand him anymore.

We said our terse goodbyes to Maxine and the kids as we piled into Albert's SUV. Reggie, much like when we were teens, called shotgun. Nick and I shared a knowing smirk over that. As the car hurtled toward Manhattan, Nick asked, "So what's our game plan?"

"I can sense where the Nameless One is," Baratunde answered. "Albert seems to think we are headed to an area called Herald Square."

"What are we doing when we get there?" Reggie asked. "I mean, except for my sidearm and the backup .22 in my ankle holster, we have nothing. I should call for backup."

"NO! IT HAS TO BE THE FOUR OF US!" Baratunde's voice boomed in our ears. "We have weapons! You are all blessed by my magic."

Before I had a chance to say that I didn't feel the least bit magical, something inserted itself into my hand. I looked down at a samurai sword that seemed to have materialized out of the SUV's upholstery. Simultaneously, two machine gun gauntlets wrapped themselves around Reggie's forearms, making him look like a comic book villain, while two .357 Magnums landed in Nick's lap.

"Why the fuck do I just get a sword?" I asked as I turned to Nick. "You're the one looking like Sonny Chiba!"

"Dude, don't you get it?" Nick said with a glee that I really didn't think matched the situation. "We're like *Ghostbusters!*"

"WHAT?!" Reggie and I shouted in unison.

"Guys, this is going to end just like *Ghostbusters!* We're going to go in, kick some ass, save some lives! Hot young girls all over us! Dude, it's going to be amazing!"

"Nothing is ever that simple," I said. "Nothing."

I was going to elaborate on why I felt less than optimistic when the car swerved, and we all took a hard turn to the left. Apparently, we had just avoided a collision.

"Hey, which one of them is driving? Albert or his great-grandfather?" Nick asked after we straightened up.

"Maybe I should drive," Reggie volunteered.

Albert didn't answer us and he didn't stop the car.

*   *   *

An hour later, we pulled up in front of Macy's at Herald Square. Any other day, four heavily armed men of color walking into the world's most famous department store would have probably led to them being killed instantly. Instead, screams greeted us as a frightened mob ran out of from the store.

"See, just like *Ghostbusters!*" Nick cried, noting the panicked crowd and the overcast sky.

"Shut up about fucking *Ghostbusters* already!" I shouted as we made our way to the entrance on 34th and Seventh.

Once inside, we seemed to have the first floor to ourselves.

"We are too late," Baratunde/Albert said with a mournful tone. "The portal is open! I can feel it!"

Albert's body shimmered, as his dark skin turned almost silver. The sword in my hand began to vibrate as if current were running through it. Reggie let out an enthusiastic "Oh, yeah!" as his gauntlets hummed.

As we made our way to the east side of the floor, the stench of sulfur hit us in a stifling wave. Then, as we each waved our hands in front of our noses, the entire store went dark. Initially, we couldn't see anything; then Albert's eyes lit up like halogen lamps. He lit our path as we cautiously walked past the expensive watches and jewelry section and made our way into the cosmetics department.

That's when we saw the first pile of dead bodies, comprised of about twenty Macy's employees who had started their day dressed in all black, spraying passing customers with perfume. They'd been torn limb from limb, some headless, others disemboweled. Something evil had gone through the trouble of switching appendages around and propping the whole thing up like a bloody performance art installation.

We stood gazing in disbelief at this horrid sight, until we heard something growl. We turned in the direction of the noise just as a gray and black mass lunged toward Nick. The thing, nearly as big as any one of us, wielded a Viking-style broad ax and bore the face of a hedgehog. As the rest of us froze in place the ax swung in Nick's direction. His belief in his *Ghostbusters* analogy is probably why Nick was able to calmly dodge the attack and simultaneously bring one of the Magnums to bear, blasting the creature in the face. It screamed, hurt, as it retreated.

I was about to congratulate Nick when a second ax brushed my left cheek, leaving a thin, bleeding gash. Without thinking, I swung the sword in the general direction of my attacker. My weapon hit flesh, and a splash of oily black blood hit me in the chest. The scream of pain from my snout-faced assailant filled the celebrated department store as we each took defensive stances.

That's when Albert's hands lit up. White fire shot out from his palms, all but disintegrating two similar creatures that had been closing on us unseen in the darkness. The hedgehog demons let off a terrible wailing as they were slowly reduced to pungent piles of ash and goo.

"That's it, I'm calling for backup! Fuck this 'only the four of us' bullshit!" Reggie said. He reached for his cellphone, but the gauntlets wouldn't let him get deep enough into his front pocket.

"No one else!" the ghostly voice of Baratunde seemed to make the floor itself shake.

"NO!"

We heard a crunching sound and Reggie yelped in pain.

"What happened?" I asked.

"My phone exploded in my pocket!" Reggie cried. "He . . . he did it with his mind! He crushed my phone with his mind! I think I'm fucking bleeding!"

I turned to my possessed friend, not sure if he or his dead sorcerer ancestor would answer me. "Why would you stop him? Why don't you want more help?" I demanded.

"That's the curse!" he shouted back. "The Nameless One must be cornered by four brothers facing him and standing to the north, south, east, and west. Over a century ago I defeated him with the other men in my family. Unfortunately, Albert has no brothers, only sisters and the three of you! That is why you're here. But now that the Gorgon is here, we must separate!"

"Separate?" I repeated in disbelief. "Look, I don't know how many movies you've seen from the afterlife, but separating is never a good idea in situations like these."

"We must lure the Gorgon here to the center of the building. Only then will the Nameless One follow him, allowing me to send them both back to everlasting hell."

The sound of glass breaking caught our attention and we all stared down into the darkness toward the Sixth Avenue side of the store. The sulfur stench intensified as two large white cylindrical protrusions wafted through the air above us. Our collective gaze followed downward as the thing stepped closer, into the light beams coming from Albert's eyes.

To be clear, I wouldn't wish witnessing the slow approach of a thirty-foot-long albino cockroach with a half-ingested human leg hanging out of its mandibles on my worst enemy. But that is what confronted us, and I quickly found myself frightened to the point of paralysis.

"So that's the Gorgon?" Nick asked. In all my years of knowing Nick, this was the first time he'd ever sounded scared in my presence. I almost didn't recognize the voice.

As the creature rambled toward us, Albert began to glow and levitate, firing more white fire from his hands. "Gorgon!" he screamed, followed by something I can only classify as a war cry. The Nameless One, a robed dark-skinned man with a beard that would make any Williamsburg hipster jealous, stepped from the shadows and began firing his own balls of fire at Albert. As the sorcerer took a position next to his giant cockroach friend, Reggie raised the gauntlets and unleashed on them. Caught off guard and wounded, both the robed villain and the giant roach retreated. This prompted Reggie to trash talk.

"Wasn't expecting hot lead for that ass, were you!" he shouted over the giant roach's hissing.

With only a sword, there was no way I was going to charge a giant man-eating cockroach. Baratunde must have sensed that. "The Gorgon's minions are killing people upstairs. We must get rid of the minions before we can defeat these two. Rescue the innocents and kill the demons!"

As much as I opposed leaving the team, I found an escalator and made my way up. I figured that I could just keep going up until I heard the distinctive sound of people being hacked to death.

Meanwhile, I could faintly hear helicopters and sirens outside, as the NYPD gathered and prepped for an assault. Baratunde may have wanted the four of us to handle this supernatural invasion on our own, but in New York City the only curse they believe in is the word "motherfucker."

After a few escalator rides, I found what I was looking for. Three of the hedgehog things had cornered some discount-seekers. One of them kept four shoppers cornered while the other two had grabbed the opposite arms of a salesperson and were pulling the man apart like a giant piece of taffy. They all stopped what they were doing when they saw me.

While visions of Musketeers and Jedis and samurais leaped into my head, I cut down the first one with a midsection blow, then decapitated the second as he tried to charge me. I was so satisfied with myself that I ended up letting the third hedgehog thing get away.

That's when I decided to make an announcement:

"Ladies and gentlemen, demons—and, yes, by demons I mean what you think I mean—have invaded this department store. So that you and your co-shoppers aren't used as hostages against my team, herein referred to as 'the good guys,' I suggest you exit this place in an orderly, non-Godzilla-movie-like fashion so that no one gets hurt. Ultimately that decision is yours, but please take it under advisement. Also, if there is any millennial trying to hang around and record this on cellphones for the sake of YouTube or World Star, my friends and I will have no problems letting you be killed."

While most of the people began making their way to the escalator, I heard my name being called. I turned toward a familiar voice and couldn't believe my eyes. Mimi Rodriguez, the Monday-to-Thursday anchorperson for the local news broadcast, was making her way toward me. She knows me because when I'm not fighting demons I'm a cameraman for that same broadcast.

As anyone who watches the local news knows, Mimi is freaking hot! Just distractingly attractive to the point of ridiculous! So much so that despite the danger and the horror surrounding the situation I still managed to feel some schoolboy crush quivers in my stomach as she neared.

"Miles, what's going on?" she demanded. "I was just shopping . . ."

I looked around and saw nothing but bras and panties on hangers and mannequins. Only then did I realize that I was standing in the women's lingerie section. *Because I'm not distracted enough without the image of Mimi Rodriguez browsing through thongs in my head.*

"Mimi, I need to you get out of here," I managed to say. "I don't want you to get hurt. Please, just get out of here. I will explain everything Monday!"

"I get an exclusive!" Mimi exclaimed.

"Oh, you'll get an exclusive, all right," I answered, quietly laughing to myself over what I really meant by 'an exclusive.'

Mimi turned to leave with the other shoppers, then turned back to me when hedgehog number three returned with reinforcements, blocking her path. They were systematically killing the other customers, making their way to us.

So there I was, a middle-aged black guy with a samurai sword standing in a pool of blood in the middle of the lingerie section in a famous department store. My Nigerian Obi Wan had gone silent, no doubt because he was still busy fighting a giant cockroach with his possessed great-grandson. My other childhood buddies were God knows where and my first rescue mission had completely shit the bed. My workplace crush was probably going to die with me, which would mean her death would overshadow mine on the evening news broadcast neither of us would ever see again.

This was definitely NOT how *Ghostbusters* ended.

The creatures closed in on us, snarling and smiling. A line of drool escaped one of their mouths and let gravity pull it to the floor. Snot ran freely from the other demon's snouts.

I held up my sword and motioned for Mimi to get behind me. Literally weeping with fear, she obliged. She clung to my shirt with a grip so firm I might have turned and asked, 'How the hell am I supposed to fight?' had the situation appeared to have room for one last witty remark.

With what must have been a desperate look on my face, I raised the sword and screamed, just as I'd seen Toshiro Mifune do in those old Akira Kurosawa movies. A sudden revelation flashed in my head. Whatever magic had given my friends and me our weapons might have provided me with the sword based on the fact that I was probably the only one out of all of us who'd even seen Kurosawa's *Seven Samurai.*

As I stood there hoping to kill at least a couple of these things to create an escape path for Mimi and me, one of the creatures screamed. It was the sort of ear-raping sound one would expect a soulless thing to make when it's being murdered. But what could be so mighty?

I half expected to see that one of my teammates had left the battle for the giant department store lobby and had come to help me. By the time I realized a black panther the size of a loveseat had quietly skulked up and attacked one of the monsters, that monster was letting out agonized wails of the damned as it melted.

The rest of the furry demons forgot about Mimi and me and moved in the direction of the panther. The panther seemed content to kill them all and reduced each of them to piles of screaming black tar with just a glancing blow from a clawed paw. Bites also proved lethal, especially when one demon tried to play berserker and charged the panther, only to get its throat ripped away by the panther's impressive incisors.

Frozen in place, I watched events unfold as if I were watching a movie. Mimi's tightened grip on my shoulder served as a reminder that I was still a combatant and not a spectator. As the last two creatures moved on the panther, I decapitated them with a strength I wouldn't have dared to dream I possessed.

"Took you long enough," the panther said.

For some moronic reason, I looked back at Mimi. Her wide-eyed face told me that she was questioning her faculties as much as I doubted my own.

"Stop trying to mate with the female and let's get back downstairs."

I closed my eyes in embarrassment. "I have to go, Mimi," I heard myself say after a beat. She was speechless, but her eyes were filled with adoration. And that's when I took my shot. I stepped forward and hugged her. Much to my delight, she hugged me back. Then, just as we were coming apart, her head tilted toward my face and our lips found each other. A full on kiss with the hottest woman I actually know suddenly made most of this worth it.

"Let's go!" the panther yelled.

We broke the kiss. "If I survive, I'll let you know on Facebook," I promised as our hands slipped away from each other's bodies. As I turned to follow the talking jungle cat, she called after me. "You better!"

As I ran toward the escalator, I snuck in one last look over my shoulder. Mimi looked almost as worried as I felt.

*   *   *

The talking panther and I rejoined the group just in time to see the sorcerer and the giant cockroach teleporting away with a flash and another sickening waft of sulfur.

"Fuck!" Reggie's voice echoed through the store.

"To the ninth floor!" I heard Albert's voice bellow.

We regrouped over the bodies, broken glass, blood, and overturned mannequins. "Why the ninth floor?" Nick asked. "Are we going after a stolen artifact, or some sacred book that we need to defeat the Gorgon?"

"No," Albert answered. "Ninth floor is where the furniture is."

With no better explanation than that, we started making our way to the other side of the floor to the elevator bank. It was around this time that Reggie and Nick noticed the panther. Under better circumstances, their reactions would have been quite comical.

"I see you've met Carla," Albert/Baratunde said. The big cat actually seemed to give my possessed friend a hello nod.

"You knew about this?" I asked as we all followed Albert to the elevators.

"Of course," Albert/Baratunde answered. "Cats and demons are natural enemies. In the days ahead they will be our allies."

As the middle elevator's twin doors opened and closed after we piled in, we heard the SWAT team making its way through the store, heading toward us.

"We're going to die," I heard Reggie say.

"No," Albert corrected. "We're leaving."

"How?" I asked. "Do you have giant falcons waiting for us on the roof, Gandalf?"

After a second the sorcerer responded. "My grandson says you've always been the funny one. And they were eagles, not falcons."

"Yeah, thanks, Albert," I said.

The elevator doors opened, revealing an abandoned furniture department. "How does this help us?" Nick asked as we stepped out into a sea of opulent dining-room sets that only the people who collapsed the US economy in 2007 could afford. "The cops are going to be up here Eric Garnering our asses any minute!"

"Look for a large mirror!" was all Baratunde said, while Reggie whined about the police and Nick and I looked around like confused children. Luckily, Carla found a beautiful five-foot-long floor mirror with an ornate silver frame and roared at us until we joined her in front of it.

"Expensive taste!" Nick scoffed after noticing that the mirror's price tag read $700. "Like all the women in my life."

Albert's hands and eyes began to glow again. At first we thought we were under attack, and we all drew weapons. But then the mirror began to shake and shimmer. In seconds, a whirling vortex appeared where a reflection had been.

Carla the Panther seemed to know what the deal was right away. As soon as the vortex filled the mirror, she jumped into it and disappeared.

"Are we allowed to ask what the fuck is going on, or where the giant cat went?" Reggie asked.

"Her owner's apartment. That's our next stop."

With that, my possessed childhood friend stepped into the vortex. After some mutual looks and shrugs, Nick and Reggie also stepped into the mirror and vanished.

That's when the one of the cops who had been coming up behind us took a shot. Glass flew at my face as the mirror shattered and the spell ended. I saved my life by using my black man's instincts—throwing the sword away and lying face down on the floor. The cops grabbed me, roughed me up a little, cuffed me, and read me my rights. Everything else went just as I've seen it on TV.

*   *   *

After being cornered by a CNN reporter for twenty minutes, Chapman received a text to meet Captain Willis in his office.

"Don't know if you care, but they're calling it 'The Nightmare on 34th Street,'" he shouted as he flung the captain's office door open.

Willis was sat behind the desk with two fortyish-looking men in black suits standing over him. None of them looked happy.

"Your suspect is gone, and it's your fault," one of the intense-looking strangers said. "You shouldn't have left him alone with a mirror. His friends came back for him. At least you made him write down what happened. You did one thing right."

Chapman noticed the yellow notepad in the second intense man's hand. "Yeah, thanks for getting this out of him. We might be able to figure out where Ford and his friends are now."

"Who the hell are you guys?" Chapman asked.

"Detective, meet Agents Smitty and Baxter," the captain said. "They're from the NSA. Apparently, the government has protocols for handling this sort of thing and we aren't a part of it."

"Those dead bodies in the medical examiner's office say otherwise," Chapman retorted.

"We've already relieved you of those," said Baxter. "By the way, as of now, no more talking to the press. You're both on a gag order."

The two started making their way past Chapman and toward the door. "Have a good night, gentlemen," Smitty continued. "Just so we are clear, if anything else leaks to the press, we will be back and you won't be happy."

"I'm sure we understand," the captain said as the two spooks exited the office.

"Anything else you want me to do?" a seething Chapman asked once they were alone.

"There's a hot Latina reporter in the lobby, looking for Ford. Get rid of her. Tell her anything that doesn't get Black Lives Matters activists down here. Just do it."

"You got it."

Chapman got to the lobby, only to find that Mimi was gone. Whether she left on her own or was prompted by something or someone else was another question added to the list of mysteries this night had provided.

Chapman shook his head and walked back to his desk. For now, he'd be a good soldier and do what he was told. Later that night, he would find himself in a bar, drinking a Scotch and soda and giving serious thought to early retirement.

Hurricane Zelda, Part IV

Kathleen Scheiner

Her children stayed home with the oldest left to babysit, Goldie, a serious, sober eleven-year-old with good sense, but still, she was eleven. There was the television, too, though Tanisha left strict instructions that it shouldn't be turned on. She didn't want them to get hysterical with the Hurricane Zelda news and start blowing up her phone at work, worried, wanting her to come home. She knew the TV would go on—an eleven-year-old, eight-year-old, and three-year-old cooped up in the apartment with crap weather and nothing to do. She only hoped they would play Xbox or watch one of their cartoon DVDs with a happy ending.

Tanisha went back to work at Beth Israel after pulling three twelve-hour shifts in a row—even longer including the extra prep time she did for other nurses before Zelda hit. Everybody who was able to had called out in pediatrics or been assigned to more critical units with all the absences. Now, Tanisha was going in under threat of losing her job, and that couldn't happen. It made her bitter, having to go to the pediatrics unit and tend to other people's children while her own ran wild at home, unsupervised, because there was nobody left in her apartment building whom she trusted to keep an eye on them.

Not planning to go in, Tanisha only did the kids' laundry this morning instead of her own, so she now wore her most hated pair of scrub pants, the ones reserved for emergencies only. A size too small, from the year before she had Bea, they pulled across her hips, leaving permanent wrinkles. Over that, she wore a scrub top printed with colored cartoon elephants, an attempt to balance out her thighs and the only kind of camouflage she could manufacture at a moment's notice.

The rain lashed at Tanisha, turning her umbrella inside out and ruining it—the good leopard one that she'd had almost a year—leaving her pants soaking from the knees down, the hems gray. It was more than rain, though: the water pierced her like hot ice, stabbing her nose and eyes, even inside her nostrils. *This is how it feels when you drown*, she thought.

Finally she got to the cover of the subway station at Jefferson and tossed her umbrella into an overflowing garbage can full of others, many lying twisted on the ground like broken flowers. Tanisha expected to find the subway platform empty with the miserable weather and dire forecasts, but once she passed through the turnstile she discovered people massed on the platform, many toting luggage. Fleeing the city, though she didn't know how they were going to get out. All planes were grounded at the airports, according to the news, and the MTA would be canceling trains soon—not soon enough in her opinion. The damn subway, though—it always ran.

Humidity made the fetid odor rise in the tunnel, a flowering like decomposing vegetables in the bin. Tanisha pulled her smock up over her nose to cut the stink and took a bottle of perfume out of her purse, squirting the air around herself to give a shield of floral fragrance.

People talked about the one thing on their minds now, Hurricane Zelda. Originally forecast to miss the city, it now bore down full force, pulsing slowly—at least that was the radar picture they showed on the news. Outside, rain sheeted down. Tanisha blocked out the chatter, sick to death about her children all alone in a sixth-floor walkup while she pulled a twelve-hour shift. And even after that, she didn't know if she had a ride home. Beneath the zizz of talk, she focused on the sound of the rain, relentless, drumming on the street above and only interrupted by the swish of whatever foolhardy automobiles passed above, not too many.

Water sluiced down from the sidewalk grates, dampening the subway station's walls and platform, trickling and dripping down into the great trough between the tracks. The water pooled there and muddied with the rusty muck already in place, and Tanisha didn't know of a dirtier thing. It was worse than any public park restroom—this was New York's toilet, the bowels of the city.

Piteous mews and squeaks came from the direction in which the train should come, and a collection of wet rats made their way down the tracks. Vicious animals. Tanisha had seen all varieties of rat bites at the hospital. They went after children, babies especially, sensing they were weak and couldn't defend themselves. These rats, though, she had never seen anything like this in all the time she'd lived in New York. They helped one another, communicating in shrieks and wails. A fat dappled gray led the pack, arrowing ahead by a few yards, and real fear twisted in Tanisha's gut.

She prided herself on being an unflappable woman, no-nonsense, able to get the job done. Inside hospital emergency rooms, she'd seen the most terrible things that people could do to one another, but never once had she witnessed rats helping each other out—those greedy things acted solo, fighting and drawing blood over a dropped Cheeto.

People around her raised a ruckus, taking pictures with their cellphones. Some chucked cans and garbage at the fleeing pack, but the rats advanced single-mindedly. They sensed something, maybe a higher-pitched frequency or a thrumming from the metal tracks.

The rats stopped collectively, sitting up on their haunches and making delicate sniffs at the air. Then the dappled gray went to the other side of the tracks, leading the pack. Once they were out of sight, people were more jacked, chattering about the rats with half-remembered, obscure data to mix in with the already terrible weather predictions. Tanisha just wanted everybody to shut up so she could have a minute to think.

A warm rush of stale air blew on her, signaling an oncoming train, and a second later, rumbling reached her ears as a beam of light shot out of the tunnel. The L train. She had to go now. She'd been hoping that the subways would shut down early and she could return to the dry refuge of her apartment, knowing she'd done everything in her power to get to Beth Israel. With the train's arrival, though, she was committed. She had to go. Otherwise, she'd be fretting every minute until the storm passed about whether she had a job to go back to.

The subway driver in the lead car looked exhausted: a doughy mannequin propped up in his compartment with dark tufts of hair pointing every which way. A clunky pair of protective earwear circled his neck.

The first few cars zipped by Tanisha, and she saw people crushed inside like vertical logs. "Shit, shit, shit," she muttered under her breath. She deserved to sit the twenty or so extra minutes before spending an entire shift on her feet, and she aimed to make it happen. Tanisha pogoed over to where the middle door of the third car would fall open, positioning herself on the left side.

The train shuddered to a stop and the doors ratcheted open. Nobody got off. Tanisha held onto the sides of the car with both arms, preventing anyone else from boarding before her. Her eyes scanned the car, and she saw two men sitting, their legs spread wide apart, while holding tented newspapers in front of them, pretending not to see the people crowded above them. A couple of women clung to the overhead rail, too nice to say anything, but Tanisha had paid her $2.75 same as everybody. She muscled over to the scant five-inch space between the men, said "Excuse me" in a voice that was anything but apologetic, and plopped down, forcing them to make room. One folded his newspaper and Tanisha saw "Zelda" in the headline.

"This bench here is made for three people," she said promptly before he could get all nasty.

The man pretended he didn't hear her and shut his eyes as if he were suddenly overcome with the most incredible fatigue.

It took five tries before the train could make its way out of the station, with everybody clogging up the doors, and each stop after that took longer and longer, as people crammed themselves into the train. Tanisha finally closed her eyes as well, seeing all the soft body parts mashed in front of her eyes, a moving wall of trapped flesh. She saw a dark mole on a midriff that looked malignant, and that was the last thing she could bear to look at.

Her ears popped as the train went into the tube underneath the East River, and Tanisha knew she had only three stops to gather her thoughts and prepare. In five minutes her peace would be over. Then the train came to a stop yet again, and the air-conditioning was cut off—always a sign that they were going to be stuck for a while. She heard groans erupt from the people around her.

After five minutes ticked by somebody cursed in a loud voice, "They raise the fare every year and service gets worse and worse," and then a man screamed and smashed his fist into something.

She jerked up immediately and held her arms out, as if she could protect people. "What's going on? Who's doing that?"

One of the young women above her looked fearfully over her shoulder. "A crazy guy." Sweat ran down the girl's forehead and her eyes widened. She was going to have an attack if she kept on like that. Tanisha reached out and tugged on her shorts, causing the young woman to look down.

"Hey, now, don't you worry. There's just one of him and all of us. Nothing bad's going to happen."

The subway started again, going in fits and starts, and Tanisha saw relief break out on the woman's face, thinking they'd be out of this mess soon. Then the subway stopped again, the lights flickering on and off, and she heard banging on the window in back of her. The woman in front of her screamed, pointing at the window. Tanisha turned around, and in a narrow alcove of the tunnel she saw three MTA workers lit up by a bare lightbulb. They pounded their fists against the window, and she could hear their muffled voices: "Let us in!" "Quick, quick!"

Tanisha got up, cramped on all sides from the people around her, and opened the narrow safety window at the top so she could hear them better. "What's going on?"

One of the men, his face so dirty that only his eyeballs and teeth showed, said, "Trouble, big trouble." He reached his grubby arm in, grabbing at her.

"Should I pull the emergency brake?" the young woman behind her asked.

Tanisha clicked her tongue. "No, don't do that. We'll be stuck down here even longer if you do. Go get the conductor and tell 'em not to move another inch, not till we get these guys in."

"Wh-who's that?"

"Never mind. I'll do it," said Tanisha and started pushing through the bodies all around her, making her way toward the middle of the train. People asked her questions, as if she were an employee of the MTA, but she just squeezed past and let herself out the door and through to the next car, praying she'd get there before the train started moving again. She'd already decided that the minute they surfaced at First Avenue she was turning right around and boarding a

Brooklyn-bound train back home. If they fired her, she'd get on at a nursing home or something. It would be less money, but she didn't want to mess around with this. Without the air-conditioning, the cars grew hot and people dripped with sweat, but she passed through easily enough, saying, "Let me through, we've got an emergency."

She saw the conductor once she hit the sweet spot, the front car, and he had the door open to his compartment while passengers peppered him with questions. "When are we going to go, man? I know you've got the information."

"I don't," he said. "I don't go until the signal lights go on—"

"Sir," Tanisha interrupted, "you've got men outside in the tunnel who need to get in. They say something bad's going down."

The conductor had been stressed with the unexpected shutdown, but now he looked positively terrified. "What's going on?" she asked in a low voice.

He shook his head. "Show me where."

Though passengers stood packed in like matchsticks, with bulky luggage here and there, a hole appeared when Tanisha and the conductor passed by, authority parting the crowds. They exited between two of the cars, precariously perched on two metal platforms joining them. The conductor craned over either side of the train, trying to peek into the alcove.

"Which side are they on?" he asked.

Tanisha pointed, and he launched himself up on the ledge alongside the tunnel, a place meant for MTA workers to stand when working on repairs and maintenance to the tube. He held his hand out for her. "You coming?"

She sure as hell didn't want to go back in and catch the panic of the others; better to stay with those who were doing. "I will. But you know something. What aren't you telling people?"

In the dim sepia light given off by naked lightbulbs scattered every hundred feet or so down the tunnel, the man looked her full in the face, trying to read her. "No radio communication," he finally said. "This is supposed to be my last run for the night. They're shutting down everything, but I haven't heard a peep in thirty minutes. That never happens. There's always somebody nattering in my ear, even if they're just singing."

Tanisha was pissed. He'd been out of contact this long and not bothered to do anything about it? "Why didn't you shut it down when that happened?" she asked. "Now we're stuck like—" She wanted to say, *Rats in a trap*, but cut herself off.

"I just wanted to get home," he said. "Same as everybody else." A long breath shuddered out of him, and Tanisha could hear a phlegmy rattle in his chest. He was sick, probably not thinking clearly. "How'd they look—the men?"

"The three I saw were okay—scared but okay. They said there's trouble, though. That's the part I don't like."

"Me neither."

The conductor stepped forward on the six-inch ledge jutting from the tunnel's edge, scooching along in the direction Tanisha had indicated. Tanisha looked at the bodies jammed in the subway car and saw condensation rising up on the insides of the windows from all the body heat. People cracked the tops of the windows, and she knew her situation was a thousand times better outside of the cars. She fished her cellphone out in case she needed its flashlight and pushed herself onto the ledge, following along.

Soon enough they reached the three men.

"What's going on?" one of them asked, his voice taking on a high-pitched, hysterical tone that Tanisha didn't like.

"Hell, I don't know. I thought you would. I haven't heard anything on the radio for forty-five minutes."

"I thought you said a half-hour?" Tanisha said.

The conductor ignored her.

"I'm on the last run before we shut down for the night, and the power just gave out."

"They closed the lock down on the Manhattan side, and we're stuck after shoring up for the storm. Worse than that, there's rats. A whole mess of them, scratching and biting as if they can get through to First Avenue. Can you take us back into Brooklyn?" asked the dirtiest of the MTA workers.

"No, no power, I told you," said the conductor.

"What's the lock?" asked Tanisha.

"Both sides of the tube under the river have a big metal plate that closes off the tunnel just in case there's a leak. We were doing the last bit of maintenance, but the locks weren't supposed to go in place until we were up out of the tube and the trains were done for the night. They locked us in," said the scared man and started blubbering.

"Are you sure about that?" asked the conductor. "There's about five hundred people on this subway. I need some answers before I tell 'em what to do, and this is a real disaster. Trying to herd people from the tube to an emergency exit? I don't think we've ever had to do that."

Two of the MTA workers moved forward on the ledge, and the conductor followed. The scared man stayed in his place at the alcove, but Tanisha followed along. The men paused a moment until Tanisha and the conductor were sandwiched between the two MTA workers, who seemed to know the tunnel intimately.

Once they cleared the train, they settled in the middle of the tracks, picking their way between the rails, boards, and other detritus on the floor of the tunnel. It was humid and hot, and the tunnel smelled dank, like rotten teeth. The two MTA workers wore helmets with headlights that they switched on, and the dim light revealed enough to make Tanisha shiver. Rusty soot coated everything, and water sluiced over their feet, coming from the bottom of the tunnel; the current seemed to intensify as they walked.

"I don't like this," said Tanisha, and she gasped when she heard her voice echo in the tunnel. *This, this, this* came back to her, magnified. When her voice died away, she took hold of herself and asked, "What about the third rail?"

"It's down," said the conductor. "That's why we're not moving. The lights come from an auxiliary source. Look at this." He took a package of gum out of his pocket, slid the cardboard cover off, and chucked it at the thicker of the two rails. It lay there, wilted, for a moment; then the streaming water took it.

Tanisha heard splashes behind her and turned to look along with the men, their headlights bouncing off the walls of the tunnel, making a strobe-like effect, before they both focused on a big black rat half swimming, half running up the tracks. The sudden brightness of the men's lamps made it squeak while its thick, ropy tail churned back in forth in the water. The company on the rails didn't scare the animal, and it skirted past them easily, not seeming to care if it came into contact with them. She swore as she felt its coarse hairs rub up against the exposed skin above her anklet sock. The rat nabbed the piece of cardboard and kept swim-hopping up the tunnel. Tanisha noticed the water underfoot rising. They heard an unearthly shriek from farther back in the tunnel, beyond the train, and didn't dare speak.

The people stuck in the subway heard as well, and Tanisha saw the front car of the train shake as people rammed the doors and windows, trying to get out. She heard splashes and grunts and shrieks, and people started squeezing out of the narrow windows, then breaking them.

"Hurry up, hurry up," said the conductor, urging their group forward, as if afraid that the crowd would creep up behind them and skin him alive.

Tanisha heard a woman scream and a crunch that she knew— bone breaking—echoing all up and down the tunnel. Again that strange, wet-sounding screech, but this time it was closer.

Cellphone lights bobbed behind her, and Tanisha heard an older woman's voice. "Oh, help. Help! Can't somebody please help her?" *Slip-slap* as those departing the subway splashed up toward her and the leaders of the group pushed on doggedly to the Manhattan side.

Tanisha turned back toward the subway and the crowd surged past her, following the light they saw ahead. They were running scared, not caring that they body-checked her as they moved forward.

Battered, Tanisha found the hurt woman, lying in the dirty water. She was young, impossibly young, her face white as chalk. Tanisha passed her cellphone flashlight over the girl, highlighting the tangled mat of dark hair that fell past her shoulders, jeans, an impractical piece of silver luggage she had been trying to haul along with her, and then her feet in sandals. One of those feet bent at an unnatural angle, pulsing blood and showing bluish-white cartilage and a sliver of bone.

"Oh, honey," she muttered and sucked her breath in.

"Help me?" whispered the woman, raising her head up. "I told my parents I'd come home. They're so worried about me."

The dirty water ran over her foot, and Tanisha knew she'd be septic for sure if they didn't get her out of here and cleaned up. People continued to run past them as the unearthly shrieking approached—"*kiiiiieeeee, kiiiiiiiieeeee*"—and they stepped on both Tanisha and the poor hobbled girl.

A heel rammed down on Tanisha's hand and she bellowed, "Watch out, watch out! Others are going to get hurt if you don't take care." That worked for maybe a minute, but people were terrified.

Tanisha took hold of the woman's silver suitcase and unzipped it while holding the cellphone in her teeth so she could see. Clothes, a Kindle, makeup, some DVDs. She took out thinner knit items and tried to make a tourniquet above the knee of the woman's bad leg; then she swaddled the broken ankle with other clothing to keep it as clean as possible and hide the injury.

"Is it bad?" the girl asked, her teeth chattering.

"It's not good, but I've seen a lot worse."

Most of the crowd had passed by now, just a few stragglers inching by, and then Tanisha heard a whole rash of screams, human voices, coming from the front of the tunnel, where everybody had rushed to. And crunching sounds, as if somebody had split open a chicken leg bone and was sucking out the marrow.

A light appeared over Tanisha and the hurt girl—a perfectly round spotlight—and Tanisha angled her hand over her eyes to protect herself from the brightness. Beneath the headlamp was the MTA worker too scared to return to Manhattan side. "Rats," he said. "A whole mess of them, I told you. I'm going back to Brooklyn. I don't care how long it takes."

"What about the people?" asked Tanisha.

"I don't care. Anything's better than rats. And when I get out of this goddamned tunnel, I'm driving as far away as I can. Texas or someplace like that. I've had enough of New York. Enough for this lifetime." He hopped the ledge and started skirting around the train the way they'd come.

The water deepened, and Tanisha hooked the girl up by her armpits and onto her lap to keep her from going under. They had to get out of here. Something had broken inside the tunnel, and she had a sinking suspicion that they'd drown if they stayed here much longer. The human screams at the front of the tunnel kept going and going, crescendo upon crescendo, but they never stopped, and more tellingly, nobody came back.

Tanisha had grown used to the stink of the tunnel, but now something even more foul assaulted her nostrils. It smelled like fish gone three days bad, a maggoty odor that rolled down from the Brooklyn end of the tunnel, like mist, accompanied by watery slaps. And a slithering.

Her cellphone flashlight reflected the rippling water onto the ceiling of the tunnel, and Tanisha saw the humpbacked dark shape the train made and then something else, something vaguely human-like cast in shadow with a body like a— She had nothing to compare it to. Meanwhile, the water rose higher. Tanisha got up from her crouch and pulled the girl, now in a semi-conscious state, toward the train. She hoped it might be dry in there, at least on the benches, but Tanisha didn't want to think yet about how she'd get the girl back in there. The water hit her thighs now, and the lights flickered and died out in the front subway car. A few screams came from those left in-side, but they were pale and faint compared to the carnage going on at the Manhattan end of the tunnel.

Tanisha felt a pull in her back; though the girl was thin and frail-looking, she had become impossibly heavy in the water. It would take everything Tanisha had to get her to something like solid ground, and all she had to go by were a few lightbulbs set in the tunnel's alcoves and the cellphone flashlight that jittered madly in her mouth.

Her light caught a gray-and-green mass emerging from the cours-ing water under the train—one, two of them. Their hair looked like wet, black dreadlocks, and from what she could see of their flesh, it was a gray, claylike color. Giant black eyes peered out of their faces, but the creatures did not blink, did not seem to show any emotion at all. With angled arms, they pushed themselves up from under the train, then drifted in the shallow water, their hands opening and clos-ing like crab claws. One of them carried the MTA man who decided he was going to Texas, and Tanisha could tell from the cloudy white cast over his eyes that he was dead.

Then that creature flapped something like a tail in the knee-deep water, a leathery gray-green tail like a fish. It swam by, an awkward movement that became more graceful as the water rose. The other reared up out of the water a few feet from Tanisha, its mouth open, showing jagged yellow-and-gray teeth, like something she'd seen once on an eel. Then it screamed—at least, Tanisha thought it was a scream—that otherworldly wailing, burbling, she had heard down the tunnel from before. *"Kiiiiiieeeeeeeeeeeeeeeeeeeeeeeeee."* It was so piercing, so ugly, that she released her grip on the girl and clapped her hands over her ears. And the creature swooped in, moving like a shark, to take the girl, holding her close to its body as it swam up the tunnel.

Tanisha had had enough. She got up on the ledge, the water lapping over her feet a good two inches, and edged her way up past the train toward the Brooklyn side. She was moving on autopilot now, as she did during all life's great emergencies. On the dividing line between life and death every day at the hospital, Tanisha knew she had to assess her tools and then act. As long as she was doing, she wasn't dying. She balanced and pushed herself forward past the cars everybody abandoned, only planning to stop at the conductor's cab. There had to be something there: a crowbar or an ax. And she'd lop through rats or human-sized fish to get back to her babies. In her mind, she repeated *Goldie, Isaiah, and Bea* like a prayer that would get her through this.

Shoal

Trevor Firetog

The First Day

Photographs of lost children, dead fathers and mothers, and unlucky siblings welcome me into the lighthouse. Graffiti adorns the walls, preaching of love and death. Prayers and incantations scrawled in dried, red paint.

I shrug off my jacket, and walk to the center of the room, careful not to step on the photographs strewn over the hardwood floor.

My eyes water against the fetid air. The salty odor of the ocean and the tang of urine hang over the room like a cloud.

I sank my rowboat, as I'd been told I should, so no one will suspect my being here. The boat is resting at the bottom of the Shoal along with my cellphone and wallet.

I wait as long as I need to. I hug myself in the middle of the room. I shiver, though the air is free of any chill.

I've been told not to sleep, because you take on the dreams of the ones who have slept here before.

* * *

You remember her, don't you?

Cool, blue eyes and lush, black hair that shimmered even without sun or starlight.

Remember your first date? All the taxis were taken that night. You rode with her on the subway.

Rain poured down and you gave her your jacket. You walked together to the High Line, holding each other for warmth. Her hand wiggled into your back pocket.

She kept looking at your lips and then back to your eyes. You knew she wanted you to kiss her, but nerves held you back.

When you reached the High Line, the rain slackened to a drizzle. The city lights pierced through the darkness to cast their glow on you.

You sat together on a wet bench, dampness soaking through your jeans. Neither of you wanted to leave yet.

She locked eyes with you and leaned closer. Your breath mingled with hers. The soft touch of her lips met yours and her tongue filled your mouth, like warm chocolate.

And she pulled away; she turned and looked back at the view from the High Line, as if nothing had happened. But a secret smile remained on the upturned corners of her lips.

You didn't say anything to her for a while. You kept stealing glances, looking at her.

Sometimes, she looked back.

*　　*　　*

The Second Day

Those memories stem from the flower-laden fields of the past. None of that matters now. Not without her.

There is no way to tell the time of night. Splinters of moonlight invade the cracks of the planks nailed to the windows.

The lighthouse has been broken into so many times the warped lock can no longer hold the door shut. I open it slowly, watching for any passing boat. It's clear. I crawl down the outside stairs to the pier, over the rocks and to the water.

I put my lips to the water and start to sip. The salt burns down my throat and splashes in my belly.

The man on the ferry told me to drink the water of the Shoal. That makes the visions come quicker, and more vividly, and last longer. But he warned me if I drink too much too quickly, I might not live to see what I came here for.

The man on the ferry told me that after spending three days at the Shoal, drinking the water, starving on the cold floors, and refusing sleep, he was finally able to speak to his mother, who'd been dead for the past six years.

He'd finally gotten the chance to say goodbye.

It is a charming thought, to say goodbye.

I go back inside.

This lighthouse has no keeper and hasn't been turned on for the past three decades. It simply serves as a landmark; a reminder for boats of shallow waters. It sits in the middle of Long Island sound, barely visible from land.

* * *

The first time she told you she saw the gray man, you thought she was joking. You had already made her your wife by now and planned to start a family.

She said she'd been seeing *it* for weeks, but she didn't want to mention anything to you, out of fear you might think she was insane.

This thing was following her, she said. A creature resembling a man, though it couldn't be one. Her voice quavered with terror as she spoke.

She said the thing watched her in the reflections of mirrors.

With skin the color of ash and bloated cheeks, it looked at her with soft eyes, almost kind, but sunken.

It never stopped looking at her.

Sometimes she looked back.

She hugged you and cried.

You didn't believe anything was there, but you couldn't say that to her.

You helped her paint all the mirrors in the house.

You promised her she wasn't insane.

* * *

The Third Day

I climb the stairs up to the lighthouse tower. Each step is covered with pellets of rat shit, and each step groans with a warning that at any moment the rotten wood might break away and drop me through to infinity.

The daylight of the third day at the Shoal has finally peeled away. Since sleep isn't an option, I crave to explore these surroundings.

My brain flutters with desperation, boredom, hunger, fatigue, thirst for something other than saltwater.

Everything feels all bendy and wavy. This lighthouse bobs in the water; it moves and sways with the current of tiny waves.

I tell myself it's not moving. My dehydrated brain plays tricks on me.

There are shadows surrounding me, twisting and writhing. I'm not scared of them. They keep me company.

I stop, for I think I heard a voice.

I call out to whoever is in the lighthouse, but even my words become shadows as they leave my mouth.

I fall. My breath abandons my body on impact. It takes a while for it to return.

The stairs seem to be an impossible task. I will try again tomorrow.

*   *   *

You promised her she's not insane, but what did you think when she pulled out clumps of hair and her scalp? What about when she yanked out her fingernails with needle-nose pliers, because she didn't want to scratch her eyeballs out from desperation?

How long did it take for her to convince you she needed professional help? How long were you willing to let your love suffer?

You refused to believe it. You saw her as she used to be: perfection. You refused to accept her paranoia. You plastered a smile across your face.

You thought she didn't see that thing following her anymore. Or perhaps she did see it, but didn't tell you.

Or did she tell you, but you didn't want to listen?

She told you she saw the thing in any reflection: the metal of a stapler, or soda cans, or the kitchen knife.

It was always there, watching her.

She told you the tuft of hair on the creature's head swayed and drifted, as if it were underwater.

But you didn't hear what she had to say. Because she was your perfect wife. Even without hair or fingernails, she was perfect.

She couldn't sit still anymore. She trembled and her eyes always darted around the room. She couldn't look at you, for fear she might see the thing in the reflection of your eyes.

But you made her look at you. Sometimes, she looked back. You told her you'd get her the help she needed.

*   *   *

The Fourth Day

I've got worms of the brain.

Life flashes before me like an old scrapbook. Memories seem crumbled, but they're there, in its pages.

Wriggle wriggle wriggle, worms munching the pages of my scrapbook.

I see her in the pictures of the loved ones on the floor. But when I look at the photos, she's never there. She waits until I'm not looking, and then appears at the corner of my eye. She likes to play games with me. Or she wants to torment me in the way that thing she saw tormented her for all those months. I hear her voice, and the scent of her sandalwood perfume enfolds me like a veil. The same perfume she wore on the day I proposed to her.

She fought back tears as she said yes. She kissed so passionately.

I touch this memory gently, smoothing it into place, before closing the book and remembering why I'm here.

Let the worms feast on the pages. Let them fill up until their bellies pop. One more day, and I won't need memories. She'll be here, and we'll make new memories together.

I puked up the saltwater I drank last night. I don't know if I need to drink more to replace it. I'm not even sure if my stomach can handle it. My next drink might be the one that makes my kidneys finally rebel against me and shut down.

My fingers feel like cotton; so do the bottom of my feet. If I step on something or press my hand to the walls of the lighthouse, the world softens at my touch.

Her laugh, sweet and sultry, echoes from the lighthouse tower.

But the steps seem so high and endless. I touch my foot to one, and like a sponge the step bends and squishes under my weight. I want to tell myself it's a hallucination, but my mind won't accept that answer.

I take another step, but it's impossible. These stairs seem to have no structure. My knees give out, and I fall and land on the hardwood floor, so soft it might have been made of feathers.

I curl against the side of the staircase and cry, for the woman I had loved and still love is waiting for me at the top of the stairs, I know she is.

Within her eyes, she holds my home.

The Shoal doesn't have a home, it doesn't belong to Connecticut or Long Island; it simply exists, forsaken between one land and the next. Civilization stands so close, yet utterly unreachable for me in my current state. So like the Shoal, I must learn to live alone, between two worlds, until I can see her eyes again. Until I find my home.

I scream my throat raw. But no one hears me, for the ocean surrounding the Shoal swallows my screams.

*   *   *

You buried her a year before you buried your parents.

She'd been nearly committed to a mental hospital, but you delayed the process. You lost some paperwork, and you gave the examining doctors contradictory statements.

You still held out hope that one day she would wake up and smile, and laugh, and put everything back to normal, and you could have a family again.

She had self-harming tendencies ever since this illusion of the gray man started, and under the doctor's request you removed anything sharp out of her reach. Despite your hatred for him, you knew he was right. She couldn't be trusted with knives or forks or tools or pens. But while you were sleeping, she went down to the basement of the apartment, with a spoon, and sharpened it against the concrete floor. It must have taken hours.

She'd done a good job for what she had to work with; you had to give her credit there. The spoon severed the flesh down the length of her wrist.

When her veins opened she tried to cut her other wrist, but she was already weak from blood loss, and she couldn't grip the spoon tight enough.

Your upstairs neighbor found her and called for you before he called the police. You saw her on her back and rolled her over carefully. Her eyes were closed but her face remained taut, as if haunted. You pressed your fingers to her neck, though you somehow knew you'd find no pulse.

She'd scribbled a note in her blood.

He's in the spoon shine.

You picked up the spoon, its edges and handle caked with her dried blood.

You saw nothing in the spoon shine, only yourself.

*   *   *

The Final Day

Even if I allowed myself to sleep, I doubt it would come easily.

The wind whistles in the gaps between bricks and wooden boards.

Images of my dead wife appear to me like those random thoughts that occur on the cusp of sleep—here one second, forgotten the next.

The sun sets on my fifth day at the Shoal. I still haven't been able to talk to her, as the man on the ferry said I would.

My brain is a flickering light bulb, threatening a moment when it'll burst and set fire to the pages of my treasured scrapbook.

If the worms haven't gotten to it first.

It's time to leave the Shoal. This isn't what I've sought. I want to see my wife again, not be teased by her image.

I'm not sure if I'll be able to make the swim back to land, but anything is better than here.

When I open the door, the wind hits hard, spraying ocean water. It's refreshing.

I lick my lips and taste it; my stomach roils from the memory of all the water drank these past few days.

I move to the rail out of reflex, knowing I couldn't vomit, for there is nothing in my stomach. The rail wobbles when I grasp it, and small flecks of rust and paint fall onto the rocks below. Clutching the railing, I tilt—against my will—further over the edge.

I don't remember letting go of the railing, I don't remember my head bursting on the rocks, but I know it must have because of all this leaking blood, but I do remember seeing her face beneath the surface.

If I opened my arms, I could have embraced her as I fell.

As I sink lower in the water, I see her yet again. She is above me, near the surface. I could reach her if I kick hard enough.

But fatigue and the loss of blood have rendered my muscles useless. Instead, I sink lower.

The water rushes into my mouth. For a second, I think I can breathe under water. I inhale as I normally do, and my lungs fill. But they do not empty.

My love is the last thing I see as my body drifts along with the waves, lapping at the Shoal.

Surprisingly, sleep does come easy.

*   *   *

There is a lighthouse in the middle of Long Island Sound. It has no business being there, for it no longer works.

It's called the Stratford Shoal. It's also known as the Middle Ground, and its place in the world is uncertain: it sits in the middle of its surroundings lands, existing in its own form of purgatory. The people who live near it simply call it the Shoal.

You see it whenever you take the Port Jefferson Ferry.

You wish you could have been able to show it to your wife. She would have loved it. She would have wanted to take photographs of it.

Murky green water surrounds the Shoal. If you're on the ferry, you can't see all the way down to the bottom.

Yet, as you lie dead in the water, you can see through it perfectly. You can see the lighthouse above you, and the stars in the sky, and the dots of green lights from passing boats.

And you can see your darling.

You can see the girl whom you let die. She reached out for your help, but you decided to wait.

You want to touch her. Kiss her. Feel her hand in your back pocket again, as together you cover your heads from the pelting rain.

But you can't do any of that. So you wait, which is something you do well, isn't it?

You see her come and go. But she is how she once was. You see her move and laugh and smile. You see her live life from the beginning, before all this happened, when she wasn't haunted.

You wait there, in the water, for a long time. Your cheeks have swollen from the pressure, and the salt water has washed your skin color away, leaving it the cloudy-gray color of ash.

You look at her with longing eyes.

Sometimes she looks back.

The Insects of Seneca Village

Jeff C. Stevenson

Now

"So, bugs . . ." Ernie said when the truck stopped at a red light. "Are you here because you find them fascinating, want to see how they keep surviving? Or do you hate them, want to help wipe them off the face of the earth?"

Jordan had taken the job with the exterminating company Bug-Out!—*"When bugs move in, we move them out! Bug-Out!"*—to make summer money for college and really hadn't thought about his position on insects.

"Neither, I guess; they're just bugs."

"No interest in bugs, huh? What are you interested in, then?"

"History, I guess," Jordan said. "That's my major."

The light changed, Ernie Riddles pressed the pedal, the truck rumbled to life. For as far back as he could remember, bugs had been his family's livelihood. His father and uncle had started the business back in 1955, then turned it over to Ernie in the early '90s. He'd never questioned why pest control was his father's chosen profession; growing up, his friends loved the idea of crawling under homes and killing insects, so Ernie was proud of what his dad did, was happy to take it over when he retired.

He stopped at another red light on Eighth Avenue, a few blocks from Central Park on the West Side of Manhattan. The traffic was sluggish, the morning already set at slow bake. The windows were down and Jordan was slightly embarrassed each time they stopped at a light. People from other cars glanced at him and smiled or smirked—he wasn't sure which. The huge logo on both sides of the truck of a huge, colorful bug being booted out of a house was impossible to miss.

"Me, I respect the bugs," Ernie said, answering his own question. "And this might sound strange, since our job is to drive them away, but I've always had a little love for their survival instincts. They were here before us, will be here long after we're gone; it's built into their tiny brains to keep on keepin' on. When they need to put up a fight, they rally to the occasion. I could tell you stories . . ."

Jordan waited, but Ernie had lapsed into silence. After a few seconds Jordan grew curious. "So tell me your favorite bug story."

Ernie smirked, his white teeth flashing like flares against his dark skin. That was what struck Jordan most when he'd come in for his interview—Ernie's bright eyes and the way his mouth sparked when he smiled or talked. Everything about the sixty-year-old man was big, optimistic, loud, like a glowing neon sign.

"That's easy. One story always comes to mind, from many years ago," Ernie said. "My daddy had told me about it happening to him and others, but I had never had a personal experience with it, until I did! Never forget your first time, right? A woman called, said she lived on the ground floor of a townhouse. Said she had slugs coming up everywhere—through her shower drain, her bathroom, kitchen sinks, her toilet. Everywhere. Somehow they had gotten into her plumbing. She was hysterical on the phone. Wanda—she was the receptionist back then—called me over, put the woman on speaker so I could hear for myself."

"You kill slugs?" Jordan asked. "Are they insects?"

Ernie glanced over. "No, they're not, they're closer to snails than insects. And yes, we kill them, too. And I'm warning you now, they are the only critters that give *me* the creeps! After I heard that woman on the phone, I knew we had to take the job. She was carrying on like her place was on fire, so we made it over there as soon as we could."

Jordan waited for Ernie to ease his way around a corner. He hoped he'd never have to drive the truck. It was oversized with all sorts of tanks, hoses, and toolboxes attached to it; he doubted he could safely accomplish the turns the careful way Ernie did.

"She was out on the sidewalk when I arrived, waiting," Ernie continued. "Had a little kid with her, refused to go back inside. My partner back then was a fellow named Dresdale Poony. What a name, right? Can't ever forget that name! And he was a bug hater, loved to see them all dead, relished vacuuming them up when we finished. Said they were amassing into communities to take over the world, needed to be shut down. Of course, I sent him inside; like I said, slugs give me the willies.

"It wasn't more than a minute I suppose before old Dresdale Poony comes huffing and puffing out of that apartment. His face . . . my God, I remember . . . his face looked sick, kinda green. He seemed to have grown older all of a sudden. I knew he had seen something just awful."

While they waited at the light, Ernie seemed to be lost in the memory. Jordan watched him, saw how the man frowned. He squeezed his eyes closed for a moment, as if trying to shut down whatever movie was playing in his head.

"Light's green," Jordan said. Ernie put the truck in gear, went on with the story.

"Dresdale was trembling a bit, like a little kid who's been spooked and can't be comforted. He kept looking over his shoulder at the townhouse. He had the jerks, too."

"The what?"

Ernie grinned at Jordan. "We all get 'em. It's that feeling a bug is crawling along your back so you flinch, fling yourself about. Usually, there's nothing there."

"What was wrong with him?"

"The woman asked Dresdale what he had seen, but he just shook his head, continued to pace around the yard in zigzags, flinching, brushing nothing off his back and arms, murmuring, keening to himself. I'd never seen him act like that. His behavior was starting to frighten the woman and her kid; the boy had nudged his way closer to his mother, she had wrapped her arms around him. I caught up with Dresdale out of earshot of the other two.

"'What's going on?' I asked. 'What did you see?' I had to grab his arm so he'd stop lurching around.

"'They're too *big*,' he finally said after I had held both of his elbows, forced him to look at me.

"'What are too big?'

"'The slugs! Those aren't slugs, Ernie.' He started to almost shout at me in a panicky voice. He rushed the words like he was in a hurry to say his piece and get out of Dodge. 'Those things are *white*. We don't have white slugs in New York! We have brown, gray, or black slugs and they're always out in a garden or in basement soil. Never in a house and *never* white!' He shuddered, broke loose from my grasp, went back to his aimless, frantic pacing about the front of the property.

"When Dresdale moved away from me, the woman approached and said, 'You're scaring me and my son.' I told her I'd find out what was going on. Man, I did *not* want to go in there, but I was the boss and had no choice. Those townhouses don't get much light. It was like going from daylight to midnight. It was murky, just a lot of yellow shadows trying to push past the grime that covered the street window. The kitchen was the first room I came to. I glanced around but didn't see much at first."

Ernie pulled up late at another stoplight, nosed into the crosswalk. He received a glare from an elderly woman who had to edge her way around the truck as she made her away across the street.

When they were moving again, Ernie said, "Not a lot of light in the kitchen, so I didn't see them at first. But I knew something was out of whack for Dresdale to act the way he had. I glanced around again. You'll learn to look out of the corner of your eye when trying to spot bugs; the flicker of a wing, the sharp scudder of a big one is easier to see and hear when you aren't looking directly at them. They're sly creatures, almost like ventriloquists with those dolls that make you think they're talking. Bugs can confuse you with their sounds, too, make you think you've found their nest when they've already moved on, leaving behind a little insect ghost town. But they're never really gone."

Impatient, Jordan asked, "But what did you *see?*"

"I stood there real quiet, just listened, waited for my eyes to adjust to the dark room. Then, all at once, I *could* see. I had missed them at first because, like Dresdale had said, they were white. Most kitchens in Manhattan in those days were painted a glossy white, so these things blended right in. The critters moved so slowly that you couldn't really say they were going anywhere, which is why I hadn't noticed them at first. There was a pile of them in the sink, squirming about. A few dozen eased their way across the counter. When I stepped fully into the center of the room, I saw that they covered the walls, the ceiling, all over the place. Their presence made the whole area sort of . . ."—he paused for a moment, looking for the right word—"*pulsate* with their tiny movements.

"Seeing them—finally *seeing* them—was enough to give you the jerks because when they were massed together like that, it really was disturbing. The ones on the ceiling were slipping loose, plopping to the floor. And they were so big—big as my fist." Ernie dropped his right hand from the steering wheel, made his meaty palm fold up under his thick fingers, then tightened it until the knuckles and veins plumped.

Jordan wondered if Ernie was making it all up to see him squirm, sort of a joke to play on the new kid. "Did this really happen?"

"God is my witness, this happened . . . and keeps happening. But that isn't the end of the story. Remember what Dresdale had said about them?"

"Yeah, that they were too big, and white."

Ernie nodded. "And something else. He said they weren't slugs." He floored the truck to sneak past a yellow light. When they'd settled back into the Upper West Side's slow stream of traffic, he glanced at Jordan. "The worst part wasn't that there were probably hundreds of them, big, and clamoring all over her kitchen and probably in the other rooms I hadn't ventured into yet." Ernie turned on the blinker. "The worst part was that Dresdale had been right. They weren't slugs. They were huge, overgrown, white maggots."

* * *

Then

It began on a summer evening—July 31, 1856.

Six-year-old Frederick Riddles was in a panic as he dashed up the dirt road. He avoided the large puddles from the earlier rainstorm because getting his clothes filthier with mud would only add to his punishment. Still, it would have been a delight to jump and splash in the pools of water. He stuck his tongue out at Manhattan Colored School No. 3 on the south side of the street as he always did. Then he made a sharp turn past the African Methodist Episcopal Zion Church. He scurried along a cluster of shacks, one-room homes made of wood, and a few three-story dwellings made of brick. He returned hellos when they were called out to him, then stopped in front of his familiar and welcoming single-story framed house. The distinctive blue porch had been constructed with siding from a feed store that had been remodeled. The white curtain with a fancy patterned border his mother had sewn fluttered in the window. The dwelling was set back a bit from the road. It was where Frederick lived with his father and grandmother.

In addition to the colorful porch, his home was easy to identify because right in front of it was what appeared to be a gigantic pile of leaves. The mound of foliage was actually a weeping beech tree, with limbs that, instead of stretching up toward the sky as expected, reached down as if gently patting the ground in search of something lost. Frederick and his friends loved playing hide-and-seek in and around the beech, since the branches that rested on the ground could be used as ladders to climb and conceal them in the upper arms of the tree.

He hurried toward the simple house: two rooms with an attached cooking shed and a primitive outhouse in the back. Frederick was breathing hard. Even though he was late—he was supposed to be home before the sun set on the church's steeple—he wanted to calm himself down before he faced his daddy and grandma. If he looked nervous and out of breath, they'd wonder why. Then they'd realize he'd rushed home because he missed his curfew. He feared upsetting his daddy more than whatever punishment Grandma Riddles would apply to his bottom. It had been a horrible few months since his mother had died; the grief and sorrow that dwelt in the house was distressing to behold, easy to arouse. The sadness made the already small home tinier and shabbier, a constant reminder of all the light and beauty Angela Riddles had brought to her family.

Even as he captured his breath and took a couple of careful steps, Frederick knew something was wrong. He could hear his daddy and grandma talking, their voices hard, bitter. He crept closer, praying their grim conversation wasn't the result of his tardiness.

"—tomorrow morning," Daddy said. "It's over. I wanted more, but all they were willing to pay was $2335."

"Greedy bastards," Grandma Riddles said. Frederick slapped his hands over his mouth in shock. He knew she'd said a bad word, so whatever they were talking about was serious and awful.

"Tomorrow morning, the police will be here and we have no choice," his father continued. "Mayor Wood has already put out notice that we are not to resist, just pack up and leave. He said six weeks' notice had been more than enough. It is time to get out."

"But where will we go? What will happen to our home . . . to this village?"

"They're going to tear the whole thing down, plow it under, Ma. I heard that they are going to purchase seven hundred acres and build a park and houses for the rich folk. This park's footprint is just going to stomp out our little town. By next year, there will be no trace of us ever having existed."

Frederick was hunched over in the near-darkness, his hands on his knees. Something was really wrong. That fluttery, nervous feeling returned to his chest; it had first appeared when his mom became ill and hadn't ever really gone away. His throat started to clog up; he knew he was going to cry. He could tell his daddy and grandma were mad. That scared him because they were usually so calm, even with Mom gone, they were always gentle and loving to him and each other.

"Your sweet mother is with the angels now, Frederick," Grandma had said after the funeral as she held him too tightly. He felt tears shaking out of her. "You must be strong now for your daddy, be a good boy, don't cause him any worry or trouble, you hear me?"

"Yes, ma'am."

Ever since Frederick's mother had died, his daddy hadn't been right. His eyes were always red as if he had been rubbing them too hard, his voice old and crackly when he spoke. He didn't sleep much, or at least he didn't snore the way he used to. Instead, there was now an eerie silence in the house at night, disturbed only when his father crept across the floorboards to sneak into the yard. He'd push his way into the protective arms of the weeping beech. Frederick would often awake to his father's mournful cries, a hard anguish that attempted to cut its way free from the leaves and branches.

"They're just going to bury our village?" Grandma asked. "Just cover us over, as if we'd never lived here?"

"Or died here," Peter said flatly. "I lost my Angela here. I can't leave her behind."

"Surely they will move the bodies. More than forty people are buried behind the church. Surely—"

"No, they're not!" Peter shouted. Frederick flinched. He hadn't heard his daddy yell or express anything close to anger in a long time. He didn't seem to have the strength for such a powerful emotion. He didn't even have the pride of work anymore—he'd stopped his barrel making after Frederick's mother died. He was bent over a lot, as if he were broken, waiting to be repaired.

Hearing his daddy yell made Frederick scared and nervous. He felt terribly alone outside. He needed the love and comfort of what was left of his family: the sweet minty scent of the horehound candy Grandma always sucked on, the familiar feel of his daddy's bristly yet soft beard when he rubbed it on top of Frederick's head. He needed to be with them. Fighting back tears, he burst into the house.

The conversation ceased, as he knew it would, but there was no scolding, no punishment. Grandma exclaimed that she had better get something on the supper table and began to move about the tiny space. With his teary, tired eyes, Daddy looked at Frederick, reached out to bring him in close for an embrace. The scratchy beard felt good on his head.

After dinner, Peter and Grandma went to her room for some privacy. Frederick knew that meant he was to fall asleep in the corner of the tiny, cluttered main area. He could hear their voices rise and fall. There was something about his father's tone that was different: he was insistent, demanding, asking his own mother for something that she seemed unwilling to give.

Several times Frederick heard his father say, "You know how to do it, so tell me so I'll do it right! I am not leaving her behind! Tell me!" Grandma protested, hushed her son, told him to keep his voice down. He continued to plead with her, demand that she tell him what he needed to know. This went on and on. It lulled Frederick into a deep, heavy slumber.

He barely woke as his father knelt by him, embraced him tenderly, rubbed his beard across the top of his head one final time.

*   *   *

Peter had visited Angela's grave every day since she died. Even blindfolded he could have found where his beloved was buried. It was close to midnight when he scuffled his way across the fenced-in cemetery that cradled so many friends and relatives. The moon was only at half-strength, as if turning away from what he was about to do.

He collapsed to his knees; the grief that clung so close to him rose up. He mourned for those he had lost and all that was about to be taken from him—his home and the plot of land he had purchased for $250 that allowed him the right to vote. Property—the very foundation of his dignity—was being stolen; it was the one thing he so desperately wanted to pass along to his only son.

His body shuddered, clenched with sorrow and rage at the thought of his beloved Angela plowed over, forgotten, all for some damnable park for the wealthy to enjoy. Everyone in the village had talked about what they had heard, how the affluent bankers, merchants, and landowners had an imagined rivalry with Europe. They envied the acres of parks in Britain, the fresh air they provided, what they called "the lungs of London." The new immigrant populations were hustling their way into lower Manhattan, and the growing textile industry made it a noisy, smoky, and unpleasant place to live. The well-heeled had simply run out of space and were inching their way up from downtown like insects overtaking and devouring a new plant. Something had to give.

Peter wiped his eyes. Breathing heavily, he couldn't help thinking about the appalling things the newspapers had written about his village, his friends, his neighbors. His wrath reignited as he recalled they had been named "squatters, simple-minded, insects, bloodsuckers, the wretched and debased of Nigger Village." They weren't simple-minded; some were educated, many could read. And the village wasn't a place for transients: Seneca had been around for decades, since 1825. Everyone was proud of how long it had been in existence. For many of his neighbors and now friends, it had been a Promised Land, a destination, a place where an African-American man could own property, raise a family. It was a desirable location, with ample fishing at the Hudson River and clean water at a nearby spring. Life in Seneca Village was rural and peaceful, in sharp contrast to the bustling streets of Lower Manhattan.

Under the dull moonlight, Peter wept because the promise and the dream were being taken away from him, picked off like the crust of a scab, leaving him wounded, bleeding. He recalled how eleven years earlier he had finally managed to bring his wife and mother from Connecticut. Once they were settled, they had tried for so long to start a family; five years later Frederick had been born. Peter loved the community of almost three hundred residents and all that they had accomplished. They had established three churches, educated their children at two schools, buried their dead at two cemeteries. They were a thriving group, building lives for themselves, something his parents and grandparents never had the chance to aspire to or even hope for. They had never been free, never had the possibilities or the opportunities that Peter did.

Now it was all being taken from him.

Insects? He'd show them . . .

Peter shook his head to scatter those thoughts. He steeled himself for what he had to do next. His legs were sore from kneeling on the dirt, but he needed to be there, close to the earth, to his Angela. He repeated the prayer as Ma had instructed him. Then he plunged his large hands deep into the soil, grateful for the rain that had fallen earlier and soaked into the ground, softening it.

He only had to dig fourteen inches before his nails scraped the rotting rosewood coffin. He brushed away the damp earth to reveal the plate on the lid:

Angela Morris Riddles died May 17, 1856,
aged 32 years, three months and fourteen days.

Tears rushed to his eyes, but this time he cursed them, blinked them away so he could see clearly. Without hesitation, he grabbed one of the rocks from the pile of freshly turned soil, stuck the lid of the coffin. It collapsed after three easy blows. Peter turned away from the sickening spoiled cheese smell that wafted from the box containing all that he loved, now decayed and crumbling. His mother said it must be the hand Angela had held forth to betroth herself to him. He felt for her left arm, lifted it out of the coffin. Her body followed. The sleeve of the dress was a dank mess of threads that slid from her limb. Even by the faint yet curious moonlight, he could see her arm was covered in mold. Startled beetles dashed off in every direction. He shook off the ones that had scurried over his wrists.

Peter looked closely. He spotted maggots feasting on what little flesh remained on Angela's shoulder and one of her fingers. With a sharp twist and a loud crack, he pulled her entire arm out of the coffin. Her body fell back, the sound of brittle kindling dumped onto cold embers. He could see what he imagined were several generations of maggots feeding on strands of tissue that clung to her ring finger. Many of the insects were fully grown; those were the ones he was looking for.

"We loved each other," he murmured into the darkness. "I had a wife, a son, a mother. We lived here once. They won't ever take that away from me."

There was only one way he could remain forever with his beloved. He had planned to be buried next to her when his time came, but that time was now, before the sun rose. They could demolish the town, build over it, but he and Angela would remain together to eternally remind future generations that they had lived in Seneca Village, that they had existed.

His mother's words, spoken less than an hour earlier, returned to him.

"If you go through with this, it will bind you forever to her and to that soil. But it will take you away tonight and you'll never see Frederick again. You will forever become what you consume, always surfacing and seeking, always reminding them of what they've destroyed. But remember, what is done can never be undone. Are you certain this is what you want? I will care for the boy, but are you certain about this?"

Peter was certain. Until he lost Angela he'd thought the phrase 'can't live without her' was an exaggeration, but now he knew it was a fact. Ma would do a good job raising the boy and the $2335 would stretch a lot further for two people than three.

He held his wife's decaying arm as tenderly as he could. Once the white maggots were close enough to his face that he could see them in the moonlight, he moved her left hand toward his mouth. He closed his eyes, bit down, began to chew.

*   *   *

Now

Jordan asked, "Why were there maggots in her kitchen? Did she have rotting food or something? Isn't that what they like?"

"Yep, or dead animals. Or dead bodies," Ernie said ghoulishly. "But she didn't have any of those. It was a perfectly clean, normal apartment."

Fascinated, Jordan asked, "So what did you do?"

"I told her the truth that she had maggots, not slugs, and they might be breeding on her property. Then I sent Dresdale in there to deal with it. I had him spray with the chemical permethrin, then he poured a bacteria compound down all her drains to eat and dissolve anything organic that had attracted the maggots in the first place."

"Did it work?"

"Yeah, but it took several days. About a week, I guess. Remember, those critters were big so it took a lot of poison to kill them."

Jordan couldn't help but chuckle. "That's all so gross. She must have freaked out when you told her."

"Yep. She moved out, too, soon after."

"How do you know?"

"Because we keep getting callbacks to the same townhouse. And it's *always* the new tenants. And it's only in that basement apartment. Not the ones on either side and nowhere else in the city that I've ever seen."

"Weird."

"You'll see how weird. We're going there now."

Ernie turned into 85th Street and Seventh Avenue, pulled up in front of a townhouse right in the middle of the block. A gigantic, ancient weeping beech tree was settled comfortably on the corner. An old green plaque with white lettering was posted near the tree. Jordan glanced at the opening sentence: *Once there was a village in what is now Central Park. It was called Seneca Village.*

"Jordan?" Ernie called out from the stoop where he stood with a young couple. Jordan quickly snapped a picture of the sign so he could read it later.

"It's really disgusting," the woman said immediately. She shuddered. "I've never seen so many slugs. They are coming up through the sinks and the toilet."

"I did all the over-the-counter sprays and pellets, but nothing works," the guy said. "No idea why they are in the house. I thought slugs were outdoor creatures."

"They are," Ernie said. He glanced at Jordan, whose eyes had gone wide. "Describe them to me."

"They're white," the man and woman spoke in unison.

"And big," the woman added, and then shivered again.

"Jordan," Ernie said, "best you check out the situation."

*   *   *

From 1825 to 1857, Seneca Village was located in Manhattan between 82nd and 89th Streets and Seventh and Eighth Avenues. It was a community . . . and then it was gone, erased by Central Park. No one knows where its residents resettled, and no living descendants of Seneca Village have ever been found.

The Grim

Allan Burd

Jack stared up at the condo complex on Thomas Street, a five-story building with four upper rows of symmetrical windows and a ground level filled with canopied shops. The building's beige hue was barely discernible between the cloak of the moonless night sky and the reflection of the flashing lights from the fire trucks and their police cars.

"The air stinks out here. When can we enter?" Sal asked him. Sal checked the Fitbit on his lean wrist and spit into the street. "It's three A.M. and I've got a prime piece of pussy waiting for me at home that I'd like to hit before morning. If you know what I mean?"

Jack glared at him. "I'm forty-five and married half that, so I have no idea what you mean. Not anymore." Jack sized up his young partner. *The bastard.* Even in his suit, you could tell the fucker was ripped. The way he used to be, he thought, before family life and the job got the better of him. "We'll go in when the professionals tell us it's clear."

A doorman held the glass door open for the burly fireman exiting the building. Jack recognized Kaufman. The seasoned firefighter carried light gear on his back and a touch of scruff on an otherwise clean face. A good sign, Jack thought, indicating the fire wasn't too bad. Kaufman lit a cigarette, took a long puff, then extinguished it under his boot on the sidewalk before approaching them.

"Evening, Detective." He gave a tilt of his head that signaled the all clear.

Jack signaled the uniformed men under his command to enter, while he and Sal hung back to gather more information. "Wish I could say it was good to see you again, but not like this," said Jack.

"Never like this," said Kaufman. He glanced at Sal. "New guy. Good. Someone to fill out the paperwork for you."

"You don't look that ruffled," said Sal.

"Fire was out before we even got here. I'd say there's minimal damage, except there's a corpse upstairs whose memory I don't want to diminish."

"Shit," said Sal.

"Aw, fuck," said Jack.

"Young too. Fucking shame. It ain't pretty either. You're not a puker?" Kaufman asked Sal, who shook his head. "I didn't think so. You don't look like a puker. Still, I don't envy you." Kaufman signaled his crew to load the gear back on the fire truck so they could pull out.

"Yeah . . . thanks." Jack patted Kaufman on the back as he left then looked to Sal. "Your dick will have to wait."

A red-vested doorman held the door wide for them as they entered the building.

"How long you been here?" Jack asked him.

"Since ten. I'm the graveyard shift."

"Have you been here the whole time?"

"I've got a bladder like a camel. Never left my post."

"Did you see anyone suspicious enter or leave the premises?"

"No, sir," the man replied. "No one out of the ordinary."

"You have video surveillance to back that up?" asked Sal.

"Of course."

"Why don't you get those recordings ready for us before we come back down. The last twenty-four hours should cover it," said Sal.

"Absolutely," said the doorman.

Jack and Sal made their way to the third floor. By the time they got there, the uniformed officers had already prepped the area, cordoning off the apartment with yellow crime tape and interviewing a couple of the neighbors awakened by the commotion.

"Aw, Jeez," said Jack, as he reached the door. He immediately placed a handkerchief over his nose to protect his olfactory senses from the pungent smell: a combination of smoke, fried beef, sizzling pork, copper, a hint of charcoal, and excess perfume. He handed an extra cloth to Sal, who turned it down.

"One tour in Iraq got me used to it." Sal lifted the tape so Jack wouldn't have to bend as far to enter the apartment and followed behind him. "Swanky digs. Very spacious. What do you think? A million? Two?"

"I don't think it matters anymore," said Jack.

His experienced eyes scanned the space: polished hardwood floors, eighty-inch TV mounted on a wall, a solid black shelf filled with tchotchkes, a square coffee table with a smattering of ladies' magazines, a long leather sofa, a bar with four stools fronting a kitchen. The window at the far end was jammed wide open to vent the room. Kaufman was right: no damage at all, not even from smoke. Other than the usual mess made by a few in-rushing firefighters, the apartment looked remarkably clean.

Jack followed the source of the offensive odor to the bedroom, where a half-charred female lay on a four-poster bed covered in scorched white satin sheets. He pocketed his hankie, approached the bedside, and studied the victim. Long curly brunette hair cascaded across her vacant pretty face. Along half her body, her melted skin melded with her silk green dress.

"That's how they found her," said a uniformed officer. "They also said every window they opened was locked tight from the inside, so no signs of entry, forced or otherwise."

Jack looked around the neat room. "No signs of a struggle, either. Most of her face escaped the flames. Beautiful girl, figure mid-twenties. Her features are intact enough for facial recognition. We have a name?"

"Tracy McRealy. This is her apartment. Got the info off the driver's license in her purse, along with her cash, credit cards, and some other valuables," replied the officer.

"So not a robbery. You smell that sweetness in the air, Sal? That's not perfume. That's cerebrospinal fluid," said Jack, sliding on a pair of latex gloves. He gently turned her head, spying the clump of blood below the sizable gash in the back of her skull. "Aw, Jeez. Good news is she didn't burn alive. Bad news is someone caved her head in . . . judging by the width and depth of the wound with something sharp and heavy like an ax."

"A hatchet," replied Sal.

"That's pretty definitive," said Jack.

"The edge of the blade is sticking out beneath her lower back. Seems to me her killer wanted us to find it. Lift her body a little more and you'll see it," said Sal, snapping his gloves on.

Jack did, and Sal signaled over two crime scene investigators who photographed the evidence, then carefully slid the blood-soaked hatchet from beneath her and sealed the weapon in a plastic bag.

Jack looked around again, noting the minimal spatter pattern. "Someone bashed her at close range and placed her in this position. It appears she didn't see it coming."

"Lover," guessed Sal. "Maybe someone who felt burned by her burned her back. If the doorman's telling the truth, maybe someone from a neighboring apartment."

"Maybe they had a fight. After our boys finish canvassing, we'll see if anyone heard any shouting," said Jack.

"Or maybe it wasn't a lover at all," came a voice from the bedroom entrance. A tall, bald black man in an overcoat stood in the doorway surveying the crime scene.

"Hey, who let him in here?" Sal asked, about to dart forward.

Jack grabbed his arm. "It's okay. He's an old friend."

"He's a crime beat reporter from the *Post*," said Sal.

"The best one," said Jack.

"The best is right. Old is right, too," said the reporter, coming closer.

"Who let you up here?" asked Sal.

"You guys were nice enough to send the doorman away, and most of the cops on this beat know me to be a stand-up guy."

"Charlie, meet Sal, my new partner," said Jack. "He's spirited. The way we used to be."

"Speak for yourself." Charlie extended his hand to Sal.

Sal showed him the gloves he was wearing instead of shaking it. "Charmed."

"I am charming," said Charlie, lowering his hand. "Damn," he added upon closer inspection of the dead body. He snapped a picture of it with his cellphone.

"Don't do that," said Sal.

"C'mon, Charlie, you know better than that," said Jack.

Charlie quickly pocketed the phone. "I won't use it. But that's only because I know you'll send me a better one," he said, smiling broadly.

"And I'm going to do that because?" asked Jack.

"Because I'm going to help you figure this one out. Care to take a walk with me, Jack? I might have some insight for you."

Jack viewed the room one more time, knowing whatever information was to be gleaned could be gleaned without him. "Yeah, sure. Sal, you take it from here."

"I'll handle it," said Sal.

Jack and Charlie exited the apartment, took the elevator down, and stepped outside the building. Jack took a deep breath, inhaling stale air that felt colder than usual.

"Does this city look darker to you?" Charlie asked.

Jack shrugged. "It's always darkest before the dawn."

"No, seriously, feels like dark times all around us."

Jack looked up. Even the skyscrapers had a pall cast over them. "The murder rate's higher. That's for shit sure."

"It's more than that," said Charlie. "These crimes I'm covering . . . they're crueler, more vicious, more sadistic, more . . ." Charlie rubbed his bald head, grasping for the right word.

"Inhuman," said Jack, finishing Charlie's thought.

Charlie shivered. "More than that, too . . . as if there's this palpable, malevolent presence suffocating this city. You notice the air feels icier and carries a foul stench. You notice the increase of degenerate scumbags leaving their crack dens and whorehouses because they feel just as home in the streets. Heck, even the rats are more comfortable coming out of the sewers lately. Everything feels worse, dirtier. Except the homeless. There's less of them. You know why? Because after livin' on these streets for as long as they have, they can sense it, an overwhelming despair, too desperate even for them. New York used to be the city that never sleeps. Now I only think that's true because people are too afraid to close their eyes."

"That's a little melodramatic, but I can't argue. What do you think is going on?"

"I think New York *was* an interesting place to live. Now I think it's a more interesting place to die."

Jack took notice of the glimmer behind Charlie's eyes. "What are you not telling me?"

"This wasn't a crime of passion. This was done as a work of art," said Charlie.

"What the fuck does that mean?"

"Her murder fits the modus operandi of a psychopath I've been tracking who's committed at least a dozen other city crimes and, unfortunately, said psycho has been clever enough to never leave even a whiff of evidence behind."

"I think we'd have noticed a pattern. Plus, I've got a murder weapon with prints on it. None of which fits with what you're telling me. What makes you think this is part of a larger series of crimes, and why the hell am I first hearing about this now?"

Charlie shrugged. "Because I wasn't a hundred percent sure until tonight. Now I've got enough to go to print."

"You're fishing for a story." Jack gave him a doubt-filled stare.

Charlie shrugged. "I'll tell you what. I can wait a few days to press my editor. Do your full investigation. Run your prints. When they don't reveal anything, then come see me and I'll tell you what I think is going on. And when you come by, bring my favorite sandwich. You'll owe me at least that." Charlie walked off into the night.

"Shit," said Jack, kicking a cockroach off his shoe and watching it skitter away unworried. "Shit." He looked back up at the condo and reluctantly went back inside.

*   *   *

Two days later, Jack held something thick wrapped in tinfoil and walked into the crowded offices of the *New York Post* as most everyone else was walking out. He slipped between the bustle and dropped the tinfoil wad on Charlie's desk. Charlie never looked up, just kept typing away furiously on his computer.

"Lean with enough spicy yellow mustard to give you an ulcer. Just the way you like it," said Jack. He produced a can of Dr. Brown's Black Cherry, placed it down next to the sandwich, and popped the tab, the fizz of released air finally gaining Charlie's full attention. "I'm ready to listen, or did you just ask me here to fetch you dinner?"

"Not here," said Charlie. He grabbed a thick file from his middle drawer, piled the food Jack brought on top of it, and tilted his head for Jack to follow him to a nearby conference room. A minute later, he closed the door and locked it.

"Very Deep Throat," said Jack. "Are you going to fill me in?"

"You ain't gonna like it."

"I'm a cop. I don't like most of the things I hear."

"Then I won't sugarcoat it," said Charlie, opening the folder on the table. "There's a serial killer stalking our city, and he, or she, is reenacting . . . no, recreating old New York City's most infamous crimes."

"You've already lost me," said Jack, his face squinting into a ball.

"Hear me out. The murder on Thomas Street a couple nights ago . . . that was a recreation of the 1836 murder of Helen Jewett that happened right on that same street." Charlie pulled copies of news articles relating to the Helen Jewett murder out of the file and displayed them on the table for Jack to peruse. "Back in the 1830s, Helen Jewett was an upscale New York City prostitute. A frequent customer of hers killed her with three sharp blows of a hatchet to the back of her skull, then set her bed on fire to cover his tracks. Check it out. Same wound. Same burn pattern. Our victim, Tracy, was even wearing a similar green dress to the one that Helen wore when she was killed, and she was laid out in the same position. Yeah . . . the old one's a black-and-white drawing, but trust me, every reference I found says her dress was green."

"Kaufman told me he thought the perp used a blowtorch," said Jack.

"For a work of art," said Charlie. He placed the drawing of Helen next to the crime photo of Tracy. "Almost identical, right? That's pretty fucked up."

"That's plenty fucked up," said Jack, reviewing the remarkable similarities of the two corpses.

"Tell me, was your victim also a call girl?"

"Yeah," said Jack. "She was an escort with some incredibly wealthy clients. We found their names in her trick book. Sal's been running them down since yesterday morning."

"He's wasting his time. But you already suspect that 'cause there wasn't a shred of evidence that anyone other than her was even there, was there?"

"The prints we found were unidentifiable," said Jack.

"Thought so." Charlie saw Jack about to speak but held up a finger. "I need you to hold your thoughts a moment. That sandwich is calling to me." He took a long bite, 'mmmm-ing' how good it was. "Damn, you did me right. And here I am ruining your whole day." He spilled more old newspaper articles onto the tabletop and lined them up, matching old articles against current police reports.

Jack took in the enormity of it. "Holy . . . start at the beginning."

Charlie chugged down some Black Cherry and wiped the excess off his mouth with his sleeve. "My beginning. Remember that case a few months back where a guy committed suicide on the rooftop of Madison Square Garden? He shot himself in the face. Based on the closeness of the gunshots, the lack of evidence of anyone else present, and the fact that the victim's fingerprints were found on the weapon as if he were posing for a selfie, no one argued about anything other than how he got up there. But you notice I said gunshots. A few weeks later, when I looked deeper into the case for a personal-interest story, I discovered that our suicide victim shot himself three times and at least one of those shots rendered his face being almost unrecognizable. How the fuck does someone shoot himself three times?

"So I started to dig. I came across another famous murder that occurred on the rooftop of the Garden. It was a different building in a different place back then, but in 1906 a man named Harry Kendall Thaw shot a guy named Stanford White on the roof of Madison Square Garden because he was screwing around with his wife. *Three times.* According to the records I could find, in the same places as our suicide victim supposedly killed himself. I brought it up to some of your brethren. They gave me a few good chuckles and sent me on my way. But the uncanny coincidence got me thinking, so I got my nose up and started searching for any recent murder scenes that might match with some other notable historical crimes. Guess what? I found a bunch."

Charlie pointed to two matching files, one old and one new. "Earlier this fall, a dismembered pregnant woman with her throat slashed was fished out of the East River. The way she was cut up and dispatched perfectly matched the 1913 killing of Anna Aumuller, a women murdered by her priest-slash-lover named Hans Schmidt." Charlie tapped two more matching files. "Shortly after that, a torso floated out of the East River. That body part belonged to a German tourist whose legs were found in the Navy Yard and whose other dismembered body parts turned up in Harlem and parts of the Bronx. That was exactly how a guy named William Guldensuppe was murdered back in 1897, same nationality, same disposal, similar locations. His murder was marked as a probable mob hit due to his alleged money laundering ties to organized crime. I think differently."

Charlie pointed to a picture of a burned-down house. "Five months ago, there was a house fire in Staten Island where they discovered a mother and her baby, not burned, but gruesomely murdered with their skulls bashed in. That was labeled a break-in gone bad, with a fire being set to burn any evidence. In actuality, I believe it's a recreation of a Christmas night murder from 1843, similar victim relationship, similar circumstances. And in every case, no leading evidence of any kind. No would-be robbers-cum-arsonists who could fuck up a crime that bad are going to be so careful they don't leave even a shred of evidence behind. But a professional artist painting a scene . . ."

"You gotta be shittin' me with all this."

"I could see a few happening the same way—bound to be some duplication along the murder train—but this many, with this many similarities? No fucking way. So I made a list of as many infamous old New York City murders as I could find, and I kept my eyes peeled. When Thomas Street came up on my scanner, I got my ass out of bed and over there already knowing what I was going to find," said Charlie.

"Jeez," said Jack with a groan.

"The interesting thing is our killer's far from perfect. He strives for accuracy, but with all the changes to the city that have occurred over time, he can't possibly get everything right. Check this one out," said Charlie, pointing to yet another set of matching crimes. "A fifty-eight-year-old former prostitute was strangled and disemboweled in room thirty-one of a hotel along the river. You guys arrested her john, a twisted puppy with a rap sheet a block long. I don't think he did it. You ever hear of a case called Jack the Ripper in America? Back in 1891, a fifty-eight-year-old prostitute nicknamed Old Shakespeare was strangled and disemboweled in the same way. Our killer got the room number right, but he had to use a different hotel because, similar to the Garden, the old one didn't exist anymore. Our killer's a stickler for details, but when the details aren't available to him, he's forced to improvise. Though he's getting better.

"Six months back a guy was shot twice in Stanwix Hall. I think that was an attempt to duplicate the botched murder of the infamous Bill the Butcher Poole from the 1850s, you know ... the guy they based the movie *Gangs of New York* on. But our guy blew it. Bill the Butcher lived through his wounds, whereas the guy who was shot died instantly and our killer didn't shoot him in the same places. I could be wrong here, but I'm theorizing that this was our killer's first attempt. I think he tried to duplicate a very famous murder and learned the hard way that he bit off more than he could chew. So in his quest for historical accuracy, he moved on to easier targets."

"So, assuming you're right, we have a sociopath on the loose painting murders in three-D like Picasso."

"Yeah, and lately he's using a lot of the color red."

Jack sat down and studied everything Charlie had. He reviewed the date order of all the recent killings along with their eerie similarities to old murders. Everything Charlie said appeared to be correct. "This is insane. Do you know the planning it takes to pull just one of these off to this level of detail, let alone this many in this short a time?"

"Kind of takes evil fucking genius to an all new level," said Charlie.

"Evil, fucking, crazy bastard is more like it. Fuck, I'm going to have to alert the mayor, assemble a task force. And that's assuming they don't push me into retirement early and label me a screw loose because no one is going to want to admit this is going on. You know, when you print this, it's going to cause a panic."

"You mean further panic. People sense something's going on. The city's already on edge."

"This is too fucked up to even think about. I should retire early. You should retire with me. My brother's got a boat up on White Lake. We'll go fishing together."

"No can do. This city's in my blood and, unlike you, I can still do my job when I get fat."

"Now you sound like my missus," said Jack, patting his pocket after feeling the vibrations from his phone. He swiped the screen and answered, "Yeah. Jack here." His face went pale to the point that even Charlie was startled. "What? No fucking way. I'll be right there," said Jack, leaning forward, his arms against the table barely holding him up.

"What was that?" asked Charlie.

"Sal . . . Sal's dead. I . . . I gotta go," stammered Jack, shaking his head.

"How?"

"He didn't say."

"Where?"

"The Empire Hotel," said Jack.

"I'm—I'm going with you," said Charlie.

*   *   *

Fifteen minutes later, sirens screaming, Jack drove his car between the barricades and parked in front of the main entrance. Two cops stepped forward to greet him.

"We'll take you to him," said one of them.

Charlie quickly moved to join them, but another officer intercepted him. "Please step back, sir. If you aren't a guest at this hotel, you're not allowed inside at this time."

"It's okay, he's with me," said Jack. The officer let him pass, and together Jack and Charlie were escorted into the lobby, where patron and staff members stared on in curiosity. "How bad?" asked Jack.

"It's fucking bad. As bad as it gets," said the officer. "I know you're a seasoned vet, but still, you're gonna want to prepare yourself."

The officer opened a side stairwell leading down to a sub-basement. The smell was frighteningly reminiscent of the putrid stench from Thomas Street, only this time made worse by the inclusion of the harsh smell of burnt hair.

"Fuck," muttered Jack, placing a cloth to his nose as his shoes scuffed along the concrete floor. Ahead of him, lying naked and headless, was Sal's body, a cavernous crimson wound across his chest exposing his cracked sternum, sharp broken ribs, meaty muscle, and a bloody mass that used to be his beating heart. Above his open neck, a puddle of coagulated blood pooled into a gel-like consistency. On a worktable off to the side rested his smoldering, unrecognizable, blackened head; patches of flesh that clung to a charcoaled skull, hauntingly perfect teeth, and some yellow goo stuck inside the empty sockets that used to be his eyes.

Charlie immediately turned and retched into a corner.

The cop who brought them down ignored Charlie. "Sal came here by himself first thing after lunch to track down one of the names in Tracy McRealy's trick book. This hotel was one of the locations listed where she met one of her clients. But nobody comes down here, so it took a while for the smell to carry to where someone noticed. He's been dead at least a few hours. A fireman spotted his head in the open furnace and scooped it out with a shovel. We didn't even realize it was Sal until thirty minutes later, when we found his badge lying in the corner."

"Jesus," muttered Jack. He put his hand over his mouth and stepped back.

The officer pointed to Sal's chest wound. "The damage was done with several blows from a meat cleaver. It's already on its way to the lab for analysis."

Charlie wiped his mouth off and walked over. Sweat dripped from his forehead, his hand trembling. "I know this crime," he whispered to Jack, a tremor in his voice.

"Not here," said Jack. "Outside." Charlie nodded and walked out of the cellar. Jack addressed all the officers present. "I want every molecule of this basement tested. I want every video feed scoured and tapped dry. We use every resource available to us to catch the bastard who did this."

A chorus of *yes sirs* followed behind him as he left the room. He met Charlie on the sidewalk outside. Together they leaned hard against the building, a sliver of moonlight piercing through the cloud cover like a dagger.

"Sorry, my friend," said Charlie.

Jack shook his head. "You think this was our killer?"

Charlie took a deep breath. "I know it was. I recently logged a case from 1902 where a guy named Tobin dragged another guy nick-named Captain Jim into the basement of the Hotel Empire and killed him exactly the same way. I'm not sure if this is the same ho-tel or not, but the name is similar enough where it has to be him."

Something caught Jack's eye, a small white object lying in the gutter. He walked over to it, bent down, and picked up the squished butt of an extinguished cigarette. For a long moment his mind churned. "Two for two," Jack whispered under his breath.

"What is it?" asked Charlie.

Jack scowled at Charlie. "Might be a coincidence. Might be something more. Go back to work, Charlie. Write a story letting the world know the hero Sal was. Not just the great cop this city lost, but the man and war hero he was before he joined us. But don't mention a peep about our serial killer."

"But—"

"No buts. I want this quiet. I don't want this sick bastard to have any idea that we're on to him. And fuck any task force. I'm going to catch this prick in the act myself and bury him somewhere so deep no one will ever find his body." Jack's eyes bore holes into Charlie waiting for a nod of agreement.

"You think you know something?"

Jack didn't answer.

"Come on, Jack. We're in this together now."

Jack nodded. "Just between you and me, okay." Charlie nodded. "Tell me, Charlie, do you know a firefighter by the name of Kauf-man?"

*　*　*

The next day, Charlie wrote a piece that made the city so proud Sal was bound to get a street named after him. And he kept his word, no mention of a serial killer. The day after that, Jack's phone rang.

"I have something on Kaufman," Charlie said over the phone.

"It has to wait. Sal's funeral is in two hours. We're lined up a mile deep."

"It can't. It's time-sensitive. I've been watching him. Late last night he left home and checked into the Park Central Hotel. And get this . . . he paid for the room with cash."

"Did he meet with someone?" said Jack.

"He did. I think he bought himself a new identity."

"You think he's planning to split?"

"All you cops will be at Sal's funeral. I couldn't think of a better time."

"Shit. You get a room number?"

"Room three-forty-nine," said Charlie.

Jack hung up the phone. He tossed his tie on his desk and left the precinct for his squad car. Soon he arrived at the Park Central Hotel, taking the stairs so he wouldn't have to waste a second waiting for the elevator to take him to the right floor. Gun drawn, he strode down the hallway, surprised to find the door to room 349 slightly ajar. Jack quietly and cautiously entered the dim room.

"Close the door," said Charlie, standing behind a cushioned chair in the middle of the room. "Kaufman's not here."

Jack holstered his weapon. "Shit. Where do you think he went?"

Charlie shrugged. "He's probably at work," he said, casually revealing the Smith & Wesson revolver he held in his hand.

"What the fuck?"

Without hesitation Charlie pulled the trigger, placing a bullet in Jack's lower abdomen. Jack yelped and fell against the bed. He reached for his own weapon, but Charlie placed the .38 special against his head.

"Don't you want to hear me out?" asked Charlie.

Jack leaned back against the mattress. "What the fuck, Charlie?"

"Do you know who was shot in this room? Arnold Rothstein. November 24, 1928. Mr. Big. The Brain. The Big Bank Roll. This big-shot mobster shot through the spleen like a common criminal by a thirty-eight caliber bullet just like the one I placed in you. But Arnold didn't die here. He made his way to the service entrance, stumbled out onto the street, and died the next day in the hospital. I would've preferred that. Heck, I would've preferred not to kill you until much later on, especially in this way because I knew this was a historical crime I could never perfectly duplicate. But I decided to make due."

"I don't get it, Charlie," Jack gasped, his breathing heavy, sweat dripping from his forehead.

"That's because you've never been the imaginative type. I'm an artist, Jack, and what's the point of being an artist if people can't appreciate your work? So I showed you my scrapbook and it was pretty great watching you appreciate it. Even better watching you appreciate in person what I did to Sal." Charlie shook his head. "But Kaufman? That was some insulting bullshit."

"Aw, fuck." Jack drooled.

"I love this city, Jack. Everything about it. The architecture, the culture, especially the history. And let's face it . . . New York's got a very violent history. Manhattan was built with blood, sweat, guts, and tears. What we have now came at a price. I'm just reminding people of that."

"You're out of your mind," said Jack.

"Not really. I like this city better when it's in a dark place, and the old days were the darkest. Killers today don't really put much thought behind it. But the murders they committed in those days . . . those were the classics."

"That's sick . . . you're sick. You're gonna get caught. Even if it's not me, someone's going to catch you."

"Maybe. Maybe not. After twenty-five years working in this city, I've learned all the ins and outs. You think it was easy getting on the roof of the garden unseen? Luckily, I've made friends everywhere . . . friends with access keys I could duplicate without their knowledge and friends I could use to con my way into places unseen. I'm smart and I'm careful."

"So that's how you got into Thomas Street," said Jack.

Charlie pshawed. "That, no. I was one of Tracy's incredibly wealthy clients. At least I made her think I was wealthy. That piece of art came at a price. But scribbling the Empire Hotel into her little book and waiting to see who came along—that one was free."

"You're a sociopath."

"Always have been. Who else could survive covering the crime beat all these years? But still, I always liked you. Would have been nice to let you walk out that door, too, just to emulate the murder of Arnold Rothstein, but . . . ."

Charlie raised the pistol and shot Jack in the forehead, killing him instantly, splattering his blood and brains on the bed. Then he wiped the room clean, planted false clues for the police to find that would lead nowhere, and left.

*   *   *

That afternoon at Sal's funeral, Jack's absence was a concern, but no one was going to stop it. Charlie sat in a pew next to a pretty blond from a local network.

"That was a great piece you wrote yesterday," she whispered to him.

"I appreciate that," said Charlie, admiring her looks, mentally picturing which victim she resembled from New York history.

She stared back at him. "I heard you were there at the crime scene. Do you have any idea who did this?"

"Take a walk with me after this. I might have some insight for you," said Charlie.

In a Pig's Eye

Teel James Glenn

I

Private parties at the Tavern on the Green restaurant in Central Park were always such surreal affairs. It was hard for California-born Jason Flood to believe he was actually only a few hundred feet from the madness of Manhattan in the artificial oasis of trees and greenery. The fact that the land for the park had been seized from local settlers and farmers who were kicked off their property, however, made it easier for the professional gigolo to understand it. It was just the way things were. And the fact that the building originally housed the sheep that grazed in Central Park's Sheep Meadow seemed completely appropriate.

Jason Flood was also a wannabe actor and arm candy for the very blonde Portia Jones, who reveled in the attention their May-December relationship garnered.

Portia, at five foot ten, was stunningly beautiful and had ample "equipment" for the chase, with large natural breasts and an athlete's graceful body; but the former chorus girl had not had a hit show in five years, and at forty-six the time showed around the edges.

Jason, a muscular, blond twenty-seven, was the exactly what the tabloids ordered to keep the aging beauty on the cover of the supermarket rags.

And that was why Portia came to Madge Dumont's shindig, despite the long-standing feud between the two stars. It would raise enough eyebrows for five more minutes of fame.

Madge, a petite, dark-haired Mediterranean beauty with a little girl pout to her artificially bee-stung lips, at forty-two still invoked the image of the oversexed high school cheerleader.

The fact that she was one of the leads on the hit TV show *Montauk Housewives* assured that there were important movers and shakers at her party. One of them, the one Portia wanted to meet, was Dr. Otto Silverhand.

Silverhand was *the* plastic surgery genius of the age, rumored to have unique and pioneering techniques, many of which he held secret—ones that kept many stars on top and in tip-top shape long past their normal "shelf-life."

The good doctor had fixed the poor quality of Madge's first implants early on in her career.

"This madhouse is a waste of time." Jason sipped on a piña colada.

"Never you mind wasting time, Jason," Portia said in a tired whisper.

Flood let a smirk slide across his handsome features. "You don't seem to mind how I waste that time below your waist."

She gave him a cold look then smiled for the public.

Madge Dumont appeared and beamed disarmingly at Jones.

"Portia, I'm surprised you accepted my invitation!" The hostess pouted. "After you turned down the—let's see—last ten?"

Portia gave a porcelain smile. "Well, even the Grand Canyon was worn down, Madge; let's just say you were the wet one here and I was the rock."

"According to all the sources I'm always wet, darling," the hostess said.

Both women genuinely laughed and the ice was broken. After that the two just chatted as colleagues.

"Uh, Madge, dear," the visitor said after a bit, "I know you look amazing and, well, so naturally so, but tell me, confidentially"—she leaned in to whisper—"did you find a way to give nature a little helping-hand?"

The dark-haired hostess looked around to see who might be close by.

"Otto Silverhand is the answer, dear. He is very strict—a diet, a workout regime, and—uh—certain practices—but, well, look at me. A regular Dorian Gray!"

Portia gave a little shrug. "I work out, I diet, I even, well . . ." The two women glanced to where Jason Flood was posing by the bar.

Madge giggled. "That kind of exercise can, uh, be counterproductive if you try too hard, darling."

"Seriously, dear," Madge added, "Otto is the answer. But he is very exclusive."

"I know," Portia said. "I've tried to get in to see him, but the wait—"

"The price of success!"

"Madge, look at me. We have knocked heads, but we both went through the wars together. You've got your hit—and you deserve it—but I just don't have a lot of time left." She leaned in to cover her face and started to sob. "I think I'm done, Madge. Really, done. There's nothing left but hag parts."

Dumont patted the blonde on the back in a sisterly gesture. "Easy, Portia, you'll undo your makeup."

"I'm sorry to make a fool of myself, Madge. I'll just collect Jason and—"

"No, stay," the dark-haired hostess said. "I'll introduce you to the doctor when he gets here. I know what it is like to need it that badly."

Portia looked at her with concern. "You—you really will?"

"Yes."

"How do you know I'm not just playing you to jump the line to this doctor?"

"Because I know these tears are real, darling. You're just not that good an actress."

Portia looked stunned for a minute, then burst out laughing.

Madge joined her and was still laughing when Dr. Silverhand entered the party.

II

Jason Flood watched Portia with some concern, afraid that the blonde might realize he was reaching his expiration date.

The business of being a gigolo was a tough one. He had to listen to Portia's whining about the good old days, listen to old music, and watch old movies.

He hated it. She kept him in Armani and a Porsche, but always at a price; she had to be there.

That was not part of his original plan. When he came to the

noisy, chaotic New York eight years ago he was sure he would launch into a stage career.

A few showcases, one speaking part on an episode of *SVU*, and some modeling jobs later, and he had discovered that his true talent was putting up with older women's wish-fulfillment fantasies.

There had been a number before Portia Jones, minor players, but by far the once-A actress was his greatest "achievement."

"I use you, you use me," was the motto of show business. Right under "Screw whomever you can and get all you can and then get out quick!"

Watching Portia and Madge in intimate whispers, he realized that maybe his meal ticket might be leaving him behind. Jason strolled over to the two divas, arriving just in time to hear Madge say, "Just let me do the talking, Portia. I'll convince Otto to move you to the head of the line."

Jason acted dumb and smiled smoothly. "Portia, darling, I brought you the usual martini."

"Madge, this is Jason, my, uh—friend," Portia said.

The dark-haired star gave a warm appraising look, and Jason automatically thrust his hips out for a few heartbeats before settling down on the edge of the chaise longue.

"Very nice to meet you, Jason," the actress said.

"You too, Miss Dumont." Jason smiled.

Just at that moment there was a commotion at the front door of the restaurant. All eyes turned to see a small parade enter from the street.

First came two muscular men. They were obviously security people who scanned the party.

Then came two of the most beautiful women Jason had ever seen: their features were so perfect, so symmetrical that they were almost demigoddesses.

They smiled and looked back behind them.

The figure they flanked was a tall, thin man wearing a coral-colored linen suit. His features were sharp with a long, thin Roman nose. His hair was worn long and was white-blond. His gaze was hypnotic.

He smiled, and when he spoke it was with a slight German accent. "Delightful to see you again, Madge, darling." He leaned down to where the hostess sat and kissed her on the lips. He let his eyes scan past Jason to settle on the blonde actress.

"Otto, dearest, let me introduce—"

"Oh, but this lovely lady needs no introduction," the doctor said. "I have followed Miss Jones's stellar career with great delight."

The blonde actress giggled like a schoolgirl.

"You flatter me, Doctor Silverhand."

"On the contrary," the suave surgeon said. "I understate. And please call me Otto." He gave a little old-fashioned European bow and kissed the back of Portia's hand.

"Otto," Flood said, forcing his way into the conversation, extending his hand, "my name is Jason."

"I'm sure," the doctor said with a cold glance. "But only my friends call me Otto." He smiled broadly and held his arm out to the hostess.

"I am dying of thirst, dearest," the doctor said. "And to mix. Would one of you care to escort me in case I get lost?"

Both women stood up simultaneously, giggled, and latched onto his arms.

"I'm sure I can help you keep on the right track, Otto," Madge said.

"And if we do get lost I'm sure we can think of something to keep us amused," Portia said with a conspiratorial grin. She looked over at Jason. "Do find something to amuse yourself for a while, Jason, dear. I'm sure we won't be too long."

"In a pig's eye," the gigolo said under his breath. His anger at being humiliated made his features brittle and his tone sharp.

The surgeon looked back over his shoulder as the trio walked off. "We shall see," he said. "We shall see."

III

"I can't eat this stuff, Portia," Jason Flood said as he looked down at the meal between them. It was three weeks after Madge's party, and things had changed.

When they'd gotten home the changes had begun. Portia altered her diet and begun Silverhand's exercise routine, which left Jason puzzled as it seemed to consist primarily of stretches and chanting. Chanting!

Madge had Ubered over several times, and the two women had sat on the rooftop pool of the condo with legs crossed humming a chant together.

Portia had taken to sleeping more than before, limiting late nights out at clubs.

This fact was not entirely a loss for Jason, as she did not insist he spend all the nights home with her and he had already begun to scope out a replacement meal ticket.

The "new" food was a strange mix of porridge-like gruel and various beans and nuts that had been ground up.

"Otto says he has to prepare my insides for the changes to happen to my outsides, Jason."

"But why do I have to eat the stuff, Portia dear. Do my outsides displease you so?"

The aging actress just shook her head.

"Is it the food or Otto that bothers you, Jason?' she said slyly. "You're jealous, aren't you?"

"Of the doc?" Jason blustered. His animal hindbrain sensed that Silverhand was threat to his comfortable nest, and he had to find a way to fight the doctor's influence. But he had to do it carefully.

"No, Portia," he said with a smile. "I only want what is best for you."

She slipped another mouthful of the strange meal between her perfect lips. "Oh my, I have to see Otto today for my blood tests to see I'm ready for the first procedure!" She jumped up from the table. "Would you be a dear and clear up the dishes?"

He watched her go, her sensual figure moving with more vigor than he had seen in a while, and realized he might have already lost to the plastic surgeon.

"I'll drive you, Portia," he called after her. "I've seen such a wonderful change in you already that I think I might want to talk to him about a few things myself!"

This pronouncement stopped the star in her tracks. "Really?"

"Yes, really," he said. "I mean, never too early to start fighting Father Time, is it?"

*   *   *

The mansion of the esteemed Dr. Otto Silverhand was a town-house on West 79th Street in Manhattan near the boat basin that had once owned by a Vanderbilt.

It was more a compound, with a "guest house" beside it that served as his private clinic with four floor-large apartments where his live-in patients recovered in privacy.

Jason delivered Portia to the driveway up front. Two suited security men stepped up to the car.

"Miss Jones," one of the sunglass-wearing guards said, "we were not informed you would be bringing a chauffeur."

"I'm not a chauffeur," Jason insisted.

"You are that and more, Jason dear." She laughed as she slipped out of the car. "But right now you are a parking attendant. Do put the car in the garage, then come inside." She didn't wait for him to respond and turned to follow one of the guards.

Jason fumed but drove the car to the spot the guard indicated. He did his best to stroll to the door of the clinic even though he wanted to stomp.

The old carved wooden door opened into an ultra-modern, anti-septic lobby that might have been in any European clinic.

A receptionist in a pastel gown met him.

"Mister Flood?" she said. She was almost too perfect, her features symmetrical and her skin baby soft and unblemished. "Miss Jones said you were interested in possibly using Doctor Silverhand's services."

"Uh, yes," he said, off-balanced by the too-perfect woman.

"Please follow me," the receptionist said. "I'm sure you will find it interesting."

IV

Jason's pulse raced as he followed the receptionist.

"This is the beginning of the process with all clients," the receptionist said. She led him into a small room where a desk and chair were located.

"You will please fill out the forms and then press that button. The doctor will speak to you afterward."

She smiled again in a vaguely sensual way and then he was alone. He felt a sudden surge of anger at the smugness of Silverhand. *To think I would need his bull—that's what gets to me,* he thought. *I'll use him; his contacts, his prestige.*

He sat down and filled out the forms. They were an odd mix of actual medical and New Age–type questions—the usual blood type, diseases or allergies, etc., but also what his hopes in life were, what physical regimen he followed, what "sins" he felt he had committed in life and his regrets, and finally why had he come to the doctor.

So I can show the world what an insufferable prig he is.

He tapped the button on the desk, and the prefect receptionist appeared.

"All done, are we?" she said. "Then we can begin a few little tests."

She stepped in to stand close to the seated gigolo and placed a blood pressure cuff on his arm.

He found that the nearness of the too-perfect woman disturbing.

She finished the blood pressure and drew a blood sample while he sat in a semi-trance brought on by her presence.

It was only when she said, "The doctor will be with you shortly. Enjoy some tea while you wait," that the spell was broken. Then Jason began to doubt the wisdom of coming into the sanctum of the surgeon.

He was about to leave when the door opened and Dr. Silverhand entered. His purple eyes glowed with energy.

"Good afternoon, Mister Flood," Silverhand said. "I see you have come to me with the thought of improving your lot in life."

"Never too soon to start, eh, doc?"

"Yes, well, let us have a seat and we can discuss your goals." Silverhand referred to the clipboard and looked up at Jason from beneath his downcast brows. "I see you eat very little meat."

"No red meat, and only lean chicken and fish, yes," Jason said, smiling. He considered slapping the smile off Silverhand's face. "You are what you eat!"

"Yes," the surgeon said. "So I've heard. Now, I see you haven't really been very forthcoming in your emotional goals. Why is that?"

"I really don't see what that has to do with tucking up a chin or disappearing crow's feet?"

"We do try to be holistic about procedures here," Silverhand said. "Such questions have value to me and my methods."

Flood regarded the man with skeptical eyes. "I want what everyone else would want—a good life, success, fun."

"Ah," the doctor said, "fun. Yes, that can be defined differently by everyone, can't it?" His smile was suddenly very eerie, and Jason felt a chill race up his spine.

"I suppose so," Jason managed to say. "But all I'm concerned with is mine."

"Yes, you would be," the surgeon said cryptically.

He gestured toward the door. "If you will accompany me I will take you to our, uh, intake room where you can begin your journey."

The two walked down a softly lit corridor to a large glass-walled examination room. There were a table, chair, cabinet with instruments, and an examination table.

"If you would disrobe, please."

Jason looked out through the floor-to-ceiling glass wall to see an indoor pool where several well-known celebrities were lounging about.

"Here in view of everyone?" Jason asked.

"Shy, Mister Flood?"

"Not a bit," the gigolo said. "But you do promise anonymity, and it seems to me prospective clients stripping buck naked in front of that audience by the pool . . ." He pointed at the window and added, "I think this is not the thing for me."

"Oh, but I think it is just the thing, Mister Flood." The plastic surgeon laughed like a plucked string. "And it is one-way glass. I always keep my promises to my clients."

Flood looked suddenly uncertain. "You can promise me that I will get all I want if I am accepted to your program?"

"I can promise you that you will get all you deserve and more," the doctor said. "And I thought you understood, you are no longer a prospective client. You are now a patient of the Silverhand Clinic."

Jason was so stunned by the surgeon's brusque manner that he complied. Soon he stood in his boxers while Silverhand consulted a computer screen on his desk. "I see you need to revitalize—a little of my special nutrient to add to your daily diet."

He approached Jason with a small glass that had a bright green liquid in it. "It is really quite tasty."

"I can't say I liked any of the stuff you gave to Portia," Jason said. "And we haven't even talked about cost. I'm not sure I want to—"

"Oh, please," the doctor said. "All the cost is taken care of by Miss Jones. You see, it is beneficial to her as it is to any of my patients when their significant other is on the program." He gave his vibrato laugh again. "And your diet will be very different from hers. No foul-tasting gruel. Just this drink twice a day; the intent of your program here is quite different."

Jason took the glass from the surgeon, sniffed it, then sipped.

"Not so bad."

"Indeed," the surgeon said, "not so bad at all. Welcome to the program."

V

Dr. Silverhand's program for Jason was a simple one: he actually prescribed less physical activity for the gigolo "to let your body adjust"; and he was able to keep eating his normal diet. In fact, the doctor had spoken to Portia and seen to it that the house was stocked with Jason's favorites. The only proviso was he drink his green shake and rest as much as possible.

When Jason asked why his program was so different from Portia's, Silverhand laughed. "Well, you are a very different case, aren't you? And your journey will be a very different path."

The aura of "hail-well-met" kinship came off the plastic surgeon in waves, and Jason felt himself oddly at ease.

Almost.

He felt that Portia was preparing to cast him aside. Still, the shakes were tasty and why would she pay for the treatment if she was going to get rid of him?

Jason also found he had little inclination to do much of anything but lounge around the pool. He didn't go out to a single club anymore.

When Madge came over for the actresses to chant together he did not even try to hit on the older, dark-haired star. He just waved hello and settled in by the pool to bask in the sun. He did it all afternoon, every day.

Weeks went by and he realized he had not left the condo at all. It alarmed him that he came to crave the green drinks. Soon, getting food and the green drinks were the only reason he even got off the lounger.

It was Friday when, as he walked past a mirrored wall in the mansion, he paused. He stared in disbelief as he saw that his skin, which was normally bronzed by the sun and had a manly texture, now seemed pale and pinkish.

What has he done to me? Jason thought. He also noticed that his rock-hard abs and lean, defined arms were now soft-looking. Undefined and almost girlish! "What has he done to me?" he yelled aloud. Jason moved to the bedroom and discovered to his horror that the first two pairs of pants he pulled from the closet were too tight!

With a sudden panic he pulled sweatpants from a drawer and threw on a baggy T-shirt and all but ran to the car. He drove across and uptown in record time. He was beyond anger now.

When he reached the driveway of Silverhand's fortress, Jason called out in a strained voice, "Let me in, I have to see Silverhand!"

The guard out front made a radio call, then waved him on.

The gigolo was almost out of the car before it came to a full stop, almost colliding with the two sunglassed guards who came from the clinic to meet him.

"Mister Flood," one of the guards said, "if you will come with me, please?"

They led Jason to a part of the clinic he had not been to before.

The guards stopped before a pink, featureless door. "Please go in, sir," the guard said.

Jason stared at the man and the door, which had no knob, and snarled, "What the hell is?" But the door slid open before he could finish. Inside a room that was as pink as the door stood Dr. Silverhand with a surgical mask hanging around his neck. He was smiling.

"Hello, Jason," the surgeon said. "I was wondering how long it would take you to come back."

"What have you done to me?"

"Merely allowed your inner nature to come to the surface," Silverhand said with a smug smile. "And we have just begun the process."

Before Jason could ask what he meant the guard behind him hit him with a Taser and everything went black.

*   *   *

The humming was the first thing that Jason Flood heard.

A low, mechanical hum that varied in pitch. Then he heard the muffled voice of Dr. Silverhand. "Ah, we are back among the sentient again, eh, Jason?"

The doctor and two Asian nurses stood over Jason.

"Don't try to speak, Jason, dear fellow," Silverhand continued. "Your vocal cords are, shall we say, out to lunch for the present." He slipped a surgical mask on.

Jason did try to speak, but could not.

"Don't struggle, Jason," Silverhand said. "You'll only annoy me more than you have already." The doctor raised a needle into Jason's view.

"Now, my little gigolo," Silverhand said, "it's time for you to sleep for a little bit—then things will get interesting for you, I should think."

VI

Jason Flood found himself swirling in and out of consciousness. He saw a laughing Portia, but he could not tell if it was a dream or she was real. Eventually the swirling vortex of color and sound began to form into the surgeon standing in front of Jason, smiling.

"I see you are with us again, dear fellow."

For a long slice of time the gigolo worked his mouth to find sound until finally he croaked, "What have you done to me?"

Silverhand laughed. "You do have a one-track mind. That is all you have asked each time you've woken up for the last three weeks."

"Three weeks?" Jason realized he was flat on his stomach and tried to move. Then he discovered his arms and legs were restrained below him out of sight.

"Yes, three weeks," the plastic surgeon said. "You recovered from the procedure even more quickly than I anticipated; bravo to your constitution!"

Jason moaned and tried to struggle against the bonds that held him on his belly. He tugged at the restraints but could not feel his hands.

Jason screamed, "You can't get away with this! There are laws—"

"Oh, please, Jason, don't be absurd," Portia Jones said. She stepped up beside the surgeon. She looked a decade younger than when Jason had seen her last. She wore a sheath dress in pale gold that contrasted with her now honey-tanned skin.

"Portia, help me," the prisoner said. "Get me out of here."

Now it was the actress who laughed like the knell of a funeral bell.

"Why would I do that, dear boy?" Portia said. "You are part of my ticket to the new me."

"What do you mean?" Jason gasped.

"What Portia is trying to say, Jason," Madge Dumont said as she stepped up beside Jones, "is that she is now a member of a very exclusive club, and there is a price to be paid beyond money."

"You are all mad!" Jason screamed. "Let me loose!" He began to rock wildly at his bonds.

"He was never very bright," Portia said with a sigh. She looked over at Madge. "Mind you, he had certain other qualities, if you know what I mean."

"Stop, stop!" Jason moaned. "Stop the joke, Portia. This is not funny anymore. Let me loose!"

The three conspirators exchanged a look.

"Jason, dear," Portia said, "you really are dense." With that the diva turned and headed out of Jason's line of sight. Madge followed, leaving only the surgeon.

"Just wait right there, Jason," Silverhand said with a snort of humor.

Then Jason Flood was alone with the nightmare. After a long time he slept, but this time he had nightmares until he woke in a sweat and out of breath.

The room was dark, evening light shining through shutters on a window to Jason's right. He listened for a long time, hearing only the distant sounds of Manhattan. He lay unmoving, lethargic, heavy, and bloated.

Still bound, he nonetheless struggled for a long time with his restraints. He only fleetingly wondered why he was secured in such an absurd position—on his belly on the narrow bench with his arms and legs pulled down below him out of sight—and worked to get free before any of the conspirators returned.

He rocked back and forth, worried about the numbness in his hands and lower legs but sure it must be from the restraints. He pulled and twisted and yanked until at last he felt his right arm slip free of the bindings.

Jason pulled his arm free and brought it up into his line of sight, intent on reaching over to undo his left arm. When it came fully up in sight he froze and his eyes went wide with horror.

"No. No. NO!!!!" he screamed.

"My hand!" Jason yelled till his voice went hoarse. At his elbow, where his forearm and hand should have been—the arm and hand he could not feel save as a numb memory—was a stump, the end of which was discolored and crusted into hardened ends. "You cut off my hand!"

The two nurses appeared and wrestled the frantic prisoner's arm back into the restraint just as Silverhand entered the room.

"You are becoming quite a bother, Jason," Silverhand said. "You really have got to just accept things, and this will move along much more smoothly."

"You mutilated me!" Jason yelled. "You cut off my hand!"

"Hands, Jason," Silverhand said. "I really don't like asymmetry."

Jason screamed again, this time an incoherent, soul-crushing sound that devolved into a burbling hiss.

"It's not as if you'll have use for them," the doctor continued in a matter-of-fact tone. "Not that you really did much with them except pick the pockets of your female victims."

The plastic surgeon waved two guards into the room with Tasers in hand. "Now you will come and meet the other members of our little family, Jason, and discover just why lovely Portia brought you to us."

The two nurses were strong and Jason weak, his muscles slack from inactivity, so they wrestled him from the bench he was on. That was when he looked down at his lower body and received another shock.

Past a bulging belly he saw that the entire lower portion of his legs were gone so that they ended where the knee should have been in the same discoloration as stumps as his arms.

The shock was so severe that Jason just began to gibber and shake as the nurses placed him on the floor so that he was now on all fours like an animal.

"Come along, Jason," the doctor said with a dark giggle. "The guests are all waiting for your debut!"

Jason waddled down the corridor, his hardened stumps clicking on the tiles, with the two guards on either side of him and the doctor leading the way. The gigolo was in a state of shock, his mind just locked up at the horror that occurred to him.

He felt his exaggerated belly wobbling beneath him and felt the shock of the contact with the floor up each of his new 'hooves.'

"You see, Jason, some of this is not, strictly speaking, necessary, you know? The amputations are purely cosmetic, as is the work on your face—but you haven't seen that yet. Still, I am such a sucker for the form of things, you know? The ceremony of it all. I do suppose in my heart I believe it has something to do with sympathetic magick and all that, eh?"

The strange parade went down the corridor and turned into a large meeting hall where a dozen people were gathered around a long runway-like ramp with seats on either side of it. As they got closer the stunned and mutilated man saw that Portia was seated with Madge and several other notables, most of whom he had no idea were clients of Dr. Silverhand.

The conversation stopped when the doctor entered the room. Then when the shambling form of the mutilated gigolo entered, the guests broke out into applause.

"Keep moving, Jason," Dr. Silverhand said. He herded the bloated amputee along with a casual foot so that Jason moved toward and up the ramp.

It was like a perverse model's catwalk, and the dazed Jason stumbled down it, barely able to focus on the smiling faces of the seated guests on either side. Beyond them Jason could see the windows looking out on the evening in the compound.

What he saw in the reflection caused a new crescendo of terror in him. In the image he was shaven bald, with a ruddy, round pink face that had a short pug nose and pointed, ears.

Then he saw the place settings before the guests and the look of desperate hunger in their eyes.

"You see," Dr. Silverhand said with a prideful tone, "part of my strict regimen for my patients is a very special diet, hence your changes." He chuckled as the guests moved toward the screaming Jason. "After all, they do call it long pig!"

Welcome to Brooklyn, Gabe

Marc Abbott

The fire roared through the church and Gabe Forrester couldn't find a way out of the sanctuary. Burning pews blocked the passageways that led to the rectory. A chain and lock around the door handles sealed the front door. The tapestries near the stained-glass windows blazed. Gabe lacked the strength to jump through the windows to his freedom.

Still bleeding from the bite, Gabe crawled down the center aisle to avoid the smoke. If he yanked on the chain, he could pull the door handles off the door. Almost there.

A figure in a white dress stepped in front of him, blocking his path. He looked up into the pale face of a beautiful woman with long black hair.

"Oh no," Gabe said. He reeled and scuttled backwards. "Please don't."

*   *   *

Gabe arrived in Brooklyn looking for a fresh start after leaving Seattle. The borough was up and coming with its mass exodus of hipsters out of Manhattan. Modern glass and steel buildings replaced Brooklyn's deserted factories in Williamsburg and Dumbo, enticing the young and wealthy. Gabe found the brownstones of Brooklyn Heights and Park Slope more appealing to his tastes. The refurbished ones were classic Brooklyn on the outside, a touch of modern on the inside.

He scored himself a third-floor apartment in a brownstone off Atlantic Avenue, just a few blocks away from both downtown Brooklyn and the subway station. It was only a hop, skip, and a jump to Manhattan, where the nightlife was always alive, but he decided to check out what Brooklyn had to offer first.

He had been to Manhattan when he was a young vampire in the '70s, and the memories of those days were still fresh in his head. The drugs, the prostitution, the promiscuity of mortals sickened him, and he went into self-exile from the city for thirty years. While he knew things had changed since then, he was in no hurry to visit the island.

Gabe didn't sleep in a coffin. He slept in a bed like everyone else during the day, but he made sure that wherever he stayed, the blinds and curtains were fully drawn until dusk. He did that in his new apartment and woke just in time to get a glimpse of the sun going down. He used *Esquire* magazine as his guide on how to dress and *Time Out New York* to pick out the best bars to go to in Brooklyn. He preferred them to the clubs. He liked good conversation with mortals.

He barhopped a linear path down Fulton Street. His good looks and wit drew the women to him. He bought just enough drinks for certain women he picked out to keep them talking. Was she in a re-lationship? Did she live with her parents or have roommates? If so, he kept moving. Those were his rules for feeding.

At a beer garden, a beautiful and wealthy woman named Hillary Muyton began flirting with him the moment he sat down. She bought him drinks, which he nursed as best as he could so she wouldn't become suspicious. She spoke of her failed marriage, her on-and-off-again boyfriend, and, after three martinis, her one-night stands.

Gabe lost interest and was ready to call it a night. He wasn't go-ing to find a victim the first night out. Then she invited him to a par-ty at her Dumbo apartment the following evening.

"I'm not sure what my schedule will be tomorrow," Gabe said.

"I have a lot of single friends and I know they would just love to meet you," she said.

"Well, if you insist."

The perfect setting. With house parties, if someone wasn't there with someone, it meant they were alone. He wouldn't have to do much work.

He called a cab for Hillary, rode with her back to her apartment, and escorted her to her door. He then scoped out the neighborhood for any hidden alleyways or abandoned buildings he could sneak off to and drain someone. Still no luck. He returned to his apartment just before dawn.

Gabe arrived fashionably late to the party. Hillary remembered him right away, surprising given the amount of alcohol she had consumed the night before. She paraded him around the room to her guests. He shook hands, shared some laughs, and kept the conversations going.

Through the open door to the balcony, a woman's eyes met his, and he knew he had to meet her. Stunning: caramel skin, smooth legs below a knee-high skirt that hugged her hips, with the Manhattan skyline as a backdrop, she might have been a fashion model for an upscale magazine. She held a glass of wine delicately and brushed back a strand of hair in her face as she smiled at him.

Gabe snaked through the crowd, eased next to her, and introduced himself.

"Adriana Fischer," she said. "Pleasure to meet you, Gabe."

"Pleasure is all mine," he said.

They laughed at their own pleasantries and discussed the changes in New York, the gentrification of Brooklyn, and his reasons for coming to Brooklyn.

"Didn't like Seattle?" she said.

"I did, but things got complicated for me there," Gabe said. "I ran into a—how do I put this?—the son of an old family enemy who still seemed to have some issues with my people."

"I see." Adriana frowned, somehow looking even more delicious. "That does sound complicated."

"Yes. Not easy to have a relationship or even start one with that going on. But that was Seattle and this is Brooklyn. I'm putting that life in the past and I'm starting anew."

Adriana smiled. She set the wine glass down and turned to him. "My boyfriend has been to Seattle. He didn't like it much,"

"Your boyfriend," Gabe said. "I see." He felt a tension headache from frustration and pressed the side of his temple.

"I'm sorry, but if I was reading what you were trying to tell me correctly, it's better that you know."

"How come he's not here?"

"He was supposed to be, but then he got called in by his supervisor. He works for Con Edison." She sipped her wine.

"He shouldn't leave a beautiful woman like you alone. I wouldn't," Gabe said.

Adriana blushed as her eyes diverted to the floor. Gabe smiled to himself. *She can't be that serious about her boyfriend if I can make her blush like that.* He stepped in close and gently caressed her cheek with his thumb. The possibility that he could still have her further excited him.

"Very charming, Gabe. I'll be sure to remind him of that."

Realizing that she was taken by him but not interested, Gabe turned to walk away. "Well, I'll leave you to the party."

Adriana grabbed his wrist. "You're leaving so soon?"

"I haven't talked to our hostess this evening." Gabe took her hand from around his wrist and kissed it.

"You're leaving me here by myself?" She blocked his path to keep him from going.

"What if your boyfriend walks in? What will you tell him?"

"We're just talking. No harm ever came from that."

Is she coming on to me or just being nice? Playing along, he took her wine glass and went to get them both a drink. When he returned to balcony, they tapped glasses and watched the Manhattan lights while talking.

At three o'clock the party died down. Gabe and Adriana left together. He decided he wouldn't feed off her. Instead, he would make a quick ride into Manhattan and grab someone coming out of a nightclub. *Was Studio 54 still around?*

"Want to split a cab?" Adriana asked.

"I'm heading to the city for a while. I'm a night person. Need to find an after-hours spot or maybe move my body at a club." His faux mambo made her laugh.

"You're not hungry? I am. How about some food?" she said.

Something stirred inside him. His eyes focused on a large vein on her neck and he curbed the desire to lick his lips.

"I could go for a little something. Any suggestions?" He kept his voice mellow.

"How about you come over to my place? Since you're new to Brooklyn, I'm sure you'd like a home-cooked meal," Adriana said.

"What about your boyfriend? Think he'll appreciate your bringing a strange man home?" Gabe folded his arms and gave her a stern look.

"I have to cook for him anyway. Besides, I think he would enjoy meeting you." She chuckled. "This is how people make friends you know."

"Uh-huh."

"Do you want to or not?" she said.

Temptation ate at him. *Was there a boyfriend?* Well, he could take them both just this once and have his fill. It would be easier than hunting the streets for a victim at this late hour.

"Lead the way," Gabe said. "But I prefer the subway."

They walked through Dumbo to the F train. Gabe paid their fare and they rode it through Gowanus into Park Slope. They walked quietly down to Prospect Park West to a tall apartment building with no doorman.

"I'm on the top floor," she said.

She's on the top floor. Not we. What game is she playing?

He followed her up to the seventh floor to an apartment at the end of the hall of a silent floor. Adriana unlocked the door and opened it to a dark apartment. The smell of lilac potpourri burned his nostrils.

"Come in," she said. She crossed the threshold and turned on a light.

Gabe looked around the modest apartment. Photographs on a chest of drawers, along with a sofa and love seat nestled in the center of the living room. A dining room table, with freshly cut flowers in a vase, sat in a nook.

He examined the pictures. Except for a photograph of a man he suspected was her father, Gabe found no picture of her and her boyfriend.

Adrian texted on her phone. When she finished, she turned to him and pointed to the sofa.

"Make yourself at home. If you want, you can turn on the television. I'll be back." She put her phone in her pocket and walked to the bedroom at the rear of the apartment.

A beautiful clock on an end table caught his eye, a valuable antique and too old for the décor of the apartment.

"My boyfriend got that when he was in Seattle. It's actually a family heirloom he went there to pick up." Adriana appeared from the bedroom in a pair of sweatpants and a long T-shirt. "He should be here soon. He always gets home before sunrise. Let me get the food ready."

Gabe nodded. The clock's chimes rang four times. He took his shoes off, placed them next to the sofa, then sat down. He promised himself he wouldn't stay long. It was almost dawn and he needed to get back to his place to rest.

Adriana brought a plate of cheese and crackers to Gabe, then tucked her legs under her as she sat in uncomfortable silence.

"Food is in the oven," she said.

Gabe still hadn't found any signs of the boyfriend. Should he take the chance? Should he make an advance and see what would happen?

So close to him. He could take her in his arms, kiss her, then drain her of her blood.

He closed his eyes and eased the storm within.

"Where is he?" Adriana glared at the clock. "Wait here."

She went back to the kitchen to check on the food.

Dawn peeped through the early morning clouds. "Damn it," he said under his breath.

Gabe got up and stretched just as Adriana reentered the room with a big smile on her face.

"Almost ready," she said.

Gabe nodded and met her halfway. "It's late and I'm tired. I should go."

"Just a couple more—"

"Adriana, you're a very beautiful woman and I am attracted to you. Now I don't know if this has been a game or what, but there are no pictures of him anywhere. No proof of a man being in here." He leaned in, ready to seduce her. "There is no boyfriend, is there?"

Gabe looked deep into her eyes and watched as Adriana became captivated by his own, the warmth of their brownness. For a brief moment it took her breath away. He knew they were changing color into a rich auburn and filling with a look of seduction.

Adriana's lips trembled. "Please, I . . ."

"Shh." Gabe placed his finger on her lips. He took her hands in his.

Adriana stared like a deer in headlights. Gabe slowly embraced her. His arms wrapped smoothly and tightly around her slim waist. His eyes stung as they turned red and he had to have her.

Forget all about the people who saw them together at the party. The father in the photo who cherished his daughter. The tenants in her building eho would know something wasn't right when they didn't see her. Her head tilted lovingly to the side and her eyes closed. He forgot everything.

Adriana's soft, warm breath blew past his ear as he brought her closer. The smoothness of her skin . . . Gabe closed his eyes. The sharp canines on his upper row of teeth grew long. He couldn't stop.

Gabe bit down into her flesh, and his lips clasped the skin as his fangs pierced the vein in her neck. The blood exploded through the small holes in her neck against his teeth. The warmth of her blood filled his mouth with its coppery flavor and coursed through his body. His insides burned.

Adriana didn't scream and she didn't fight him. She planted her hands on the back of his head and held him there. Gabe fixed his lips onto her neck and drank harder. Slowly her hands began to slip away from the back of his head. Her pulse slowed and her body went limp. Just as gently as he had bitten her, he removed his fangs from her neck.

Blood trickled from his mouth. Gabe ran his tongue across his lips, cleaning the residue. An inhuman groan of satisfaction escaped him and his eyes rolled back in his head. Sated, his eyes turned back to brown, and he looked at Adriana's peaceful face. He caressed her cheek. As he placed her on the sofa he noticed a long shadow stretched from the front door. A chill ran down his spine.

Standing in the doorway was a stocky young man dressed in street clothes carrying a book bag and holding his cellphone. His mouth wide open from shock, he dropped the book bag and stared at Gabe. He didn't say a word.

Gabe laid Adrianna down and slowly backed away as he made note of the window to his right. The boyfriend took a step into the apartment, put his phone in his pocket, and closed the door. He moved to Adriana's body slowly.

Gabe kept a close eye on him. He'd had his share of fights against men whose women he had killed. While vampires did have the strength to snap a mortal man's neck in seconds, men were relentless when they were enraged.

When the boyfriend knelt next to Adriana, a thin stream of light from the window illuminated his face. For a split second, Gabe thought he recognized the man. It wasn't until he lowered his head to look at Adriana's neck that Gabe saw the tattoo of a serpent coiled around a crucifix. He knew the symbol, the crest of the Kinkead family, a clan of vampire hunters that dated back a century. He was the one who had come for him in Seattle. At the moment Gabe could not recall his name, only that Kinkead's people took their time to assess a situation before retaliating against a vampire.

"Is she dead?" the boyfriend said. Gabe didn't answer. The boyfriend slowly looked up at him. "Did you drain her?"

Gabe hesitated. "I didn't know she had ... she didn't tell me." Gabe's nerves made him heave and clutch his stomach, but he didn't throw up.

The man slowly rose to his feet. "Answer me."

"Okay, listen. I lost it. I didn't intend to kill her,"

The boyfriend exhaled a sigh of relief. "Good. She is dead then." He made the sign of the cross above Adriana's body, then turned and started to walk out of the room. "Patience. Always patience. Patience is pure and patience is strength."

Gabe moved toward the window.

The boyfriend stopped and calmly asked, "Where are you going?" He smiled, extended his arm to a closet door, and opened it so fast it startled Gabe.

A stainless-steel sword protruding from an ivory handle glimmered inside. The boyfriend pulled it from the closet. He slammed the door and stood before Gabe, tapping the side of his pant leg with the sword.

"Missed you in Seattle," he said. "I'm Malcolm Payne, descendant of Luscious Kinkead."

"You're the grandson of Carson Payne—the one who killed the vampire Gerard Lord during the riots in Harlem in the Sixties," Gabe said.

"You know your history, Gabe Forrester," Malcolm said. "I heard you had come to town. Welcome to Brooklyn." Malcolm took his phone from his pocket. "She texted to tell me she had found you. Must have been in my notes again. It's my fault. I should have never let her in on what I do." He wiped away a tear before it could run down his cheek.

"You're going to try and keep me from leaving, aren't you?" Gabe said.

"I'm going to kill you. Probably not tonight because I can see you're going to run, but I will kill you. In fact"—Malcolm tossed the sword to the floor—"I won't even use the sword."

Malcolm pointed to the window as the sun started to rise. Gabe saw his own shadow growing on the floor. With his eyes blazing red, he bared his fangs, hissed at Malcolm like an angry cat, then crashed through the window.

Glass rained down onto the street along with droplets of blood that sizzled in the dawn's light. Gabe jumped the wall to Prospect Park and looked back at the window once he was under the cover of trees. He saw Malcolm looking down at him. Gabe ran deeper into the park to hide.

Gabe didn't dare go to his apartment. Instead, he returned to Dumbo and hid inside an old coffin in the bowels of an abandoned factory that once manufactured them. He had seen the place while scouting out places to take his victims. Since he had fed off Adriana, he could last several days without needing to feed. In the meantime, he would wait before trying to leave Brooklyn. Malcolm was a good hunter. He had tracked him and run Gabe out of Seattle with ease. If he left now, Malcolm would find him quickly. Better to allow him to find and raid his apartment. Gabe would then run while Malcolm tried to figure out his next move.

Patience. Be patient like Malcolm and you'll get out of this alive.

By his calculations, Gabe had hidden for two days. Most of that time he spent sleeping. Finally ready to leave, he pushed on the lid of the coffin. It wouldn't open. He shifted his body and used his shoulder; it still wouldn't budge.

Gabe slid his fingers into the grooves where the lid and the body of the coffin met. He felt around until he found space to put his fingers between them. The catch. He pushed it over and pushed on the lid again. He peered through the crack. A small flicker of light tormented his eyes. The smell of incense forced him to stifle a sneeze. With more pressure, the top cracked and the lid opened. The sound echoed around him.

Around the coffin, burning candles gave off a warm glow. Behind him, a large crucifix hung over a beautiful altar. High ceilings made the sounds of his movement echo. The large pipes of an organ, sticking out of the walls, hummed a single tune.

To Gabe's right, Malcolm sat at the organ. He played a D flat and stared at Gabe with smirk on his face. Gabe spun around. Pews, the confessional, and a small chapel area, all covered in a layer of dust. A floor lost in debris and dirt. Somehow Malcolm had dragged his coffin into an abandoned church.

"A church? You brought me into a church?" Gabe chuckled. "Who do you mistake me for, Dracula? That's the oldest myth about vampires. We're not afraid of crosses or holy water. This isn't going to kill me."

Malcolm stopped playing and stood. He carried no weapon as he approached Gabe.

"They're going to gut this place, can you believe it? I think they're going to demolish it. What a shame," Malcolm said. "I didn't bring you here thinking it would kill you. I know all the truth and legends. For example, I know that you can move around in daylight, but direct sunlight will boil your blood until your veins explode. I know that only very old vampires can actually fly, just not long distances." A devious smile grew on Malcolm's face. "I also know that to become a full vampire anyone bitten needs to drink from the vampire who attacked them."

Gabe raised a single eyebrow. "I don't get where you're going with this. But—" He attempted to climb out of the coffin and couldn't. His legs bound by rope. The rest of the lid was shut so that he couldn't see it. He tried to shake himself loose, and failed.

"What did you do to me? What's got my legs?" Gabe's eyes burned a glassy red color. "Tell me what you've done."

"When I started, my grandfather pulled me to the side and said, 'Malcolm, you know what makes a vampire such a difficult opponent to face? They're patient creatures.'" Malcolm crossed in front of the coffin as Gabe watched him. "They lie in wait like a spider in a web; then, when the time is right, they attack with precision." Malcolm made a fist as he passed it across his face. "I had to learn that kind of patience. The kind handed down through the centuries. You see, you vampires always assume we're going to cut you up. But no, not this time. Your death won't be so swift."

Malcolm walked over to a door that was near the confessional. He opened it then strolled back to the coffin.

"Why don't you let me out and face me man to man?" Gabe said.

"You think I've been waiting all these days to duel with you? Far from it. Tonight I kill you with the result of my patience."

Gabe laughed as he worked his feet free from their bonds. He jumped out of the coffin and seized Malcolm by the throat. Malcolm didn't fight back. He stood there taking the chokehold.

"See what your patience has earned you?" Gabe said. "Your guard is down and your—"

The sound of feet shuffling interrupted him. Malcolm shifted his eyes toward the sound. Gabe looked as well.

Walking toward them, in a flowing, ghostly white dress, came Adriana. Her skin was pale as a new moon, her lips chapped and cracked. Her eyes had thick, black circles under them, making her favor a raccoon more than a human being. Her beautiful hair had been combed back and tied into a long ponytail. She looked frighteningly beautiful.

Gabe slowly let go of Malcolm and stared at her. She stopped halfway to them. The light from the candles danced across her eyes, bringing out a red glow. Malcolm's heart dropped at the sight of her. He had been in this position before, looking into the eyes of a beautiful woman who had fallen victim to the bite of the vampire. He never thought someone he loved would become a soulless shell looking back at him.

* * *

"How do I look, my love?" Adriana smiled, her voice soft and gentle.

"You look beautiful." Malcolm walked to her and kissed her on the cheek.

Gabe took a single step toward her. Their eyes locked. Her smile fell, replaced by a look of curiosity. Slowly she folded her hands together and watched him.

"I thought she was dead," Gabe said. "You said she was dead."

"Yes. She is dead. Dead to me as the woman I once knew. The woman I once loved." Malcolm sighed as a tear formed in the corner of his eye. "But my patience has paid off."

Malcolm had kept Adriana hidden until she turned. In that time, he hunted down Gabe, tied him up while he was asleep, and brought him to the church. Then he just waited for Gabe to wake.

Gabe shivered. No running or attempting to leap out of a stained-glass window was going to prevent the inevitable from happening.

"She's been waiting to see you. She got all dressed up for you, Gabe. By the way, she hasn't eaten yet," Malcolm said.

Adriana tilted her head slightly and smiled, her long fangs exposed as she hissed. She raised a finger. "You did this to me, Gabe. You bit me and you left me to starve." She walked toward him. "I am so hungry. So very hungry."

"Stay away from me," Gabe said.

"Feed me. Nourish me."

Gabe bent at the knee, a maneuver that signaled he was going to try to leap toward the ceiling. Adriana was on him fast; her fangs sank deep into his neck. Gabe sailed backward, slamming into the coffin before falling over. Adriana gripped his shoulders tightly, pinning him down. Her jaw locked to Gabe's his neck. His blood spattered the floor.

Gabe pushed Adriana hard. She sailed through the air and crashed into a row of pews. He sat up clutching his wound. He and Malcolm locked eyes.

Malcolm picked up a candle, walked over to a tapestry, and set it on fire. A pile of pews blocking a passageway came next. Smirking Malcolm then climbed over another set of pews blocking a second passageway and torched them from the other side, trapping Gabe and Adriana in.

Gabe crawled down the center aisle to get to the front door and avoid the smoke. Before he could reach it, Adriana stepped out from a row of pews and blocked his path. He scuttled backwards and pleaded for her not to attack.

When she motioned toward him, he rolled over on all fours and crawled back to the steps of the altar. He started to feel weak. He sat down on the bottom step and saw that Adriana had not chased him. She stood in front of the door, blocking his only way out. Then he chuckled to himself as he remembered something Malcolm had said in his apartment.

"Welcome to Brooklyn," Gabe said. "Yeah."

Machine Gun/Latté

Amy Grech

Poised and ready,
a tall, lean
National Guard
Soldier, dressed in
full camouflage regalia,
stands at attention
on the main concourse
of Penn Station in
New York City.

In his right hand
he clutches a latté,
frothy and warm,
in a white
Starbucks cup.

His left hand
hovers above
a machine gun,
slung over his shoulder,
cold and commanding,
sleek and menacing.

His trigger finger twitches,
roused by a jolt of caffeine.
Fuel for the fight.

The Spouting Devil

Meghan Arcuri

God, I'm hungry.
    Eat the fish.
    I don't want the fish.
Spring swirled and whirled and spun and twisted and rose. The water, her home, moved with her. Mini-whirlpools formed all around, the fish darting in and out of them, jumping through them, playing in them. Then the fish came to her, tickling her fingers, her arms.
    Get away from me, you little shits.
She shook them off, and they dashed away. She had no time for games.

It had been too long.

She was famished.

She was agitated.

She needed to be sated.

The sky illuminated in a flash, a bolt of lightning fracturing the blackness.

Thunder boomed, wind howled.

This, of course, only revved up her need, whipping her into a frenzy. The water churned, white caps forming on her creek.
    Dial it down, Spring. Or start eating the fish.
    I don't want the fish.
    I wish you'd eat the fish.
    Of course you do. You're a no-fun Goodie Two-Shoes.
    That's generally what a conscience is.
    Go away.
The fish would nourish her, but they would never truly satisfy

156

her. Only one thing could do that.

Spring sank into the water, the whirlpools stilling, the fish swimming to the bottom. She floated at the top and waited. Waited and waited. More thunder and lightning. The rain assaulted the surface of her creek.

I'll never get what I need in this weather.

Yes, feasting on her one, true desire was wrong. The physical and emotional pain that followed could be unbearable. But Spring didn't care. In the moment, it tasted so damn good. The way it rolled around on her tongue and down her throat. One of the best feelings ever. She shivered in delight.

It also kept her fuller than those stupid fish did.

Between the cracks of thunder and the whistles of the wind, a sound blared. Again and again and again.

What the hell is that?

Within seconds, the answer presented itself: a horn.

Held by a man.

Hot damn! Now we're in business.

Leave him alone.

Why should I?

He's an innocent.

And I'm starving.

"They come!" the man said, heading toward Spring's creek. "They come for us!"

He blew the horn again.

Shut up and come to me.

Spring rose again, anticipation coursing through her. Thumping heart, rapid breathing. She could nearly pass for human, but for her skin and hair: her translucent skin rippled and flowed like the water in her creek; and her hair contained varying hues of aqua and green and purple. Her face, her limbs, her heart and lungs, however, all resembled those of a woman. Of course they worked differently, what with her being able to breathe underwater . . . and with her being a demon.

The man stood on the bank of her creek, at the northern tip of Manhattan Island. Rain pelted him, his hat and clothes soggy and sticking to his rotund frame. Brass horn at his pudgy, little lips, he blew and blew his alarm.

Candles lit the homes of other people on the edge of the island. Some men stood in their doorways, pulling their nightclothes close to them in defense of the wind and rain and cold.

"What say you, Anthony?" one of the men shouted.

"The British! They are headed this way. I must get word to our countrymen to the north of the creek."

"In this weather? You are mad!" said the man who was not Anthony. "The creek is a devilish fright on a good day. She's even more foul of temper on a night such as this."

You ain't seen nothing, baby.

Spring spun and writhed, the water crashing on the bank. Her eyes began to glow, the white light reflecting off the surface of the water.

She closed her eyes. She needed to settle. When she opened them again, they had returned to normal.

The trumpeter looked across the expanse of her creek to the land opposite Manhattan Island. He seemed to be weighing his options.

Come on, Fatty. Do it. Keep coming this way.

He looked behind him, then back in front.

"I must warn them," Anthony said.

"Then Godspeed."

Anthony pulled off his hat and his overcoat and threw them on the bank.

That's it. Just one step closer . . .

"Despite the spewing Devil, I will persevere!" he said and blew his horn.

The fat man ran into her.

Yes . . . yes!

She swirled and whirled again, her waters churning and spinning and tossing everything in their reach.

The man lost his footing, his knees crashing into the rocky bottom. He cried out, a worried look on his face.

Yes! It's time.

Maybe you shouldn't

Maybe I should.

You know what happens when you do.

No matter how I answer this, you're going to remind me, aren't you?

Yes.

I knew it.

Your organs start to bulge, making things very uncomfortable for you.

Not that uncomfortable.

The last time you did this, you had a massive headache and your lungs got so big, you could barely breathe. And then there were your eyes . . .

Oh, they were fine.

If by fine, you mean protruding and hideous, then I guess you're right.

Har-har.

You could eat the fish.

I could.

Then do it.

No.

Do you want to be just like your mother?

You had to go there, didn't you?

Well . . . she did have the same cravings as you, didn't she?

Spring's mother inhabited the creek prior to Spring. She was a kind and gentle mother, but she loved humans just a little too much. One day, when Spring was very young, her mother had overindulged and died. Leaving Spring all alone.

She was weak. She couldn't control herself.

Maybe. But at least she had you before she died. You don't even have any offspring yet.

Thanks for reminding me. You're such a ray of sunshine.

No. I'm just your better half.

Whatever. I'm still hungry.

Eat the fish.

But this human is right here. Fat and bloody. Afraid and hurting. Ripe for the taking.

I'm not going to stop you, am I?

Not unless you have another human in your pocket.

I don't.

Then you're not going to stop me.

At least I tried.

Yes, now you can rest easy.

But can you?

Shut up.

Time for the kill, Spring needed to change forms. She went with her favorite: the shark.

She swam toward the fat man, scenting the blood coming from his knees.

Sweet, delicious blood. Sweet, delicious fear.

He regained his footing and swam further out. Putting his trumpet to his bloated lips, he blew one last note.

She circled and circled.

You're sure about this?

I thought you were sleeping.

I was just pretending.

Go back to pretending.

What about the bulging?

Bulging, schmulging. It'll be fine.

Are you sure?

Absolutely.

Spring sank her teeth into his leg, the plump flesh providing little resistance. Blood and pain and fear flowed.

Oh, god. Oh, Jesus, this is better than any fish.

She shuddered—over and over and over—as she pulled him under and took him to her cave to devour him.

*   *   *

In addition to giving her delectable nourishment, Anthony also gave Spring a new name. From that moment forward, the humans referred to Spring's creek as the Spuyten Duyvil, the spewing or spouting Devil.

The pronunciation—SPY-ten DYE-vil—tickled her, and she would often say it again and again, just for fun.

She would always think of herself as *Spring*, however, for that's what she ultimately was. True, she lost her temper on occasion, but only when she was really, really hungry. And she kind of loved the new name and its implied bad-assery. It was way better than the lame name her mother had had: the sitting-down place.

What she did not kind of love, however, was the physical pain she had to deal with after consuming a human.

Like the morning after poor, delicious Anthony.

Spring woke with difficulty breathing, the pressure in her chest heavy and terrible.

And her eyes. Jesus, her eyes. When she rubbed them to relieve the pain, they felt bigger than they ever had. She tried to blink, but her eyelids wouldn't work.

She darted to the surface to see her reflection in the water.

Oh my god!

Both eyes were huge, almost popping out of her head. The right one was bigger than the left. And it kept growing and growing and growing.

Make it stop!

She fanned it with her hand and splashed water on it, but it continued to swell.

It stretched and itched and burned. All the while growing and growing.

Then it exploded.

Blistering pain filled the right side of her face. Green and purple fluid, warm and gloppy, slid down her cheek.

Holyshitholyshitholyshit!

She stuck her face in the cool water. It helped to ease the scorching agony.

Stay at the surface: the fresh air will help. And get spatterdock for your eyes.

Floating next to Spring was some spatterdock, the water lily with the pretty, yellow flower, known for its healing properties. Her mother had taught her that. She grabbed its green leaf and put it over her right eye, now no longer her eye.

The burning began to subside.

What the hell just happened?

You ate a person.

I've eaten people before. This has never happened.

He was a lot bigger than the others.

This is terrible.

Now you know why I tried to stop you.

Why didn't you try harder?

Spring . . .

You could have.

Spring . . .

All I'm saying is, if you'd tried harder, my eye wouldn't have exploded.

Mm-hmm.

Mm-hmm, what?

Nothing . . .

Oh, shut up and just say it.

Say what?

Don't be coy. Say it.

Fine. I told you so.

Feel better?

Not as good as I thought I would, but good enough.

My eye is gone!

Be happy it wasn't anything else.

Thanks for the comfort.

Thanks for losing control . . . you know how you can prevent anything worse from happening, don't you?

Don't eat the humans?

Don't eat the humans.

But they taste so amazing. And not just their meaty goodness. Their fear, their pain, their anger. That's what makes them irresistible.

Your mother thought that, too. Your dead mother.

Wow. Harsh.

Just sayin'.

Spring had mixed feelings about her mother. She'd been weak, succumbing to her urges, leaving Spring to fend for herself all too soon. And Spring hated her for that.

But she had also been sweet and loving and had shown Spring the ways of the creek. They'd studied the fish and the plants, her mother helping her to remember their special properties. Even with a proclivity for humans, her mother had been an amazing teacher and had always given comfort to Spring when she needed it. Spring would be lying if she said she didn't worship that part of her.

My mother had her flaws, but she was pretty great, too.

You miss her.

I do. Especially right now. She'd help me, tell me what to do. I want to see her.

If you keep going the way you are, you might get your wish. In the afterlife.

Really harsh. Why do you have to be like that?

Because your eye exploded. I don't want anything else to burst. And I don't want you—us—going to the afterlife any time soon.

You're protecting me?

That's what a conscience does. Especially when a mother can't.

That's pretty nice of you.

Yes, yes it is.

*   *   *

Spring managed to behave for some time. As much as she loved gorging on people, as well as their fears and anxieties, losing an eye had sucked.

Many years after Anthony, on a cold winter evening, the earth shook and the water rippled. A long, loud sound pierced the air.

It was a whistle, and it came from one of those new metal contraptions that had been passing Spring's way with more and more frequency.

A train.

Car after car after car.

Each one full of humans.

Excitement flowed through Spring. She whirled and spun, the water gathering around her like the skirts of a twirling ballerina. She jumped into the air and dove back into her creek, swimming along the surface, dancing among the fish.

Are you trying to draw attention to yourself?

Maybe.

She swam to the bottom, then dolphin-kicked her way up, bursting through the surface, spinning 360 degrees, and sinking back down into her creek.

Or maybe I'm just excited.

Maybe you see a train full of people, and you're thinking of falling off the wagon.

She swam west of her creek—to the Hudson River—to get a better look. She adjusted the spatterdock leaf, which she now wore permanently to cover the gaping hole on the right side of her face. A few clicks to the north raced a beautiful, glorious train.

Wagon? What wagon? I don't see any wagon. I only see a train.

With your one good eye?

That was uncalled for.

Just reminding you what can happen when you lose control.

Losing her eye had been one of the most painful and horrifying experiences of Spring's life. Fortunately, she'd grown used to living with one eye. It had been a challenge at first, but time had allowed her to develop new ways of seeing, moving, and existing.

It had also allowed her to forget how bad the pain had been.

She thrust herself into the air again, the water spraying all around.

You must stop. They will see you.

It's near dark. They'll see nothing. And so what if they do see me? No one would believe them, anyway. These humans are too serious.

They are not too serious to get a closer look.

And we wouldn't want that to happen, now, would we?

No, we wouldn't. Because of—oh, I don't know—your eye?

I've gotten used to it. I'm fine.

If by fine, you mean permanently handicapped, *then I guess you're right.*

Har-har.

The train drew closer and closer, its glowing headlight penetrating the dark. Each car had huge windows revealing oodles and oodles of people. In one car, some men were drinking and laughing and drinking and smoking and drinking and patting one another on the back. One man's face slid down the window, his eyes closed, mouth wide open. Perhaps he'd had a bit too much. In another car, a young man and woman sat shoulder to shoulder, enthralled in each other's company. Perhaps they were lovers?

Spring's heart raced, and she clapped her hands. The humans

were positively delightful.

The tracks of the train curved sharply in two spots, both by Spring's creek. As the train went around the first curve, Spring swam from the Hudson back to her home.

One man in a bowler hat looked out the window in Spring's direction.

He was attractive. Curious. And meaty.

Let's give him a show.

Spring, please. Don't. You've been so good.

I just wanna see what happens.

She rose into the air, the water spilling down her waist like a glorious waterfall. The surface before her reflected a white light, the one coming from her eye.

Spring, stop.

No!

The man saw her. He watched her, mouth falling open. She spun twice and waved at him.

He yanked some sort of line above his head, and the train screeched to a halt, right in the middle of the second curve of the tracks.

Spring lowered herself back into her creek.

You've done it now.

I have, haven't I?

Through the windows, chaos had erupted. Some of the men in their top hats and coats continued to drink, laugh, and make merry, while others—whose faces had soured—ran to the front and back of the train. The man in the bowler continued to stare at Spring. She continued to spin and dance for him.

Another man exited the back of the train with a lantern and headed up the track from where they'd just come, toward the first curve.

A second whistle sounded. Not from this train, but from another.

The man on the tracks yelled and screamed and waved his lantern up and down.

The whistle sounded again, louder and longer than before, as the other train appeared. It rounded the first curve and headed toward the second. It sped down the tracks, moving too fast to stop.

Its whistle blew, its brakes screeched.

Then it rammed into the first train. Metal moaned and groaned and buckled. The last two cars of the first train crunched up into each other.

People screamed. Bodies flew. A few of them landed close to Spring's creek.

She bathed in the pain and fear. Her eye glowed brighter and brighter. She whipped around and around, then swam toward the edge of the water.

Blood and flames covered the banks of her creek. As she moved closer, four bodies came into view. They lay near each other at awkward angles. Were they dead? Alive? It really didn't matter; they'd be fresh enough. She would have to change forms to grab them.

Don't do it.

You're still here?

I'm always here.

Believe me, I know.

Don't do it. You're going to go too far. Just as your mother did.

She got sloppy. Didn't know when to stop. I do.

Why don't you do one better and not start at all?

Do you feel that pain, that anguish, that beautiful, sweet horror? I want it.

But what about the pressure in your chest you're sure to feel? What about your other eye?

I don't care.

Spring changed into a serpent—a large sea serpent—and slithered along the bank of her creek.

Two bodies lay unmoving, skin black and blistered from the fire. One of them was missing its legs from the knees down.

Yuck. A little too well done.

She glided past a top hat and leather boot to get to the next body. It wasn't as badly burned, but it was small, delicate. Probably a woman. Maybe one of the lovers? Her long coat and frilly, pleated skirts had been thrown up to reveal skinny legs.

Maybe.

The next body was bloody, broken, and beginning to char—its clothes had caught fire. It was much larger than the last body. Definitely a man.

And he was alive.

Bingo!

Spring coiled her tail around the body.

Pain, terror, and anger filled her. She shuddered and trembled. Before she went over the edge, she slithered back to her creek, dragging the body behind her.

When she pulled the man into the water, she changed back to her regular form. As he drowned, his distress and despair skyrocketed . . . as did Spring's pleasure.

Let him go.

You're kidding, right?

You're going to regret this.

I don't care.

You will tomorrow.

Then I'll deal with it tomorrow.

So will I . . .

* * *

Spring woke in the middle of the night wanting to die.

A burning, twisting sensation filled her chest, the pressure ten times worse than last time. She swam to the surface to take in some air, but she could barely breathe.

Wheezing, she crawled onto the bank and got on her knees. She pounded her chest, but the pressure only increased, her breathing becoming more labored.

She looked to the plants to ease her pain, but she couldn't remember which ones helped with breathing. Her mother would know. She needed her mother.

Maybe consuming spatterdock would help. Before she could put it in her mouth, however, searing pain bloomed in the right side of her chest. Her lung was shredding.

She couldn't scream.

She couldn't cry.

She couldn't breathe.

Then she blacked out.

When she came to, morning had broken. Water from her creek lapped at her feet.

The right side of her chest still burned, still throbbed, but she was able to take some shallow breaths.

What the hell just happened?

You overindulged.

One human is hardly overindulging.

One?

Yes, one.

Looks like someone blocked out the details of her . . . feast.

What do you mean 'feast'?

You really don't remember?

No.

After consuming that first human, you went back up for seconds. And thirds. And fourths.

I ate four people?

Yup.

I don't remember eating four.

That's 'cause you were frenzied, blind drunk on fear and anguish. It was a nightmare for those people up there: the fire, the chaos, the wounded and dead bodies everywhere. After they got over their initial shock, they worried the trains would explode and spent half the night throwing snow on the flames. But you—you reveled in it. Fed on the dismay and chaos. Rolled around in it like a pig in its own filth. You've never lost that much control.

Are you sure it was four?

Yup.

Spring threw up everywhere. The vomit—full of water and fish and quasi-digested human parts—made her throw up some more. She tried to swim back into her creek, but her limbs wouldn't move.

The only good thing throwing up did was to relieve the pressure in her chest. Breathing was difficult, but she could get air in. She lay on the grass and rocks, aching and panting.

You must get back in the water before someone else sees you.

I can't.

You must.

After throwing up some more, Spring pushed herself back into her creek.

Feel better?

No.

Good.

You're so mean.

I'm not mean. It's called tough love.

It sucks.

So does watching you do this to yourself. To us.

I'll be better.

You said that last time.

My lung exploded! I'll be better.

Last night was the worst I've ever seen you.

Was I as bad as my mother?

You didn't die, so no. But you were close.

Why did she have to die? I miss her.

I know.

I wish we were together.

You want to be dead?

No . . . I just need her.

Yeah. But she can't help you. Only you can help yourself. Do you think you can stop?

I never want to feel like this again. I don't want to lose my other lung. I can't.

Or we'll die.

Or we'll die.

Then you must stop.

Okay . . .

Good.

* * *

For many more years, Spring was true to her word. The humans, of course, did not make it easy for her: they swam in her creek, built multiple bridges across it, and even changed the shape of it so more ships, and thus more people, could cross her. She had a few near-misses—some drunken construction workers, a derailed freight train, even a dog. Luckily for them, though, no one had died.

The delicious human stress and anxiety sated her at times, but it had never been potent enough. Eventually her hunger caught up with her.

One morning she woke with a need more powerful than she'd felt in years

I'm famished.

Try the f—

I don't want the damn fish.

Even though she didn't want the damn fish, she ate them anyway, half-heartedly chewing and swallowing them.

But the fish weren't working.

Spring left her creek and swam up the Hudson, past the town now bearing her name—Spuyten Duyvil. Maybe a good, hard swim would help.

As she moved through the cold, crisp water, a whistle blew. She swam to the bank of the river. The ground rumbled and vibrated.

A train was coming from the north.

She twisted and dove and played with the fish, then she headed back toward her creek.

Careful, Spring.

Why?

You know why.

Okay, fine.

She slowed herself down, floating on her back and inhaling a shallow breath.

But the whistle sounded again, and the train blew by Spring. It flew along, whipping up the dead leaves that had gathered along the tracks.

Spring rolled back onto her stomach and chased after the train.

Spring . . .

What?

You know what.

It's a train. I love trains.

Mm-hmm.

And it's moving fast. I love fast trains.

You love your remaining eye, right? And your lung?

Yes.

Then slow down.

Spring sighed and swam to the bottom of the river. She stayed underwater until her lung burned and some of her need had subsided.

When she surfaced, the train was next to her. She'd caught up to it underwater. But she had to work hard to keep up with it. Was it moving faster than it should be?

Soon it became a game of cat and mouse, which, in turn, made Spring more excited. Whipping through the water, letting the train beat her, catching up to it, passing it, doing it all over again. Spring's desire, her appetite, grew and grew.

The first curve by her creek approached. Usually the trains slowed for it. But not this one. This one hummed along, racing and chasing Spring. She jumped in and out of the water.

Spring, no! They'll see you.

But I want them to. I need them to. I need to feed on their pain, their fear. Them!

Do you want to die?

No.

Then stop.

It's been so long.

You will die. Think of your mother.

I always do . . .

Spring dove under the surface again, temporarily tamping down her hunger. But the whistle blew again.

Ever her siren song.

Spring exploded from the surface, water cascading behind her. The engineer looked out his window and saw her. She held his gaze, her eye glowing. He looked dazed, entranced.

The train rounded the curve.

The whistle blew.

The brakes screeched.

Rescue Shelter

David Sakmyster

As soon as she entered the shelter, roughly pushed inside along with a horde of panicked residents, Roshella Jackson knew that this old school gymnasium would be where the *Baka* would finally come to claim her soul.

She surveyed the open floor and the townspeople as they madly rushed to claim beds and blankets or stood on lines for Red Cross packages. This would be her tomb. There was no escape. The hurricane—the one they called Sandy—could not have come at a worse time. Nearly eighty-five, she had warded off the *Baka* for sixty-two years, and she had been approaching the natural end of her life.

Freedom. It had been so close . . .

Roshella turned and tried again to fight the human tide crashing in on her from the crowded hallway. She could feel the bitter wind stinging at her face, screeching after those who sought refuge from the imminent catastrophe. It didn't matter to Roshella. Nothing mattered—except that she had to make it back to her house.

To sanctuary.

A big white man with a baseball cap grabbed her shoulders and turned her around.

The touch nearly threw her into a panic. *Was it him?*

But then she studied his eyes and saw that she was safe, for the moment at least. "Please," she croaked over the howling wind, the distressed voices and wailing babies. "I got to get outside. I got to—"

"Sorry," the man said without even looking at her. "No one's going back out until Sandy's come and gone." He brushed past her, mumbling, "Shoulda' left yesterday when you got the warning."

The last few stragglers ran inside, and a Red Cross worker pulled both doors inward. The heavy slam echoed in Roshella's ears like the ringing of a morose funeral bell. Next, the worker wrapped a heavy chain around the bars, securing them with a thick padlock. When the lock's bolt slid into place, Roshella's gaunt shoulders dropped. She hugged her arms and stared down at her shoes. Alone, she stood before the door and watched it tremble and rattle with the wind. Outside, something heavy tumbled over and rolled into a wall.

Maybe, she thought with a glimmer of hope, *it* couldn't get in. These doors appeared to be the only exits. She turned and glanced around the gym. There were restrooms at the far end of the room, in the locker rooms, and there was plenty of food, wrapped in foil care packages. They had all they needed to wait out the storm. Perhaps the *Baka* was locked outside.

With a resigned sigh, she bitterly recalled how she had been removed from her house this evening. Her neighbors had come just before eight with the relief workers to drag her from her home, kicking and hollering up a mighty fuss. They had dismissed her as a raving invalid, and had ignored her urgent demands that the protective talismans and wards at least be taken along as well. Even her one friend—Jeralyn Hillman, who did Roshella's shopping—didn't understand, or chose not to believe. They were all too young, Roshella thought sadly. She was the last, the only one old enough to recall the events of 1955. No one remembered or even cared anymore; belief in voodoo was a thing of the past—gone, along with Roshella's youth.

They all thought it was just southern nonsense. If anything, a by-product of her Louisiana upbringing, before her parents—children of slaves from Haiti—fled for the safer havens of New York City, with her as a young child.

This northern city was filled with a profusion of the mundane, where the teeming population, the endless concrete and the sprawling towers left no room for even the thought of magic. And the evil that existed here—sometimes in plenty—at least was of the natural sort, the kind that could be countered by a gun or a jail cell.

But Roshella knew better. For what hunted her, there was nowhere to hide. Never was.

A shudder ran through her bones as a numbing thought crossed her mind:

Maybe it was already inside.

She backed up a step, reaching an unsteady hand to the door. Her heart moaned like soft thunder in her sunken chest as she scanned the entire gym, looking at faces and bodies, seeking any hint that would give the *Baka* away. Fortunately, her vision was still as perfect as it had been back in 1955, her eyes the only organs that still worked, at least adequately, in her otherwise decrepit shell.

"Who ya lookin' for, lady?"

Roshella jumped. Holding her chest, she looked down at the child with the big green eyes. He was a Creole like herself, she saw at once. A bright-looking young boy of not more than seven or eight, dressed in tattered dungarees and a white T-shirt with some rock band's emblem on it. "What?" she stammered, regaining her composure.

The boy blinked at her. He fidgeted with a watch on his left wrist. "I thought maybe you was lost, and lookin' for someone."

"Lookin'," Roshella said, nodding. "Yeah, you might say I was lookin' for someone."

The boy's eyes widened. "Can I help?"

Roshella shook her head and leaned against the door. "Nah, boy. You go on back to your mama and papa. They'll be worried about you."

"No, they won't," he insisted. "They're right over there." He pointed a tiny finger to a group of seven people sitting on a floor beside two beds. He waved, but his parents seemed too preoccupied with a flailing, bawling toddler to notice.

Roshella sighed and looked around the gym some more. Again the terror crept into her bones, chilling her resolve. And, with a sigh of futility, she realized she wasn't even sure what to look for. It had been so long, and the *Baka*, according to the legends, had no true shape, but instead assumed a more innocent, passable form when it came for its victim.

"Come on," said the boy, tugging at her cloth dress. "Let me help."

Roshella stared at him in a new light. *Could it be him?*

The thought lodged itself precipitously at the edge of her sanity. "What's your name, boy?"

"Taddy," he said with an impish smile. He put his hands behind his back. "Taddy Chance. I'm eight years old. I'm in the fourth grade. And I play first base on the Little League team—the Nassau Lions." He looked down and closed his eyes. Sniffling, he said, "We was s'posed to play today . . ."

"Hush, chile," Roshella said, reaching out and setting a tentative hand on his shoulder. He jumped back, momentarily startled. She relaxed. This wasn't the *Baka*. He was just a scared young boy, thrown into a tense and demanding situation. She imagined that, in the next few hours, he would do a lot of growing up. "You'll get to play your game another day," she said. He rubbed his eyes and blinked up at her. She had a sudden inspiration. Maybe he could help her.

"Taddy, this your school?"

"Yes ma'am. It is."

"Tell me, boy, there be another way out of this gym?"

Taddy frowned, then looked over his shoulder, eyeing the boy's locker room. "Yeah!" he said, spinning his head around in the excitement. "There's a boiler room under the lockers. I was only down there once, hidin' out from Tim and Jake—they're in the fifth grade, and they beat me up almost every Thursday after school. . . . Anyway, when I went down there once, I ex-caped out through an exit door down there. Came out in the back parking lot where the buses usually wait . . ."

"That's great," Roshella said. *It could work*, she thought. She could get out and make it back to her house before the storm hit. Her chances were far better in her own basement than here, where the *Baka* could strike from any source, out of any shadow. At least at home she had only to contend with one threat—the natural one. She squeezed the boy's arm. "If you really want to help ol' Roshella, you could take me there."

Taddy frowned. "But . . . you can't go out now."

"I have to," Roshella said in a low voice, wondering how much to tell the boy to convince him. "If I stay here, I'm gonna die."

Taddy's eyes bulged. "Why? Do you need medicine? My grandma almost forgot her pills. Papa had to run back to get them."

Roshella grinned. "Yes, Taddy. That's it exactly. I left my medicine at home, and—"

"Wait right here!" Taddy shouted. "I'll go get Papa. You can tell him where your house is, and he'll go get your pills and come right back."

Roshella shook her head, and tightened her hold on Taddy's arm. "No, chile," she said with a deep sigh. "I gotta tell you the truth. There ain't no medicine."

Taddy looked confused. "No medicine? Then what?"

Roshella pulled the boy after her as she made her way to the bleachers and took a seat on the bottom level. She sat Taddy down on the floor in front of her. After a quick check to make sure they were relatively alone here in the remote corner of the gym, she fixed her weary eyes on the boy. She hoped that he would understand. Children often accepted things they could not fathom and believed in things that adults, with their logic and reason, denied.

"Listen to me, Taddy Chance." She leaned toward him, balancing her bony arms on her legs. The way he sat there with his knees hunched up under his chin, giving her his complete attention, gave Roshella the impression that he was an excellent pupil.

"There be something—either here in this gym, or just outside those doors—that's come for me. It wants my soul, Taddy. And it's gonna kill me for it."

Taddy gasped; his mouth hung open as he craned his neck and fretfully looked around the gym. "Where is it?" he asked in a breathless whisper.

"Don't know," Roshella replied. "You see, it be an evil spirit—a *Baka*. And it can make itself look like anything." Her eyes glazed over, as she drifted back into the past. "Early on it come as an animal. First it make itself into my dog, which been dead two years. Then as a robin. Sometimes it come as a stray cat, crying to the moon and the stars while it scratch at my window every night for a month.

"Over the years it got stronger, and began to shape itself like people. Once my cousin come to the door, bringin' gifts. I start to open it, but something about her eyes don't look right. And so I slam the door and sprinkle the powder over the sill, and I go and hide. Sure 'nuff, two days later I get a letter from my Julia. She in Paris, where she be for eight months."

Taddy looked scared. "Is this spirit just after you?"

Roshella took a deep breath. "Yes, child. It's just after me. Been after me sixty-two years now. It ain't never given up. You see, once it's been called up by a *Bokor*—that's an evil sorcerer, as we called 'em in Louisiana where I was raised—it don't ever stop until it gets its victim."

Taddy bit his lip. "Even if the bad sorcerer dies?"

Roshella nodded. "Oh, yeah. The *Baka* don't care. You see, chile, I gone and kilt that *Bokor* right after I learned what he done called up after me—all because I refuse to be his woman, this after he try to force himself on me. I march right into his fancy little white house on Long Island, and I sprinkle the Fugu powder all over his food." She smiled, looking off over Taddy's shoulder, remembering the day. "1955 that was, boy. Doctors then din't know no better. Thought he was dead, when he really just pear-a-lized. They bury him that same day . . . bury him alive." Her cracked, withered lips parted in a toothless smile.

"And then," she continued, blinking herself back to the here and now, "I made ready for the *Baka*. With talismans and powders, potions and glyphs, I sealed off my house to it, and I waited."

Taddy whistled. "Sixty-two years. Wow!"

"Yeah," Roshella murmured, lowering her head. She began to feel the toll that fear, along with the move from her home, were taking on her tender frame. "Sixty-two years," she sighed. "Ain't never left the house."

"Until now," Taddy said, shaking his head. "Cuz of Sandy."

"I almost beat it," Roshella said after a minute of silence. "If'n I die a natural death, my soul go free." Her eyes blazed with a sudden burst of strength. "And that's what it's all about, boy. The soul."

She spread her arms and looked down at herself. "This body? It's nothin. I was beautiful once. Not a man in town din't want me, one time or another. But none of that matters. Youth be gone before you know it."

She leaned forward and touched his chin with a bony finger. "The soul—that be forever. And that be worth fightin' for, and holin' yourself up in a house all your life, if thass what it takes."

Taddy vaulted to his feet and grabbed her wrist. "You'll be safe in your house?"

"Oh, yes," Roshella said. *That is, if Sandy don't knock it down.*

"Then, come on!" he urged. "I'll get you out. But it's gotta be quick. If you get caught in the storm, you'll get kilt."

"Maybe that's not half-bad," Roshella said, struggling to her feet. "Probably shoulda let myself die a long time ago and cheated the damned *Baka*. But no, Roshella's a stubborn old woman who won't go without a fight. And now, I've gone and let it have a chance at me."

"We won't let it get you," Taddy said, letting go of her and running off ahead. "Meet me at the stairs in the locker room." He then sprinted around his family and sped through the bedraggled men and women who sat with hopeless expressions, shaking their heads. Some prayed, others wept softly.

Roshella stepped gingerly past them, anticipating a restraining arm at every step. Would it manifest itself as a gurgling whisper, a fetid breath in her ear, or an icy talon at her throat? She brushed off the thought and hurried toward the lockers. With each step she realized that, no matter the conditions outside, she had to chance it. There was no sanctuary here, among this collection of whimpering, distraught people who fretted and moaned about their lost possessions and the years of hard work put into their homes. *Years*, she thought, scoffing. *What were they compared to eternity?* Right now, Roshella felt no kinship with anyone here; though miles from their homes and hours from losing all they had ever owned, every one of these haggard individuals still retained the deed to their most valuable possession, while hers remained in question, as it had for sixty-two years.

She stopped short to allow a young girl with long black hair to dart in front of her, followed by her brother, screaming for her to wait. When she looked up, she felt a twinge of panic.

Someone was watching her closely.

She saw him out of the corner of her eye: a tall black man dressed in khaki pants, green shirt, and a camouflage jacket. He stood at the Red Cross table, hands in his pockets, intently staring in her direction. Roshella froze. Time seemed to grind to a halt. The background noise faded to a barely audible murmuring. The bustle of activity slowed and people moved sluggishly, as if underwater. He became the central object in the room, the radial focus of all points;

and her gaze immediately shifted to his location, where she knew he was smiling, waiting patiently for her to see him.

Don't look at him, Roshella told herself. *Not even a glance to let him know you see him. Just keep walking. Slowly.*

She was only ten feet from the entrance to the boys' locker room. As usual, there was no line here as there was on the girls' side. She could walk right in without anyone stopping her.

But not while she was being observed. If she was right, and the *Baka* had seen her, she wouldn't last a minute down there. She shuddered, wondering what it would do to Taddy if he tried to protect her.

She needed a diversion, something to distract the *Baka* while she slipped away.

No sooner had the thought crossed her mind than the diversion occurred. Roshella heard a great commotion: angry shouts and screams, a heavy crash. She risked a glance and saw the young girl who had run past her sitting on her floor with a pile of care packages sprawled around her, the table knocked on its side, and her brother backing away nervously. The big black man angrily scolded the children while he bent down to retrieve the fallen items. He looked up briefly, and for a split second, between the hurried shapes in the crowd, their eyes met and a sliver of absolute fear ripped through Roshella's mind.

Seeing her chance, Roshella moved as fast as her thin legs could carry her. With one quick look to reassure herself that the accident still held everyone's attention, she slipped into the locker room, rounded the corner, and headed for the third door on the left, marked STAIRS.

*   *   *

She was four steps down in the dark stairwell, the door slamming shut behind her, when she noticed the smell. Musky and damp, it hung oppressively in the still boiler room air. It was familiar, Roshella thought, and for some reason a memory of her childhood sprang up—a painful, long-repressed memory of the squalid streets of the Louisiana back-country where she had learned, the hard way, how to avoid death and abuse, how to mix the potions and write the glyphs that would ward off the evil spirits, and how to protect herself against the more natural, but just as evil threats.

The memory froze her completely, one foot just touching the bottom stair. Around the corner, the light from a single bulb cast furtive, malevolent shadows across the bare walls. Something scraped and dragged itself across the floor. One shadow moved, and a gaunt, impossibly tall outline stretched on the closest wall, arms at its side, head bent.

"T-taddy?" Roshella whispered.

The shadow tittered, retreated, and seemed to melt and fold in on itself, absorbed into the larger shades.

The scraping sound again.

And then a cough. "I'm down here!" Taddy called. "Come on. You're almost there."

Something creaked upstairs, a locker slamming. Footsteps approaching. The *Baka* had followed her too quickly, she realized. The diversion hadn't been enough. Roshella took the last step and dropped onto the cold, dusty floor. The smell hit her again; it was almost overpowering—as if something had died down here weeks ago and no one had found it. She imagined a cat trapped behind the pipes, dying of starvation, its rotting corpse feeding the very rats and mice it used to hunt.

She moved into the room, watching her shadow glide over a row of barrels and crates. The bulb hung from a thick wire in the center of the cramped boiler room, in front of a work bench and a wrought-iron furnace, not more than ten feet in front of her.

"Taddy?"

Suddenly she recognized that smell and knew what it meant. It had never been that strong during the past sixty-two years, but maybe the power of the talismans had been keeping it in check. Now, however, the spirit was on its own turf and free to expend its full power. She had made an error in judgment.

It was down here. With her.

Her terror surged, escalating from the pit of her stomach. She turned to consider the stairs and wondered if she could make it back up. As she turned her head, the shadows around her suddenly lurched, evaporating and re-forming themselves, turning inside and out. She looked back and saw the light bulb swinging violently, whipped around in a furious gale. But the air was still, and the putrid stench stronger than ever.

A soft, childlike giggle emanated from the shadows behind the furnace.

Roshella backed up into the bannister. She clutched at her shawl. "Oh, God . . . Taddy?"

The darkness parted and the small boy skipped out, a fawning smile on his pure, silken features. His brilliant green eyes glittered and dazzled in the jerking light, the darkness caressing his face for a split second before yielding to the returning brilliance. He stepped into the center of the room, under the swaying bulb. Never taking his eyes off her, Taddy lifted his arm and raised himself up on the tips of his toes.

Roshella couldn't be sure in the spastic light; it might have been an illusory trick, but it seemed Taddy's arm stretched an unbelievable distance, over twice its length, to reach into the path of the bulb. On its return swing, the bulb glided directly into his open palm. Taddy held onto the bulb, steadying it for what seemed like slow, agonizing minutes, before releasing it. Not once did the playful grin crack or waver under what must have been intense pain.

Roshella forced herself to take a breath and swallow. Fear had dried her mouth and constricted her throat.

Slowly, Taddy pointed past the stack of hurdles and the disorganized crates, to the back of the room and the flickering green exit light. "There it is," he said in a whisper. "The way out." His smile fell and his eyes turned cold—but just for a moment. Then the youthful smile was back. "Hurry," he urged. "I hear the storm comin'. The rains are fallin' already—just listen."

Taddy cocked his head and closed his eyes, concentrating on the sound of the rising storm. Roshella couldn't hear a thing over the pounding of her frail heart. She looked at the child and felt her doubts crack and slip away. He was just a boy. He'd played a trick on her; that was all. He was in fourth grade here, and he played Little League. Surely the *Baka* wasn't crafty enough to make up such a story. And besides, Taddy's family was upstairs in the gym. She saw him wave to them, didn't she?

Yes. But they didn't wave back . . .

She pushed off the bannister and took a step toward the exit.

Taddy's eyes were still closed, his head nodding to an invisible, far-off beat. Another tentative step. She was committed now. She had to go, whatever the consequences. Turning her back on the boy, she threw herself ahead, stepping around crates and over netting and ropes. The glowing green sign called to her, a beacon of hope. So close . . .

"*Roshella.*"

The word froze her in her tracks. It was the inflection of the voice: the grinding, guttural sound that was not quite a whisper, but loud enough drown her ears in a sea of pain. Her feet seemed to act on their own, turning her body around. From the damp, dark rear of the boiler room, within an arm's reach of the release bar for the door, Roshella lifted her eyes and looked upon the *Baka*.

Taddy's body had changed. It was thinner, his clothes torn and hanging loose around the bony frame. His ridged spine jutted upwards from under the shirt, coming to a point behind his head. His shoulders, likewise, rose to sharp points, the bony tips ripping through the fabric. As Roshella watched, his hair grew, and long strands fell past his face and dropped to the ground or hung under his eyes, now narrow, vertical, and feline. His bony arms extended, hanging down below his knees, the fingers ending in long, sharp nails that stabbed their way out from his skin. And his jaw chattered insistently, clicking away, joined intermittently by the wet, smacking sound of a thick, black tongue slopping around in a cavernous mouth.

Roshella gasped. "The Loa preserve me . . ."

The Taddy-thing shook its head and in a wave of descending hair said, "Not this time, my lovely Roshella. I've been more than patient."

Roshella tried to take a step back, but couldn't. "Please," she whispered, knowing well the futility of arguing with a *Baka*. "Let me go. Just this once . . ."

The *Baka* threw its head back and roared its laugh. Its skull was now hairless. And the black, leathery scalp writhed and bubbled up in a frothy, putrescent liquid. Its eyes blinked, then bulged at her, the black pupils expanding to capture her terrified reflection. "Patience I've had. Not generosity—never that." It spoke in a grim voice, then advanced on her, talons clicking, the forked, black tongue slithering over its lipless mouth.

Roshella raised her arms in a vain attempt to ward off the sixty-two-year-old curse. She felt the creature's heat, its foul breath in her nostrils. Bile roared to the tip of her throat.

At the top of the stairs, a door slammed open and a voice shouted down, "Hey! Who's down there?"

The glistening claws stopped, inches from Roshella's face. With a snarl, the *Baka* whirled around on its powerful legs and leaped to the ceiling, where it latched onto the maze of pipes. Its long arms moved swiftly, and in two great swings the *Baka* had reached the dangling light bulb. Roshella saw a pair of khaki legs running down the stairs just as the black talons encircled the bulb.

The light went out with a hot blue spark and a puff of glass shards. A complete shroud of blackness enveloped the boiler room.

Roshella heard a hiss, similar to escaping gas, but with a certain mischievous edge. The concerned relief worker let out a surprised cry—abruptly cut off and followed by a series of heavy thumps on the stairs, then one long, blood-curdling scream. The death-cry freed Roshella from her paralysis and gave her the impetus to grip the iron bar and struggle against the fierce wind in forcing the door open enough to squeeze through. She plunged headlong into the parking lot, where the wind shrieked its rage and belted her back against the stone wall. The pounding rain instantly drenched her and numbed her to the bone. In the violent gale, small pebbles and shards of gravel tore at her face and stung her eyes.

Over the howling wind, she couldn't hear herself scream as she edged along the wall. Peering through the slick curtain of rain, she saw the exit to Broad Street, nearly forty yards away and, further along, three streetlamps bending over in the wind. One shattered and blew out as she watched. Catching her eye from another angle in the flooded parking lot, a telephone pole split and fell, slamming against the roof of a station wagon.

Never gonna make it, she thought with a sudden rush of despair. It was over. In a minute the door behind her would open, and the *Baka* would come shrieking after her. With its speed, she wouldn't even make it to the street, let alone to her house. And, in this gale, she doubted that her seventy-year-old excuse for a home would be standing much longer; her talismans would soon be hurled to the wind and scattered over Nassau County.

As she cleared the building and rushed into the parking lot, she slipped and tumbled painfully onto her right hip before sprawling into a deep puddle where the pavement dipped and cracked. Lifting her face from the cold pool, she blinked away the water and looked back through the downpour.

The boiler room door blasted open, almost torn from its hinges. She couldn't tell for sure, but it looked as if something dark and twisted sprang out from inside and flattened itself against the ground, coupling with the deeper shadows. Roshella gasped, spitting out a mouthful of rainwater. She tried to rise, but her broken hip wailed in protest. Helpless, she watched as the black form leapt from the ground to a point high on the brick wall.

A burst of lightning ripped through the night, revealing the clawed, spiderlike thing scuttling across the wall, its determined green eyes gleaming in the flash of white light, its jaws chattering, its rubbery skin glistening in the rain.

Roshella flailed in the puddle, desperately trying to shut out the pain and force her rebellious body into motion. She made it to one knee.

Twenty feet in front of her, the base of another telephone pole cracked. A shower of sparks fell. In a fleeting thought, Roshella wondered if those inside had just lost their power.

Out of the shadows, the *Baka* glided into the faint light from one of the remaining streetlamps. It crouched, drawing itself inward, preparing to leap.

Something buzzed angrily over Roshella's head, and a heavy snap cut through the wind. She lifted her face to the sky and at once realized she had to move, had to get out of the way before—

The *Baka* hurled itself into the air, unfettered by the tremendous wind, and flew straight at her. It landed on all fours with a heavy splash, its extended snout and slavering fangs inches from Roshella's throat. The green eyes sparkled and the black tongue flicked out.

"Now I claim what is mine," it said, without malice or pleasure. It was only fulfilling its pledge, completing the task assigned to it over six decades earlier. Just one act, and it would be free to return to its lightless home, bearing the old woman's soul.

Water streaming off her face, Roshella turned to stare into the

Baka's paralyzing visage. She gathered her will, tapping into the well of courage that had propelled her since this all began. "It ain't yours to take," she said as her body relaxed. It was over, she knew—out of her control. She spread her arms as wide as they would go, closed her eyes, and waited.

The *Baka* was momentarily confused by her lack of fright. But it was not an issue to dwell on for long; and in the next second, it opened its jaws and bent forward . . .

Something crashed nearby—a loud, thunderous sound, and over it, an angry buzzing.

The live power cable, spitting out bluish-white sparks, dropped right between the old woman and the creature, splashing into the puddle.

The electrical surge threw Roshella and the *Baka* together, and in a blind embrace they danced like spastic marionettes to a death march. Roaring in pain and frustration, the *Baka* thrashed and kicked, in a frenzy trying to free itself from the electrified pool and the dead woman who wouldn't let go.

Throwing its head *back*, the *Baka* howled and screamed in protest, until a final jolt hurled the pair three feet away, onto dryer ground. Immediately tearing loose of Roshella's death-grip, the *Baka* pushed away and stood to its full height. Looking down at the woman and the steam that rose from her scorched flesh, the *Baka* grunted, its features molding into an expression of disgust.

It had failed. The woman was at peace, having cheated the old *Bokor* after all.

Feeling the long-anticipated pull—the irresistible tug on its tether to the underworld—the *Baka* snarled and raised its fists to the heavens. The wind roared and the rain intensified, relishing in the triumph of the natural world over its spiritual counterpart. And in one sudden, blinding moment, a jagged trail of lightning licked across the underbelly of a madly swirling cloudbank. The fierce light dazzled in the creature's eyes an instant before it departed, and stayed with it as an afterimage for many countless years in a much darker place.

Blood Will Tell

JG Faherty

I signed the contract and returned the pen to Jenson. The grand estate, so much like the mansion I'd grown up in across the river in
Sleepy Hollow, was officially mine. Thirty acres of property outside
the village of Rocky Pointe, nestled between the Hudson River and
the Ramapo Mountains. A day's ride by carriage to Manhattan, it was
as secluded as a castle.

"Congratulations, Peter. It's fine place." Jenson tipped his glass of
brandy to me. A celebratory drink, 'for good luck,' he'd called it. I
was happy to oblige.

"Thank you."

"I hope you'll be comfortable here. It's different from the towns
in Westchester. Still a lot of wilderness. Bear, bobcat. In fact, rumor
has it people have heard wolves recently." He stated this last with a
wink and a porcine smile, and I knew he was trying to give me a
playful scare.

"I prefer the isolation," I replied. "That's why this side of the river
is perfect. Westchester has grown too cosmopolitan. Soon it will be
nothing more than an extension of Manhattan."

I poured us another glass. Outside the wide windows, the first
rounded edge of the moon peered over the treetops.

"Have I ever told you how I met my wife?" I asked.

"Wife? I didn't know you were married. Do tell."

"It's quite a story," I said, handing Jenson his glass.

*   *   *

When the girl emerged from her mother, it was as if she intended to remain cloaked in secrecy, much as her mother's arrival from

Romania had been. Born in the dead of night, in a dank basement, she entered the world hidden behind a mask of pale flesh.

The blue caul stretched from the top of her head to her feet, like the birth sac of an animal. The vein-ridden tissue distorted the baby's features, as if a creature from another world were trying to push through a wall of the thinnest rubber. Tiny arms and legs kicked in a palsied St. Vitus's dance, and I watched the outline of the mouth open and close in silent screams.

Three people surrounded mother and child: the midwife, her assistant, and the man who'd accompanied them to the filthy, earth-floored room.

My father.

A fourth pair of eyes—mine—watched from behind a pane of glass. When I'd heard the midwife's shout that the baby was coming, I'd run outside to peer through the tiny, dirt-encrusted window set into the foundation.

Upon seeing the caul, the midwife stepped back, hands making the sign of the cross over her ample chest. Father, a hairy, bearded brute with arms and neck thick as tree trunks and a head square as a stone block, shouted at her to "Cut the damn caul off, you foolish woman!"

For a moment I thought the midwife might faint. Her face went white, but she got a grip on herself and picked up a small scissors. Ignoring the mother, who screamed and writhed on the table, she pushed the scissors into the pulsating veil of skin and cut it away in quick strokes, then severed the umbilical cord.

The midwife hoisted the baby by the legs and slapped its rump. The gulping mouth froze in mid-gape, and then the most awful wail emerged. Freed from its abnormal hood, the baby's face seemed fine. Beautiful, in fact.

As soon as the girl-child began to cry, Father nodded and went to the head of the table. The mother had her arms outstretched, and though I couldn't hear her words, I felt sure she was asking to hold her newborn child.

Father turned so that his tall, broad-shouldered body faced away from me. His muscular arm moved once, after which he stepped backwards with more speed than I would have believed possible for a man of his size.

Dark liquid erupted outwards from the woman on the table. At first I thought she was vomiting, until I saw the blood pouring from a gaping hole where her throat had been.

The midwife's young assistant put a hand to her mouth, and I believe she would have screamed, but Father shook his bloody weapon, a barber's razor, at her. She looked away and Father said something to the women before stalking out of the room.

The midwife turned her back to the gruesome scene on the table and began cleaning the baby with wet cloths.

*   *   *

Upstairs in my chambers, my door securely locked, I fell into bed without bothering to remove my clothes, unaware of how my muddy pants soiled the linens. No matter how tightly I squeezed my eyes closed, the woman's murder played over and over in my head, like the silent films the movie houses show today. But unlike those films, what I saw had both sound and color.

I slept poorly for several weeks after that. I kept dreaming of Father coming for me with his razor.

My sister was several years old before I could look at her without reliving the night I witnessed her birth.

*   *   *

"Piotyr, come quickly, I want to show you something." Daniella stood in my doorway. I knew from her tone there was no ignoring her.

I closed my book and rose from my chair.

"What is it, sister? I have exams to study for."

"This will only take a moment." Her downy-fine hair, so pale as to be almost white, moved with a life of its own as she tilted her head up at me.

Unlike Father and me, Daniella stood tall and thin. At age seven she already reached my shoulder. In all respects we couldn't have been less alike. I sported thick, curly, dark hair, the same as our father. My eyes were so brown as to be almost black; hers were two perfect circles of winter-blue ice. I was calm and quiet, while Daniella had difficulty sitting still for more than a few minutes.

Now, in her excitement, she switched back and forth between English, which Father had insisted we both learn, and our native Romanesti. "*Grabă!* Hurry! Before they are gone."

Tugging me by the hand, she led me through the empty halls of our home.

They? I was unaware of any visitors.

Instead of heading downstairs to the front entrance, Daniella brought me to her bedroom. She drew back the curtains and opened the balcony doors. The January wind blowing off the river bit our exposed skin and whipped Daniella's cornsilk hair across her face as we peered over the brass railing.

Six wolves cavorted in the snow. Although I'd never seen one alive before, there was no mistaking these creatures for dogs. They were wild wolves, great hairy beasts. Five had fur colored in grays and browns. The sixth, the largest of them all, stood out from the others. Its coat was darkest black, and in the last rays of the evening sun it shone with hints of purple.

Daniella waved a long-fingered hand at the dancing beasts. "*Salut!* Hello!"

I expected the oversized canines to flee when she called to them, but instead they stopped and lifted their heads toward us. The midnight-colored one, who seemed to be their leader, sat back on its haunches and raised a paw larger than my own hand.

"See, Piotyr? He is saying hello!" Daniella clapped her hands, as she was wont to do whenever a burst of happiness came over her. Her azure eyes sparkled with glee.

I tried to speak, but my voice failed me. I coughed, then tried again. "Sister, how can this be? Wolves are animals of the forest, not the city." My first thought was they had escaped from a zoo; that would explain their actions as well as their lack of fear.

"This is not the first time I have seen them," she confided. Rosy circles stood out on her pale cheeks, although whether from cold or excitement I could not say. "They visit me every month. Always when the moon is full and round. They dance and play for me."

"You never told me about this." I was angry and more than a little afraid. How could she keep such a thing to herself?

"*Îmi pare rău.* I am sorry. But he told me not to tell anyone. Then today, he said I could summon you."

"He? Who is this he?" Even as I asked, I feared the answer to my question.

Daniella aimed a thin, delicate finger at the dark wolf. In the advancing night, he was a shadow upon the snow.

A menacing shadow with green, luminescent eyes.

"Their *căpitan*. He talks to me."

I wanted to ask what she meant, but a knock on the bedroom door startled us. It was Miryam, our housekeeper, calling us to supper.

"We will be right there," I responded. When I looked back, the wolves were gone. Only their footprints remained.

Daniella and I went inside. As I closed the doors, I stared at the ribbon of forest separating our home from the banks of the wide Hudson River. Floating above the trees was a great, bone-white circle.

From somewhere in the darkness came a chorus of howls.

"Listen, Piotyr," Daniella whispered. "They wish to tell you things, important things."

I drew the curtains shut and pushed her away. "Stop your nonsense, sister. Wolves cannot speak. Now go and ready yourself for supper."

My appetite that evening was poor, and I finally excused myself, saying I had studies to attend to. Father, himself something of a scholar, waved me away without a look. Daniella's eyes burned into my back as I hurried from the room.

From that night forward, I kept my windows shut and the drapes drawn. Each month, when the muted howling of Daniella's wolves reached my ears, I retreated to the library or the kitchens. There I secluded myself, hiding from the voices of the wild creatures cavorting on our lawn.

As bad as their cries were, it was worse to hear Daniella answer them. Her lilting voice would echo through the cavernous rooms of the house as she conversed with them for hours.

If I happened to be in my bedroom, I would press my hands over my ears and speak loudly to myself. I couldn't bear to listen. Her communion with the wolves terrified me.

Even more terrifying, sometimes I felt as if I could almost understand them as well.

* * *

Most of the time our house was a wonderful place to live. Father was well off, and he devoted a good portion of his energies and wealth to our happiness.

But for me, there existed a dark cloud that cast a cold shadow over our blessed existence. Once a month Father would leave us for three or four days, with no explanation for his absence.

Without fail, those were the same nights when Daniella conversed with her wolves.

The continued visits of her wild creatures troubled me to the point where I finally broached the subject to Father, but he only laughed.

"Do not be afraid to experience new things, my son. You would do well to listen to your sister. There is much to learn that cannot be found in your books."

He placed one massive hand on my shoulder. Curling, dark hair filled the spaces between his knuckles like some miniature forest. "Be a man, Piotyr, not a shrinking violet."

After that, whenever I tried to speak to him about the wolves, he would just shake his head or ignore me.

Eventually I found other ways to distract myself from the nocturnal visits of the black beast and its pack. Books and music became my companions. Daniella teased me about this and often tried to coax me back to her rooms to converse with her friends.

Fear lent my resolve stubborn strength, though, and I did not budge from my stance. Daniella would sulk and pout as she always did when she could not get her way, but her general good spirits could not remain down for too long. By the next morning she would be my friend again.

So things continued for several years, until the day of Daniella's sixteenth birthday.

The day I learned the truth of our family.

* * *

I've said that Daniella and I shared a disinclination to associate outside of the family. Father had raised us in the traditions of the old country, and we found little in common with our schoolmates.

Aside from required social gatherings, we kept to ourselves. And why not, with so much entertainment available at home? Many of our days and nights were spent roaming the hallways, rooms, and basements of our home, or exploring the nearby forests and riverbanks.

I suppose it was inevitable our friendship would grow to something more.

Since the day of Daniella's birth, I'd been aware we did not share the same mother. My mother had died when I was three, succumbing to illness soon after we reached America. Father never brought up the subject of Daniella's parentage, but I knew the truth. I'd seen it with my own eyes, that horrible night in the basement.

However, I instinctively knew not to reveal my knowledge to Father. Some secrets are best left untold.

Daniella was a different story. When I was thirteen and she but eight, I told her the truth of our kinship, after swearing her to secrecy. She cried, but never doubted me. If anything, the knowledge of Father's despicable act brought us closer.

Perhaps that is why neither of us felt any guilt when we shared our first kiss, me at sixteen and she a precocious eleven. We both knew it was wrong, but when our lips touched, the world around us seemed to disappear.

From then on we were inseparable. Contrary to what you might think, ours was not a relationship of debauchery and lustfulness. Most times we played together as of old, with but two simple changes: several times a week we would find a place to ourselves and practice the art of kissing.

And I joined Daniella in speaking to her wolves.

From the moment we began our innocent but illicit affair, my ability to understand the four-legged guardians of our home increased tenfold.

Usually we conversed with Reggnyak, the black-furred pack leader. He welcomed me with a canine grin and a wagging tail. The others—Chook, Hrenstraal, Omal, Koo, and Baa—rarely spoke.

Reggnyak would regale us with tales of their adventures in the wooded lands well to the north of Manhattan and Westchester, where they made their home when not visiting with us. I asked

Reggnyak once why they had come to us. He said Daniella had called to him. More than that he refused to reveal.

We never let on to Father the extent of what we did, with the wolves or each other. Nor was he aware when our love grew from childhood to adulthood, even as we ourselves did.

Daniella, fifteen and already well blossomed into womanhood, came to me on my twenty-first birthday. She entered my bedroom late at night, waking me with gentle caresses to my neck and ears. I opened my eyes and found her face hovering over mine.

"What are you doing here?"

"I have one last present for your birthday, dear brother," she whispered.

She untied her nightdress and let it drop to the floor. Perfect she was, even at her age. Her full breasts were snow-capped mountains in reverse, dark peaks on white hills. Her hands were silk as she explored me, her skin butter-smooth to my touch. We were both virgins, but our lack of experience did not hinder us.

Afterwards, we declared our love for each other as more than half-brother and -sister. We devised a secret plan. Once Daniella was sixteen and old enough to marry legally, we would leave the house and start a new life together.

"Three months, Piotyr? I do not know if I can wait that long," my beautiful one said, her rose-colored lips brushing my neck as she spoke.

"We must."

She nodded. *"Da înţeleg."* Daniella had never lost her habit of mixing English and Romanesti. "I understand."

We lay in each other's arms until the sun's first rays reddened the sky.

"I must go," she said. *"La revedere,* my love."

Daniella began dressing, then paused.

"What is it?" I feared she had heard Father in the hallway.

"Listen." She pointed to the window.

It was Reggnyak, calling softly from the lawn below.

"Bun venit!" His words were for me, but they made no sense.

Welcome.

*   *   *

Three months passed with agonizing slowness, but finally the day arrived. Daniella's sixteenth birthday, her entry into adulthood.

Father came to me as I dressed for our evening meal. His thick beard, now tinged with gray, framed a serious expression.

"Piotyr, we must speak. I have kept secrets from you, secrets about our family, and about your sister."

His eyes widened when I said, "Father, I know your secret. About Daniella's mother, and the basement. I've always known. I was there, *de par iv*, you bastard."

Brave I was to say such things to this man, who could still break me in half with one flex of his massive arms. But I did not care. In the morning, Daniella and I would be gone.

My surprise was turned back on me as he first smiled then laughed. "You think murder is our family's secret? My son, that is but the beginning!"

He proceeded to tell me an unbelievable tale. How his line had descended from wolves and he was the last of his clan. Out of necessity, he had married my mother, whom he referred to as 'ordinary blood, not one of the *vircolac*.' Which made me a half-breed.

"Because of this," he said, "your true nature cannot rise until you are blooded by a female of our race."

He explained how he'd arranged for his men to have a full-blood from another clan kidnapped and brought to America, so he could make her with child. His idea was to father several sons and daughters, in order to establish our race anew here in America. He'd chosen the wilderness north of Manhattan because it reminded him of our homeland yet remained within easy traveling distance of a large city should he ever need to flee.

"The only flaw in my plan," he said with a scowl, "was Daniella's mother. She hated this place. Hated me. Had I kept her alive, she would have slaughtered innocent people and brought the same unwanted attention down on us that led to the demise of our people in Europe."

"So you killed her."

"Yes. Being a leader means making hard choices, my son. As you must do now."

"What do you mean?" I asked.

"To take your rightful place as one of the *vircolac*, the people of the wolf."

It was my turn to laugh, because I thought I understood what he was telling me. "You are too late, Father. The wolves already speak to me." I crossed my arms and puffed out my chest, unaware my youthful arrogance had me following the wrong path.

"Foolish child," Father shook his head. "Anyone of the blood can do that. But only a full blood, or one bitten, can do this."

Before my eyes, he began to change. His arms grew even larger and longer. His thick, matted hair lengthened and became straight and coarse. The long, thin fingers of his hands, so adept at playing the piano or carving a turkey—or slicing a throat—curled inward, turned dark and callused. Black, knife-like claws sprouted from their tips.

His voice, always deep, held a menacing growl when he spoke. "Our people do not just listen to the wolves, Piotyr. We *are* the wolves. This is what your sister will become tonight. Because it will be her first time, she will be ravenous, eager to kill. Only I, as her pack leader, will be able to control her when she delivers the bite that will finally allow you to transform as well."

"What?" My sister, a monster like him? And now he wanted me to risk my life to become such a thing as well?

"*Nu!* Never!" I ran past him, my only thought to leave this place, take myself far away from the madness.

A howling roar chased me as I raced down the hall. Father had completely changed into his beast form and was coming after me!

Down the wide steps of the main staircase I fled. Instead of the front door, which led to a wide-open lawn, I ran to the back of the house, desperately hoping to lose myself in the woods between our property and the river. I was ready to throw myself into the icy waters and let them wash my body all the way to Manhattan rather than become part of Father's evil plan.

My breath came in harsh gasps, and fire burned in my lungs. But the ache in my chest had nothing to do with my fear or exertions.

Rather, it was from my broken heart, as I realized Daniella and I would never be together. I was human, and she was something else.

I pushed open the doors to the garden. My goal was in sight. If I could make it . . .

A powerful blow struck my back, knocking the breath from me and forcing me into the autumn-dead flower stalks and brown shrubs. Claws pierced my shoulders like arrows as inhuman arms lifted me to my feet.

The creature that had once been my father pulled me close. No remnant of humanity remained. Long whiskers trembled as the thing drew back pink lips, exposing gleaming white teeth. Frothy white drool hung from its mouth.

I shouted my pain as its nails dug deeper into my flesh. I tried to push away, but the iron grip tightened further, holding me fast.

A flash of movement caught my attention. Father's grip on me loosened, and he let out a high-pitched bark. I kicked free from his claws, my skin tearing as I fell to the ground.

Gasping for breath, I regained my feet, then froze when I realized I stood in the middle of a battle.

Reggnyak and his wolves had come to my rescue!

In his *vircolac* form, Father had the advantage of size, but the pack had strength in numbers. They darted in and out, biting here, clawing there. When Father turned one way, a wolf would charge from the other side and attack his exposed hindquarters.

Father roared, the wolves howled, and I screamed at them to kill him. Finally, a wolf I didn't recognize, a long, thin animal with shining silver-white fur, closed its jaws on Father's leg and tore the muscle so badly that the limb collapsed.

Father went down under the pack's onslaught. The white wolf finished it, tearing Father's throat open and spilling his blood onto the hard, dead ground.

When it was all over, I expected Reggnyak to converse with me, but it was the new wolf that came forward and growled out a single word.

"*Frate.*"

Brother.

My sister. Just as Father had promised, she was now one of the *vircolac.* Father's blood dripped from her muzzle, and her sides heaved from her exertions.

I wanted to run, but I could not move. Her eyes, so like her human ones, crystal blue and full of love, mischief, and joy, held me in place.

"*Soră.*" The word came out of my mouth, even as I realized the awful truth. "*Îmi pare rău.* I am sorry, sister-love."

As much as I loved her, I could not let her bite me, transform me.

So I turned and fled.

*   *   *

Jenson, well into his third brandy, stared at me as I stopped speaking and poured myself another glass.

"That was quite a tale!" he finally said, a sheepish grin forming on his pudgy lips. "Why, you should be a writer."

I tipped my glass to him. "What, like Shelley or Stoker?"

"Indeed. But what of your real wife? When will I . . ." His voice stopped as the library door opened.

Firelight reflected off feather-soft, silver-white hair.

"So this is where you have been hiding. It is getting dark outside, *a mea amator,* my love."

I smiled. "Mister Jenson, this is my wife. Daniella."

Jenson's mouth opened, but no words came out. Daniella took his hand in both of hers, her long fingers wrapping around his sausage-like counterparts.

"*Salut,* Mister Jenson. Thank you for finding us this house. I know our children will be very happy here."

Jenson cried out and struggled in Daniella's grasp, but could not break free of the claws that pierced his flesh.

I put down my brandy as my body began to change.

"It turns out an exchange of blood is not necessary to bring about the change. Any of the body's fluids will do."

Outside, our children began to howl. Somewhere in the forest, their Uncle Reggnyak and his pack answered.

"As they say, Mister Jenson, blood will always tell."

The Lady in the Sideshow:
A Circuspunk Story

Charie D. La Marr

Every summer on the weekends, the people of New York flock to Coney Island. They fill the beaches and crowd the wooden boardwalk, eating Feltman's hotdogs and vanilla custard. They scream and laugh as they ride the wooden rollercoaster, The Cyclone. They strain to reach for the brass ring as they ride the B&B Carousel at Luna Park. They hold their girls tight while they ride the Loop-o-Planes and the Octopus.

But there are other things they come to see.

The barker lures them in from the boardwalk, urging them to pay their ten cents and come inside the Dreamland Circus Sideshow. It looks like a castle, with its turrets and bright banners flapping in the ocean breeze. On the way in, they stop for an ice cream soda for five cents in the land they call the Nickel Empire. They're lured inside by the undeniable urge to see those God forgot—the freaks of nature, the absurd, the hideous. Year after year, they return to see them. Lionel, the Lion-faced Man. Violette, the Limbless Woman. Zip the Pinhead. They're all inside, waiting to titillate some, make others swoon and faint, and guaranteed to send the youngest home with a week's worth of nightmares.

They have seen them before, yet they willingly hand over their dimes to step inside on a hot, sunny Brooklyn afternoon. What has changed over the winter? There are rumors of a four-legged woman. Twins, really, sharing one body. What new oddities await them inside?

Once inside, they wince at two-headed fetuses, forever floating in a bath of formaldehyde. They gasp at the malformed. They shake their heads at the unfortunate and walk away.

There is another addition this year. Last year's fat lady has passed on. Her funeral made all the papers—the *Daily Mirror* even printed a picture of her body on the front page, tucked inside a huge, custom-built casket. Mayor La Guardia himself eulogized her. Her fellow freaks served as her pallbearers when they laid her to rest in two plots at Cypress Hills, doing their best to hoist the load and hide their faces from the gawkers.

This year there is a new one. She sits on a settee three times the size of the normal, her thick feet wide apart. One hand rests on her knee, as does the other elbow as she bends forward, her face all but obscured under the mounds of flesh. She wears the ruffled dress of a child and a large bow in her short, curly hair. The image is laughable. A large Shirley Temple doll. A bulbous Baby Snooks.

They stop to look at her, and she looks back at them with a challenging gaze.

"She's bigger than last year's, don't you think?"

"That one died, I read. Suffocated in her sleep. Saw her picture in the *Mirror*."

"Look how the legs of the chair are bending under the strain! Can you imagine if they broke and she fell? Nobody could get her back up again."

She motions, and three men come to her aid. Two take her arms and one gets behind her, barely managing to reach under her armpits. They shift her position.

She passes wind loudly. The smell of rot and decay fills the room. Women cry out in disgust and put their handkerchiefs to their noses. Children gag loudly and pretend to vomit as they laugh. Men chuckle and look away.

She grins smugly.

"What are you looking at?" she calls out. "Ain't you never passed no wind before? Huh, Missus? Too much of a lady to pass a little gas?"

The woman grabs her husband by the arm and pulls him away. On the platform, she cackles and opens a box of chocolates tucked down beside her.

People shake their heads self-righteously. Look at what she's doing to herself. It's nobody's fault but her own. She makes her own choices. She doesn't have to be like that if she doesn't want to.

From behind her eyes dulled by cataracts, she can read their thoughts.

"Is that what you think, lady? Do you really think a box of bonbons did this to me? Ain't you never had no bonbons before? Sure you have. And yet I don't see you sitting up here for all the world to stare at. You ever wonder when this started, or how? You ever think maybe I come from big-boned stock? Or do you think most of my kin end up in the slaughterhouse? That I'm not even as human as the likes of you."

A boy throws his hot dog at her. It slaps her in the side of the face and mustard drips down her chins. People point fingers and laugh.

"You pay ten cents for that hot dog at Feltman's, son? Shame on you throwing away good food like that. We're just getting over a Depression, or haven't you heard? Didn't you learn nothing from that? How many of you got the quarter it costs to ride on that Cyclone these days? Factories don't pay you that much no more, do they? Wildcat only costs a dime, I hear. Scares you just as good as the Cyclone, I suppose. How many hours you gotta work in a sweatshop to afford a day here at Coney? Me, all I do is sit here and look at you, and I bet I out-earn all of you!

"Oh, it's easy to look at me and judge, in't it?" she asks, wiping off her chin and licking her fingers. "Easy to think the Good Lord put me here so you can pay your ten cents and gaggle. Do I make you feel just a little bit better about yourselves? 'I may not be perfect, but at least I'm not like her,' you say."

She begins to cough, a deep, wracking cough that brings up a handful of blood-tinged mucus and phlegm that she wipes on her dress as she snorts the rest back down her throat. She sits quietly for a few moments to catch her breath. Her heavy chest rises and falls. Her hands cling to the arms of the settee so tightly that her fingers turn white.

"Feel sorry for me or hate me, don't make no difference to me. You paid your dime, you got your rights. Only things you know about me is what it says on the billboard poster. Caroline—that's my name. Sweet Car-o-line. But what do you care? Ain't you got no questions for me? You know you do. How does she fit into the outhouse, you wonder. How does she wipe herself clean? How does she fit on the train? Do they put her with the animals? No bed can hold me, I'm sure you all agree with that. Bed her down in straw with the livestock. Good enough for her.

"And what do they feed her? Do they fry her up half a dozen chickens at night with a pot of mashed potatoes and a dozen ears of corn? Two or three apple pies for dessert? Or do they just slop her down with the animals? You wonder? And what did you have for dinner last night, Mister? The Missus, she feeds you well?"

She motions to the men, and they come back to adjust her position again. It's physically exhausting and leaves her panting. She pulls a Chinese fan out of the side of the chair and fans herself.

"Hot in here, ain't it? Or is it just me?" She laughs to herself and slaps her knee.

"Well, now's the part when I'm supposed to entertain you folks. Give you your ten cents' worth, as if you didn't get enough already. Them three baby goats stuck together and floatin' in a jar was worth the money all by themselves."

She leans back and sighs. "Folks, the truth is, I ain't got no talents to entertain you with. Used to play some harmony-ca, but I ain't got the wind for that no more. All I got is what the Good Lord gave me, and while you may think it's an awful lot, truth is it ain't much at all. Two arms, two legs and a head—same as you. So I'll just sit here and y'all make sure you get a real good look so's you can talk about me tomorrow.

"'Did you see her?' you'll ask your friends. 'Positively disgusting, wan't it? You see the way she was puttin' those bonbons away? Were you there when she coughed up all the bloody goo and used her dress for a hankie?' Oh, you'll talk about me tomorrow for sure."

She laughs again. The laughter gives way to another hacking cough that brings up more bloody gunk that she adds to her dress. The men move her. She fans herself more.

"Make sure you see it all, folks. Although a lot of you will be back later in the week. Don't think I don't notice when the same ones come back for another look, because I do. Just like you're watching me, I'm watching you. And I sees things. Some of these fellas, they'll be back later on with a different lady on their arm. You think I miss that? You think you're the only one he takes roller-skating over at Steeplechase? Think again.

"And I can tell you now which of you ladies is holdin' it all in with the corset and girdle they buy over at Klein's when they think nobody's watching. The ones who undress in the dark so's their husbands won't say nothing about how their girlish figures is gone.

"And how many of you kids paid the dime and how many of you snuck in here when nobody was looking? Ain't ya got nothin' better to do, ya little Micks? Shouldn't ya be standing on the street corner pushing the *Post* or the *Brooklyn Eagle*, taking your earnings home to your ma?"

She stops and looks at each one of them before moving on to the next as if, through those cataract eyes and folds that almost cover them, she can see everything.

"You got your laughs for today. So be on your way, ladies and gentlemen. You saw what you came to see. You can walk away feeling a whole lot better about yourselves now that you seen me. Go on, get on your way. Go look at the tattooed lady for a while. I validated all of you. I made your sad, empty lives just a little bit better. I earned that ten cents you left at the door. Go on, move along. Others are waiting to take your place. They need to be validated, too. The BMT's waiting to take you back to the Lower East Side and your miserable lives in tenements that smell like stinkin' onions where babies cry and you'll be lucky if you make it to thirty without catching that tuberculosis and dead by thirty-five. Come back and see me if you need more hope for the future. Go ahead and spend your dimes, if lookin' at me makes you feel better about yourselves. Don't make no difference to me. You want to feel you're better than me, go right ahead."

The crowd standing before her mumble as they collect their children and shuffle on to the next exhibit.

"Mama," says a little girl in a straw hat and a crisp starched white dress with a sailor collar and a blue bow, "I didn't like that lady. The one they had last year was a whole lot funnier."

"Maybe next year's will be better," her mother says, dragging the little girl away. "They don't last long, you know."

Pink Elephants: A Murphy's Lore Tale

Patrick Thomas

It started out like an old joke. A man and a mouse walk into a bar. The guy has the mouse on a piece of string as if it's a leash, and the mouse is a Great Dane that shrank in the dryer. The mouse, of course, doesn't appreciate being led around by the neck and is running back and forth, trying to get loose. The man, already three sheets to the wind, is trying to keep the mouse walking in a straight line, a task he can't seem to manage himself. The guy stumbles across the room, immensely proud of himself for some reason.

He managed to find the bar, more by luck and touch than by sight. The stench of his breath made me glad no one in Bulfinche's Pub was smoking at the moment. The guy had enough alcohol on his breath to become a human flame thrower.

"Bartender, c'mere," the man said, slurring his words.

"Morning," I said.

"Is it?" he asked, looking at his wrist. He was unable to figure out the time, so he shook his hand and held his wrist up to his ear to listen for ticking. Hearing nothing, he put his arm down and sighed disgustedly. If he had only asked, I could have solved his problem. His watch was on the other hand. "You know something? I refuse to drink with strangers."

"Really?" I said, half smiling.

"So you have to tell me your name," the drunk said, smiling as if he had made the funniest joke ever.

"Name's Murphy," I said, extending my hand to be shaken, not stirred.

The drunk managed to grab my hand on only the second try. "Nice to know you, Murphy. My name's Marty."

"Pleasure to meet you, Marty."

"Really?"

"Actually, that remains to be seen. What can I do for you today, Marty?" I asked.

Marty shifted his weight and half fell off his bar stool. Righting himself, he mumbled, "Guess."

"Get you a drink?" I suggested. Marty was too drunk to notice the sarcasm.

"Bingo! How'd you know?" he asked, appearing to be as genuinely amazed as a five-year-old watching his grandfather pull quarters out from behind his ears.

"I'm a professional. I'll bet you a buck I can guess what you're drinking," I said. Marty fumbled in his wallet, pulled out a dollar, and slapped it down on the bar top. The movement unseated him again, but he landed on his feet.

"Deal," he said, retaking his seat on the bar stool.

"Bourbon, right?" I said.

"Amazing! How'd you do that? You psychic or something?"

"Nope, I'm not psychic. Just have a good nose," I said, pointing to my right nostril, then picking up the bill and putting it in my pocket. "Straight up?"

"Yes. You're sure you can't read minds?" Marty asked, looking down at the frantically running mouse. He had gotten his leash tangled up in and around the legs of the bar stool. Marty bent down and picked up the little rodent, petting him gently. The mouse either relaxed or was filled with such fear he didn't dare move.

"What's the deal with the mouse?" I asked.

"He's my bodyguard," said Marty. He added in a confidential whisper, "I'm being followed."

"By whom?" I asked.

"Pink elephants," replied Marty.

"Of course," I said. "I should have known."

"I want to buy my bodyguard a drink. Milk or whatever mice drink. I also want to buy my other friend a drink."

I looked around. There was no one near us in the pub. "Friend?"

"The talking dog," said Marty.

"Does he tell you what's on the top of a house?" I said, waiting for the old punch line, when a familiar canine head popped up on the stool next to Marty's.

"Not unless you ask," said the furry trickster god, putting his front paws on the bar. "Hello, Murphy. Bowl of whiskey, please."

"That's no dog, that's my strife," I said. It went right over Marty's head. We have a unique clientele here at Bulfinche's Pub and the furball was a regular. "Hello, Coyote. What brings you by?" I asked, putting a bowl of whiskey in front of the divine canine and a saucerful of milk in front of the mouse. Coyote lapped up his drink, but the mouse ignored his.

"My new friend Marty, who has been so kind as to offer to pick up the drinks," said Coyote.

"That's right. What's the damage on the drinks?" asked Marty.

"For you and the rodent, nada. First-timers get a drink on the house. Bulfinche's tradition. Furball's a good friend of the boss, so he gets a discount." I told Marty the amount and he paid up, plus a nice tip. I liked him already.

"So explain the bit about the mouse being your bodyguard against pink elephants," I said. If Coyote was involved, this was going to be good.

"Sure. I'm here in New York from Cleveland for an accountants' convention. Yesterday I went out drinking with some buddies from college that I hooked up with. I decided to head back to the hotel to catch some z's. It was early, but we'd been drinking since noon. I got lost and ended up at the Lincoln Tunnel. There was a crowd around and I was a little drunk." And the Empire State is a little building. "I tried to cross the street, but tripped over something and fell on my face. When I got up, I was facing a herd of pink elephants. For some reason there was no traffic, so I ran down the middle of the street. The damn elephants followed me for two blocks. I couldn't get back on the sidewalks because of the crowds. When I turned the corner they followed me all the way up to 32nd Street. I ducked into Penn Station and they stopped following me. I don't think they could fit on the escalator."

"Poor pachyderms. Not being able to get into Penn Station must make it hard for them to commute to work," I said, trying not to laugh.

"I guess. Anyway, I took the subway and got off a few stops away, but I knew they were still following me. I didn't dare go back to my hotel," said Marty.

"That's the first place they'd look," I said.

"That's what I was thinking, too. So I've been wandering around Manhattan, scared spitless that the elephants would find me. Luckily, I located an open liquor store and bought a bottle of bourbon to keep me company. I found a comfy park bench with a nice newspaper and spent the night there. This morning I ran out of bourbon, but I ran into my friend the talking dog. He helped me out."

"Did he?" I asked skeptically.

"It is my nature, you know," said Coyote, looking up and feigning innocence. If a canine could look shifty, it was Coyote.

"What did he do for you?" I asked.

"I told him my problem with the elephants, and he was wonderful. The mouse was his idea," said Marty.

"I bet it was. How much did he charge you for it?" I asked.

"Only two hundred dollars," Marty said.

"I hated to part with it," said Coyote, "but Marty's plight moved me. I even sold it at a discount. I practically gave it away."

"It only took him five minutes to go home and get it," said Marty.

In a whisper, Coyote confided in me, "Actually, that's how long it took me to lift one from a pet shop around the corner."

"What, you didn't hunt one down yourself?" I whispered back.

"Too much effort. And before you go squealing to Paddy, I left a few bucks for the rodent," said Coyote. The boss frowns on ripping off innocent bystanders. Guilty ones are fair game.

"And how does this mouse act as your bodyguard?" I asked Marty.

"Simple. I knew the elephants weren't afraid of me, so I figured all was lost. That's when the doggie reminded me that elephants were afraid of mice. So if the elephants come after me again, I'll just send Squeaker here out after them. Isn't that right, little buddy?" Marty asked the mouse, picking it up again. Squeaker tried to run away, but couldn't break Marty's grip.

"Brilliant," I said.

"Thank you," said Coyote, overly pleased with himself.

Marty seemed delighted by the turn of events. With enough booze in the blood, I guess anything can make sense.

"Excuse me, where's the restroom? I gotta see a man about a dog. No offense," added Marty, looking at Coyote.

"None taken," replied Coyote.

I pointed Marty toward the bathroom, and he stumbled away.

"I gotta admit, Coyote, you've outdone yourself this time," I said.

"Yes, I have," said Coyote. "I love being me."

There's one thing I've learned about Coyote in the time I've known him. He can be a nasty SOB, literally, but not without a good reason.

"So what did the guy do?" I asked. Coyote stopped lapping up whiskey with his tongue, lifted up his head, and smiled.

"Swindled a widow out of her savings, about fifteen grand. Not much, but it was all she had, except a Social Security check every month," said Coyote.

"Let me guess. She's part Indian," I said. Technically, I'm supposed to say Native American, but it always sets Coyote off on a speech about the only truly native Americans having four legs, so I just skipped it.

"One-sixteenth Cherokee," said Coyote.

"Only one-sixteenth and she prayed to you?" I said. Coyote is one of the few deities who still answers prayers personally, provided he likes what's been asked. His favorite kind are the ones that let him even a score.

"Good sense transcends race, Murph. Besides, I don't get all that much notice in the prayer department these days. I gotta pay attention. Beggars can't be overly choosy."

True enough. "So you're getting her money back?"

"Yep. A little at a time. So far, I've gotten two thousand for the mouse alone."

"But he said he paid you two hundred," I said.

"He did. Several times over. First I convinced him he was so drunk he was seeing double, so he paid me four hundred dollars. Then I kept reminding him that he forgot to pay me and he paid again. It's worked five times so far," said Coyote.

"Impressive."

"Thank you."

"So Marty has no idea that the elephants he saw were with the circus?" I said. Whenever the circus comes to New York, for free publicity they stage a parade with all the animals heading through the Lincoln Tunnel and up toward Madison Square Garden, where the circus performs. Madison Square Garden also happens to be right on top of Penn Station. This year the elephants had been colored pink, via harnesses with special lights, for a "mystical creatures" theme. The horses wore unicorn horns, the gorillas were supposed to be Bigfoot, and so on.

"Nope. You haven't heard the best of it," said Coyote.

"What?"

"When Marty walked in here, I stopped at a pay phone and called Roy and Rumbles." Roy G. Biv and Rumbles were clowns in the circus and regulars here at Bulfinche's, at least when they were in town. "They are on their way with a special package."

It took a second to sink in. "No way."

"Way."

"I find one part of that story hard to believe," I said.

"Which part?" asked Coyote.

"You finding a pay phone. And using it. Where do you keep the change?"

"I borrowed Marty's credit card," said Coyote. "I called Ryth's 900 line and told her what I was doing." Ryth is a succubus who used to work here as a waitress after she ran away from Hell to marry an angel. She saved up her tips and opened her own sex phone line business. Her husband Mathew still works here as a dishwasher. "I left the pay phone off the hook. Marty should be looking at a several-thousand-dollar bill. I've been following him for days without his knowing it. Found out all sorts of stuff, some of which should interest his wife, whom he's already cheated on twice since he's been in New York. I took video, which I'm sending her, along with the number of a shark-like divorce lawyer."

"You are really going after this guy," I said.

"I checked him out. He has gotten rich by pulling scams on people who can't afford to lose the money," said Coyote. In his mind, it's okay to swindle some money from the rich, as long as they have more or are downright nasty. "Not just widows, but parents investing money for their kids' college education, couples trying to save for houses. The guy is bad news. He sets up a dummy corporation for them to buy stock in, which soon goes bankrupt, when in fact he really 'invested' the money in his personal account in the Caymans. By the time I'm finished with him, he's going to be penniless."

Seemed reasonable, I guess.

Outside I saw a circus truck pull up and into our parking garage. I walked over to the door to the garage, along with several other patrons who had been listening in on our conversation. Rumbles helped Roy down and then into his wheelchair. Roy became a paraplegic after a high-wire accident at the circus. Roy rolled in while Rumbles got something large and "pink" out of the back of the truck. I doubted very much if either of them had actually asked permission to bring the cargo.

"We'll be ready in a minute," Roy said, his clown face aglow with mischief.

"Murphy, hide the mouse," Coyote said. I ran back behind the bar and slipped the little fella into an empty beer pitcher. Roy wheeled himself over to the bar as Marty was coming out.

"Hello," Marty said.

"Hi," Roy said.

Marty leaned over the bar and waved Coyote and me over as if he was going to tell us a secret.

"That short redhead over there is kind of cute, but she wears way too much makeup," whispered Marty. Roy had his long red hair tied up in a top knot and his clown makeup on. "I'd tell her myself, but I don't want to hurt her feelings."

"I understand," I said, holding my breath so I didn't chuckle.

"Hey, Marty, when you going to pay me for Squeaker there?" asked Coyote.

"I thought I paid you," Marty said, downing the rest of his bourbon.

"No. You said you would when you came back from the bathroom, didn't he, Murph?" said Coyote.

"You did," I confirmed.

"I did? Okay," said Marty, reaching into his wallet and flashing a wad of cash, at least a few thousand dollars. Normally, I would have warned him about flashing that much money, but I didn't. There was no way Coyote was going to let him get mugged while he still had a dollar Coyote hadn't managed to get his paws on. "Here ya go, doggie."

Marty slid two hundred-dollar bills across the bar to Coyote.

"Here ya go," slurred Marty.

"Marty, I think you're seeing double again. There's only a hundred dollars there," said Coyote.

"Are ya sure?" he asked. Turning to me, he said, "How much do you see there?"

"One ten-dollar bill. There's only one zero there," I said. Coyote raised an eyebrow and smiled.

"Really?" he asked. I nodded. "I really am drunk."

By convincing him he was seeing hundreds as tens and that there were half as many there, we managed to get Marty to count out four thousand dollars. With a quick paw movement, Coyote secreted away the money, although I couldn't tell exactly where.

"Murphy, you show a lot of promise," whispered Coyote.

"Thanks," I whispered back.

Marty looked around and noticed his bodyguard was missing.

"Hey, what happened to Squeaker?" he said.

"Didn't you take him in the bathroom with you?" asked Coyote.

"I don't think so. Squeaker!" Marty yelled, running back into the men's room. There was the sound of frantic searching before he came out again. "Oh no! I must have flushed him down the toilet."

"Poor guy," I said. "What a way to go."

Marty started crying. "I killed him. I didn't mean to, but I killed him. I'm a murderer."

"It's okay," I said. "He always said he wanted to be buried at sea. At least he got his wish. Part of him will always be with us, as long as we remember him."

"You're right," said Marty, his tears stopping as suddenly as they as had started. He picked up his glass. "A toast to Squeaker."

"To Squeaker," we said. Marty drained the rest of his glass.

"Doggie, can you get me another bodyguard?" Marty asked. "Please?"

"Sorry, Squeaker was one of a kind," Coyote said.

Marty sniffed sadly. "Yeah, he was, wasn't he? I better get back to the hotel."

"You'll be okay?" I asked.

"Sure. I'm sure the pink elephants have forgotten all about me. Maybe I was just too drunk and imagined the whole thing," said Marty.

"That's the spirit," Coyote said. He wasn't about to let Marty go far.

"Bye, everyone," Marty said. "Thanks for everything."

We wished him well. As he walked out the front door of the bar, everyone in the place rushed over to the window. Roy was even recording video. Marty turned toward the parking garage. We all ran to the door that led into the garage for a better view. As Marty crossed in front of the entrance, a trumpeting noise burst into the afternoon air. Marty turned slowly until he was facing a several-thousand-pound pachyderm lit up with rose-colored lights.

"No! The pink elephants found me! Help me, Squeaker!" Marty yelled, looking up to the heavens in hopes that his tiny bodyguard would drop out of the sky and save him. When that didn't happen, he turned and ran down the street screaming. We watched him until he ran out of sight. Poor Marty looked as if he wouldn't stop until he got back to Cleveland.

Everybody Wins

Lisa Mannetti

ANXIOUS? DEPRESSED?
THINKING OF SUICIDE?
Now, there's help. Our 24-hour line connects you ONE ON ONE
With a New York State Certified Suicide Counselor

That was as far as Sally Grimshaw read. She punched in the phone number.

"We're here for you," a young woman on the other end said. Sally began explaining, talking faster and faster. Her black moods, her low self-esteem (and what good did it do to *know* it was low self-esteem? As if knowing could make you feel less like shit).

"I want to die," Sally finished.

"Mr. Vinny can see you in twenty minutes—"

"See me?"

"Certainly." The woman rattled out an address in the West Eighties. "Can you get here?"

"Yes. Thank you. God bless you, yes—"

"Don't worry about your hair, your clothes—don't worry about a thing. Just get in a cab and come right now."

Sally hung up and rushed into her old trench coat, throwing it on over a flannel nightgown. She snagged an oversized worn black leather pocketbook from the hook inside the closet door.

Five minutes later she walked into a cold gray day and wishy-washy December flurries. But she had hope, she told herself. Now there was hope.

*　　*　　*

212

"I'm forty-seven and I've never even had a date." Sally snuffled into a white Kleenex tissue. "I hate my job. I think they're going to fire me because I call in sick a lot. I can't help it." She twisted the soft paper to shreds, as if it might prevent her from breaking into hysterical sobs. "Four years ago at my high school reunion, not one person remembered me . . ."

Mr. Vinny ("No last names here, please") held up a pudgy hand. "It's a tough old world, that's God's truth, Sal." Gold pinkie ring gleaming, he was paging through the three or four sheets of paper that were Sally's file.

Mr. Vinny's office was painted dark salmon. A huge aquarium built into the wall behind his antique desk added turquoise sparkle. He closed the folder and walked toward her.

"So, Sally, how were ya gonna do it? Huh?" Mr. Vinny sat on the edge of his desk, one loafer dangling. "Pills, a gun, a dive out the window, what?"

"Pills, I guess—"

"Shit, you take pills, maybe you'll get the job done. More likely you'll wake up one morning in Bellevue, and you'll be lucky if you don't end up a vegetable in a wheelchair." He got up and paced a step or two, hands clasped behind his back. "Nope, it's not efficient." He stared at her. "I don't like inefficiency."

Sally wasn't sure what he meant.

"Ya know, nobody can tell you when it's time to check out—I mean, look at you." He suddenly whirled around and snatched her file, flapping it in her face. "Overweight, nobody in your life—not even a cat. Your life is a shitpile, and nobody knows it better than you. So whaddya say? Have you had enough, or what?"

"I thought—" She stopped. Confusion mounted inside her. She touched her thin brown hair and knew she looked bad. "I hate all of it," she whispered.

"Right. That's my point. But ya' know, it's not easy to kill yourself. I could show you a dozen files about how tough it is."

"Yes," she said. She had botched everything else—killing herself would be no different. She felt the hot flash of embarrassment and knew her face had turned the ugly purple-scarlet of a wine birthmark.

"Guy holds a gun to his head," he mimed, "but who knows? Maybe he chickens out at the last second. Anyway, whammo-slammo. 'Cept he don't die, he just ends up with a dent in his right temple and pissing his pajama bottoms because his fuckin' catheter fell out, only he don't know it, 'cause there's no feeling from his neck down. Hoo-boy, and he thought he was depressed *before*." Mr. Vinny smiled, his face broadening to a double chin.

This wasn't a place that coddled or pampered; they were going to make her realize what a terrible decision suicide was. "I guess it's a bad idea."

"No, it's a great idea! But amateurs . . . unless you got like Jack Kevorkian on the spot, there's no guarantees. You get amateurs involved, it's not efficient. It's bad business."

"Oh," she said. Confused, she clutched her purse a little tighter.

"So what do you say, Sal? Should I pencil you in on my dance card or are you gonna stay miserable?"

"In? You mean like a program?"

He was rustling papers. "I got a guy here needs to be taken out, Sally, and you could—"

"Taken out? I—I . . . What?"

"The bastard's been beatin' the shit out of his wife, the kids. He's lappin' up the booze. He's got millions, and he's still as stingy as a whore's alarm clock. But his wife—she's a woman who understands good business, so she came to us for help. And what I want to know is, are you willing to kill him at the same time you kill yourself?"

"But—"

"We guarantee you go—no messy half-assed attempts. The lady gets her hit. Everybody wins." He paused. "Sal?"

"You're the Mafia, aren't you?" she said.

He leaned forward, his bulky arms supporting his weight, hands resting on the arms of her club chair, his heavy chin an inch from hers.

"There *is* no more Mafia." He backed away and she breathed easier.

"Between the last three or four asswipe mayors, what we *used* to call a hit man wouldn't touch a contract. Too much risk. There's no loyalty these days. But there are still people who need services. See? This woman needs a service—and you need a service. She paid for it, but for you it's free. And when it's done there'll be one less creep friggin' up the world."

He paused. "Uh, I was referring to the shit-sucking gentleman. Not you, of course. You're goin' to your heavenly reward."

"I don't know. I mean ..." She squirmed in her seat, the thick nightgown wadding into a lump between her fleshy thighs. "How would I ... ?"

"You drive?"

She nodded.

"Smacko." He brought his hands together in a thunderclap. "Head-on collision. We pump you through-and-through with your drug of choice. Guaranteed lights out and you won't feel a thing after the first ten seconds."

"No, I couldn't!" In her mind she saw glass spewing in a slow arc like water droplets from a fountain. She heard the ripping clang of metal, felt the thud of the impact hewing her instantly, saw blood.

"You disappoint me. I thought sure you'd go for the car." He sighed. "You could shoot him. Him and the assholes he hangs with. Have you had target practice? 'Cause we can arrange lessons at the local shooting range—"

"No guns," Sally said.

"Tough shit. Gun it is."

"I think I should go now."

"I don't think so," he said. "Not unless you want to have a messy accident ... because I got ten lonely guys and five world-weary pre-menopausal ladies like yourself that's gonna call me before the close of business today." His smile was too wide, his teeth too prominent.

She understood at once. One of his other cases, a would-be suicide, would do her in. A small scritchy noise—the sound of a cornered ferret—pushed its way past Sally's lips. But so what? Death was what she wanted anyway.

"Wouldn't it be better to have time to make your preparations, write your note, call your mother? Get some closure on the mess of your life?"

"No!" She started to get up, but the menacing look on his face told her to sit. She was in a trap, caught under the bell jar of her own neurosis. She was making herself sick and depressed. Was her life so terrible that she couldn't snap herself out of it?

"'Cause you can walk right out the door, if you want—but you won't know when the knife's gonna go through your cheek in some cold alley, and there'll be no time to get your shit together. And no guarantees you'd die. Nope, no guarantees. Except the guarantee that you'll suffer."

"Mr. Vinny—" Sally said.

"Just Vinny now." He smiled. From his desk drawer he removed a plain manila folder and opened it. "Sign here."

A single sheet of white paper with black print like flea dirt came at her. At the bottom was a line marked with a huge blue X.

Sally signed.

*   *   *

A half-hour later, she left with photos of "John Doe," his thinning gray hair offset by a neatly trimmed, silvery mustache. He was wearing a tuxedo in all the pictures.

She hailed a cab back to her apartment.

The contract was totally illegal, she thought. But she had no doubt Vinny would see she kept her end of the bargain.

The last words he'd said to her were *Happy New Year.*

"Happy New Year," Sally said, sliding the key into the scratched brass of her door lock and letting herself in. "Happy fucking New Year."

Inside the apartment she opened her black purse and took the greasy towel wrapping off the .22 Ruger. Its serial numbers had been filed off.

Tomorrow she was scheduled for practice at the shooting range at 8 A.M. sharp.

Vinny told her if she didn't show, he'd begin to have doubts about her intention to honor the contract. And that would be too bad.

Sally picked up the gun and aimed at an age-browned lampshade in her tiny living room. She pretended it was Vinny's double-chinned face.

"Pow," she said, and then she let the hand holding the gun fall to her side. How could she think there was any help for someone like her, or that anyone cared? How stupid could a person be?

*   *   *

"I can't." Sally wept into the phone in her galley kitchen. "This man's never done a thing to me!"

"So what? He's hurt plenty of people. And that's all you need to know. You'll be doing the world a big favor."

"I went to the shooting range." Her tears were coming harder now. "I just know, Vinny, I just know. I mean, the minute I take the gun out in the restaurant, someone will see me, I won't be able to shoot, I'll wind up in jail!"

"No, you won't, Sally." His voice was ice. "You'll never see the inside of a jail."

"All right," she sighed.

"Good girl. The Moon Over the Tiber Ristorante. Nine P.M. sharp. Saturday night the twenty-third and no later. We don't want to ruin his kids' Christmas Eve. It's a big night with Italians."

The phone came down with a *thunk* in her ear.

It was two days until the end of the world.

*   *   *

She stood outside the restaurant. The crosswinds veered madly around the corners, and she shivered. Garlands of colored Christmas lights sparkled through the fogged glass of the Moon Over the Tiber's red door.

She pushed on the door, and a gust of steamy air scented with garlic assailed her. It was so warm it was almost tropical. Sally shivered again.

A phone call from Vinny this morning had included her final instructions.

She was to take Doe out first, and any baggy gentlemen dining with him were fair game. But no grandmas would get shot because *we're not fuckin' barbarians, capisce?*

Doe, then the linguine-slurpers. And she was told not to worry. Since she refused to use the gun on herself, all she had to do was clamp down on the little yellow capsule she'd been told to keep between her back teeth. A little blood might leak out of her mouth, but hey, that was it. She'd seen the photos of all those crazy cultists from Guyana, right? Cyanide was a sure bet.

It lay like a dollop of dentist's gel in the gutter between her cheek and her teeth. She'd been afraid she'd inadvertently clamp down on it too soon.

If that happened, the Lifespan Treatment Center was going to bring her mother in for bereavement counseling.

Sally stood in the cramped foyer, hesitating. The gun in her purse felt like an anvil.

Have dinner, Vinny told her. *We want to keep our clients happy. But don't pay for it—you don't want anybody seeing the gun before you yank it out. Stand up like you're gonna use the can, then let 'er rip.*

She'd left no note. Nothing in the dog-eared diary she called a journal about being angry or feeling crazy or having a gun. There would be no clues.

A waiter wearing a long dark blue apron over his suit showed her to a table. Twenty feet or so away, John Doe was sucking clams from the shells. There was a white napkin tied bib-style around his neck.

"Wine, Signora?"

"Yes. A bottle of Pinot Grigio."

"Bene." He scribbled onto a small pad.

She ordered fried calamari, a Caesar salad, stuffed cannelloni, and tiramisu for dessert.

Sally fingered the empty wine glass on the table in front of her. The wine would taste damn good, she thought. Then she suddenly realized the capsule was in her mouth. How could she eat or drink anything with the capsule in her mouth?

She waggled it out and placed it gently in the under the rim of her bread plate. She would shovel it back in right after the tiramisu, just before the check, just before ... Yes, she sighed, that would work out fine.

The waiter brought the wine and uncorked it. "How festive," Sally said, taking a sip and nodding assent.

"Si," the waiter said, fussing over the glasses, rearranging the tableware, the glowing votive lamp.

The waiter hurried off again.

The condemned woman ate heartily. At least it was a great restaurant. The calamari had been delicious.

Sally was into her second forkful of Caesar salad when she realized the waiter had taken away the bread plate.

The capsule was nowhere on the table.

Panic seized her, and she shifted the short white vase with the single red carnation, the silverware, skimming her finger around the underside of her salad plate. She even lifted the tablecloth and peered at the floor.

It was gone.

It must have disappeared when the waiter cleared the appetizer and dipping oil. Oh, hell, did it matter? The capsule was probably already in a big industrial garbage bag, invisible in a soggy mess of half-eaten cream tortes, tossed lemon slices, and limp parsley.

It wasn't as if she could ask for it back. *Oh, waiter, I'll take the check and my cyanide capsule. I'm afraid of guns, you know.*

Sally stifled a snort, drank some more wine, and ate dripping romaine lettuce, mopping the dressing with the half-eaten slice of crusty bread she'd left perched on the salad dish.

She glanced at John Doe. He was with three other men. They were eating provolone and fruit.

Everybody wins. It was so much like her own dreary, wrecked life.

Everybody else wins, she thought, *but not me.*

And she was tired of it all, tired of being the loser, watching everyone else get what they want. Was she tired enough to do anything about it?

She ate the tiramisu but her appetite was gone, and the food was no more than dust and the steely taste of gunmetal in her mouth.

And Mr. Doe became everything she hated about herself. If he was as disgusting as Vinny claimed—disgusting enough for Doe's wife to want to have him killed—then who was Sally to argue?

She pulled the gun out of her purse as she stood and aimed it at Mr. Doe's face. His startled expression disappeared a moment after she pulled the trigger. His dinner companions never had a chance to react as she easily dispatched them one after the other.

She was a natural at this.

The handful of restaurant patrons had fled, leaving Sally alone with her four victims. Killing them had been shockingly liberating, and she realized she finally had a talent for something in her wretched life. She smiled as she wondered whether or not she could get away with this.

She planned to try. It was incredibly fortunate the cyanide pill had been lost. Perhaps more than fortune. Perhaps fate.

She turned to leave, to begin a new life.

From out of the shadows her waiter approached, his gun drawn. She could tell he'd been crying.

"I'm sorry, miss," he said. "I have to. I signed a contract."

He pulled the trigger.

Edna's Soul Kitchen

Elizabeth Crowens

Edna Meeks drew in deep a breath. "I love the smell of Bed-Stuy in the morning!" she exclaimed. The sun bounced off the cracked pavement, with the searing scent of summer smog and grime. The cameraman panned over to focus on Edna's Soul Kitchen, then over to a table packed with a dozen trays of delectable samples of her catering.

Edna hid her nervousness while she tiptoed off to the side. Fidgeting with her compact, she whipped out a Victorian-era perfume bottle that dangled on a tarnished brass chain around her neck. Then she dabbed the precious gravy-like concoction inside into the aged hollows of her cheekbones, blending it in before anyone noticed, and tucked it back inside her well-worn vintage dress.

Arthur Kildare, the NY1 news reporter, spoke into one of Edna's fried chicken drumsticks, mistaking it for his microphone. He laughed, switched hands, winked at the camera, and said, "Congratulations for being awarded a city contract to feed homebound senior citizens in Brooklyn. How long have you been here?"

"Soon it'll be my fifty-year anniversary, and I'm still going strong," Edna boasted while onlooker, Mr. Chan, who owned the Chinese takeout across the street, gave her an envious look. "Took over my daddy's business that'd been here before that."

The cameraman gestured the *cut sign* in front of his throat.

Edna continued. "You know Junior's restaurant was featured on *Seinfeld.* So was that Soup Guy. Hey, if anyone out there wants good old-fashioned soul food, you know where to find me."

"Well, Edna, judging from what I've tasted, you've got some lucky people out there about to get some real downhome cooking. For NY1, I'm Arthur Kildare."

*　　*　　*

The reporter stuffed the rest of his fresh buttered biscuit into his mouth, and his cheeks puffed out like a chipmunk. With more effort than expected, he choked it down and jogged off with the cameraman toward his van parked on the corner of Nostrand and Lafayette Avenues.

A *Brooklyn Eagle* photographer ran up. "Ma'am, please . . . one quick shot."

Mr. Chan barged in, took one look at her fried chicken, and sniffed with disgust. "On the news, too? So Edna, you think you're a big shot now."

"Go check on your Kung Pao whatchamacallit, *Genghis Kahn*," Edna said, shoving him aside. "Or tell General Tso that he's lost the war. By the way, that MSG you put in your food will give you age spots. The photographer wants a picture of me, not your ugly face. You're just jealous because I got the city contract and you didn't. Now scat!"

Edna's bobby-pinned, blue-tinted gray curls were corralled into a ragged, spiderweb hairnet, making her appear like a middle school lunch lady, but she put her hand on her hip and, with a great big grin, she mugged for the camera like a sexy pin-up girl.

"You said that your soul food is the secret to your longevity. Isn't it packed with salt or sugar, grease and lots of cholesterol?" the photographer asked, taking a bite into her honey-dipped fried chicken. For a quick moment he had a look of distress, but finally gave a hard swallow.

"Hasn't killed me yet. My daddy lived to be one hundred and four." Did Gumbo put out the right stuff? *How come the reporter and photographer had so much trouble swallowing?*

"Bless his heart," he replied and kissed her on the forehead before leaving.

And I've managed to stick around even longer, Edna said to herself as she anxiously took her compact out of her apron pocket, along with her tarnished heirloom locket containing a fading tintype photo of her when she was child standing alongside her father. She took one hard, woeful look in the mirror. *"But I need something stronger."*

*   *   *

The next day, her kitchen assistant plopped a copy of the *Daily News* on her countertop.

"So what's in the news, Gumbo?" she asked. "They've been promising to print an article on me for a while now."

"Ma'am, I don't know why you keep calling me Gumbo. My name's Jason, and you know that."

"I like calling you Gumbo," Edna replied, patting him on the back. "Suits you better."

He rolled his eyes, resigned that as long as Edna was his boss, she'd call him whatever she wanted.

"Yo, Edna. Check this out."

Edna read it out loud. "'Mysterious deaths of eight Brooklyn seniors. Four in Bensonhurst and four in Brighton Beach died from what authorities think are food-related illnesses.' Those neighborhoods are on your delivery route."

"You know how silly some old-timers get," Edna explained. "Often they keep food for years and forget all about it. Probably gobbled down expired stuff way past its shelf life."

*   *   *

The following morning started out with a *boom, boom, boom!* The front glass doors to Edna's catering establishment almost shattered as two fists pounded on them and a strong voice demanded entry. Edna rushed up front from the back kitchen. She fumbled for her keys and opened the front door.

"Is something the matter?" Edna asked as she let the two officials inside and relocked the door behind them. Her rival, nosey Mr. Chan, the Chinese restaurateur from across Bedford Avenue, stepped outside his restaurant to light a cigarette and have a closer look.

"Good morning, ma'am," said the taller one. "Sorry to disturb you, but we're representatives from the New York City Health Department. Food poisoning is going around. Many of those who've fallen ill are also recipients from your senior meals project. This could just be coincidental, but we'd like to rule out that the contamination could've come from here. Do you mind if we have a look?"

Edna was so nervous that she pulled out a sponge and wiped up every little crumb and spill on the countertop. "I'm a busy lady," she said, "but I guess I don't have a choice."

The two health inspectors snooped around, took notes and snapshots, and asked her permission to take random samples. She tried to remain calm, but fear caused the fine hairs all over her neck to stand on end.

"Officers, I've always been one of those chefs that samples my goods as I go along, and I've never gotten ill," Edna explained.

"What about that guy in the back?" the shorter one asked.

"Gumbo? You don't suppose that my boy is trying to kill off anyone with the Curse of the Voodoo Stew, do you?"

The two men struggled to hold back their laughter.

One of the inspectors handed her his card. "Call me if you catch wind of anything. Meanwhile, we'll send these samples off to the lab."

"Good day, ma'am," the men said in unison and headed out.

"I plan on keeping my Grade-A sticker," she shouted, as they got into their car.

"Gumbo, can you help load those meals into the truck?" she called out.

"Aye-aye, Captain!" he said, giving Edna a salute.

"What do you think of our driver?"

Gumbo reached over for a stack of cellophane-wrapped disposable trays containing the seniors' meals. "Def? Guess he's all right. Why?"

Edna growled. "He and I . . . guess we have a love-hate relationship. Sometimes I get the impression that he thinks he's the boss instead of the other way around."

"How so?"

"Always telling me that my cooking needs a bit more heart and soul. What the hell is that supposed to mean? Well anyway, I don't want to catch you eating any of my stuff."

"Not even an itty bitty taste?" Gumbo asked. "It always smells *soooo* good."

"I pay you plenty. Besides, we need to keep everything separate—the meals for the seniors from the regular catering business. Uh—cheaper ingredients in the senior deliveries. It's a matter of economics. Look, for an extra fifty do you mind tidying up near the garbage cans? Either some stray dog or a homeless person has been makin' a mess back there. You know where the brooms, mops, and buckets are."

Gumbo started gathering the supplies, but a few items seemed to be missing. "Ma'am, do you have any idea where your minivac disappeared? Your drinking straws, too."

Edna shook her head and tried to hide the look of guilt on her face.

"Gumbo, you're smart. Don't know what straws have to do with clean-up duty, but you'll figure a way around it if my minivac doesn't turn up. Improvise. I don't want rats."

"Sure thing, ma'am, but isn't that what Po' Boy is for?"

As he opened the back door, an orange-striped tomcat sauntered in. He bore a resemblance to Morris the cat from the famous TV commercials. Edna bent over and picked him up, giving him a hug.

"Did those health inspectors trouble you earlier?" Edna asked.

"Oh, was that who those guys were? No, just flashed their badges at me and left me alone. I was busy, so I just ignored them. Why?"

"Hmmm, surprised they didn't say a word about the cat causing some kind of health code violation," Edna said.

The front doors opened again. This time it was Mr. Chan looking upset, but his scowl softened to a smile when he reached over to pet the cat.

"Okay, *Charlie Chan*, why the hell were you spying on me?" Edna demanded.

"Health inspectors went over to my place before yours. You didn't tell them I was slaughtering cats?"

Edna sneered. "Isn't that what you all do in your back kitchens?"

"There are plenty of customers to go around. Stop smearing my reputation. I'll show you receipts from my wholesale grocers if that'll make you stop. Or maybe I should borrow him," he said, picking up the tabby. "If I return him in one week that means I didn't turn him into Moo Goo Gai Pan."

Edna grabbed Po' Boy out of his arms and hollered, "Get the hell out of my kitchen!"

Mr. Chan left with a slam of the door. Edna patted the beads of sweat from her wrinkled neck with her thinning handkerchief. Once again she fished out the trusty vial she hid inside her dress, dabbed some of its contents on her face, and tucked it away.

With a sigh of relief, she turned her attention to her furry friend. "Gotcha chicken livers today, sweetie," she said as she went over to her cutting board to retrieve the treats. "Yum, yum. Tastes a lot better than the canned stuff, right?"

Edna coaxed the feline to follow her out back. Gumbo went over to the trays of her famous red velvet cake for the senior meals project. Earlier they had been set out to cool, but the driver was waiting and he needed to load up the truck. Upon closer inspection he noticed an oozing red liquid looking like blood.

"Edna, did you put too much coloring in these today?" he shouted. "Edna?"

He shrugged. "Guess the old lady has been working me too hard. There's been so much more to do around here since we took on that extra gig."

*　*　*

After Edna's television interview aired, people took the train all the way from the Bronx to sample her culinary treats. When Gumbo arrived that morning, he held up a copy of the *New York Post*.

"Did they print my review?" Edna asked.

He shook his head. "No, but listen to this. 'Arthur Kildare, 52, well-known reporter for NY1 television, was found dead in his home near the Great Kills section of Staten Island. So far, the coroner's findings are inconclusive. However, rumors that the cause of death might be an unidentified blood disorder or food poisoning are circulating. Oddly enough, slivers of chicken bone were found lodged in his throat. Recently, Kildare did a news story for a local caterer . . .'"

For a second she was worried again that Gumbo put out the wrong trays during her interview. Best not to bring it up. Nothing could be done now, but Edna was quick on the draw to come up with a brilliant excuse.

"Why on earth do they call an upscale neighborhood Great Kills?" Edna asked, cutting in and deflecting the conversation. "Sounds like a slaughterhouse. Wait a minute; it says he was visiting a catering company. Probably my competition over by the Kingston Throw-up subway stop."

Gumbo doubled over laughing. "Edna, I think you mean Kingston-Throop."

"Naw, I like to call it Kingston Throw-up, because that's what I think of Winnie Lester's cookin'. If anyone's dyin' of food poisoning in Brooklyn you can bet it came from her neck of the woods."

* * *

The following day, Edna was thrilled to find a write-up in the Food Section of the *Daily News*.

"Serve Up Some Soul. Don't feel like cooking? Let Edna do it for you. Edna Meeks brings Southern flavors to Bedford Stuyvesant. When asked if she planned to retire, Edna replied, 'I'll cook till the day I die. Nothing can keep me out of the kitchen.'"

"That's more like it," she said with a sense of satisfaction. She continued reading as Mr. Chan passed by her front window. She showed off the newspaper and laughed.

Once he and Gumbo were out of sight, Edna rushed into the restroom and stared with trepidation into the mirror.

"I'm aging way too fast."

She panicked as she plucked out that antique glass vial and began her ritual by pouring a reddish, viscous substance into her hands. Then she spread it all over her face like a beauty mask.

"Damn it! I should never have tried to commit that recipe to memory," Edna muttered to herself in contempt. "If I weren't so paranoid that Gumbo would find out what I've been doing and report me to the police, I wouldn't have tossed it out. Heart and soul? Why do I need more heart and soul? My body and beauty might be defying time, but my memory is *still* living in the nineteenth century."

Counting on her decrepit, mummy-like fingers from one to one hundred, she swallowed the rest of the goo, wincing as it oozed down her skinny little throat.

"At least this crap doesn't taste like embalming fluid," Edna said to herself.

Moments later, this mysterious substance sucked right into her pores and vanished. She licked her lips, tightened her apron strings, and left to check on the cat.

*   *   *

Weeks went by and business was better than ever, but Gumbo was even more disturbed about those mysterious deaths happening all over Brooklyn. That *Brooklyn Eagle* photographer, who had come to Edna's the same day as Kildare, also died.

When Edna's driver arrived, she made an announcement. "Today I'm going to tag along with Def on one of those drive-bys."

"You mean one of those ride-alongs," Gumbo laughed. "A drive-by is a shooting."

"Heavens, not one of those!" Edna replied, embarrassed. "Yeah, I want to keep an eye on Def. Something not quite right about that boy."

"Maybe I should go instead," Gumbo said. "All sorts of unexpected customers have come in since you became famous. Did you ever hear back from those food inspectors?"

"No, you're stayin' behind. Def and I are a team . . . on a mission, but often I feel like we're undermining each other."

"Whatever," Gumbo said, raising his eyebrows.

A white van pulled up to the curbside. Edna stood outside of the front seat passenger door expecting Def to act like a gentleman and open it.

"Back seat, ma'am," Def said in a low baritone.

"Don't you start giving me orders!"

"No room up front."

Curious, Edna pressed her nose against the tinted window glass and stretched every bone and muscle of her age-shrunken body to look inside. "What the—? Looks like you got a stash of chitlins and pigs' knuckles inside a bunch of giant pickling jars. You better not be taking stuff from my kitchen when my back is turned."

Def grunted. He escorted Edna over to the truck's rear, and with a hefty tug he slid its side panel open. With care she put her unsteady foot on the running board and climbed in. A steel mesh barrier separated her from her driver, also making it difficult to see anything he concealed up front. She moved over a few loose prepackaged meals that didn't fit on any of the racks in the back of the van, reached for her seat belt, and tried to get comfortable.

When they arrived in Bensonhurst, Edna made two dozen deliveries. Edna was thrilled to assist the elderly men and women, but they didn't reciprocate her enthusiasm, especially the ones who wanted Italian food instead of good old Southern cooking. Many gave her mean stares. Some doors were shut in her face. After that they headed over to the Russian section in Brighton Beach.

The ringtone on Def's smartphone started to play the first few bars from "Heart and Soul," that silly tune that seemed to be everyone's first song they'd learn when they played piano.

"Ah, that means there's one more . . . for Mr. Boris."

"Oh, yes, I almost forgot." Edna smiled, winked, and unfastened her seat belt. She joined Def to deliver that final meal.

When the two of them returned to her catering company, Edna handed Gumbo extra cash, and he agreed to clean up out back. While she prepped the next day's menu, he inspected the stew that she left simmering.

"That smells more like beef stroganoff. My mind must be playing tricks on me."

"You better not be tasting that stew!" Edna yelled from the back. "If you're that hungry, go across the street and pick up some pupu platter from Mr. Chan!"

"Haven't seen him around for a few weeks," Gumbo replied. "His wife's been minding the place."

"Good riddance," Edna replied. "Such a damned busybody."

Gumbo shrugged his shoulders, washed his hands, hung up his apron, and left.

* * *

Disturbing headlines kept showing up in the local papers. A memorial was held for that newscaster. Mr. Chan was nowhere to be seen, but cops stopped by twice. Edna got so rattled on their second visit that she had to change her incontinence pad. The health inspectors also made a surprise appearance. Their tests were indeterminate, but for now she was off the hook. At the end of each day, Edna continued to receive a poor reception from her senior meal recipients but paid it no mind.

A few days later, Edna and Def pulled up to Sophie Rostov's

place in Brighton Beach.

"I'm making the delivery this time," Edna insisted and hopped out of the van. "You're screwing everything up."

"No, Edna. You're the one who can't get your own recipes right," Def said.

"You're supposed to be my partner in crime. We're supposed to be working together, not fighting against each other. My anti-aging serum—it's not working," she replied, taking one last look in her compact mirror. She shivered at the thought of deteriorating further.

"Yeah, yeah, yeah," Def blabbered to himself as he rummaged through the van for Sophie's meal. "She's always right. I'm always wrong. She'll eat those words soon enough."

Edna rang the outside bell to the building. No one answered. She rang it again and waited. No response. A mom with a whining toddler let her inside. Mrs. Rostov's apartment was at the end of a long, dark hallway. A multicolor palette of paint peeled off the walls. A bare bulb overhead light was burned out. Mrs. Rostov's doorbell outside was painted over so many times that it no longer worked. With hesitation she reached for the knob, and the front door automatically creaked open.

"Mrs. Rostov, are you there?" Edna called out with her squeaky voice.

No response.

Edna cautiously stepped further into the woman's home. Curtains were drawn, with rays of blaring sunlight occasionally peeping through breaks in their heavy damask fabric. She waded past tall stacks of old, dusty newspapers and magazines. There was an unpleasant sour smell as soon as she opened the bathroom door, but no one was in there. Edna could barely distinguish the toilet and the bathtub from the dozens of stacked boxes squeezed into that tiny slot, but on the wall was a mirror, and she couldn't resist examining her decaying face.

"Oh, God," she said in dismay. Her cocoa-colored complexion had become almost translucent, looking more like a paper-thin parchment dug up from an ancient tomb. Hideous purplish-blue veins poked through its delicate surface. She pulled out her locket with her father's photograph and tried with all her might to refrain from crying.

"Daddy . . . the immortality potion . . . it's almost perfected. I only wish we could've enjoyed it together."

She wiped away her tears and snapped to her senses with sinister determination.

"Mrs. Rostov?"

Edna poked her nose into the bedroom. Empty, except for more piles of floor-to-ceiling yellowed newspapers, even on the bed. She was relieved that she hadn't found her buried alive in piles of unwashed laundry. Then Edna headed for the kitchen, which had two entrances both closed off by doors. She tried the first door, the one located off the hallway, but that one had been permanently sealed shut from decades of paint filling in the cracks. When she tried the other one off the dining area the doorknob rotated back and forth, but as Edna tried to push in the door she met with resistance.

"Sophie, what's going on?" she called out with concern, when the door wouldn't budge.

"Go away!" Mrs. Rostov cried.

"It's Edna Meeks, the owner of Edna's Soul Kitchen. We've been delivering your daily meals. Is everything all right? Can I enter?"

"I thought I was doing myself a favor when I signed up for food delivery. My daughter called me all the time, worried that I'd accidentally kill myself if I continued using my gas stove. She thought I'd either knock into one of the knobs and gas myself to death or blow the whole building up. But every one of my friends has dropped dead after you've come and visited them."

Edna pushed the door open. Before she had time to utter another word, Mrs. Rostov took a knife from her silverware drawer and pointed it at Edna. Edna put the woman's meal on the countertop. She pulled out a vial of poison green liquid from her pocket and poured it into her meatloaf.

"My driver will get impatient if we keep him waiting," Edna said.

The woman was mortified. "Stay away!" she cried out in panic, still pointing her knife it at Edna.

Edna took a fork from the silverware drawer, plunged it into the dinner, and held out a bite-sized morsel closer to Mrs. Rostov's quivering lips.

"I'm going to live to be one hundred . . . no . . . more!" Mrs. Rostov shouted in defiance.

A dark hulking shadow appeared, filling the only open doorway. With her free hand, Mrs. Rostov reached for a flashlight. Edna's driver had his dark hoodie drawn up and still hiding most of his ghoulish features, but as he began to partially unzip it, the letters A-N-G-E-L were revealed on his black T-shirt.

"Def, I need some assistance," Edna said, turning in his direction. "If I throw you an extra fifty, do ya mind takin' out the garbage? Filet her first. That'll help."

"Mrs. Rostov," Def said, "I don't know how you managed to ward me off with pepper spray last month, but when you had that bout with pneumonia--"

"I didn't like it over there," Mrs. Rostov complained, cutting him off. "Meals in the afterlife taste worse than cat food. When I had a stroke after my husband died, I raised such a fuss that they sent me back to Brooklyn. They were glad to get rid of me."

"You've eaten cat food?" Edna asked. All she could think of was about her own cat, Po' Boy, and how he always preferred kitchen scraps over stinky canned stuff.

"Yeah, Nine Lives. My stupid husband told me that if a cat had nine lives, I could have nine lives, too, if I ate that brand."

The Harbinger of Darkness took out a cordless wet and dry minivac that had been hidden and stuffed inside his loose hoodie. He flipped on the power button and out bellowed a deadly electronic roar.

"You bastard!" Mrs. Rostov shouted with venom in her voice, pointing her knife at the van driver. "I'll be damned if you take me now!"

But her threats were idle ones. Def pointed his portable vacuum cleaner in her direction. With the oddest *whoompf* that couldn't be described by mere words, a filmy duplicate of the victim disengaged from its host, as the infernal machine rapidly sucked her soul inside.

After her vital essence was extracted, Mrs. Rostov collapsed on the floor and was covered with ectoplasmic slime.

"Gumbo wasn't all that farfetched when he suspected a bunch of my straws missing," Edna cynically remarked. She plucked a drinking straw from one of her many deep pockets and slurped it up with gusto. Edna fetched her trusty compact and wiped off the gunk that still stuck to her mouth, but this time she was more worried than usual when she examined her reflection in its mirror.

"The essence of Mrs. Lentini added the perfect Italian accent, and Mr. Boris? Let's say he lent the right zest from the Ukraine, but—"

Once again, Def's ringtone sounded off, playing "Heart and Soul."

"What's the matter with your phone?" Edna asked, a bit confused.

"I've got two customers on my roster today. We just took care of the first one," he said, pointing to the remains of Mrs. Rostov on the floor.

"Then where the hell's the second?" Edna asked.

"I warned you that you needed more heart and soul in your secret stew."

"What's that supposed to mean? You're not the boss, I am."

"You're next on the list," he said, pointing his skeletal hand in Edna's direction.

"That's ridiculous! My time can't be running out. Not yet. I've almost perfected my formula," she argued. "I want to live forever!"

Def bent down, clutched Mrs. Rostov's sticky head, and with unfathomable strength snapped it off her corpse. With blood spurting everywhere and showering Edna, he stuffed it into his extra-large hoodie right next to the minivac. Then Def grabbed Edna by the crook of her arm and escorted her back to his van.

"This time you get to sit up front," he said, as Edna wrestled him with every ounce of her strength.

Def opened the front passenger door, threw her down, buckled her seatbelt, and strapped her in with a bit of duct tape for good measure. Edna screeched in terror as she caught a closer glimpse of Def's motley collection of pickling jars on the floor. Behold! There was the gruesome head of her rival, Mr. Chan. No wonder he hadn't been pestering her in the past few weeks!

To her horror, she recognized Mr. Gambino, the neighborhood locksmith. It was rumored that he'd been knocked off by the mob when he disappeared. Next to those monstrosities were several other clear containers filled with an array of sundry organs, preserved eyeballs, and stray fingers, as well as human knuckles and "chitlins" from

Def's *lost souls* kitchen. Def picked up an empty one and stuffed Mrs. Rostov's head inside.

"Do you have any last words, ma'am?"

"Who's gonna run my kitchen?" Edna cried out, flailing and kicking her legs as she was still tethered to the seat. "You're going to have to put up with a damned nasty fight if you want to drag me to hell!"

"That can be arranged," he replied with a gruff laugh.

But instead of using the minivac to add her soul to his collection, he reached out his deathly hand toward her sagging breasts.

Slowly he pierced her soft flesh as if he were stabbing a fork through Jell-O. He continued to penetrate through her chest cavity until he grasped her anxious, beating heart and yanked it out with a swift jerk.

"All your stuff needed was a little bit of *heart and soul.*"

"Heart and Soul." Def's ringtone went off playing that infamous song, and another soul was there for the taking. He held up her heart like a precious ruby, examining his prize that pulsated and continued to beat along with the rhythm of his pernicious melody.

"And no one argues with Death, the Master Chef," he said, having the last wicked, bellowing laugh. "Because I am the boss of Hell's Kitchen!"

Then he opened his bony jaws as wide as a snake and swallowed her still-beating heart whole, as it continued to thump inside him.

The Grim Reaper climbed back into the driver's seat and started up the ignition. The engine sputtered and coughed, looking as if it was also going to die, but it finally turned over. He recklessly rolled over a curb and continued toward the Verrazano Bridge.

"Death and dessert on the highway of life," he laughed, as he and his collection of lost souls barreled down the road. Everyone was on their way to that final destination . . . the one where all the refuse in the Big Apple lies . . . the one where the last rays of sun kiss their last goodbyes . . . of shattered promises and thwarted dreams . . . the ultimate dumping ground of the chewed-up dog toys and broken light bulbs . . . the trash and the trifles . . . expired medications and kitty chow past its shelf life . . . where all the castoffs go that great slaughterhouse in the sky. Gone and buried—now a park-in-disguise, Def headed for the great landfill . . . at *Fresh Kills*, Staten Island.

Eyes Left

Jack Ketchum and Edward Lee

Happy Hour at the World Cafe. 69th and Columbus.

At 4:30 after work that was where we came. Neal from his studio and John from behind his camera over at ABC and yours truly from She Who Must Be Fed—otherwise known as Microsoft Word. Pretty much every day. There were other regulars who'd come and go, but we three formed the core of it. We'd stand there talking at the bar, drinking and munching trail mix with Neal feeding the juke a couple dollars now and then to keep the blues and country flowing and so that John wouldn't start in with his goddamn Frank Sinatra.

You had to be careful with John and Sinatra. He'd play a whole CD and sooner or later he'd be singing along.

And we watched the ladies, of course.

Today was Neal's day On Point.

"Eyes left," he'd say.

That was what we did. Stake our claim on the liquor industry, tell jokes and bitch about life in general and listen to sweet blues and watch the women walk by along the hot summer sidewalk. We'd been doing it for years.

The only difference now was that some of the women were dead.

The women. They're the first, best reason to love summer in New York City. The sidewalk outside the big plate-glass window on Columbus brought along an endless procession of them—almost as though they were walking by just for us, just for the appreciation radiating out from inside. Sure, I know what you're thinking. A bunch of horny sexist pigs. Reducing women to the sum of their sexual parts. But it's not like that at all. At least not for me. For me there's a kind of reverence to it. All that beauty and diversity. All those blessings to our little lonesome planet walking around in shorts and tanks and halters. I'm serious.

You ask me, the best that fifty-one percent of the human species has to offer can be found right here in the City. L.A. just can't hold a candle to it. Neither can Boston or San Francisco. You don't believe me? Come over to the World Cafe sometime and sip your Bud and keep your eyes on that window.

Of course it's a little different now.

You can mostly tell the dead by the grayish look to the skin or of course if they've been mutilated in some way but from the distance of bar to sidewalk not by much else. You might notice that the hair had little sheen maybe. That the sun didn't catch it right. But you had to get up close to see the clouded eyes or the blue fingernails and you didn't usually want to get that close. If you did, that was what your sidearm was for. And none of us had shot one in a long time, male or female, old or young, and didn't care to.

The dead walk briskly in Manhattan, just like everybody else. Thing is, they have no place to go. The law protects them now, at least to some extent, but they're not allowed to work or have careers. They get food stamps, welfare, public housing. I pretty much always felt sorry for them. Sure, a small percentage get out of line now and then, would rape somebody, mug somebody, rob a liquor store. But no more than the living.

Most of the bum rap they got came from the cannibalism thing. That's what the crazy ones would do—kill regular folks and eat them. There was a lot of hysteria over that at first. That's when the mayor revoked the Sullivan Law and passed the concealed-carry ordinance. But once the Army retrieval squads rounded up the crazy ones you didn't hear much about cannibalism anymore. Hardly ever.

Fact is, the dead don't seem to fuck up any more than the living. It's a simple, primitive prejudice against a minority, nothing more. Sure, you wanted to be careful, just like you wanted to be careful of a lot of things and people in New York. But I'd stopped carrying my own gun a long time ago. A lot of us did.

Still, it was a kind of like a game with us, a bar contest.

Seeing who could pick out the dead ones.

"Eyes left."

This one sure wasn't dead. Chestnut hair tied back long and gleaming, tan shoulders glowing in the sun. Curve City too, if you know what I mean. The silky dandelion-print dress seemed spun on-to her. Low cut and no bra.

"Jesus," said John, "are those nipples or fuckin' spark plugs?"

John could be crude, but he had a point, so to speak. Her nipples were extremely elongated and hard, as if they wanted to spike through the fabric.

"If they're spark plugs," Neal said, "maybe they need to be re-gapped. Know a good mechanic?"

"Notice that nipples are back this year?" I said. "For a while you hardly ever saw them."

John nodded solemnly. "It's a good thing. It's a godsend."

Then she was gone and two pretty smiling Goths walked by dressed in black, chrome nubs glittering in their vampire-red lips. *It's eighty degrees out there and they're wearing black.* They were holding hands.

"You gotta love this town," I said, smiling.

We turned back to our drinks and talked about Tom Waits on the juke. Neal had seen him fall off his piano stool in Nashville. Whether it was part of the act was still open to question.

"Eyes left."

John let out a low whistle. "Can you say *chest fruit?*"

"No, but I can say mammiferous," I said. "Can you?"

"What she needs," said Neal, "is an exemplary and thorough breast examination, care of Dr. Neal, to be promptly followed by regular pants-sausage injections on a daily basis."

"What if she's a vegetarian?" said John.

"Then I've got a plantain that'll change her life."

"You guys are terrible," I said.

"Listen to him," John said. "We're terrible and *he's* standing there cross-legged."

Then it was back to the drinks and talk again. Cigarettes had gone up nearly fifty cents. Rent control was once more being threat-ened in the legislature. ABC grips were considering a walkout. The usual New York bullshit.

Then "*Eyes left*" again.

"Call it," John said. "Dead or alive."

"Alive," Neal said, but then his squint grew narrower.

I knew she was dead before she was halfway by the window. "Dead," I said. Easy on the eyes at first, sure. But then you caught the autopsy staples showing in the gap between the top of her jeans and the bottom of her peach blouse. She glanced in at us and you could see it in the eyes.

"The winner!" said John. "Anna, get this gentleman another Dewar's on me and another Heiny for myself."

"What am I," Neal said, "chopped liver?"

"And a plate of chopped liver for Dr. Neal of the exemplary breast exams."

These guys. I mean, you can't take them anywhere.

Anna knew us all pretty well by then though and poured refills for everybody. No chopped liver made an appearance. We drank.

"Gustavo told me a story last night," Neal said. "About those apartments over the flower shop. Hey, where the hell were you two guys last night, anyway?"

John shrugged. "I was home doing the Sunday *Times* crossword puzzle and listening to ole Blue Eyes. What, you go out *every* night? I had to work today. Not everybody's an *artiste* and makes his own fuckin' hours. Some of us gotta work in the morning, y'know?"

"I was on the computer," I said. "Online from about ten to midnight. They did another Dead Chat last night."

Neal made a face. "Why do you bother with that shit?"

"He's a voyeur," John said, "of the dead."

"No, I just like hearing what they have to say. And let me tell you, they have some stories. When they start writing novels I'm *really* fucked."

"*Eyes left.*"

We looked. "Hubba-hubba," Neal said.

A real head-turner. Tall and sleek with mile-long legs walking along like a runway model in this sheer off-the-shoulder top and flowing organdy dress. Lots of jewelry and fiery red hair.

The redheads always get to me.

Behind us Anna laughed. "You perverts! She's *dead!*"

She was right. When she turned her head you could see the long unhealed gash along the side of her throat. As if somebody had tried to cut her head off but didn't quite make it.

John groaned.

"So much for hubba-hubba," I said.

Neal ordered a plate of fried calamari and Anna went to place the order with the kitchen. We watched her too. Anna was quite a looker herself but way off bounds. You didn't mess around with your bartender.

"So? Like what?" John said.

"Huh?"

"Those stories you were talking about. These Dead Chats. What's so fuckin' interesting?"

"Okay, take this guy last night. Ninety-two years old, starved to death in his own apartment. Got out of bed one morning, got dressed, wanted to take a leak, but his bedroom door wouldn't open. He starts yelling for his nephew, who lives with him. Nephew's only sixty-four. No answer. So the old guy opens his bedroom window, takes a four-story piss, then goes back to pounding on the door and yelling for his nephew. Who still doesn't answer."

"Where's the nephew?"

"I'm getting to that. So this poor guy's trapped in his bedroom with no phone and no food and nothing but a John Grisham novel to keep him company. Can you imagine that? He's trapped in there for a week with John Grisham. So finally he just lies down on his bed and dies."

"So then he comes back, right?"

"Right. And you know what they say. Sometimes they're stronger than when they were alive. So he pushes at the door and this time it opens. What's been blocking the door is the nephew. He's dead on the floor from a heart attack."

"How come he didn't come back like the old man?"

"No brains."

"Say *what?*"

"See, the nephew had a plate in his head from a war injury. So when he fell down from the heart attack his head slammed into the radiator knob. Pops the plate right out of his skull along with half of what's inside. Rats made short work of whatever was left."

John laughed. "I dunno whether you call that good luck or bad. For the nephew, I mean."

"Got me. Depends on your point of view, I guess. Most of them seem pretty content, though. At least they're walking around."

"Eyes left! Quick! Man, is that one hot dish or what?"

John and I looked. Then gagged.

"Yeah, one hot dish of ground chuck," John said.

"Prick!"

She was roadkill in a sundress, probably pushing three hundred pounds and all of it rot. One eye was gone and so was her lower lip. At least she'd done her hair up nice. Neal was having a good old time, though, laughing at our expense.

"Now that's what I call a wood-killer," John said.

I had to look away. "Jesus, I bet she leaks, leaves a trail of drippings. There oughta be a law against the ones like that."

"The dead aren't toxic, remember?" Neal said. "Nobody knows why, but they're not. So there's no reason there should be a law, you bigot. Come on now. The dead are people *too.*"

He was mocking me. I probably deserved it. I could get a little preachy sometimes on the subject of the dead. There were laws to protect them these days, and I agreed with those laws. A lot of people didn't. But sometimes it got to be a little much even for me, seeing the really maimed or rotten ones like this. I once saw a guy walking down Broadway carrying his guts in front of him in a wicker basket.

Wasn't pretty.

"You were saying something about Gustavo and last night? Something about the flower shop?"

His calamari had arrived in front of him, and Neal was nibbling the batter off a piece of squid to expose the gray-black tentacle. That wasn't pretty either.

"Oh, yeah. Last Saturday he's sitting here in the bar tossing back a few tequilas and notices a couple of squad cars pull up over there. They don't have their lights on or anything, but he just happens to notice them, and while he's talking up some woman beside him he keeps an eye on them. Comes from growing up in Spanish Harlem— you watch the cops. Anyway, they're no sooner out of their cruisers than the old lady who runs the flower shop comes out and she's yammering away and keeps pointing up to the third-floor apartment over the shop."

"That apartment's been empty for years," John said.

"You bet."

"So what happens next?" I said.

"The cops—four uniforms—go up into the apartment and they're in there a while. The old lady's still outside wringing her hands and looking like she's gonna have a heart attack right then and there. So Gustavo says fuck it, leaves his drink on the bar, and walks over and asks the lady what's going on. The lady tells him that she keeps hearing this loud banging sound coming from upstairs. She's spooked. The apartment's wiring is bad and nobody's supposed to be up there. She's too scared to check it out herself, so she calls the cops.

"Finally they come back down, and three of them are carrying kids wrapped in blankets. Little kids. A few minutes later an ambulance arrives. Turns out the kids are a year old, two years old, and about three years old—two boys and the oldest one's a girl. Their parents went dead two days ago, OD'd on heroin, and then came back with brains so fried they were totally retarded, wandering around and jabbering and bumping into walls. But that's where they were living, in the old apartment over the flower shop. Squatters, sneaking in and out at night."

"So they died. And came back . . . ?"

"Five days later. But for those five days . . ."

"Oh, shit. Nobody to take care of the kids. They're lucky they didn't starve to death."

"Right. And the apartment's a total shithouse. Gustavo talked to one of the cops and I guess it was pretty grim. Garbage all over the place, clothes and dirty diapers and human shit all over the floor. The three-year-old told them that they were drinking out of the toilet bowl. Sinks hadn't worked in years."

"What'd they do with the parents?" John said.

"Dead junkies walking? Took 'em straight to the ovens. Can you believe it? Stuff like that happening right across the street?"

"So what was the banging sound?"

"Huh?"

"The banging sound the old lady heard."

"Oh, Jesus, yeah. The three-year-old was whacking cockroaches with a hammer. That's what they ate."

My stomach went sour. John was shaking his head. But it was just another case in point as far as I was concerned. Some people were total fuck-ups, alive or dead.

Even after the roaches-as-baby-food story Neal still had the munchies. He ordered two more sides. Oysters on the half-shell and grilled octopus.

I ordered another drink.

I guess we were all getting pretty tanked. The ass-end of Happy Hour was long gone and it was getting dark. We listened to Jagger singing "Midnight Rambler" on the juke. The bar was filling up. Now that the sun was going down most of the action was coming in. Down at the end, Madeline was sitting with her current squeeze and we heard her laugh at something he said, the same phony laugh she always used on them, a lawyer's laugh, dry as a ten-page brief. Madeline drank zombies. She thought that was pretty funny.

"Be honest," John said. "You ever make it with one?"

"With a dead woman?" I shook my head. "Never. But Burt did. You know Burt, he'll fuck damn near anything."

Neal laughed. "Burt? That psycho's so perpetually horny he'd probably fuck this plate of octopus."

"Better finish it quick then," John said, "case he comes in. Burt say it was any good?"

"Said it was damn good, actually. Wasn't what he expected, her being dead and all. I guess it got pretty lively. Of course he had his Colt under the mattress just in case. He said they're not cold inside the way you'd think. More like room temperature."

"Stands to reason," John said.

"Get one at high noon this time of year, I bet she cooks," said Neal.

"But what about winter? Be like sticking your johnson in a Slurpee."

"It'd be different, that's for sure." He shrugged and sucked down an oyster. Then his eyes bugged and he swallowed fast. *"Eyes left,* gentlemen," he said. "I mean *really* left!"

We looked.

"Christ in a coffeeshop," John said. "*She looks like . . . she looks just like . . .*"

". . . *Daryl Hannah*," I said. "Oh my god."

And for a moment I thought the tall willowy blonde peering in through the window really *was* Daryl Hannah. The resemblance was utterly uncanny. The long wild hair, those thick parted lips, that graceful neck, those big bottomless eyes.

Neal damn near knocked over his Scotch.

"She's looking right at us!" he whispered.

She was.

I was loaded enough to shoot her a smile and raise my glass. Neal and John just gawped at her.

"Know what, fellas? I'm not sure she's looking at *us*," John said. "I think she's looking at *you*, slugger!" He slapped me on the back. Hard. Scotch spilled. Ice tinkled in the glass.

But he was right. It was me she was looking at. Our eyes held for a moment.

And then she was gone.

John slapped me again, easier this time. "Don't take it too hard, old buddy. You know the babes. One minute you're Mr. Chick Magnet, you're fucking Fabio for a second, and then . . ."

"Chopped liver," said Neal.

"That's right, chopped liver. Maybe she caught one of your two gray hairs. Thought you were old enough to be her daddy."

"I *am* old enough to be her daddy."

"Nah," said Neal. "She took one look at our man here and realized he was out of her league. That she's outclassed all the way. Huffed off probably to pout about it."

"No, she didn't," said John. He was looking over my shoulder.

"Huh?"

"She didn't huff off. She's coming in."

I turned, and there were those eyes on me again, directly focused on mine like lasers coming toward me. There was something deliberate and almost predatory about the way she walked. The designer jeans were so tight they looked sewn onto her hips and legs. Long,

long legs. *Daryl Hannah legs.* I get my share I guess, but I knew I didn't deserve this. God was either smiling or laughing at me. I didn't know which.

She stopped directly in front of us, and her gaze took us all in.

"Who's got the balls to buy me a drink?" she said.

"Why does it take balls?" I said. First thing that came to mind. The Scotch speaking.

"Because after a couple I might be more than you can handle. When we go back to my place, that is."

I guess we all came pretty close to losing our drinks through our noses on that one.

Bar-tramp, I thought. Either that or a prostitute. Though I'd never seen a whore who looked as good as she did. But when they came onto you that hard, you knew something was wrong. Ordinarily it was an instant turn-off. Not with her, though. Not with some Daryl Hannah look-alike. With this one it went the *other* way. You just had to play it through. See where it went.

"You sure know how to make an impression, lady," John said.

"Thanks. I'll have a Hurricane. Who's buying?"

I was. I introduced her to John and Neal and told her my name. She shook hands like a man, hard and abrupt.

"And you?" I said.

She laughed. "You care about my name? You guys really give a damn about my *name?* Come on. That's not what you care about."

The smile softened it some, but she was still being an asshole. Haughty, arrogant, maybe buzzing on something stronger than a Hurricane—whatever the hell that was. Maybe even crazy. In a bar you got used to seeing them now and then.

She asked what we did for a living. Another turn-off under most circumstances, asking right off the top that way. But we told her. *Artist, cameraman, writer.* She didn't seem particularly interested or particularly uninterested either. Just seemed to take it in. Normally you tell a woman you're a writer the next question is what do you write. Not with this package. She nodded and drank and pretty soon the first one was gone so I ordered her another.

Her long slim fingers plucked at a piece of Neal's grilled octopus and she swallowed it down. Didn't ask. Just took. *Her privilege.*

John offered her his bar stool. She said she'd stand, thank you. And that was fine with us because leaning on the bar the way she was her breasts were straining one way through the tank-top and her butt the other. In those jeans it was a sight to see. She was beautiful.

I didn't like her one bit. But she was beautiful.

Her blond hair glowed, a luscious fog about her head. She smelled like musk and roses. Her eyes were so damn bright they seemed to blur like neon whenever she moved her head.

Men are from Mars, they say, *and woman are from Venus.* War on the one side, love on the other. Well, sometimes that's simply not the case. Sometimes it's the woman who wants a conquest, sexually speaking. Wants sex the way a man will. Doesn't care to be wined and dined, doesn't want to hold hands in the park and get flowers on Valentine's Day, couldn't care less for kissy-face and all that lovey-dovey bullshit.

She wanted what we wanted. You didn't see it every day. It was intriguing.

"I know what you're thinking," she said to me.

"Huh?"

"I know what you're thinking. You do play the game, don't you? Most of you guys do."

"What game? What am I thinking?"

Her entire face seemed to give off light. "You're thinking, *'Is she or isn't she?'*"

I just looked at her. I didn't know what the hell she was talking about.

"Is she or isn't she *what?*" John slurred. By now he was piss-drunk.

Her gaze scanned us.

"Is she or isn't she dead?"

She reached over for Neal's cocktail fork and *no!* I thought as she buried the fork into the wide-open palm of her left hand, slamming it through like a ball into a baseball glove, and suddenly I could see the tiny pitchfork tines sticking out the other side.

No blood.

She didn't even flinch.

She just kept looking at me. And smiled.

"Fooled you, didn't I. All three of you."

I think we breathed then. I know what we must have looked like, open-mouthed, staring down at her hand while she pulled the fork out again and tossed it on Neal's plate. There were still a couple of oysters there. She held her hand up and turned it, showing us the bloodless punctures.

"Fooled us?" Neal said. "Ma'am, that's an understatement."

What you have to realize is that for us this girl was a fucking bombshell, and I don't just mean in the looks department. If anybody in this freaky city were experts on telling the dead from the living we figured it was us, or at least that we were well into the running. And we didn't have a clue—not with her. She was right. She'd fooled us all completely.

"Your skin?" I said. "Your hair . . . ?"

"Diet supplements. Magnesium, Vitamin E and Potassium mostly. Some of us are learning." She sighed. "Okay, boys, who wants to blow this pit-stop and get on with it?"

"Wait a minute," I said. "If you're dead, how come you're drinking . . . whatever the hell it is you're drinking and—?"

"Eating octopus?" Her eyes narrowed. "You believe everything you hear? What? *We* can't go into bars but *you* can? We don't like a drink now and then? You buy into all those moronic stories about how we can't eat anything but human flesh? Isn't that the same thing as saying all Irish are drunks, all blacks like watermelon? I'd hoped you guys were a little more evolved than that."

I saw her point. She was whitebread just like us, but now that she was dead she was different too; she'd slipped into a new minority group—and one we little understood. So who were we to make judgments about her?

"It's a different society now," I said. "We hear things about you, you hear things about us. I guess the only way any of us is going to get it right is to talk to one another."

"Oh, gee, isn't that sensitive," she laughed. "Get real. You don't want to understand the dead any more than we want to understand you. There's plenty of what I guess you'd call common ground, though." Her eyes went to my pants. "Isn't that what this is all about?"

She was putting it right on the line. I wondered why the living so rarely did that. Why we always played these goddamn games.

"I hear you," I said. "You call it."

The next piece of octopus she picked off Neal's plate she seemed to swallow whole.

"Okay. Who's going home with me?"

The question was for all three of us, but she directed it straight at me. *Those eyes again.* A beautiful, perfect dead girl's eyes.

"Who wants to know what it's really like . . . *to do it with someone like me?*"

I finished my drink and called for the tab. "She's not beating around the bush," I said, sounding a whole lot more confident than I felt. "Gentlemen? Neal?"

He shook his head. "I'm a married man, boys. No can do."

"John?"

His face went blank. You could practically hear his brain ticking off the countless possibilities, all the pros and cons. Then he stood up.

"I'm there," he said.

We paid and followed her to the street.

It was hot that day, but the night seemed hotter still. The streets were more crowded than usual, a forced march of bar hoppers searching out liquid relief.

"If you don't mind my asking," I said, "how did you . . . ?"

"Die?" The question didn't faze her. "Brain tumor. Simple."

I wanted to ask her more. It was common wisdom that it was the brain that mobilized the dead and that destroying it was how you put them down for good. So it stood to reason that any damage there, like a tumor, would at least cause some dysfunction. But she was functioning perfectly. I wondered why.

I didn't ask, though. Too clinical, too damn anti-erotic. And we were moving along at the fast pace she set for us like a couple of slightly woozy dogs trotting behind their mistress.

Booze, beauty, and forbidden sex. It'll make a dog of you every time.

"Can you believe we're actually doing this?" I whispered to John.

He shot me a look and a grin. "Well, *yeah!*"

"I dunno . . . something's not right."

"Hey, you're the one who's always mouthing off about how the dead should have equal rights. So what about equal *shtupping* rights? She wants some action, we're the guys who're gonna give it to her. And she's the one who asked for it. So what's the problem?"

It made sense, I guess.

He nudged me. "And if she gets froggy? Relax." He flipped up the front of his shirt, and I saw the snubnose stuck in his belt.

"Come on, guys," she called over her shoulder, her voice lilting like a song. "I mean, exactly who's dead here?"

She lived in a split rowhouse up on 89th and Amsterdam. Welfare housing. Not exactly a total dump but pretty damn close. Her high heels tapped up the stairs. You could smell piss faintly in the dimly lit stairwell—*did the dead still piss?*—and half-erased graffiti swirls decorated the walls. Nothing to deter us. Not when you could look up and see that Class-A butt riding up and down in those jeans. We were beyond the point of no return now. That primordial toggle in the male brain had been switched to the *on* position for the duration.

She unlocked triple deadbolts. It looked like somebody'd smeared shit on the door. I hoped it was just more bad graffiti. Then she opened the door and switched on the lights and stepped inside. For a moment we just stood there.

"You gotta be shitting me," John said.

Inside it looked like the Presidential Suite at the St. Regis. Whatever *that* might look like. Russet wall-to-wall carpet, long sable couches, finely crafted Hepplewhite furniture, and one of those fifty-inch-screen tube TVs in the corner. Some pretty high-end art hung from the walls and the curtains could've been Byzantine tapestries.

We stepped inside.

"Some joint," John said.

Our hostess didn't respond. She just stood there appraising us while we moved into the room and looked around. I finally stated the obvious question.

"I thought that . . . that the dead lived on public assistance."

"Only because that's all that people like you will allow us."

"Come again?"

"Hey!" said John. "What's this 'people like you' bullshit? You invited us here, remember?"

"True. I don't have to appreciate your politics though, do I?"

"No, you don't. Though my buddy here's a liberal Democrat. But how about you cool it with the big bitch attitude, okay? Be nice."

She nodded, smiling. "Okay. Back to the subject. You wanted to know how I can afford all this, right?"

"Yeah."

She slipped the tank-top up over her head. Underneath she was naked.

And perfect.

"How do you think?" she said.

John groaned. "Ah, I should've known. A fuckin' hooker. Hey, are we fuckin' morons or what?"

"That's not the deal," I told her. I was seriously pissed off. "You came on to us and all we did was go along. We don't pay for it."

"You will tonight," she said.

She slipped a big semi-auto out from behind the phone stand by the door in less time than it takes me to swallow. The gun had a long black can on the end of it. A silencer.

She pointed it at John. "And Johnny," she said, "don't even *think* about pulling that little pea-shooter in your belt. Between your shirt and your beer-gut that thing's been harder to miss than what passes for your dick. Thumb and forefinger, champ. Take it out and drop it on the floor. Slow."

John hesitated. She cocked her gun.

"If you don't, I'll punch so many holes in you you'll whistle when the wind blows. Count of three, tough guy. One, two . . ."

He parted the shirt, reached down, and dropped the gun to the floor.

"Now wallets. Toss 'em over here by my feet."

We did that too. You didn't have to have a doctorate from M.I.T. to figure out now how she'd furnished her apartment. She wasn't a whore, she was an armed robber, luring guys to her apartment and then ripping them off.

A *dead* armed robber.

And we knew what she looked like. And we knew where she lived. She wasn't letting us out of here alive.

John looked at me and I looked at him. And I thought we were saying something a whole lot like goodbye when she fired the shot into his chest. The silenced report sounded like a single light clap of hands. He went down like a wall of mason blocks. She'd hit him directly in the heart, blood arcing a yard up out of the bullet hole.

I watched the arc dwindle. To nothing.

"I hope you sad fucks have some decent credit cards."

Now the gun was on me. She was enjoying this. Her nipples were as long as thumbnails. I wondered if she'd always been this way or if the tumor had turned her vicious.

"Listen," I said. I was shaking. "We can work this out somehow. We can—"

"Shut up." She fired two more rounds into the side of John's head. The side of his skull blew off and brains like old clotted oatmeal flecked with red were suddenly all over the floor.

I understood the russet carpet.

"Wouldn't want him to come back, would we? The world's a better place without that drunken troll."

All I could do was stand there expecting to die in seconds. I couldn't move. I felt stupid and slightly sad, as if I'd lost an old friend. And not John, either.

"So now me?" I managed to say. "Just like that?"

She laughed. "You mean, 'after all we've had together?' Not necessarily."

She was holding the gun almost lazily—the way you'd hold a phone receiver you weren't exactly going to use right away. But there was a good ten feet between us. If I went for it I'd be dead on the floor right next to John.

"You can't get out," she said. "The door locks automatically, the windows are barred, and you can yell and scream all you want to, but let me tell you, the neighbors won't complain."

Of course not. The neighbors were all dead, like her.

"So what do you mean, 'not necessarily'?"

She shrugged a smooth bare shoulder. "Whether you live or die depends on you."

My stare told her I didn't get it.

"I see assholes like you every day. We're not even people anymore, to you we're not even human. We're nothing more than a bunch of animals."

"That's not true. Yes, there are tons of bigots out there. But I've been trying to tell you all night long, *I'm not one of them.*"

I was pleading for my life, not my principles. And she knew it.

"Sure you are. You're no different. Liberal Democrat, my ass. The proof is the fact that you're here in the first place. You goddamn guys, you all think it would be a riot to have sex with the dead. Something to laugh about, something you can brag about to your buddies. Well, guess what? Here's your big chance."

She ran her finger down the gun barrel.

"And if you do a real good job, I won't kill you."

It was crazy. It made no sense. It was what we'd come here to do in the first place, and now she was turning it into some kind of weird life-and-death challenge. But could I believe her?

What choice did I have?

Strangest thing was, I knew I could do it. Even with the gun in her hand. Even with John dead on the floor. I could put the blocks to her then and there. I looked from her mouth to her breasts and I was hard already.

Maybe death and fear *are* aphrodisiacs.

I took off my shirt and dropped it to the floor. I slid off my belt and dropped that too. "All right," I said quietly and took a step toward her. She started to laugh.

"You should *be* so lucky!"

Now I really was lost.

"Not with *me*, you jackass." She reached for a door back near the drapes that opened to a block of darkness. "Mom? Billy? Come on out."

Their stench preceded them. I could barely breathe.

"Mom burned up in a car accident," she said. "My brother Billy drowned in the Hudson. But they both came back. I take care of them now."

They shuffled across the room, knelt awkwardly at John's body. The woman had no face at all, just char. Her body looked like a skeleton covered with blackened bacon. The boy's flesh was mostly green and hung slack now that he'd lost his floaters' bloat over a naked ribcage that seemed stuffed with meatloaf. Two eyes gleamed from a mottled blood-pudding face. And what we'd heard about the dead—that they were sometimes far more powerful than they'd been in life—was true. Effortlessly these two palsied ruined creatures opened John's gut and pulled things out of him and then for a while there was nothing but munching noises until she broke the silence.

"Mom likes it hard and fast," she said. "But not *too* hard. You know, pieces could fall off. You've got to be careful."

The faceless thing looked up at me through black clotted eyes and did something with its mouth that might have been a smile. I could see the crisped breasts, the scorched sex between its stick legs.

"And Billy's gay. Try to get him off with your mouth, otherwise he's gonna put the whole thing up your ass. Ouch!"

Already its cock was getting hard. The glans looked like a spoiled green tomato.

They both began to crawl in my direction.

"You're the one who wanted to have sex with the dead," she said. The gun was cocked and pointed at me. "So get to it."

She kept her promise—she obviously didn't kill me. So I guess I got it right. They keep me in the back room now with Mom and Billy, shackled.

I hear her bring in other guys all the time. None of them last long. I hear a *pop* and that's the end of them. So far I'm they're favorite. I figure she must have singled me out after all that evening at the bar. And the sex? It's horrible, sure, it's hideous. But it's better than being their next meal. You'd be surprised what you can do if it means staying alive just one more day.

But their appetites are . . . awful, tremendous.

My only hope is that Neal's out there somewhere looking for me. Looking for his buddies, John and me. That he's got the cops onto it, maybe. That somehow, against all odds, he'll find me. That maybe one of these days she'll slip up, make a mistake—she'll go by the World Cafe again and Neal will be On Point that day at the big plate-glass window watching the ladies go by in their short summer skirts and tees and tank-tops and see one who looks just like Daryl Hannah.

Eyes left.

Meantime it's winter now. The City's cold in winter.

And it's very cold in here.

Tales of the White Street Society: The Hairy Ghost

Grady Hendrix

We arrived at the White Street clubhouse at a quarter after eight and were led into the dining room by the inscrutable Charles, who promptly whisked our topcoats away into the mysterious bowels of that great brownstone. Our host, Augustus Mortimer, welcomed the three of us and we dined well on the club's excellent fare, none of us mentioning the nervous excitement we felt at being summoned, once more, to convene this meeting of the White Street Society.

After dinner, we retired to the murky clubroom where Lewis stoked the fire into a crackling blaze while Mortimer distributed Russian cigars. Drake, his whiskers trembling with exertion, applied himself to the cork of a dusty bottle of excellent brandy and then passed around snifters of the amber liquid as we settled into our accustomed places. Mortimer raised his snifter and solemnly intoned: "Spirits for spirits," and we simultaneously raised our glasses and drained them. The bottle was passed again as Mortimer addressed us.

"You will be surprised to learn that my absence of the past several weeks did not take me to sunny Spain, underdeveloped Mexico, nor balmy Italy. Instead, I have been, gentlemen, in Cow Bay, that epicenter of filth in lower New York."

"Whyever for?" Drake cried, expressing the astonishment we all felt.

"Wherever the veil of our world is drawn back and glimpses of that other, uneasy shore are revealed. Wherever spirits haunt the steps of man, where time runs backwards and dogs mutter, wherever the weird and mysterious bedevil our material plane, there shall you find me, bedeviling right back. And, for reasons incomprehensible to the sane and hygienic, this time the veil was drawn back in . . . the ghetto."

We all shivered.

"I have never encountered a case as blood-chilling as this one. Never have I, except perhaps once in Majorca, had my sensibilities been so affronted as in a sodden tenement on Little Water Street. There, in the filthiest conditions imaginable, I confronted the worst case of the supernatural run amuck that I have ever had the misfortune to witness."

"Worse than the Infant Aerialist?" asked Lewis, precipitating a chill to pass around the room at the mere mention of that silent marauder.

"Worse, my old friend."

"Worse than the Devil Cat?" I asked, my tongue stumbling over the hideous name of the demonic presence that had terrorized a buttery in Connecticut and almost cost Drake his life.

"Nothing is worse than the Devil Cat," said Drake.

"My friends, it is a case worse than that of the Levitating Head of Al Arak, more insidious than the Humming Book, more demonic than even the Devil Cat, dear Drake. This, my friends, is the only time you shall hear told of the Hairy Ghost. And you are the more fortunate for it."

We settled back into our chairs, hearts pounding, ears straining to catch every word as Augustus Mortimer recounted to us the following bizarre narrative.

THE TALE OF THE HAIRY GHOST

"One morning, overtaken by hunger and fatigue, I abandoned a rather pointed letter to the *Times* and repaired to a nearby hotel for breakfast. There my gaze happened to fall on a day-old newspaper. Imagine how upsetting it was for me to read on the front page an account of the self-murder of one Dr. Ebenezeus Hagedorn in a hideous establishment known as Weeping House in the slums of Cow Bay.

"Dr. Hagedorn and I had served each other, unofficially, as consultants on difficult diagnoses, usually through the post as he is the possessor of a singular personal odor: like that of a large, sweating cheese. Being Italian, it is to be expected, but even after years of association I was unable to acclimate myself to his unpleasant bouquet.

"The article described, in rather poor taste, the discovery of Dr. Hagedorn dangling lifeless from a noose, in a cramped and fetid chamber, helpfully supplying me with the greasy abode's address. I intended to report it to the health authorities, perhaps encouraging them to burn it to the ground and incarcerate its occupants in lunatic asylums and prison cells, when a tiny paragraph at the bottom of the column caught my eye.

'The doctor was found with a great quantity of paper currency upon his person, but otherwise he had no possessions save the clothes he wore upon his back.'

"Why should that alarm you, Mortimer?" Drake asked.

"Because nowhere does it mention his lucky lodestone."

"Lucky lodestone!" ejaculated Lewis.

"Yes. Hagedorn never went anywhere without a tiny lodestone in his right front trouser pocket."

"Could it be theft?" I asked.

"Why take the stone and leave the paper currency?" said Drake.

"It could have fallen out," I replied, trying to bring reason to this room.

"That is possible," said Mortimer, "were it not for the fact that the lucky stamp nailed to the heel of his shoe was also not mentioned."

"Worn off," I said.

"And the tiny gypsy charm he carried attached to his watch fob?"

"But the watch itself was missing, according to your article."

"Then what about the splinter of the true cross this fanatical papist wore beneath his shirt?"

"Perhaps he didn't put it on that day?"

"Or the vial of blessed water he carried in his waistcoat pocket?"

"Carried away by rats."

"Then there is the tiny magnet he wore on a leathern string concealed beneath his copious beard. What of that, Algernon?"

"That, I admit, is very strange. But might not all this be the work of rodents or light-fingered police officers?"

"Perhaps my boundaries of the fantastic are not as broad as yours, my friend," Mortimer said. "To me, a Dr. Hagedorn shorn of his numerous charms and talismans is a Dr. Hagedorn awry. And so, after finishing my breakfast—which was quite excellent, I might add—I took myself down to Cow Bay to demand answers to this mystery."

"Was it—was it in the Five Points?" Drake asked, naming the very black, beating heart of corruption and poverty in New York.

"Not in the epicenter, my friend, but very nearby."

"But how did you get there?" Drake asked.

"I tramped southwards, down Manhattan Island. Thriving gaudy neighborhoods gave way to blighted streets overseen by dead-eyed buildings and crammed with a species of animal that bore only a passing resemblance to humanity. Gangs of children, maddened by depravity and rum, bit and tore at one another. Human excrement rained from the sky, spilling out of empty windows by the bucketful. Insensate women lay sprawled in doorways, their garments disheveled so as to reveal gruesome portions of biology.

"I finally arrived at a tall, narrow structure like a vertical kennel, sagging between its two more robust neighbors. An obese, unconscious Irishwoman, sprawled on her back, blocked the front door. I looked about for someone who might grant me alternate access and settled on a pinch-faced hag running her hands through the filth beside the rickety wooden steps.

"'Old hag, tell me—' I began.

"'Yew wanna see the death room? Cost yew a nickel,' she said.

"I was rather taken aback at this crude reception, but the loathsome creature misinterpreted it as an attempt at haggling.

"'Four cents then, an' tha's as low as I go.'

"Unsure of how to respond, I fished four pennies from my pocketbook and without a word she led me around to the side of the building, through a rough woollen blanket tacked over a hole in the wall of Weeping House, and into its putrescent interior.

"The house was black as pitch, unlit by windows, and all around me in the dark I could dimly perceive sleeping bodies. The floor was be-slimed with filth, and with every step it oozed up almost to my shoe mouth. Pale faces leered at me out of the dark as I passed. The smell of boiled cabbage was strong and oppressed my soul. We passed through room after room, packed with pallid shapes moving suggestively in the darkness. I observed leaking buckets of filthy water over which harlots would raise their skirts and relieve themselves, and into which children would dip tin drinking cups. The house was permeated with a sense of the collected dregs of humanity up to something vicious, secretive, and disgusting.

"After winding through these intestinal corridors for some time we arrived at a door. The old witch brusquely pushed it open and stepped aside.

"'I doan go in,' she said by way of reply to my unspoken query.

"'Madam, I thank—' But before I had finished my courtesies she was but a dim shape, scuttling away from me down the hallway and swallowed up in the darkness.

"I shook my head at the typically Irish rudeness of her manner, and then stepped into the room, which was little more than a closet, illuminated by one broken and dispirited window. The walls were covered with graffitoed crudities and childish attempts at anatomical diagrams. I even found a hole in the planking, beneath which was a rat's nest containing five blind ratlings, Hagedorn's lucky lodestone, and the leathern strap with the magnet on it which he wore beneath his beard."

"Aha!" I said. "It was the rats!"

Mortimer dismissed me with a languid wave of his hand.

"I have no time for rats and talk of rats," he said. And he continued.

"I looked around this forsaken room and wondered what on earth could have brought such a great, albeit odorous, man as Hagedorn to this pit of poverty. I must admit I was tempted to join a reform movement and burn this filthy hovel to the ground immediately if I had been sure that cremation would not have released harmful gases into the atmosphere.

"A creak of the flooring caught my attention and I turned sharply, expecting to find my guide creeping up behind me with a jack-black in her hand and murder in her Irish eyes. Instead, I beheld a waif with a waxen pallor, protruding bones and papery skin, crouching inside the doorway. Her furtive creeping was arrested as she saw me. Raising herself up to her full height she fixed her watery eyes on me and said: 'Harry don't like you.'

"I was about to strike her for her insolence when her face slackened and she swooned. I stepped forward to catch her, then noticed spittle running from her mouth and stepped back just as quickly to avoid soiling my clothes. Fortunately, she was very light and the fall did her no great damage. With an empty room at my back, an unconscious child at my feet, and no way of locating my guide or escaping from Weeping House, I was in a tight spot.

"After due consideration I decided to make for the street. Unfortunately, the dim hallways proved to be more than my match, and I found myself passing deeper and deeper into the filthy core of the house. Ghoulish faces babbled 'Arby, arby 'ose' at me as I ran by, and I saw such scenes of depravity in my peripheral vision that I shudder even now to recall them.

"Finally I heard distant voices raised in excitement and directed my steps toward them, eager not to lose this spoor of humanity. It shames me to confess it now, but I was not a little afraid at this point that I would never see daylight again. When I rounded that final corner and saw a knot of broken-down inebriates gathered around a doorway my heart raced as if confronted with the Heavenly Host itself. A cry of greeting on my lips, I stumbled toward this clump of excrescence who were mumbling to themselves and staring down at a fallen form. They turned and stared at me in terror as I approached them, and my relief turned to dismay as I recognized the fallen figure as the emaciated trollop who had assaulted me earlier. She had somewhat recovered and was in the doughy arms of my guide. Turning her baleful gaze upon me, she coughed up a sticky, brown substance.

"'It's all right,' I said. 'I'm a doctor.'

"'She sez yew left her on the floar,' snarled my elderly Virgil.

"'She is obviously hallucinating. She's a sick girl and belongs in a sanitarium.'

"'She's got fits, that's awl,' the creature said.

"'She seems well enough now. Tell me, Miss . . .'

"'Miss Kathy,' the girl said.

"'Miss Kathy,' I said, kneeling in her general vicinity. 'Tell these . . . people how you attacked me and fell to the floor on your own.'

"The wizened crone who had brought me into this hellhole narrowed her eyes.

"'She says yew left 'er on the floor. What kind of man be ye oo'd do sech a thing to an innercent child like 'er?'

"The crowd of derelicts mumbled assent from behind yellowed falls of unkempt facial hair. I realized instantly that I must take charge of this situation or risk being trampled and sodomised."

"Sodomised?" cried Drake.

"Yes, dear Drake, for it was immediately clear to me that this crowd was composed in no small part of sodomites. Their lack of energy, their sallow skin, their unkempt hair: the sure signs of sodomy were writ large upon their broken bodies.

"'Look here, you old harridan,' I said, drawing myself up to my full height. 'I am a gentleman and a doctor and I am used to being addressed with the respect due my position. Now show me to the kitchen. We shall lay this hapless creature on the table, boil some water, and examine her. Then,' and here I made my eyes flash quite menacingly, 'you shall answer some questions.'

"My speech had the exact opposite effect to what I had intended. The woman cursed and formed her hands into claws, and the men shuffled forward *en masse*, many of them wielding boat hooks and cudgels. I retreated until my back was pressed against the door frame. They continued their lethal advance, and so I shot one of them. Crying out, he fell backwards and his fellows froze as one. They looked at their fallen comrade and then withdrew to a respectful distance. I could tell the attitude of the crowd had changed significantly.

"'I am here to help you,' I said.

"'You shot Fergus,' an unseen voice protested.

"'Only in the shoulder. Now carry this girl to the kitchen.'

"'You'll shoot us.'

"'No, I won't.'

"'We're going to call the coppers.'

"'He'll recover.'

"'You still shot him.'

"At that point, the unfortunate Fergus awoke and bestirred himself, mumbling in his incoherent Irish brogue. A wave of relief passed through the crowd.

"'You see, I told you he'd recover. When I leave this place I shall take Franklin with me, and I shall employ him in my household as a coachman, and he shall never want again. I so solemnly swear.' The crowd was greatly moved by this fine promise. 'Now bring the girl to the kitchen. I shall follow!'

"So with the lack of efficiency that is the hallmark of the Irish race we made our way to the greasy, soot-blackened kitchen of this hellhole. The filthy creature who called herself Kathy was fully conscious by the time we laid her on the rough, splintery trestle that served as a kitchen table, and despite my instructions to the contrary, she attempted to rise.

"'You there,' I said to my guide.

"'Mrs. O'Hanlon,' she said.

"'Mrs. O'Hanlon, make this beast hold still,' I said. 'I'll make it worth your while.'

"So saying, I tossed her a penny and she raised a wooden ladle and delivered Kathy a great rap on the head that dropped her flat upon the table. Flush with success, she rapped the unconscious Kathy on the head again, then raised her arm for another blow.

"'That will do, Mrs. O'Hanlon. Now boil some water and remove these rogues from the room. I require utmost privacy for the acts I am about to perform.'

"'I rapped 'er two times,' said Mrs. O'Hanlon. 'Yew owe me another penny.'

"'Very well, you beast,' and I threw the penny into the hall. The disgusting woman ran after it, fighting for it with her fellow tenants as wild pigs will over a small helpless child, giving me the opportunity to close the plank door and secure the baling wire hook upon its latch. I pulled my leather work gloves from my coat and set to work.

"I shall spare you the gruesome geography of this unfortunate mongrel's body, but there were several points of interest: a strong, greasy smell of pork was upon her; her skin was unnaturally smooth and clean around her most animalistic regions; tiny bruises covered most of her thighs, both inside and out; and needle scratches were much about her neck, ankles, wrists, and stomach.

"Finished with my examination, I covered the girl and unlatched the kitchen door. The populace of the house stood outside in the dark, sooty hallway and turned their hairy, blank faces toward me as I spoke.

"'There are interesting things in this house, for a man of learning and education like myself, and I wish to study them at my leisure. I shall rent a room in which to work. Here, old crone,' I said, passing a dime to Mrs. O'Hanlon. 'Take my lodgings out of this.'

"A murmur went through the dense knot of inebriates as the coin flashed in the firelight from the kitchen.

"'I do not want any obstacles to my work, nor do I intend to smooth my stay here with liberal dispensations of currency. I am a doctor and I am here to help you. Do I make myself clear?'

"The murmuring turned dark and ugly.

"'What's 'e say then?'

"'E's not going to pay us?'

"The largest, and ugliest, of the crowd stepped close to me, pushing me backwards with his puffed-out chest.

"'Look 'ere. The way we see it, yoar our boarder and you owe each of us a coin like the one yew gave to Mrs. O'Hanlon 'ere.'

"'I do not.'

"'Yew do.'

"'I'm warning you, Mick, don't put me in a position where I must do you harm.'

"'What'd yew call me?'

"'Stand down, sir,' I said firmly.

"'I'll stand down yoar arse!' he roared.

"And so I shot him.

"He went down like a load of coal, and the crowd rushed forward like a surging wave to tend to their injured companion.

"'You'll notice that I have only wounded him in the leg,' I pointed out.

"It was Mrs. O'Hanlon who finally pushed herself forward and shook her gnarled and crooked finger in my face.

"'I expect yew'll be givin' 'im a job in yer house next, sir.'

"'Oh yes, he shall be employed as a footman and I shall pay him three dollars a week.'

"An admiring murmur rippled through the gaggle of miscreants, but did not take hold. Their eyes were still hard.

"'And I shall give him free room and board.'

"With that the floodgates opened, and they clapped their bleeding companion on the back in a congratulatory fashion, which caused him to grin through his bloody teeth. Somehow he managed to smile up at me.

"'God bless 'ew, sir.'

"'Nonsense. You're a hardy fellow. You shall fit right in with my staff. Now, if there's nothing further to discuss, I wish to establish an examining room here by the kitchen fire and examine each of you in a scientific manner.'

"Hours later, my joints stiffened with exhaustion, my fingers and ears grown cold, two pairs of leathern examining gloves soiled beyond reclamation and burnt in the fire, I looked up from my last subject to see that night had fallen on the house as if it had been submerged in a brackish lagoon. Unwilling to die for science, I rejected Mrs. O'Hanlon's offer of a bowl of greasy water dotted with floating gristle, and retired to my room upstairs where I pored over my notes late into the evening.

"My clear penmanship combined with my colorful writing style made the situation instantly clear to me: many of the pathetic residents of this overgrown hovel shared similar symptoms. The men bore scratches and bruises around their nether regions. The few women—many of whom had to be sluiced with water and have their matted hair removed with a knife before I could even determine their gender or age—bore the same symptoms, but no scratches were found on any but tiny Kathy. Nor were the unspeakably animalistic regions of the other women as clean, or as bruised, as Kathy's.

"I sat back and lit a cigar while pondering this enigma, and realized that I still did not know the identity of the Harry whom Kathy had mentioned. Determined to spend not a minute more in this stinking pile than I must, I launched myself into the bowels of the house to find Kathy and question her severely. To this end I brought with me a short length of leather filled with shot to make a sturdy yard-long cudgel. A crude weapon, but an essential diagnostic tool.

"The hour was late and the sound of drunken squabbles echoed through the house. Suddenly, an increase in the smell of rotten garbage informed me that the kitchen was near, and from behind its door I could hear a wet sucking sound. On stealthy feet I approached and peered around the jamb to be greeted by a most un-Christian sight."

"What was it, man!" said Drake.

"It was the young ragamuffin, Kathy, in a state of complete dishabille. She was standing next to the kitchen table, illuminated faintly by the orange glow of the dying hearthfire. And here is where this story takes a turn toward the grotesque, gentlemen. In her hand she was holding a cake of bacon fat and she was slathering her body with it. Rubbing the greasy block all over her limbs and torso, and around her darkest unspeakables. She performed this activity with no small measure of excitement, briskly and sensuously lathering her body.

"I was struck dumb, but had the presence of mind to secure my grip upon the cudgel. She soon finished her oleaginous chore and dressed herself lightly in rags. My heart leapt into my throat as she moved directly toward the doorway where I lay watching. In one deft move, I leapt into the deepest shadows. Kathy walked out of the door, looking neither left nor right, and quickly made for the interior of the house. I followed her as best I could. It was a task of no small difficulty to keep her in sight as she darted through the dim interior of the sleeping ghetto as if she had been born there.

"Our journey came to an end at the suicide's dormer of Dr. Hagedorn. The girl plunged into the room and closed the door behind her. I pressed my eye immediately to the keyhole, and through it I observed the mean apartment in which this girl was conducting her rendezvous with the unknown."

"What was she doing?" asked Lewis, unable to contain himself.

"She was undraped—standing in the center of the room, lit only by a cheap tallow candle that cast its sickly yellow glow on her skin, which was shining brightly with bacon grease. She turned herself this way and that, as if dancing to unheard music, exposing every inch of her flesh to the moon's blind eye. Little sighs and moans escaped her parted lips, and I quickly realized that she was not alone."

"Not alone!" cried Drake.

"Not alone," continued Mortimer, "for on her flesh, her resilient youthful flesh, were indentations. They moved with a purpose and in an orderly path from her neck and shoulders to her back and stomach and then to her bestial protuberances. It was as if an invisible hand were kneading her flesh like dough. Where it moved, the bacon grease disappeared as if it were being pulled into the aether by whatever invisible force roamed freely over her body. Hours passed before she was deposited in a limp heap on the floor. She was panting and gasping, quite nearly unconscious, as dawn's watery light crept in.

"Desperate to interrogate her, I flung open the door and knelt by her side.

"'Kathy! Kathy!' I cried, roughly shaking her shoulders. Her eyes, half-closed and glazed with a lustful exhaustion, could not focus on me, but I snapped her head to and fro until she turned it in my direction and bestowed me with a sickly, satiated smile.

"'At was Harry,' she mumbled, and then dropped into unconsciousness. Unwilling to be discovered like this yet again, I left her on the floor and retired to my room to record the nauseating events of the evening.

"The next day, I made my way to the kitchen. No one was present except what I took to be the normal human garbage, sucking great portions of rough barley porridge into their horrible maws. I enquired as to Kathy's whereabouts, and after enduring many lewd and suggestive innuendoes I was informed that she was in an undisclosed location doing piecework. Hours later she returned to the Weeping House, her fingertips red and sore. Without giving her a moment in which to order her thoughts, I pounced. Using logic and reason, I soon had her isolated in my rooms, sobbing and in no condition to dissemble.

"'Kathy,' I said, 'I saw you in the kitchen last night, and I saw you go to Dr. Hagedorn's room. Do you remember this?'

"She shook her head.

"'Liar! You told me that you had seen Harry, and that he had assaulted you. You smeared yourself with grease and performed lewd gyrations.'

"Her beady eyes, sharpened with tears, fixed me with a wanton look.

"'Did yew like seeing that, sir?'

"'My God, no. It was like watching animals in the barnyard. However, as a doctor I was compelled to observe it carefully.'

"'Yew liked it, dincha, sir?'

"'I want to know who Harry is, and why you smeared yourself

with bacon grease, and exactly what was going on in that room. I want to know all these things, and you will reveal them to me posthaste!'

"My thundering put her in a pensive state of mind. She bit her lips, she twisted her hands, she squirmed in her chair. Finally, she took a great breath and spoke:

"'I don't know.'

"'Oh, for the love of God! Are you a sentient being? Shall you go from the cradle to the grave without even the simplest perception of your surroundings? Tell me what is happening here or I shall beat it out of you.'

"'It's 'Arry, sir. 'E likes lickin' the grease off. It tastes good to 'im, sir. Please don't beat me, sir. I'm tellin' the truth, so 'elp me.'

"I looked into her stolid eyes and realized that she was telling the truth, but I decided to thrash her anyway to confirm my hypothesis. After a few minutes' frenzy I sat down in a chair.

"'Kathy, I now believe that you are telling the truth,' I said, panting. 'So you must help me to capture this Harry.'

"''E won't like that, sir.'

"'No, I suspect he won't. What is he? Does he speak to you?'

"''E whispers things in my ear when 'e's lickin' off the grease, sir, but I canna be sure if I'm hearin' things or if 'e's really saying them.'

"'Let's assume that he is saying them. What is he saying?'

"She told me, and I blushed.

"'That's enough of that. How long have you been visiting Harry?'

"'Quite some months now, sir. 'E leaves me very tired.'

"'And are you the only one who has relations with Harry?'

"''E tells me that 'e goes after all the boarders—th' menfolk an' th' women. But I'm 'is favorite. 'At's what 'e tells me.'

"'And what do you think Harry is?'

"'I t'ink 'e's a ghost, sir. Only . . .'

"'Yes? Speak up.'

"'Only 'e's very hairy and I dinna know that ghosts were an 'airy lot.'

"I had never heard of this before, yet it stands to reason that if an individual possessed a large quantity of hair in his life, then in death his mind might shape his ectoplasmic form so as to resemble hair in order that he might feel as if he were still bound to this earthly plane. A paper on the phenomena of post-mortem hair would be most informative and educational.

"'May I go now, sir?'

"'Oh, no. You're not going anywhere, Kathy. You're going to get some rest, and tonight we shall capture this Hairy Ghost.'

"'I t'ink 'arry will not like 'at, sir."

"'I tend to think the same. However, I am a man of science and am disinclined to allow the objections of others to stay my hand.'

"I dismissed her, drawing forth a promise to meet that evening in the kitchen where she would apply the bacon grease and we would go together to dear, late Hagedorn's room to speak severely with Harry, the Hairy Ghost.

"That night, after the house was asleep, I dragged the protesting Kathy out of bed and brought her to the kitchen. There she coated her body with bacon grease while I averted my eyes. She warmed to her task, and I had to walk quickly to keep pace with her as she practically ran to the room designated for her ectoplasmic assignation.

"She proceeded into the room and stood in an over-eager attitude in the middle of the rude apartment, whilst I lurked outside the door, cudgel in hand. I did not have long to wait before the noxious spirit made its presence know.

"The first sign was a slight glassiness to the girl's eyes, followed by a line of spittle that appeared to run from the corner of her mouth. I swiftly noticed the telltale imprints of the invisible form pressed upon her flesh, and soon it was making its presence known most gratifyingly. Her debauched sighs and carnal moans merely augmented my resolve, and I tightened my grip on the leather cudgel in my hand. I waited until things had proceeded to a point most inappropriate before my sense of decency recoiled and I was propelled into action.

"I leapt into the room with a cry, and the spirit instantly ceased its mauling of the girl's nether regions. Sensing the phantasm's hesitation, I brought my cudgel down on the area which I judged to contain the invisible beast, and I was rewarded with a tactile shudder as my blow struck home. And then several things happened at once.

"Kathy dropped to the floor, insensate; an unearthly cry pierced my ears; and immediately the spirit manifested itself. And its appearance turned my soul to ice.

"There, writhing in lurid agony upon the floor, was a short creature, perhaps two feet tall. It was covered with red, wire-like hair on every inch of its exposed flesh. A bristling beard sprung from its acne-scarred face, as did a pair of bushy eyebrows, and long tufts of untended hair, the same shocking red color, unfurled from its nostrils and its ears. On its head it wore a green cap, and a stained leather apron covered its body. Its feet were shod in shiny leather shoes with bright brass buckles, and it was, upon first glance, a man—a small man. A small man with red hair and green clothes. Judging by my surroundings and the ethnic swamp in which these people lived, I should have guessed earlier that what plagued this house was nothing less than the Cluricaune, the Lurikeen, the Irish blight, the potato homunculus: the Leprechaun. This randy, common fairy had been sating its lust on the good, albeit disgusting and filthy, people of this boarding house; depositing in them the seed of its drunken lusts and taking from them their vital fluids, as well as the bacon grease lapped from the flesh of young Kathy.

"The Leprechaun growled and launched itself at my knees. I beat at it with my cudgel, but the little demon was too devilishly quick for me. My center of gravity is quite high, which those who know me will admit makes me an exceptional dancer; but it is a distinct disadvantage when doing battle with Leprechauns, gnomes, or Black Forest dwarves, whose low stature gives them the gravitational advantage. The creature upended me with its attack on my lower body, and I sprawled across the floor.

"It crawled up my trousers as I lay prostrate and snatched and grabbed at my johnny, attempting in a stupor to unbutton my trousers. A most debased scheme flashed in its bloodshot eyes, foul, Gaelic mumblings dribbling from its thick, chapped lips. I threw the hideous thing against a nearby wall, but quickly it was back upon me, and I had to beat it off with my cudgel, dealing myself several glancing blows in the process.

"Our battle raged on and the sound of splintering wood echoed throughout the house and drew a crowd of on-lookers. As this sleep-addled throng pushed into the doorway I managed to stagger to my feet and struck at the leaping Leprechaun as it ran from me. It pulled out its prodigious member and urinated at me from a great distance, spattering my clothing with its foul-smelling bile. I lashed out at it with my cudgel, smashing the floor and delivering not a few blows to its johnny, legs, back, and head.

"I freed my pistol from within my jacket and had the creature's square, Irish head in my sights when, with a leap, it landed on the nearest bystander and ran up his nightshirt. It was one of those foul drunkards whom I had seen earlier, an elderly man whose body bore the ravages of premature aging brought on by drink. Now this poor unfortunate had a randy Leprechaun beneath his clothing, trying with all its might to sodomize him. I struck at the vulgar creature through the wastrel's nightdress and managed to drive it out, but not before rendering its victim unconscious. The tiny, evil sodomite leapt at the other members of the impromptu audience, and they ran about in circles, screaming. Several times I fired my pistol at it and lashed out with my stick, until in the confusion I managed to catch hold of the filthy beast's ankle with one hand.

"Triumphantly I lifted it into the air, carefully keeping it far from my face. It twisted itself upwards and gnawed at my hand with its needle-sharp teeth, producing daggers of agony in my arm. But I had steeled myself for this, and I called out to Mrs. O'Hanlon:

"'Stoke a fire in the kitchen hearth, old hag. Hurry! Stoke it bright and hot.'

"She stumbled ahead of me as I raced through the black hallways. I leapt over the bodies of dissolute alcoholics passed out with fear, and I pushed past staggering half-wits whose terror had reduced them to drooling idiots. All the while, the Leprechaun snapped and bit at my hand, tearing my flesh to bloody shreds.

"I arrived in the kitchen to find the fire barely smoldering and Mrs. O'Hanlon struggling to open a bottle of cheap gin. Knocking her to the floor, I wrested the gin bottle from her and threw it into the hearth, where it exploded into roaring flames. The hearth was now crackling as merrily as the gates of hell, and the degenerate fairy struggled mightily as it perceived my plan.

"'Ar, me boy. Don't yew wan' ta fine me pot o'gold? I can promise ye treasures th' laiks of which ye've never seen! Ye've caught a Leprechaun, m'boyo, an' ye've airned yerself a booty. Let me go an' claim yer due.'

"But a lifetime of reading and intellectual cultivation has made me a cruel man, and so I tossed him into the blaze. The Leprechaun staggered across the hot, gin-soaked coals, consumed by flames, beating its arms helplessly at its burning body. Some of the heartier tenants were peeking around the door frame by now, and Mrs. O'Hanlon was bestirring herself as the smell of scorched corned beef filled the room. All eyes were drawn to the blazing hearth and the stumbling shape within.

"Suddenly, with a savage scream, the blazing Leprechaun launched itself at my throat. It sailed out of the hearth, its flaming arms outstretched, its eyes burning red in the middle of its blackened face, a hateful cry upon its scorched lips. The crowd stumbled backwards in horror, and Mrs. O'Hanlon fell to the floor and covered her face. I calmly drew my pistol and with one shot neatly decapitated the vile thing. Its headless body fell to the floor, while its shaggy head sailed backwards into the fire, where it crackled and popped for some time.

"Sensing that the drama had passed and that shortly I would be petitioned to part with more money and listen to the further ramblings of degenerates, I left that vulgar house and made for fresh air and safety. But as I clopped down the wooden front steps of Weeping House onto the muddy track of Little Water Street a sudden consideration brought me to a halt.

"Was not the Irish problem really a Leprechaun problem? These foreigners seemed to have brought their own supernatural oppressors with them to our great country, and now they were paying the price. I thought of savage, yet fair, Mrs. O'Hanlon. Of brave, lewd Kathy. Of the horrible Leprechaun that had turned this house into a den of wanton buggery. Acting on a sudden surge of sentiment, I brought out a box of matches from my waistcoat and burned Weeping House down. It caught quickly and its flimsy framework went up like a torch. I watched it burn for some time, bemoaning the fate of the poor Irish who came to our shores so full of hopes and dreams only to have them dashed by Leprechauns, and then I returned to my apartments uptown, where Charles prepared for me a wonderful meal in the French style and I had a hot bath with plenty of carbolic soap.

"But there is one thing that haunts me still. Before I left Little Water Street I saw their eyes. Hundreds and hundreds of them, staring out at me from chinks and crannies, through broken windows, from under mounds of dung: Leprechaun eyes, blazing with hatred. I saw them and counted their number, and my blood froze in my veins. They are a blight, and one day they shall overrun us all. They shall tear down our churchs, our art galleries, and our great halls of government, and make of them a muddy swamp of degeneracy. They shall usurp democracy and decency and goodness and make us all nothing more than human cows which they shall milk for food. They are our reckoning. They are the wages of sin. They are our doom."

Mortimer's tale was finished, and we sat in stunned silence until the clubroom clock striking twelve roused us from our grim contemplation. One by one we took leave of our host.

I was the last to go, and on the front stairs of 44 White Street I took Mortimer's elbow and had a confidential word in his ear.

"Look here, Augustus, if there's a fund for the extermination of these monsters I am good for a substantial contribution. But it must be for their complete and total eradication—nothing less."

"No, Alegernon," Augustus said with a rueful smile. "There are too many of them. It is too late for extermination now. We must put our faith solely in God. And in these."

And he drew back his waistcoat and showed me two pistols tucked into his trousers.

We said our farewells and I walked out onto the cold city streets. New York was silent, and my thoughts were troubled. A stiff wind was picking up from the east. I could not believe that the Lord had abandoned us to this Irish blight. He would hear our prayers. He would deliver us from evil. Turning my steps homeward, I resolved that, come morning, I would go to church and light a candle and offer up a fervent prayer for the salvation of our souls—after I had purchased a pair of pistols.

The Long Lost and Forgotten

J. Daniel Stone

South Williamsburg, far as one can go before they swim. September says the calendar, but summer won't shut its greasy legs to let the cool breath of autumn roam free. Here it is far too quiet to be considered part of metropolitan New York, even with Manhattan's lights slathered like grease upon the shoreline, or the endless adventures that live within the abandoned factories.

Two hooligans prowl the streets looking for fun or trouble, most likely a little of both. Their friendship was founded upon a mutual love of creation, perpetual laziness, and ridicule of the current art scene. They had been introduced by their lovers and quickly found that their obsessions complemented each other quite well: the girl's painful poetry to the boy's surreal art.

Tyria was fair and driven by anger; Dorian was dark and wretched in nature. But when the two of them put their heads together they could spin straw into gold, turn creative energy into defiance, and unravel the entanglement that we call reality.

"I really hate Brooklyn," Tyria said.

Dorian looked at her with eyes made of dark stone. "Then why do you live here?"

"I'm in a much better neighborhood than this."

"Horseshit." Dorian tugged at the piercings in his lip.

Tyria looked at him square in the eyes. "Is your boredom killing you finally?"

They stopped walking. Dorian lit a joint, inhaling a spicy cloud of THC that put his mind into a more patient state. The smoke swirled about everything, claimed the air. Tyria watched him with disdain, lit a hand-rolled cigarette. They both enjoyed the full minute of silence, losing each other in the dreams that lived behind their eyes.

Dorian broke the silence. "I've something on my mind."

Tyria rolled her eyes, put on her black Ray Bans. "Entertain me then, *Dangerous Dorian.*"

"Hate that name."

The way Dorian looked upon Tyria was a most maddening sight. It was not admiration, protective instinct, or even lust. It was fascination. His almond eyes bowed to her every move and word. He was Tyria's greatest admirer and, admittedly, wanted to cut open her head and live inside her.

But Tyria would never say how much Dorian marveled her. He was a unique painter with a macabre slant that put all his competition to shame. When you entered a gallery you knew immediately that the one painting that rubbed you the wrong way was a Dorian Wilde original. It was his unique technique, the relationship he developed with the paint brush: one moment you could be looking at Dorian's work—the sure admirer—but then all of a sudden find that your God-given free will is no longer yours and that Dorian's work is staring *into* you.

"Out with it," Tyria said.

Their walk had taken them to edge of the borough so that the sulfuric smell of the East River tongued them passionately. Unstable territory, Tyria knew, as peace on this side of the street was intermittent and drug deals were exchanged like currency. Popular real estate had yet to enslave this part of town as it had done the north side, probably because the pavement was so uneven and that the creepy warehouses were hunched together in attempt to hide from the neighborhood's volatile populace. And then something caught her eye: *Salvage Warehouse*, in bright pink aerosol paint.

"Isn't that—?"

"Oh, yes," Dorian said. "And look."

He pointed at a flickering window. There, Tyria saw something dark. Not shadow, nor a shred of universe, but something *wrong*. It looked back at them, into them, the face of something forgotten, lost. Dorian didn't waste a moment, taking out his sketchpad and pencil, immediately drawing parabolas on the page. There was no true way to make sense of the horrible thing, but his hand always moved before his brain, circles and dull ends and spirals before he realized that something had taken shape: a mouth, a cyclopean eye, and a tail. Tyria grabbed the sketchbook from his hand and threw it on the ground.

"What was that for?"

"Not everything wants to model for you," Tyria hissed.

"Don't you want to see it?"

"Not for the life of me."

But that was not where her rage was stemming from. Somewhere inside she was scared as hell, and the only way she knew how to protect herself was to get mad; she knew there was no backing out of this, not by a long shot. Dorian's mind was set and he would do something terrible.

"You coming?" Dorian said.

"Fuck my life."

The front door was bolted and the side entrance was gated off with rusted barbed wire. No matter, as Dorian was already scaling the fire escape, dropping his hand for Tyria. Though she huffed and puffed, she took his hand and he pulled her up without effort. They faced a window that was cracked by sun and snow and moonshine.

"Thought you had the key to this place," Tyria said.

"Where's the fun in that?"

Dorian's fist easily punched through. They climbed in carefully, throwing pieces of glass onto the metal staircase. The floor below them was a dark maze of spired gates, X-ray films, antique keys, desks, ornate light fixtures, art supplies, and stone animals. No light inside but what reflected off the river, and as Dorian illuminated his cellphone, Tyria saw one of the stone animals turn its head away.

"I'm not going any further," Tyria said.

"Don't be shy."

Dorian took her hand and pulled her in.

*   *   *

From 1980 to 2000, the Architectural Salvage Warehouse was the only place in Brooklyn that accepted the remains of demolished structures from around the city. Precious detritus revered by historians, nostalgists, and even bloggers; priceless ghosts of a past that was unable to be preserved since institutional Alzheimer's became somewhat of the norm in New York City.

For restorers, this warehouse was a place they could call home, a luxury their craft hardly ever had. Griddles, fire pokers, and street signs could be melted down to create something more modern, or simply restored and put up for sale to anyone who appreciated the painstaking work. But to developers, the once city-operated business was just taking up space on their future goldmine.

It didn't matter what relics were stored inside, or how much cultural legacy could be wiped clean if and when it was demolished or sold to the highest bidder. It didn't matter that the origins of each item could no longer be traced as fiscal constraints had cut staff down each passing year, which meant that bookkeeping had been grossly overlooked.

Thus, the landscape of the Architectural Salvage Warehouse changed from historical heaven to sudden purgatory. The lights cut out and the doors were sealed. Everything began to collect dust. Pieces of history piled upon more pieces of history, and once put inside, no item would ever find its place in the world again.

*   *   *

It was a summer to remember, insofar as summers are to be remembered. Dorian's art had sold well through July, and his first four shows in August put so much extra cash in his wallet that he was able to pay the rent two months in advance. The leftover cash was invested in craft beer, completing his Black Sabbath vinyl collection, painting the brick walls of his loft silver and black, and more art supplies, natch.

Riding on the success, a local Brooklyn paper called *Eyesore* ran an article about Dorian. Within it the writer theorized that if photographs were an inexhaustible source of material for Francis Bacon, than reality—even nightmare—was for Dorian Wilde a depthless well of inspiration. How else could the oils have bled together with such vigor, or the jaws of a fossilized abomination snap open? Dorian made his audience question the external world in effort to justify their own perversions.

But popularity soon dwindled as it always seems to do, that white-hot moment of stardom cooling so fast there was no point in trying to redeem himself. If you don't keep up with the in crowd—if you don't make small talk and smile—they stop buying. Self-promotion was an act that Dorian knew he could never ace, and so now he was suffering the repercussions. Luckily for him, Tyria only lived ten minutes away by foot, which eased the transition from sky-rocket to skyfall.

"When will the artist ever be challenged?" Tyria said, sliding her finger across the centerfold of the magazine.

"Do you not live in the same world as I?"

Tyria smiled. "The rational world or—"

"The one that forces us to pay rent to slumlords and buy food because we can't grow it ourselves in this city."

"You sound bitter."

Dorian snapped his face toward the sun, and the reflection caught Tyria right in the eyes.

"I have to get a fucking job. Do you know how that feels?"

"No," Tyria said, wincing in preparation for Dorian's reaction. "And don't call me a brat because Adelaide takes care of everything."

"You're very lucky. Leland, as you know, is upstate on that fuck-ing Zen retreat. I have to find a quick way to get paid, quicker than schmoozing."

"Leland didn't leave you any cash because you were doing so well when he left."

Dorian took a sip of his early morning IPA. "Yeah, well, he also didn't give me a fallback plan, and I guess that's partly my own fault."

"Hey, you wanted the rock star life, but artists rarely enjoy all the sex and drugs. The rock 'n' roll is there for sure, but without the glam."

A spoken-word poet by nature, Tyria almost always had the up-per hand in any conversation they had. Though her talents stemmed from a tragic childhood, having lost her innocence too early in life because of a father who showed his love by touching his only daugh-ter in places no girl should be touched, she had those memories to thank for her passions even if they weren't the greatest. But this is why Dorian and Tyria were friends, and this is why they would continue to work together so long as they dreamed.

"The fuck am I even good at?" Dorian looked at his studio door, which had just creaked open slightly. "Everything in that room contains the life I need. No more, no less."

Tyria lit a Camel. "I ain't ever setting foot in there again. Too much fucked-up shit happens."

"You say that like it's my fault."

The small talk went on for another two hours. Brainstorming and surfing the Internet for job postings, Craigslist and LinkedIn, two web platforms Dorian never thought he'd find himself needing. By moonrise Tyria was a six-pack in and Dorian switched to a wine that stained his tongue red. Another hour flew by, and maybe it was the rush of beer drunk, or the fact that she hadn't laughed so hard in a long time, but Tyria made Dorian a promise to hook him up with a guy Adelaide used to buy her dope from.

"I don't want her hanging that over my head," Dorian said.

"I'll make sure she doesn't."

"Yeah, good luck with that."

The hook-up was an Italian relic from the north side, Johnny-No-Thumbs, aptly named because he had lost both his thumbs to garden shears after not making good on a gambling debt he owed a certain family. After that incident, Tyria said that Johnny had left the wise-guy stuff behind and went all-out American hustler, buying buildings on the south side while they were cheap, housing a junk-yard, a factory that made propellers, and using one of the buildings as a storage facility of the strangest nature.

"If ya want work you gotta work for it, ya lazy bum," Johnny said to Dorian. "I hear yous a good guy, but I also know you make weird shit up."

"I'm a painter," Dorian said.

"I don't know nothin' about painting, but what I do know is that I got shit lying around and nobody to clean it up."

Johnny was a small man with an abysmal demeanor. Whatever guilt or empathy Dorian had felt about his radial nubs had faded to the reality that for an indeterminable amount of time he'd be slaving eight hours a day hauling shit he couldn't care less about, ultimately taking time away from him being an artist. But cash was king; emotional livelihoods had to wait.

Work started on the hottest Sunday of the year. The sun blazed against Dorian's back, and he hated himself for wearing his *Ozzfest 2001* tour T-shirt and black jeans from *Yellow Rat Bastard*. By the end of the day he had never felt so abused, never seen his skin so red, or his dark hair stick up in so many directions. He wanted to choke Tyria for all this stress, but the crisp $100 bill in his back pocket was something he could get used to.

Though he felt completely out of his element due to the humiliation of the job, not to mention the language barrier of the immigrants—the fact that they laughed at Dorian and made fun of him under their breath—these things could not touch the electrifying inspiration he felt when he first entered the building at the loading entrance.

The warehouse on Berry Street lay in the shadow of the Williamsburg Bridge, nestled grotesquely between a bar, a junkyard, and two small apartment buildings. A brick-and-mortar time capsule unlike anything he'd ever seen. No museum could compare. Literal pieces of the city were inside of it: torn-down façades, shredded subway tracks, antique doorknobs, and stained glass that would never see the light of day again if the current administration had its way. It had no respect for the past and no hope to restore it. Whatever made its way inside the warehouse was to remain, to decay, to gather dust.

Johnny was paid a handsome salary to keep these strange keepsakes away from the general public. While some of the stock—like the original street signs or skeleton keys for padlocks that secured the first storefronts of the city—remained priceless, there were some items that Johnny had mentioned that rubbed him the wrong way. He was not a believer in echoes and specters or ghosts and goblins, but he figured that since Dorian always walked around with a rain cloud over his head he'd be into some of the spookier things that the warehouse stored.

"I'm a man of Catholic faith. I grew up reading the Bible, which I will say has some scary shit in it. But I never seen anything like this," Johnny said.

"I don't believe in spooks either." Dorian finished his Marlboro and crushed it against the warehouse's metal door.

"Yeah, right," Johnny said. "Here's the key if you ever want to check it out when no one's around. Tell Ty I said hello."

That night he tried to call Leland but couldn't get through. When he called Tyria, Dorian could feel the immense annoyance in her voice. Adelaide was in the middle of painting her nails, but he let it all out anyway, going over and over about the warehouse, as he supposed Tyria would like the idea. But five minutes into the conversation she slipped an invisible **DO NOT DISTURB** sign between them by hanging up.

He would have to do it alone.

It was the ass-end of a typical Brooklyn night, the East River scintillating and Manhattan's glass and steel façades seemingly unreal. He checked all his things before leaving his apartment, didn't need much other than his backpack, a fresh sketchpad, and two number two pencils. He weaseled his way west on South 4th Street, making a slight left on Berry, stopping directly in front of the warehouse.

The building had been freshly tagged, something Dorian hadn't seen earlier in the day. Swooping white paint and black bubble letters—the beginning of some kind of mural against the establishment, from what he could make out. He fished his pocket for the key and had to give the lock a few good twists before he heard the rusted cogs unhinge to let him in.

The warehouse had changed, stretching further than he remembered, which was damn near impossible but somehow plausible. Maybe it was just too dark inside. For a good five minutes he couldn't bring himself to walk fully inside; wary of something that hadn't even shown its face yet.

He used his Zippo lighter to guide him into the labyrinth, barely enough light to get him to one side of the main room. Immediately he tripped over pieces of sheetrock, smelled insulation and the cinders of buildings that had been brought down by fire. Sounds infiltrated his ears from all parts of the room—not wind, not rodents, nor even the wings of insects. Just sounds. He placed the lighter on the floor and opened his sketchbook, blindly drawing all the things he was hearing.

When his pencil broke through the pad he knew that there would be no hole to prove it. Now his hand was going in, deep into the mouth of something he could not see. He heard a footstep, cloven hoof made of stone, and the sound of mortar being chewed by steel teeth. The Zippo light blew out, forcing Dorian to take cover in an old glass phone booth. When he sat down to catch his breath he accidentally pulled the chord out of the phone—

—as something on the line began to speak.

*   *   *

Third Wednesday into August, and the swelter had hooked itself so deep that nobody could escape their own stink. On the street odors mingled madly, everyone holding their noses, bags above their heads to block the sun but their hands burning against UV-B rays.

Down below the surface there was still some candlelight left in the old book shoppe. Tyria had been perusing its aisles since dawn, transporting herself into multiple galaxies far, far away, ones that would never change inside their paper bindings and flimsy parchment. Opening a book is sort of like opening a wound, splitting memory: always there to haunt you, it just needs the right touch.

Now her stomach began to growl and her head started to ache; her tattoos itched, especially the bright green ouroboros around her left wrist. She wanted a cigarette. But she was safe in these long halls, a strategic move to partition off Adelaide's clinginess and Dorian's madness as there was no cellphone service down here. No way for them to poison her mind with their rhetoric, their aches and pains, their artistic debts to various entities and organizations. As much as Tyria loved Adelaide, and as much as she respected Dorian, she did not have to be at their every beck and call.

The library was permeated with stillness, and this was duly noted in the titles that were never rotated, its technologies never updated. Poetry was still in the back, prose in the front, and textbooks were off to the right. Time stood still down here, plain and simple.

But the books were special, this place not open to the public—not for decades—now privately owned but no upkeep to be had. Each shelf seemed a mile long and several miles high, and Tyria found herself sometimes staring so hard that the books seemed to glow with age and wisdom, sway to the music of the stories that lived within them.

"Why haven't you been returning my calls?"

Tyria nearly jumped out of her skin, swinging at the sound that came out of the darkness. Her fist caught a corner shelf, knocking down several books and unleashing clouds of dust and cobwebs. Tyria listened for the voice again, taking two steps back before something warm and fuzzy came over her, like being drunk, an embrace she knew all too well.

"How the fuck did you know I was here?" Tyria snorted.

Dorian let her go, stepping back so that she could fully see him. "You're not too hard to find when you only like being at one of two places."

His clothes were worn down, his wingtip boots ripped at the toes. Black ink was smudged across his chin, which made his teeth appear way too bright. He looked as if he hadn't gotten sleep in years; Tyria could see the fear and apprehension in his eyes. How bad had the job worn him down? How much more would he be able to take? The blue-collar life was not for him.

"Are you okay, Dorian?"

Nails in his mouth, red slime on his lower lip. "I'm fine. I just need to talk . . . is all."

"I'm sorry I haven't called you back," Tyria said, her guilt now showing. "It's just been a weird time for me."

"What could be so weird that you can't tell me?"

Tyria lit a hand-rolled cigarette. "It's got nothing to do with you. It's all me. Just need to be alone."

"You'll really want to be alone when I tell you what I've seen, things your nightmares can't even create."

"Don't flower it up, Dorian. Just out with it."

And so he went into bitter detail of the encounters. How the warehouse changed when viewed from the inside or out, how it seemed to be its own little world. It had a sky, a shoreline; it made sounds as if it were digesting bad food, and it had its own gravitational pull. Tyria took a seat in the closest chair she could find, losing Dorian in the dim light.

"Sounds?" Tyria said, shaking her head.

And then he pulled a book down from the shelf, proof in his hands that something was following him, trying to tell him something. A queer title, something about a Great White Whale, and when Dorian opened the first page the book misted Tyria's face. She smacked it out of Dorian's hand, but upon landing on the floor it began to vomit water. She bent down and shut it.

But Dorian wasn't finished. He pulled more books off the shelves. Carter's wolves bayed and Grimm's Fairy Tales smelled like a forest. Butterflies and will-o'-the-wisps were let loose from the imprisoning pages of another book. A grotesque hand reached up, grabbed Tyria's hair, and tried to pull her in.

"The phone rang," Dorian said. "And I'd already pulled the out the cord."

Tyria's eyes widened. "What the fuck was that?"

"Adventure," Dorian said. "I want to go back . . . *with you.*"

"Don't you work there?"

Dorian moved his hair away from his face. "I do, but you're not understanding me. Those things . . . those forgotten pieces of history . . . they don't want to be lost, or forgotten. They want to go on and they're trying to tell me why."

*   *   *

The rain started with no warning, settling on the old roof loudly. A heavy whistling cut through the broken window, bringing with it pelts of warm summer water. Lightning spread pale veins in the sky, its luminescence crawling across the floor and through the grate of the metal staircase so that Dorian could see the entire warehouse as if it were during the day, even if for a moment.

"That's not where it should be," Dorian said, picking a rotary phone up from off the floor and putting it back on a shelf.

Something feathery crawled across his scrawny body, and it made him suddenly understand how insignificant he was. Might it be that the visible world was only the size of a single subatomic particle stitched into a vast quilt made up of a billion atoms, a cosmic spiderweb where dimensions and physical law did not hold sway? This made Dorian take a step back, look deeply into the warehouse's contents to see nothing but a big dark blanket, a blanket he wanted, and needed; one that he would certainly unravel.

"You gonna move or what?" Tyria said.

He trotted across the metal staircase, using the wall as his ful-crum and the light from his cellphone as an assistant so that he wouldn't bust his ass. Upon landing on the ground floor the phone was immediately drained of battery; he tried his Zippo, but the flint was no longer functioning. Tyria silently descended, puerile in her beliefs—so said her resting bitch face.

"The fuck is that horrible stench?" Tyria said. "Did something die?"

Dorian could not have dismissed the odor if he tried. It was a smell that was born and bred in mystery, one that had been living in his olfactory sense for quite some time, though he had failed to real-ize it until now. The mingled scents rocketed up to his brain, spread-ing fire between his ears. He knew them as well as he did his reflection in the mirror: old things, dead dreams, and settled night-mares; something fecund while at the same time rotting.

"Feels like I'm in a bad movie."

Tyria her own light, pale hair and neon Converse sneakers, bright tattoos to lead them on the road to nowhere. But her glow did not stretch far enough into the warehouse, for as much as its spidery fin-gers could illuminate, there was just as much darkness to swallow it. Dorian could see that this made her uncomfortable, and he almost felt sorry for bringing her even though she had caused just as much mischief for him in the past. When he let that thought settle, all feel-ings and remorse had simply vanished.

Dorian attempted to light a cigarette. "Fucking thing isn't work-ing. The flint is . . . gone."

Tyria turned sharply. "What do you mean gone?"

Dorian shrugged his shoulders. "It doesn't work."

"I just bought that for you, there's no way it could have—"

Sudden noise, not a bang or a knock on the metal door, not any-thing coming down the stairs: the rotary phone was turning. Dorian heard the dial spin, the receiver ring. Tyria grabbed Dorian's arm—immediate signal that she was going no further, that she would not feed into any of his games no matter how true they were. And then the phone hit the floor with a sound like bottled thunder, while thunder itself bashed the sky bloody.

"You never said why you wanted to be here," Tyria said. "Is there a purpose?"

"Must everything we do have a purpose?" Dorian stepped inside, tapped the rotary phone with his wingtip boot. "It's dead as dead can be."

"Our minds are playing tricks."

"No. They're talking to us."

"Bullshit, Dorian."

"Step in further with me."

Dancing through the accumulated dark, as if to tease Tyria that this archaic sanctuary was completely safe, that nothing in here could hurt her, but certainly they could try her tolerance. She continuously rolled a cigarette between her lips, so dry that Dorian could see blood on the filter. But his wayward movements guided him now, brushing against cornerstones and clay pots, kicking up dust bunnies and soot, sailing deeper into the labyrinth of pipes and rocks.

"Don't get lost," Tyria said.

Dorian's boot smashed through a canvas that was dry as a sepulcher, then through the whorled intricacies of stained-glass windows. Tyria bent down and picked up some of the glass, a wild spiral in her hands, looking deeply into a piece the color of an open ocean. Dorian saw Tyria's eyes change colors, and so he pressed his finger gently against the glass and drew a shape into the dust, a mouth of some sort, an orifice with teeth. The second he removed his finger he heard something growl.

The glass shattered as it hit the floor.

And now his hands, those gifted hands, searching for something else, falling against something warm, a hole in the wall too big to comprehend, too alive to make sense. He pulled himself further into the warehouse, giving up his own will for something he didn't quite understand. He stepped onto wooden paneling that had certainly been ripped from the floor of an old Victorian Flatbush mansion, then balanced himself on freighter crates so that he would not fall atop the pieces of metal waiting for him as if they were a bed of nails.

From up here the rain was insignificant. The universe was crushing in on him. Tyria looked small but fierce in her stance, pale eyes watching Dorian, bright shoes kicking glass away from her warpath. Behind her, he saw the outline of a rising Baphomet, and just as he was going to scream he realized that it was just a stone bull, half of its face lathered in soot from some fire in the past.

Dorian's hands gleamed as the sky exploded again, dripping light into the warehouse's window. The stained glass sparkled and the floor looked as if it were steaming. For a brief, holy moment he glimpsed the space where he had felt that alien warmth, to confirm now that it had come from no hole, but a statue of Mother Mary with a vulgar red orifice graffitied between her genuflecting hips.

There was blood on his hands.

"That's just vile," Tyria said.

"Now you see what I mean?" Dorian smirked.

"Get down here and do it again . . . draw something—"

The stone bull snorted, dragging cloven hooves across the linoleum. Tyria braced herself as it darted, barely managing to jump to the side before it bashed into the wall, forcing itself to crumble into pieces. Dorian made his way down and picked Tyria up, nose bleeding and tears in her eyes. But there was no fear in her; there was only absolute clarity. She wiped her nose, then scrawled poetry on the floor.

"This is how I make my mark," Tyria said.

Behind them, a blighted grandfather clock began to chime, the handles frozen at midnight or noon, depending on the light, the sound reverberating throughout the warehouse. It slid beneath Dorian's feet with a strange force, ran up every wall until the sounds coalesced in the air. Dorian held his ears as Tyria continued to write, digging her nails into the floor, engraving her reality into this unstable one.

"I can't take this shit," Dorian said. "It's driving me nuts."

Tyria looked right up at him. "Then you know what to do."

"What?"

"Draw, you fuck. Draw something so they stop."

Dorian had nearly forgotten that he had his backpack on, but it was what was inside that mattered. The pad was fresh, smelled as if it had just been cut from the tree. The pencil was beaten up, but it would do the trick even with the intermittent lightning. With the sound of the clock and of Tyria's screams, Dorian unleashed something inside of him that he never knew was there.

His hands had taken him deep in the center of the page. Spirals into circles into an endless vortex. The paper gave way; his hand went in, losing the pencil. Pain found Dorian near his elbow, to which he saw that shards of stained glass ringed edges of the paper like teeth, digging into him; maybe trying to keep him. At the sound of his scream Tyria was up on her feet, pulling Dorian's arm, tattoos peeling back.

"Don't touch me!" Dorian pleaded. "Let it take me."

The burning ran all the way up his arm, pain swirling into his head. Tyria took a step back, but this time moving into territory that also did not want her to leave. A spired gate unfurled, pulling free from concrete, pinning her down no matter how much she cursed, no matter how much she fought. The metal kept her in place.

Now Dorian's arm was inside the paper mouth, but a familiar pain was rising through him, forcing his fingertips to tingle. Then he heard the tattoo needle, saw the electric socket implode with sparks as the pain reached its white-hot threshold. It all made perfect sense. They were becoming part of him.

When he pulled himself free there was no blood and no more pain, as if what had just happened was a bad dream. The rain stopped and the lights of the warehouse buzzed to life, throwing out the shadows and echoes so that Dorian now saw that the entire space was empty except for Tyria, who was sprawled across the linoleum with a bleeding lip, red-stained teeth in her pseudo-smile.

"It's all gone," Tyria mumbled.

Dorian looked at his right arm, which was now taken over by a miraculous new tattoo, one that would continue to tell the story of history past, of a city taken over by new administrations and people who did not appreciate what had brought them to the greatest city in the world, that the change they bring, though rooted in New York's history, should not pride itself on erasing everything they built.

Dorian, with this new smorgasbord, would now be able to keep it in his heart.

Contributors

THE AUTHORS

Marc L. Abbott is a novelist, playwright, short film director, and storyteller. His written works include the stage play *A Gamble of Faith*, the YA novel *The Hooky Party*, and the children's book *Etienne and the Stardust Express*. His short horror film *Snap* was an official selection at several film festivals such as Coney Island Film Festival, Macabre Faire Film Festival, and the NJ Horror Con Film Festival. He was also nominated for three best actor awards for his role in the sci-fi short film *Impervia*. He is a Moth StorySlam and GrandSlam winner and has been a featured storyteller at Tell It: Brooklyn, The Dump, What Are You Afraid of, Barbershop Stories, RISK! and BadyHOUSE Storytelling Concert Series. He currently has two one-man shows under his belt, *Love African-American Style* and *Of Cats and Men: A Storyteller's Journey*. Born and raised in Brooklyn, he still calls the borough his home. Visit his website www.whoismarclabbott.com for more on his work and future appearances.

Meghan Arcuri writes fiction and poetry. Her short stories can be found in various anthologies, including *Chiral Mad* (Written Backwards), *Chiral Mad 3*, and *Madhouse* (both from Dark Regions Press). She also has a story in the forthcoming *Borderlands 7* (Borderlands Press). She lives with her family in New York's Hudson Valley. Please visit her at www.meghanarcuri.com, facebook.com/meg.arcuri, or Twitter (@MeghanArcuri).

Alp Beck was raised in Italy and Cuba. She writes in all genres but prefers horror. Her essays have been featured in the *New York Times* and the *NY Blade*. She prefers the short story format and is working on a screenplay adaptation of one her tales. You can find her most recent story in the anthology *Hell's Grannies*, edited by April Grey (Lafcadio Press). She is hard at work on a fiction series, including *Eyewitness* and *The Underride*, a project with her co-writer, Laurie Jones.

Allan Burd writes imaginative thrillers in a mix of genres. His novels include *The Roswell Protocols* (which has been described as *The X-Files* meets Tom Clancy), *All Hell* (an action-monster-murder mystery with werewolves and more), and *Blood Cold* (a global adventure mission that goes from Yeti high in the mountains to the dungeons of a legendary castle). For more information, please check out his books on Amazon.

Elizabeth Crowens, writer of alternate history and Hollywood suspense, won First Prize in the Chanticleer Review 2016 Goethe Awards for Turn-of-the-Century Historical Fiction for *Silent Meridian*, also a finalist for the 2016 Cygnus, Paranormal, Ozma/Fantasy, and Eric Hoffer Awards. She is a member of the Horror Writers Association, Mystery Writers of America, Sisters in Crime, and Broad Universe and writes a column, "The Poison Apple," for BlackGate.com.

A lifelong resident of New York's haunted Hudson Valley, **JG Faherty** has been a finalist for both the Bram Stoker Award (*The Cure, Ghosts of Coronado Bay*) and ITW Thriller Award (*The Burning Time*), and he is the author of five novels, nine novellas, and more than 60 short stories. He writes adult and YA horror, science fiction, paranormal romance, and urban fantasy. Follow him at www.twitter.com/jgfaherty, www.facebook.com/jgfaherty, www.jgfaherty.com, and jgfaherty-blog.blogspot.com/.

Trevor Firetog is an author/filmmaker from Long Island. He has worked on short stories, novellas, comic books, and film scripts. When he's not reading on the beaches of LI or scavenging used bookstores, he's usually working on a ton of other projects, including a novel. Find him on Twitter @TrevorFiretog.

John C. Foster's novel *Dead Men* was published by Perpetual Motion Machine Publishing in 2015 and his novel *Mister White* was published by Grey Matter Press in 2016. His debut collection of short stories, *Baby Powder and Other Terrifying Substances*, and *Night Roads*, a sequel novel to *Dead Men*, were published by Perpetual Motion Machine Publishing in 2017. His stories have appeared in numerous magazines and anthologies, including *Shock Totem*, *Dark Moon Digest*, and *Dread—the Best of Grey Matter Press*, among others. He lives in Brooklyn with the actress Linda Jones and their dog Coraline. For more information, please visit www.johnfosterfiction.com.

Patrick Freivald is the four-time Bram Stoker Award–nominated author of the Ani Romero and Matt Rowley novels, dozens of short stories, and the *Jade Sky* graphic novel (with Joe McKinney) in *Dark Discoveries* magazine. He keeps bees and teaches physics and robotics not too far from Canandaigua, where he lives with his beautiful wife, parrots, dogs, chickens, way too many cats, and several million stinging insects. You can find him on Facebook, Twitter, Instagram, and at patrick.freivald.com.

Teel James Glenn has had stories in over 100 magazines, including *Black Belt*, *Crimson Streets*, *Fantasy Tales*, *Mad*, *SciFan*, *Sherlock Holmes Mystery*, *Spinetingler*, and the esteemed *Weird Tales*, as well as anthologies in many genres. He is winner of the 2012 Pulp Ark Award for Best Author, and his short story "The Clockwork Nutcracker" won best steampunk story for 2013 and has been expanded into a novel. His website is: theurbanswashbuckler.com.

Amy Grech has sold over 100 stories to various anthologies and magazines including *Apex Magazine*, *Beat to a Pulp: Hardboiled*, *Dead Harvest*, *Deadman's Tome Campfire Tales: Book Two*, *Expiration Date*, *Fright Mare*, *Needle Magazine*, *Real American Horror*, *Shrieks and Shivers from the Horror Zine*, *Space and Time Magazine*, *Tales from The Lake: Volume 3*, *The Pale Leaves*, and many others. New Pulp Press published her book of noir stories, *Rage and Redemption in Alphabet City*. She is an active member of the Horror Writers Association and the International Thriller Writers who lives in Brooklyn. Visit her website: https://www.crimsonscreams.com/. Follow Amy on Twitter: https://twitter.com/amy_grech.

Grady Hendrix has written about the Confederate flag for *Playboy* magazine, terrible movie novelizations for *Film Comment*, and Jean-Claude Van Damme for *Slate*. He has covered machine-gun collector conventions, written award shows for Chinese television, and been published everywhere from academic journals to television schedules. His novel *Horrorstör* has been translated into fourteen languages, and his latest novel, *My Best Friend's Exorcism*, is now out in paperback. He wrote the War of 1812 horror movie *Mohawk*, directed by Ted Geoghegan (*We Are Still Here*), which premiered at Montreal's Fantasia Film Festival. His latest book, *Paperbacks from Hell*, a nonfiction history of horror paperbacks in the '70s and '80s, won the Bram Stoker Award.

Erik T. Johnson writes speculative fiction from Old School Brooklyn. Trespass is his middle name. Erik has appeared in more than sixty literary periodicals and anthologies, including the #1 Amazon bestseller *I Can Taste the Blood*, a five-author novella collection. Erik's short fiction collection *Yes Trespassing* has been well received by the press and authors alike. Visit www.eriktjohnson.net for blog updates and links to Erik's Twitter, Instagram, Amazon Author Central, and Facebook pages.

Hal Johnson is the author of several books, one of which, *Fearsome Creatures of the Lumberwoods*, is pretty much just like his story here, but literally twenty times as long.

Jack Ketchum is the author of thirty-one books, thirteen of them novels, five of which have been filmed to date—*The Lost*, *The Girl Next Door*, *Red*, *Offspring*, and *The Woman*, the last of which won him and Lucky McKee the Best Screenplay award at the Sitges Film Festival in Spain. He is the five-time winner of the Bram Stoker Award, most recently for Lifetime Achievement. In 2011 he was elected Grand Master by the World Horror Convention. His new novel with Lucky McKee, *The Secret Life of Souls*, was published by Pegasus Press in 2016, and his collection *Gorilla in My Room* was published by Cemetery Dance in 2017. In 2015 Dark Regions Press published the 35th Anniversary Edition of his landmark novel, *Off Season*.

Distantly related to Mary Shelley, **Charie D. La Marr** has created a genre called Circuspunk (listed at Urban Dictionary) and written a collection of short stories in the genre called *Bumping Noses and Cherry Pie* and a horror novel called *Laugh to Death*. She also wrote a bizarro novel (or Nyzarro as she calls it—the New York version of Bizarro), *Squid Whores of the Fulton Fish Market*, and a satire, *Everybody Wants a Piece of Candi*. She participated in many anthologies, including the heavy metal anthology *Axes of Evil*, JWK Fiction's *Memento Mori*, *Bones*, *Indiana Crime*, and *Ugly Babies 2*, *In Vein* (for the benefit of St. Jude's Hospital), *Ripple Effect* (for Hurricane Katrina relief), Oneiros Books' *CUT UP!*, and many others. She was selected to participate in the 2014 Ladies and Gentlemen of Horror—as one of fourteen new voices in the genre. She won a challenge anthology *Vampz vs. Wolvez* (JEA Publishing) with her vampire story "Nothing Is Forever." She is most proud of working with an Iranian translator, translating Booker Man Award–winner *Vernon God Little* into Persian—which became a bestseller in Iran. A redhead with a redheaded attitude, she lives on Long Island with her mother and son and fur children Bailey Corwin and Casey Daniel Tibetan Spaniel.

Edward Lee is the author of over fifty books and numerous short stories and novellas. Several of his properties have been optioned for film, while *Header* was made into a movie in 2009. Lee has been published in Germany, Poland, England, Romania, Greece, Austria, Russia, France, Italy, and Japan. Recent releases include *Terra Insanus*, *The Haunted Dollhouse*, and *White Trash Gothic*. Currently he is working on *White Trash Gothic, Part 2*. On the side, he makes his own low-budget comedy horror videos at https://vimeo.com/user22091649. Lee lives in Largo, Florida. Visit him online at edwardleeonline.com. On a particular note, Lee was close friends with the late award-winning novelist Jack Ketchum since the late-'80s. "Eyes Left" is one of their many collaborations.

Lisa Mannetti has won the Bram Stoker Award twice: for her debut novel, *The Gentling Box*, and her short story "Apocalypse Then." She has also been nominated five additional times in both the short and long fiction categories. Her story "Everybody Wins" was made into a short film (*Bye Bye Sally*), and her novella "Dissolution" will soon be a feature-length film; both directed by Paul Leyden. Her work, including *The Gentling Box*, "1925: A Fall River Halloween," and *The Box Jumper*, has been translated into Italian. Her most recently published longer work, *The Box Jumper*, a novella about Houdini, was not only been nominated for a Bram Stoker Award and the prestigious Shirley Jackson Award, it won the "Novella of the Year" award from This is Horror in the UK. Visit her author website: www.lismannetti.com; her virtual haunted house: www.thechanceryhouse.com; and watch "Bye Bye Sally," starring Malin Ackerman: https://www.youtube.com/watch?v=pkuvRpoKrAA&t=73s.

Monica O'Rourke has published more than 100 short stories in magazines such as *Postscripts, Nasty Piece of Work, Fangoria, Flesh & Blood, Nemonymous,* and *Brutarian* and anthologies such as *Horror for Good* (for charity), *The Mammoth Book of the Kama Sutra,* and *The Best of Horrorfind.* She is the author of *Poisoning Eros I* and *II,* written with Wrath James White, *Suffer the Flesh,* and the collection *In the End, Only Darkness.* Her latest novel, *What Happens in the Darkness,* is available from Sinister Grin Press. She works as a freelance editor, writer, and book coach.

Patrick Thomas is the award-winning author of the beloved Murphy's Lore series and the darkly hilarious Dear Cthulhu advice empire, which includes the collections *What Would Cthulhu Do?, Cthulhu Happens, Cthulhu Knows Best, Have a Dark Day,* and *Good Advice for Bad People.* Among his nearly forty books are *Exile & Entrance,* a slew of urban fantasies that include *By Invocation Only, By Darkness Cursed, Fairy with a Gun, Fairy Rides the Lightning, Dead to Rites, Rites of Passage,* and *Lore & Dysorder;* the steampunk-themed *As the Gears Turn;* and the science-fantasy space adventures *Constellation Prize* and *Startenders.* He co-writes the Mystic Investigators paranormal mystery series and *The Assassins' Ball,* a traditional mystery, co-authored with John L. French. A number of his books were part of the props department of the *CSI* television show and one was even thrown at a suspect. His Soul for Hire story "Act of

Contrition," included in *Greatest Hits*, has been made into a short film by Top Men Productions. Drop by www.patthomas.net to learn more.

David Sakmyster is the award-winning author of more than a dozen novels, including *Jurassic Dead* and *The Morpheus Initiative*, a series featuring psychic archaeologists (described as "Indiana Jones meets the X-Files"). He also has an epic historical adventure, *Silver and Gold*, the horror novel *Crescent Lake*, and a story collection, *Escape Plans*. His screenplays *Nightwatchers* and *Roadside Assistance* have been optioned for production. Visit him at www.sakmyster.com.

Kathleen Scheiner is a freelance writer, editor, and proofreader with a taste for horror and dark fiction. She lives in Brooklyn, and her nonfiction has appeared in *L'Ecran Fantastique*, *Toxic*, *Publishers Weekly*, and *Dance International.* Her novel *The Collectors* was published in 2013, and her short fiction has appeared in *Memoirs of Meanness* and several anthologies. She is also a mentor with Girls Write Now, helping high school girls from underserved neighborhoods in New York City become the next generation of horror writers.

Jeff C. Stevenson is a professional member of PEN America, an active member of the Horror Writers Association, and a finalist for the Best Published Midsouth Science Fiction and Fantasy Darrell Award. Jeff has published more than two dozen dark fiction stories and has been included in anthologies alongside Clive Barker, Ramsey Campbell, Richard Chizmar, Jack Ketchum, Brian Lumley, Adam Nevill, Graham Masterton, Edgar Allan Poe, and Algernon Blackwood. Jeff is the author of the Amazon #1 bestselling *Fortney Road: The True Story of Life, Death and Deception in a Christian Cult.* His first novel, the supernatural mystery *The Children of Hydesville*, will be published in the summer of 2018 by Hellbound Books, which will also publish his suspense thriller *I'll Come Back to Get You* in late 2018. Jeff also writes mainstream fiction under the pen name of Mary Saliger.

J. Daniel Stone writes from New York City, where he was born and raised. He is the author of the urban horror novels *The Absence of Light* and *Blood Kiss*, the collaborative stand-alone novella *I Can Taste* *the Blood*, and the short story collection *Lovebites & Razorlines*. In 2016 he was selected by readers to be included in *Dread* (the Best Horror of Grey Matter Press). He writes under a pseudonym to keep the wolves at bay. Find him on Twitter and Instagram @SolitarySpiral.

Steven Van Patten is a celebrated writer and Brooklyn native. He has written four novels; *The Brookwater's Curse* trilogy, about an 1860s Georgia plantation slave who becomes a vampire; *Killer Genius: She Kills Because She Cares*, featuring a hyper-intelligent black woman who becomes a serial killer, was nominated in the category of Best Mystery/Thriller by the African-American Literary Award Show. The sequel, *Killer Genius 2: Attack of The Gym Rats* will appear in 2018. His short horror fiction is popping up everywhere, including *Hell's Kitties* and *Shadows of Deathlehem*. There is even a children's book, *Rudy's Night Out*, which is based on the childhood of one of the characters from the *Brookwater's Curse* series. He's also one of the hosts of the Beef, Wine and Shenanigans podcast, an Internet radio show that comically explores the person of color perspective of nerd culture and all things horror, science fiction, and superhero related. SVP can be found on Facebook by searching his name and under @svpthinks on Twitter and Instagram.

THE COVER ARTIST

Joseph Sigillo is a Long Island native and a graduate of New York City's School of Visual Arts with a BFA in Illustration. His graphic design career spans nearly thirty years and includes a diversified portfolio that encompasses work from book covers to logo design. In addition to his freelance design company, PixelLogic Studio, Joseph's day job is the Creative Director at Grey Packaging Inc., a display and packaging manufacturer. Specializing in the music and entertainment industry, he has worked with clients such as Sony Music, Universal Music Group, Disney, and HBO. In his spare time, Joseph enjoys sketching and visiting New York's finest museums with his family.

THE EDITORS

James Chambers received the Bram Stoker Award for his original graphic novel, *Kolchak the Night Stalker: The Forgotten Lore of Edgar Allan Poe*, and his short story "A Song Left Behind in the Aztakea Hills" was a Bram Stoker Award finalist in the short fiction category. He is the author of *The Engines of Sacrifice*, a collection of four Lovecraftian-inspired novellas that received a starred review from *Publishers Weekly*. His tales of horror, crime, fantasy, and science fiction have appeared in many magazines and anthologies. He has also authored several novellas, including the dark, urban fantasy novella *Three Chords of Chaos*, *The Dead Bear Witness*, and *Tears of Blood*. He edited the comic book series *Gene Roddenberry's Lost Universe*, *Isaac Asimov's I-Bots*, and *Leonard Nimoy's Primortals* as well as illustrated fiction anthologies based on Anne McCaffrey's *Acorna* and *I-Bots*. He has also edited many nonfiction books on a variety of topics. *He is online at* www.jameschambersonline.com.

April Grey edited numerous novels during her stay at Damnation Books. She went on to become the editor of the Hell's series of anthologies: *Hell's Bells*, *Hell's Garden*, *Hell's Grannies*, and *Hell's Kitties*. She is currently working on her fifth Hell's anthology. April has also written several novels, including *Chasing the Trickster* and *St. Nick's Favor*, and many short stories that can be found online and in print through Amazon and B&N. She is grateful to HWA for all the opportunities it presents for producers of dark fantasy and horror.

Robert Masterson, professor of English at City University of New York's Borough of Manhattan Community College in New York City, has authored *Artificial Rats & Electric Cats*, *Trial by Water*, and *Garnish Trouble*. His work appears in numerous publications and websites. He holds degrees from the University of New Mexico; the Jack Kerouac School of Disembodied Poetics in Boulder, Colorado; and Shaanxi Normal University, the People's Republic of China, and his work has taken him to the PRC, Japan, Ukraine, and most recently India as a student, reporter, writer, and teacher.

CPSIA information can be obtained
at www.ICGtesting.com
Printed in the USA
LVHW021706300720
661978LV00013B/924